C000083701

THE ISLAND

MARY GRAND

B
Boldwood

First published in Great Britain in 2021 by Boldwood Books Ltd.

Cover Design: Head Design

Cover Photography: Shutterstock

A CIP catalogue record for this book is available from the British Library.

Paperback ISBN 978-1-80048-182-4

Large Print ISBN 978-1-80048-181-7

Hardback ISBN 978-1-80162-973-7

Ebook ISBN 978-1-80048-183-1

Kindle ISBN 978-1-80048-184-8

Audio CD ISBN 978-1-80048-176-3

MP3 CD ISBN 978-1-80048-177-0

Digital audio download ISBN 978-1-80048-178-7

Boldwood Books Ltd
23 Bowerdean Street
London SW6 3TN
www.boldwoodbooks.com

To my sisters and brother, Anne, Janet, and Gerald, with much love. Thank you for being the best family and friends I could wish for.

PROLOGUE

Adrenaline numbs the pain of the car keys digging into the palm of my hand. No breeze comes off the sea. Remnants of a scorching day hang in the air.

Hiding in the darkness, I peer at the church door, lit by the feeble night light in the porch, waiting.

Unexpectedly, the church door opens. Stop. It's the wrong person. What the hell are they doing here?

I step back as they come towards me, hold my breath; they are so close now. I can imagine the warmth of their breath on my cheek. Oblivious to my presence, they move on, down the path towards the main road, and I return to my position, staring at the church door.

The church clock strikes one, the sound bouncing off the grave-stones, and I see the lights in the church being switched off; the door opens again. He's coming out. This is it.

I get in the car and push the keys into the ignition. I hear the clink as the stone-heart key ring knocks gently against the other keys. I wait, timing is everything. No headlights, no engine... yet.

He's coming this way. That's it. Now he's walking down the path.

Quickly: engine on, accelerator hard down. Thud. It's over so quickly. I screech to a halt, get out of the car. Something catches a slither of light. I check – he's dead.

Job done.

1

The tunnel was stifling apart from the occasional slither of sea breeze squeezing its way through the cracks around the windows. Two lanes: one for people leaving the island, one for those arriving. Juliet, in the latter, was aware of people behind her getting frustrated, but she was weighed down with her backpack and pulling a large suitcase: she couldn't go any faster. She wanted to tell them that she wasn't some tourist, she was the real thing: an islander returning home. Despite the sickening dread that had gripped her from the moment she received the phone call, she still felt a child-like flutter of excitement at finally coming home to her family, her island.

Juliet emerged from the tunnel and hit a wall of brilliant sunshine, crowds of overconfident 'yachty' types, shouting, their voices clashing with strains of live music and gulls screeching above. The masts of sailing boats jangled, their furled sails white against the blue sky, and the air was thick with the smell of alcohol and 'street food'. It was Cowes week.

Juliet was forced to make a diversion around a large group of youngsters who were far too busy impressing their friends to make way for her.

'Hi. Over here, Juliet.'

She waved to the taxi driver. Although she'd not seen him since leaving school years ago, she recognised him. Juliet grinned, grateful to see a familiar face.

The taxi driver was Mike, who used to live in her village. She had suffered him messing about on the school bus for years. However, she was impressed to see him open the boot, come towards her and take her bags. She held onto the large brown leather handbag.

'At your service,' Mike said, smiling as he opened the passenger door. Her heart sank – she had wanted the protection of the back seat.

'My God, its chaos,' she commented.

'Bloody Cowes week, eh. Still, good for business. It's the hospital, then?'

'You know about Dad?'

'It was in the paper this morning.'

Juliet breathed deeply, of course it was, and if it had been in the weekly island paper, then everyone knew.

They soon left the crowds behind and were on the main roads that led out of Cowes to the main town of Newport. Juliet was struck by how quickly her last two years were disappearing, and the feeling of 'never left' returning.

'I've always said that road your dad was on was dangerous; there should be more passing places. People speed something awful along there,' Mike commented.

Juliet wondered how much the paper had said about her father's accident. Mike soon answered that.

'Still, I don't think your dad was feeling, well, quite himself.'

Juliet cringed. So, they'd mentioned the drinking; that would get the island talking. She could hear them all: 'I never knew he was a drinker. He always seemed such a decent sort of man.' She clenched her fists in frustration, wanting to shout at Mike, 'He isn't like that,' but she couldn't bear the pitying look she would get in reply.

Fortunately, Mike changed the subject. 'So, have you been on holiday?'

'No, I've been away for two years, teaching abroad in China.'

Juliet turned and looked out of the window. She wasn't in the mood to chat and Mike took the hint.

It didn't take long to drive to the hospital, and Juliet's sense of dread grew as they parked outside.

'Here's my card,' Mike said. 'We're the hospital's nominated taxi service. If you or your mum need a lift any time, night or day, give us a call.' He gave a sympathetic smile. 'I know Mum would want me to send her love to you and your family.'

She knew he meant it, that is exactly what his mother would have wanted him to do, and that, she knew, was the flipside of the closeness of the island.

'Thanks, Mike.'

Mike handed her the bags. 'Hope your dad's all right,' he said, but the serious tone in his voice indicated he knew how ill he was.

Juliet tried to swallow the deep sense of apprehension as she walked towards the hospital entrance. 'Intensive care,' her mum had said. The words filled her with alarm; they were always preceded with something awful. 'They're not sure if he'll make it...' She used the hand gel, rubbing her hands hard together, headed for the lift, glanced down the list and found it: ICU.

Walking along the corridor, she passed visitors and medical staff milling around, and then turned a sharp right. It was quieter here, a short passageway leading to a row of plastic chairs outside the main entrance to the ward and on these sat her three sisters.

Her internet connection in China had made video calls impossible and most of her communications with the family had been by email or text, with only the occasional telephone call. Seeing them now, they looked older, rawer than the pictures she had stored in her mind. They weren't huddled together; they each sat slightly apart, each an individual.

Mira appeared to be staring unseeing into the distance, but she immediately spotted Juliet, leapt up and raced towards her. Their hug was clumsy but warm.

'You've cut your hair,' Mira signed and spoke simultaneously, her eyes bright, smiling.

'Yours is the same,' replied Juliet and reached out, touched the long brown untidy curls. Juliet glanced around. 'How are things?'

Mira shook her head, with both of her hands she made a wringing gesture over her heart, the sign for heartbreak, and, as so often, Juliet felt the sign said so much more than the words.

The whole family had been using British Sign Language since Mira had been diagnosed Profoundly Deaf at the age of three, they spoke and signed at the same time. Mira's speech and lip-reading were extremely good, but British Sign Language was her first language.

Juliet glanced at her eldest sister, Cassie, sat very upright, her hair scraped back into a tight ponytail, arms crossed, legs wound around each other, one foot tapping rhythmically on the floor.

Cassie glanced at Juliet; her mouth flickered in recognition.

'Thank God you're finally here,' wailed Rosalind, who, even at nearly twenty-one, held out her arms in the familiar gesture of the 'baby sister' waiting to be hugged and catered for. However, she appeared even more glamorous than when Juliet had left her, with expertly tanned legs and tinted blonde hair.

Juliet put her bag down and went to Rosalind. 'I'm so sorry, I came as quickly as I could.' She leant forward and signed to Cassie, 'How is Dad?'

Cassie glanced over in her direction. 'Critical. He's been like it since the accident on Monday evening, four days now,' Cassie signed in the same way she spoke, clipped and sharp. Today, there was an extra edge and nothing passive about the aggression in her words. She clearly meant that Juliet should have come sooner, cared more.

'We know it's a long way to travel,' interjected Mira, as always trying to smooth things over.

'I took the first flight I could get from China. What was Dad doing driving at that time of night anyway?' Juliet signed to Cassie.

'He'd gone up to the Downs, looking for owls or something. If he'd not been drinking—'

'Mum said he crashed into a barn?'

Cassie nodded and then stood up. 'I have to make a phone call; I'll be back soon.' She stalked off down the corridor.

'Can I see Dad?' Juliet signed to Mira.

'Of course.'

Juliet gently unpeeled Rosalind and handed her to Mira. She moved to the doors of the ward.

'Mum is in there now. He might not open his eyes or speak,' Mira said.

Juliet felt a sickening dread, a knot in her stomach. She felt guilty that part of her wanted to run away, but this was her father. Of course, she must see him.

She pushed open the door. There were six beds, but they were spread out. Unlike so many wards where the nurses seemed invisible, here they were everywhere, quietly, efficiently, going about their work. The sound of machines, purposeful steps, no shouting, no unruly children or groups of families: this was serious.

A nurse came straight to her.

'I'm Juliet. I've come to see my dad.' Juliet instinctively lowered her voice as if she were in a library or a church.

The nurse nodded, indicating where Juliet's mother was sitting. 'Your mum said you were on your way.'

As Juliet walked towards her mother, she tried to avert her eyes from the other patients and yet, at the same time, found it impossible not to glance at them.

Her mother was sitting like Cassie had, very upright, very still. She was wearing a sensible blouse and skirt.

Juliet touched her shoulder. 'Mum?' She felt a shudder of shock.

Her mother turned to face her. She never wore make-up. Her face was lined but soft, and today her light brown eyes were screwed up in pain. Juliet felt a wave of despair, closer to panic than grief, as, for the first time, she fully understood how ill her father was.

Her father, a quiet gentle man, lay, eyes closed, lost among the machines. There were superficial grazes on his face; his grey hair, still thick, stuck to his head.

Her mother stood up and gave Juliet a desperate hug. 'They've just given him his pain relief. He might be able to chat a bit, but he had a long talk with Rhys first thing, and then Cassie. I've just been sitting here while he rests. I'm so glad you made it.'

Juliet flinched. The words 'made it' were like a punch to her stomach, reminding her how close to that invisible edge between life and death her father was.

Her mother leant forward and touched his hand.

'Ian, Juliet is here.' Her mother spoke gently but firmly.

His eyes slowly opened. Deep grey-blue, vital, and alive; at odds with such a destroyed body.

After giving his hand a reassuring squeeze her mother hugged Juliet again, then quietly left the ward.

Juliet sat down and pulled the chair a little closer to her father's bed.

'Dad.' She reached out, touched his hand. It was too cold.

Slowly he turned towards her; their eyes met. Each soaked in the sight of the other.

'Juliet,' he spoke, the words soft, slightly slurred by the medication, a whisper of a smile on his lips. 'My sunshine.'

She felt the tears burning her eyes. Shards of glass in her throat made it hard to swallow. 'I'm home now, Dad,' she said, her voice shaking.

But then the smile melted away, his eyes screwed up in pain. 'I've made such a mess of everything, I'm so sorry.'

'No, you are a great Dad.'

'I wanted everything to be perfect for the four of you. You were happy, weren't you?'

'Of course, we had a wonderful childhood. Remember all the times we've walked on the Downs, watched the kestrels hovering, waited for them to swoop down. And the larks, way above us singing. Remember you said to me, one day you will draw as beautifully as they sing. They were the best times, Dad – and we will go again, soon.'

His eyes for a moment let in the light. 'They were. I have been lucky; my life has been rich.'

Juliet hated that her father was slipping into the past tense. 'And we're going to have lots more good times, Dad. Autumn will be here soon. We'll see the swallows gathering up on the Downs ready to fly away for the winter, hear the tawny owls fighting for territory. Dad, there is so much we can do together. And it's Rosalind's birthday, she'll be twenty-one, imagine that.'

She saw the muscles in his face tighten, the light faded from his eyes. 'I wanted to tell you all everything on her birthday, put everything right.'

Juliet was confused. 'What do you mean? Put what right?'

'The past, I would have, but then...' He screwed his eyes up in concentration. 'When was my accident?'

'Monday, the day of your birthday.'

'Yes, it was Monday when I realised I would never be able to tell any of you the truth. It broke my heart.' Juliet saw a tear weave its way down the side of his face and onto the pillow. She had no idea what he was talking about but was desperate to comfort him.

'Whatever it was, Dad, you are not to worry about it now, we need you to get better.'

'He should have had a life. I am sorry now; he was too young to die.'

Juliet blinked at the sudden turn of the conversation. 'Sorry, Dad, who died?'

'Harry.'

'Harry?' she questioned, wondering who her father could mean.

'Maddie's son.'

'Oh, that Harry,' said Juliet in surprise. 'He died years ago Dad.'

'The island never forgets; the past never goes away.'

Juliet frowned, upset that her father seemed so ill at ease. She glanced over at a streak of blue sky she could see through the window at the end of the ward. 'It's really sunny today, a good day for an early-morning swim. When I was little, we'd go down first thing, wouldn't we, before all the holidaymakers; we'd have the beach to ourselves. Who knows, maybe Mira and Rhys will have a little one soon, your first grandchild? You'll be able to take them down with you.'

Her father's eyes opened wide. 'I spoke to Rhys earlier. I needed to tell someone. I am so tired of carrying everything; it's so lonely being forced to keep secrets.'

Again, Juliet, disturbed by her father's agitation, attempted to reassure him. 'I can't imagine you had much to confess, Dad, but I hope it helped. Rhys is a good listener; it comes with the job of being a vicar, I think.'

'But it didn't help; it was a mistake,' he replied, despair and anxiety coating his words.

'Oh no, I'm sure—'

'You didn't see his face. He panicked, he was scared, and now I don't know what he will do.'

Juliet's lips trembled as she tried to force a reassuring smile. 'Dad, nothing you could say would have upset him that much.'

His voice cracked with pain as he spoke. 'And it's a lot for him to take on. I should have thought about that. I don't want anyone else to know. Don't let him tell Mira; he can't tell anyone.'

Juliet sat forward, laid her hand on his. 'You are not to worry about anything. Rhys won't tell anyone what you said, Dad. He may be married to Mira, but as a vicar he understands about keeping things private.'

Her father strained to lift his head off the pillow; his eyes were burning. 'Tell him to try to let it go, bury it at sea.'

'Okay, Dad, it's all right,' she said anxiously. 'I'll talk to him. I'll take care of everything.'

He gave her a sad smile. 'You always do. Watch Mira, she needs to look after herself now. Rosalind is unhappy, and Cassie...' He paused. 'Like I said, it's so lonely keeping secrets, she needs you more than you think. And then your mum,' his face softened, 'you are everything to her, forgive her.' He laid back and seemed to relax. 'Have you been drawing?'

'Yes, Dad. Remember all the times me and you sat together in the workshop? We'll have to do that again when you come home.'

Again, his eyes widened in alarm. 'Don't let Rosalind have her box, she mustn't have it.'

Mystified, Juliet answered, 'Um, okay.'

'And the key, the one I gave to Mira, get rid of it.'

Juliet blinked; she had no idea what he was talking about, but she wished she could help him relax. She spoke gently as she said, 'I will take care of everything, Dad.'

The words of comfort, however, failed to soothe him. If anything, he became more agitated. 'You must be very careful. Anyone can kill.'

Juliet sat up, alarmed; was her father delirious? She glanced around to see if a nurse was close. But she felt his hand move under hers and looked back at him.

'I know what I am saying. I'm sorry, but I have to warn you. You think you know them, but you don't, even people close to you, even family.'

'Dad, no one we know would hurt anyone.'

'Anyone who has the motive can kill. And if they have killed once, they can kill again. Remember that.'

Juliet scratched the back of her hand, digging her nails in hard. She felt hot; her heart was racing. The words and the intensity with which her father spoke was horrifying. It wasn't like him; he was the one she turned to for comfort and reassurance.

Her voice shook as she said, 'Dad, please. I am home now. I promise you; everything will be all right.'

He let out a long breath. When he spoke, his voice was weaker, the words came slower. 'If it all comes out, it will break them, but you are strong. It will be down to you to look after them all.'

Juliet's eyes burned with tears, her throat hard, too many emotions making it difficult to swallow.

'I don't feel strong, but I will try to be brave, Dad.'

Juliet saw his shoulders relax into the pillow. He closed his eyes, his breathing slowed down. His skin was paler, and she knew then that he was leaving her. Desperately, she squeezed his hand and said, 'Don't go, Dad,' but she knew it was useless, he was slipping slowly through her fingers and there was nothing she could do to make him stay. She felt a hand on her shoulder and turned to see her mother.

'I'll sit with him for a bit now,' her mother said gently.

Juliet stood up and her mother took her place.

'I'm here Ian,' she heard her mother say. Her father didn't open his eyes, but there was a whisper of a smile on his lips, no words needed now between him and her mother.

Juliet walked away quietly, not wanting to disturb them. As she went, a nurse glanced over at her parents and gave Juliet a sad smile. Juliet knew then that she would not hear her father's voice again.

Outside the ward, Cassie had returned and was sat in her chair.

Mira looked up, a glint of hope in her eyes but Juliet shook her head.

'Is Rhys around?'

'He's in another ward. He went to see one of his parishioners. I'll go and get him.'

Juliet sat down next to Rosalind, who was scrolling mindlessly through her iPhone, but not typing.

Eventually, Mira returned with Rhys. As always, he wore his clerical collar; he was never off duty. Usually he walked quickly, purposefully, with the slightly self-important air of a doctor on call. But today he appeared to be almost sleepwalking, as if he could walk straight into a wall, fall down a step, without noticing. However, as he came closer, he seemed to notice her.

'Ah, Juliet, welcome home.' His words were coated in a deep, silky Welsh accent.

Juliet stood up, and they faced each other, but didn't hug.

'Mira told me you've spoken to your father; that's good,' he said.

'Yes. He had a long talk with you?'

Rhys removed his glasses and rubbed his eyes. 'Um, yes, but, well, I don't know...' He replaced his glasses and looked around.

Juliet wondered what exactly her father had said to Rhys, but now wasn't the time to ask. She sat back down, and they all waited in silence in that timeless world you enter when you go into a hospital. Finally, her mother came out, tears falling down her cheeks. Cassie stood up, put her arm around her.

'We can all go in,' said her mother.

They walked slowly onto the ward. Juliet saw the screens had been pulled around her father's bed, and she reached out, grabbed Mira's hand. The machines were silent, her father lay motionless, his eyes closed.

He'd gone; her father had left her. Juliet's body started to tremble. She covered her face and broke down. There was no need to hide the pain, the panic, from him any more.

Juliet felt an arm around her. She knew it was Mira and they hugged each other; her mother, Cassie and Rosalind were together, each comforting the other. And then, to one side, she saw Rhys standing alone. Their eyes met. She saw a flicker of compassion, but his gaze went back to her father and he stared at him.

She looked at her mother and sisters, stood together. Why had her father made that comment about not knowing the people close to you? Of course she did.

If only she could forget that look in his eyes, if only she could dismiss all he said as the ramblings of a very sick man. But she couldn't; her father had meant every word. And with that certainty came fear. Because if her father's words were true, there were secrets she knew nothing about, and the future had become an uncertain, frightening place.

2

Juliet suggested a taxi home, but her mother, who seemed, as always, unnervingly in control of herself, had insisted on driving them.

Rosalind and Cassie were travelling together; Mira and Rhys had to pick up something at the vicarage but would be with them soon.

Juliet was relieved to be driven in silence; she needed to still the emotions raging around inside her head. She looked out of the window, and soon the business of the town roads was replaced by the quieter roads of West Wight, and she remembered that this small diamond-shaped island had many facets. Back in Cowes, it was loud, brash, over in Sandown and Ryde, it would be a bucket and spade, chip-smelling family holiday, but over here, she had always believed, was the real soul of the island.

Over here, it seemed to expand, become endless. The squawking gulls of the tourist towns were transformed into things of beauty, gliding across empty sky, their white wings spread, catching the sunlight. Nature was free, could breathe here. Away from the crowded pubs, coaches and tacky souvenir shops, the island could be itself.

As she soaked in the sights, Juliet could feel her breathing slow, her mind still, and she could hear the island whisper, 'You're home.' Juliet could have cried with relief; it hadn't forgotten her.

Eventually they approached the village. They drove past the thatched pub that Juliet had worked in as a teenager and arrived at a crossroads. To their right was the road leading to the village church where Rhys was vicar, but they turned left down the main road through the village, past houses, and a small green with a tiny stream where they held the annual duck race.

At the bottom of the street was the junction onto the busy military road, and across from that the beach and the sea. Juliet's family home, an old farmhouse, occupied a large plot on the corner. It faced the sea, and there was a sprawling front garden surrounded by hedges and trees, giving them their privacy.

Juliet's mother pulled into a small parking area behind the back of the house. There was very little garden here, and no one used the old back door. And so, once out of their car, Juliet had to pull her case a short distance along the pavement-less road until they reached the garden gate that led to the front of the house.

Her mother was about to open the gate when Juliet saw one of the neighbours come towards them.

'I am so sorry to hear about Ian's accident,' she said to Juliet's mother.

'Thank you, Kath. I'm afraid he passed away this afternoon.'

'Oh, Helena, I am sorry. Such a lovely man, you must all be devastated.' She smiled at Juliet. 'I'm glad you're home to look after your mum now. You've been gone a long time.' She turned back to Juliet's mother. 'Now, anything we can do, you know where we are.'

Juliet's mother thanked her, and they pushed open the gate.

'Well, that's told the village,' her mother said with a sad smile.

The gate squeaked open, and Juliet stepped onto the long gravel path that ran the length of the front of the house.

Juliet glanced at the expanse of garden, flinched when she saw her dad's workshop and the old oak tree next to it. It wasn't a tidy, planned garden, but rambled, with apple and pear trees down the bottom where they would make dens and have picnics when they were children. The smell of salt and seaweed reminded them the sea was very close by, and their dens would be decorated with shells and pebbles.

The house had been built on in a haphazard way over the years. The front door was far to the right, the rest of the downstairs taken up with windows into the large kitchen diner. Juliet looked up and saw her bedroom window, tucked above the front door and the wooden gate – prime position to watch everyone coming and going on the long summer evenings when any time before ten felt far too early to be in bed.

Her mother unlocked the porch and the inner front door. The porch was full of the usual clutter. Juliet was pleased to see her wellington boots neatly standing next to her dad's, but then the pain shot home. The whole house was going to be like this, constant prods and reminders that her father had gone.

As she stepped into the hallway, there was an uncanny silence. Her father had been a quiet man, so why did the house seem to shout his absence? It was as if it was in mourning.

The hallway was scruffy with old oak parquet flooring, white walls. There was that individual smell that every house has, the one you only notice when you have been away. She breathed it in, then heard the deep ticking of the grandfather clock. Like the smell, it was so intrinsic to the house that it largely went unnoticed in the daytime. It gained its significance for Juliet at night, when she would lie in bed, even as an adult, counting the ticks, the chimes on the hour.

Her eyes were drawn to a framed picture on the wall.

'Where did you find that?' she asked her mother, feeling emotion tighten her throat.

Juliet stepped closer to the picture. She'd drawn it in her teens, even then preferring pencil to paint. The four sisters were sat together on 'their beach', Brook Beach, and even now, Juliet could hear the seagulls overhead, the shouts of other children playing, running in and out of the sea. Rosalind sat, the princess, her white golden curls shining, little chubby legs stretching out from her short pink dungarees, while Juliet, aged ten, was close by filling a bucket with sand ready to make sandcastles for the baby to knock down with a spade. Mira, eight, was watching sand seep through her fingers. Apart from them sat Cassie, nearly nineteen, serious in shorts and T-shirt, reading a book.

'I have so few pictures of you all together,' said her mother, 'and that was such a happy day. As I get older, it's good to be reminded of days like that.' Her mother looked around as if the house had become a stranger to her. Juliet saw the vulnerability, a confusion she'd never seen in her mother before. 'Um, now, put your things there, you're in your room, of course.'

Juliet felt a wave of relief at the words 'your room'. She guessed everyone, whatever age, when they went to their childhood home, wanted to find that they still had 'their' bedroom. Of course, it would be more practical for the room to have been turned into a guest room or a study, say, but what you really wanted was for it still to be your room, a place that gave you access to your history, your childhood, that showed you were still that child.

'Come and have a drink.' Her mother glanced at Juliet's case. 'Where are the rest of your things?'

'This is everything. I was determined to come back as I went, with everything in one case.'

Her mother smiled. 'Rosalind takes more than that for a night away. You might as well leave it there for now.'

The kitchen was to the left of the front door, and Juliet, leaving her suitcase in the hall, automatically followed her mother, still holding her handbag. Juliet passed the large living room. Being at the back of the house it was quite dark and her parents still only had the one, small television. Filling one shelf of the bookcase was a beautiful set of the complete words of Shakespeare, each play, each book of poetry in its own leather-bound book. They had belonged to her grandmother, handed down to her mother.

The room next to it was Cassie's music room, and Juliet glanced in. On the wall were photographs of Cassie playing the violin, and in the cabinet, cups and awards; the room was a shrine to Cassie. Juliet looked away, and went into the room opposite, the kitchen. As she entered, she blinked; it was lighter than before. She looked over and recognised why. New patio doors led out onto the garden. 'Wow, when did they happen?' She was irrationally upset that her parents had made changes to the house while she was away.

'Only about a month ago. It was something I always wanted when you were all little instead of always having to go in and out of the front door. This would have been so easy. I was thinking with Dad retiring soon it would be useful for him getting to his workshop.' Juliet looked out at the old wooden building, her father's sanctuary. Her mother took a deep breath. 'We should have done it before... you always imagine there will be more time.' She walked over to the kettle and filled it up.

The kitchen was two rooms knocked into one and retained that feel. To her left was the functional end, with cooker and cupboards, but at this end was the old pine table and dresser. Juliet put her handbag on the dresser as she always had done.

'What have you eaten?' asked her mum.

'It's okay, Mum. I ate bits on the journey.' She saw a tiny look of disappointment; her mother needed to know she was making things better for someone.

'There is cake in the tin. I made some fruit one. Your dad's favourite—'

'Let me make us a cup of tea, Mum.'

'No, I'll make it.' Her mother spoke sharply, but Juliet guessed she was only just holding on, and this was something concrete to ground her in the house.

Juliet sat at the table, feeling again like the little girl after school being given squash and biscuits.

'You've cut your hair,' said her mother, blinking. 'The first of my girls—'

Juliet smiled at being called a girl at thirty. 'I felt like a change. Do you like it?'

'It suits you. I suppose Mira always wanted hers long to hide her hearing aids, not that it would bother her now. Cassie needs to be able to tie hers back for playing the violin, but the only one I'd be really upset if they cut their hair, is Rosalind. You all are so dark, but she, well, she is like Rapunzel, long fair hair...'

Juliet thought someone looking on would think how odd it was that these two people, who had lost a husband and father just hours before, should be talking about haircuts, making tea. But then sometimes something is so huge the only thing to do is talk about the trivial, a kind of survival tactic.

Juliet's mother screwed up her eyes and scrutinised her. 'It's been good for you getting away, but, of course, it's lovely that you are home. Now, I know you said you wanted a break from teaching, but I saw your old job at the high school is vacant – they're still advertising. You could give them a ring, maybe even go on a temporary contract?'

Juliet heard the eagerness in her mother's voice. Now more than ever, she knew how much her mother would want her to move back to the island. She had to be gentle. 'I don't think so Mum. I have some possibilities of work on the mainland, nothing definite, but I won't be going travelling again.'

Her mother sighed, looked out of the window. 'Me and your dad had planned to go out to Verona in November.'

'I didn't know—'

'It was going to be a special holiday. You know, I was sixty in February, and Dad was sixty-five on Monday. We'd planned a holiday for the autumn when he'd retired. I know the weather might not have been great, but neither of us are much for the sun. He was going to take me to see the balcony, you know, where Shakespeare got his inspiration for Romeo and Juliet.' Her mother gazed out of the window unaware of the tears on her face.

'It would have been wonderful, Mum.'

'It was a kind gesture from your dad. He was never that fussed with Shakespeare, or holidays for that matter.'

'And he let you give us all Shakespearean names.'

'I know. My mum, your grandmother, would have been so pleased. I used to get teased about the name Helena when I was a child. All my friends had names like Sarah and Susan, and they saw my name as a bit fancy. I was lucky. People were starting to give less traditional names by the time you were born. I love all your names. I do wish Cassie and Mira hadn't shortened theirs. Such pretty names. At least you and Rosalind have kept yours. I had an awful feeling you'd end up as Jules and Rosy.'

'I like my name. It's a bit different, and somehow Rosalind's suits her much more than Rosy. She's too dramatic for a Rosy.'

Her mother sniffed. 'I'll have to cancel the holiday. It's covered by insurance, but I wish we'd gone before. I so wanted to see it with your dad. It's too late now.' She made tea in the bone china tea service that had belonged to her parents, set out matching cups and saucers, poured the tea and placed the cake tin on the table, but neither of them opened it.

The grandfather clock in the hallway chimed four in the afternoon. Juliet realised how tired she was. It felt so much later. There was too much of this day still to get through.

'He was waiting for you,' her mother said.

Juliet felt her throat tighten with tears at the thought of her father clinging onto life so he could see her one final time. 'I wanted to get here quicker. It was a nightmare gathering all the things together to return home so quickly and I don't think I'd really grasped quite how urgent it was.'

'I didn't want to scare you and you never know, do you.'

Juliet sipped her tea. 'But, Mum, I don't understand what happened, why Dad even had this accident. I knew he had a problem with drink before you were married, but he's not drank for years; I've never even seen him drink alcohol...'

Her mother carefully put down her tea. As she did, Juliet could see her hands shaking. 'There have been a few times; binge sessions up on the Downs. Like when he lost his dad. He was devastated, found it hard to cope. He'd walk up to the Downs then and drink, come back, hours later, but, as I say, it was only a few times.'

Juliet was shocked. 'I had no idea.'

'I'm glad. It's my job to protect you.'

Juliet's mind started to drift back to her conversation with her father at the hospital. 'I suppose it can be hard for a parent to know what they should tell their child and what they should keep to themselves.'

Her mother sat back. 'Is there something on your mind?'

Juliet paused. Surely now wasn't the time, but then her mother added, 'You can tell me anything. Is it something Dad said?'

'He said some very odd things, Mum, and I don't think it was just the side effects of the medication.'

Her mother blinked quickly. 'I see, and what did he say?'

'He said there were things he'd wanted to tell Rosalind, but he'd realised he couldn't. He talked about wanting to put things right. It was like there was some secret he'd been keeping all these years. Mum, do you know what that was?'

She watched her mother, waiting to see how she would react. But, as usual, her mother's face remained impassive as she spoke.

'Listen to me carefully. Dad was rambling. You need to forget all this, don't worry your sisters about it. Promise me.'

Juliet gave a cursory smile and her mother patted her hand.

'Good. Now, we won't talk about it any more.' Her mother habitually closed down conversations and sometimes Juliet would fight it, but today was not the time to do that.

'Okay, Mum.' She glanced over at the birthday cards on the dresser and smiled. 'I see my card to Dad came. I know the day ended in a nightmare, but did Dad enjoy any of his birthday?'

'Oh, yes.' Her mother sniffed, shook her head and then said, 'Dad went to work as normal at the garage. You know how he is, even with retirement coming up, still working long hours. He was late back. He rushed home and then, in the evening, we had a meal.'

'And he was happy then?'

'He was a bit stressed. We had a few words.'

'A row?'

'Oh, nothing like that. It was lovely to be together. Rosalind stayed in for once. She goes out so much now, usually in Cowes or over to Southampton for the evening with the girls from the beauticians. Cassie came down from London Sunday evening. She's got the week off from orchestra. They'll have to extend that now, won't they? Mira came on her own. Rhys had some church meeting. Having three churches means three times the meetings. Of course, we didn't have you, but we did have someone to cook for us.'

'Gosh, that's fancy.'

'We didn't pay caterers. No, it was Rhys's sister, Anwen. You know, she moved over here after Rhys and Mira's wedding. She's a chef, very good. She did beef wellington, your dad's favourite. He seemed to enjoy it, but then after the meal he said he was going out.' Her mother covered her eyes. 'If only I'd stopped him.' Her mother unpeeled her hands from her eyes, clasped them together on the table. 'They found his flask in the car; it contained more vodka than hot chocolate.' She rubbed the thumbs of her clasped hands together. 'I can't believe he won't be here for Rosalind's twenty-first birthday and he'd worked so hard on her musical box. It's beautiful.'

Juliet interjected, 'Oh, the musical box. Dad said he didn't want her to have it—'

Her mother's face creased in confusion. 'I can't see why not.'

'I don't understand it either, he didn't explain why. Maybe he didn't think it was finished?'

'No, he was happy with it. What an odd thing to say. I still think she should have it.'

Juliet blinked. 'I don't know. He was adamant.'

'You girls all treasure yours so much, don't you? He might have been confused.' Juliet saw the desperation in her mother's eyes and then her mother started to cry. 'It's the last thing he will have done for her.'

Juliet put her arms around her mother, felt the shuddering tears. 'Let's not worry about it now.'

Her mother nodded. 'I can't think straight about anything. I don't know what's important and what's not any more. I feel so lost without him.'

'We'll look after each other.'

Her mum pulled away.

'How have the others been this week?' Juliet asked.

'Cassie's not one to fuss, is she, but she's been very supportive; she's not moved from my side. Mira is a natural in hospitals, but, of course, her and Rhys are busy, so she's been in and out.'

'And Rosalind?'

Her mother smiled. 'She's a butterfly, on her phone, talking about the drama to all her friends. But her grief is real. She's younger than you all in her ways as well as her age, isn't, she?' Her mother sipped her tea.

'Dad talked about her, about them all. He asked me to look after them.' Juliet paused and then said, 'He was worried about the things he'd told Rhys, was anxious he didn't tell anyone. Do you know what they spoke about?'

'I am not too sure, but I'll have a word with Rhys. He'll keep it to himself.'

Juliet saw her mother stroke the handle on her cup. Her finger-tips were shaking, and she felt, as she had with her father, the need to comfort and reassure her mother.

'Okay, fair enough. So, something a bit more exciting. In her last email Mira told me she had a surprise to show me. Do you know what it is?'

Her mother nodded vigorously. 'Yes. I do, but I mustn't spoil it.'

At that moment, Juliet heard a car pull up at the side of the house.

'That must be Rosalind and Cassie,' said her mother.

Juliet heard the car door bang and then Rosalind and Cassie walked past the kitchen window. Her mother opened the patio door to let them in.

Cassie was pale but held herself very upright. And Juliet was struck again by her similarity to their mother, both so reserved, tightly bound.

Rosalind rushed past her and flew to her mother.

'I can't believe it,' she said. 'It's not fair.' She started to cry again.

Her mother cuddled and soothed Rosalind. 'I know, darling.'

Cassie stood to one side, her clothing monochrome as always, the only flash of colour the red gemstone on her finger. Juliet wondered if she should go and hug her, but everything in Cassie's stance shouted to keep away.

'We're not going to leave him there, are we? Dad hated hospitals,' said Rosalind.

'It's all right. I shall arrange for him to be taken by the funeral directors. He will stay there until the funeral.'

Juliet watched Rosalind. Maybe she was the normal one. The rest of them were keeping everything inside, but not Rosalind.

Juliet's mother closed her eyes; she was clinging onto Rosalind as much as Rosalind clung to her.

It was then Juliet heard barking outside.

She could see Rhys and Mira through the kitchen window, but it was not until they came into the kitchen that she saw the dog.

'My God! Who is this?' signed Juliet, kneeling down and stroking the dog's head.

'This is Lola. We called in at the vicarage to pick her up. Poor thing, she has been left for three hours. We never leave her that long—'

'She's so sweet.'

'She's from an organisation called Hearing Dogs for Deaf People, for me she is mainly a companion. She's wonderful. Dad loved her.'

'I love the little red tabard. She's a cocker spaniel, isn't she?'

'That's right.'

'White and black, and look, it's like a little moustache, she's a sweetie.'

'I think she may be my best friend, very easy to chat to.'

'What do the people from church make of her?'

'They love her. It's the same with the people in the care homes;

they want to see her more than me. To be honest, I think most people do these days. It's got people talking about me being Deaf as well. Some of them are learning to sign. We have a screen now on Sundays. You wouldn't believe what a big step that was for some of them. Oh, and we have a loop system in each of the churches. So, it has gone well, hasn't it?' She looked up at Rhys.

Rhys looked down on her, blinked, his mouth half open, but he didn't speak. It had always seemed odd to Juliet that her sister had ended up marrying a vicar. Mira had hardly been to church since she was a child. However, she had always been passionate about looking after other people and had obviously found Rhys had the same caring side when they met. The vacancy for a vicar in the village had come about when Rhys left theological college and he'd come first as a curate and then stayed on as vicar to a group of local churches.

Juliet watched Lola stroll over to the corner of the kitchen, where, for the first time, she noticed a small dog basket and bowl.

'She's been made at home here,' said Juliet.

'It seemed a good idea. Mira can drop her off then whenever she wants,' said her mother.

'You sound like an indulgent grandmother,' laughed Juliet.

'It's the nearest I've got to grandchildren. She's such a wonderful companion. I lost the battle for Mira to be allowed a dog at university, but I'm so glad she has Lola now.'

Mira went over to her mother, gave her a hug, acknowledging the years her mother had fought for her; from her diagnosis, her right to sign as a child, to have support at school, a note-taker at university. Her mother was always there.

'What will happen to Dad's things in the hospital?' Rosalind asked unexpectedly.

'I will have to go there to collect the certificate and Dad's things tomorrow.'

'When can we hold the funeral?' asked Juliet.

'The doctor said it will depend on what the coroner says. Of course, there will be an inquest, but that could take some time.'

'There will be a post-mortem?'

'I think so, but the police don't feel there's a lot to investigate. The doctor apparently signed the death certificate. I'll see what he wrote tomorrow. We might not even have to go to the inquest. I don't think we will have to wait long for a funeral.'

Juliet walked to the window. 'I hate to think of him up on the Downs on his own.' She turned. 'They are sure he was alone, aren't they?'

'Yes, I don't think he even got out of the car,' said her mother. 'There were people parked there in a campervan. They saw Dad's car arrive, and then drive off. Obviously, they weren't watching him the whole time, but they said they only saw one person in the car.'

'They should have gone and seen he was all right.'

'But why would they? A man sitting in the car drinking from a thermos?'

Juliet tried to shake the picture of her father alone in the car. 'I wonder where he got the vodka. We never have anything other than the odd bottle of wine here.'

Her mother fiddled with her wedding ring. 'He went into the supermarket at Freshwater before going up to the Downs. The receipt was in the car.'

'Juliet,' said Cassie, her voice sharp, 'Mum doesn't need you picking over that evening. He had his birthday meal, and we were all together and that is a good memory—'

Juliet glanced over at Rhys, but he stood very still, unspeaking.

'But Dad was upset, something had happened that day—'

And then she saw it, a look between her mother and Cassie, an invisible thread of understanding. She'd seen that look a thousand times before, but, and maybe it was the effect of being away, for the first time she wondered exactly what it was about.

'Leave it,' said Cassie, and this time there was something close to panic in her voice. 'It's hard enough losing Dad. Don't make it worse.'

Juliet flinched at Cassie's words but, glancing around, saw no one was going to defend her.

Instead, her mother said, 'Cassie is right. There's nothing more to be done,' and she firmly slammed the book closed on the conversation.

Cassie walked over to her mother. 'We're going to organise a beautiful funeral for Dad.'

Juliet stood on her own, watching them: Mira stroking Lola, Rosalind cuddled by their mother, Cassie standing to her other side, stern, unsmiling, her arm around protectively her.

She noticed Rhys had quietly left the kitchen and was outside sitting alone in the garden, so she went out to see him.

He had taken off his glasses and was rubbing them hard with the edge of his sleeve. Juliet sat next to him.

'What did Dad talk to you about in the hospital?'

He looked at her sideways. 'He talked about a lot of things.'

'I found some of the things he said to me rather disturbing.'

He looked up at her. 'Your father had a lot on his mind.'

Juliet felt they were playing a kind of verbal chess. 'I am sure he told you a lot more than he told me. With me it was hints and warnings. I think he was talking about some family secret. I just asked Mum about it, but she said to leave things alone, you know what Mum is like.'

'I do,' he said, giving a half smile.

'So, does she know everything Dad told you?'

He looked away. 'I don't think so. Not everything.'

Juliet touched his arm. 'Look, I know Dad wanted you to keep it to yourself, but I am curious to know what he said. I'm not just being nosy; it sounds really important.'

Rhys nodded. 'It is, and your father has left me in a real dilemma. I am very conflicted. I promised not to tell anyone what he told me, and usually I would feel that was right, but this is different—'

Juliet grasped his arm. 'Did Dad say anything to you about someone killing someone?'

His eyes widened; he took a breath and looked away. 'I can't talk to you about this, not now.'

'So, he did?' she pressed.

'Juliet, I can't say anything, certainly not yet. I have to take time to think and pray about this. Firstly, I made a solemn promise to your father and I have never knowingly broken my word. And, secondly, I have no idea what the implications of exposing things will be. I have to do the right thing.'

Juliet felt a wave of fear. She wanted Rhys to reassure her, to make the things her father had said feel less important, and yet he was making her more afraid.

He turned to her, patted her knee. 'I'm sorry. I should be offering words of comfort to you now, not be taken up with my own problems. You have just lost your father and I know how close you both were. You must take time to grieve, leave all this other stuff to one side.' He looked at his watch, stood up. 'I'm sorry, I have to go and see a couple for a wedding preparation session. Life goes on, doesn't it? I'll come back as soon as I can.'

He walked quickly out of the garden. Rhys clearly knew things she didn't, and she was torn between wanting to know what they were and the fear of what they might be.

Juliet went inside and, to avoid the others, she headed for the hall-way, picked up the suitcase she'd left in the hallway and took it to her bedroom, the room she used to share with Mira.

Mira had never found it easy to sleep. Once she took her hearing aids off at night, she didn't have the comfort of the sounds of family around the house, the grandfather clock, her mother in the kitchen. As far as Mira was concerned, the lights went out, it was silent and she was alone, so she would cry, get out of bed and wander, looking for company.

It was their father who suggested Mira share a room with Juliet, and it had been during those years that a very special bond had formed between them. Like twins, they instinctively developed their own dictionary of simple signs, their own language, even before Mira and the family had learned British Sign Language.

Juliet looked around the room at the two single beds, the night-light that had cast a cosy glow over the room still plugged in. Of course, it had been many years since they had used it, but she had never wanted to remove it.

Juliet went to look out of her window. In front of her lay the expanse of the front garden and her father's workshop was tucked away to the right and Mira was sat alone on the bench next to it.

Juliet turned her attention back to her room. Next to her bed was the musical box her father had made her for her twenty-first birthday. The wood was beautifully carved, and on the side were slots for photos: pictures of her as a baby, a child, a teenager, and an adult. Her father bought the musical movements from Germany, a special tune for each of his daughters. Juliet wound the delicate key on the base and lifted the lid. 'You Are My Sunshine' played and the music tore her in two. She hugged the box, sat on her bed, and sobbed. For a brief moment, that final conversation was forgotten, and she was consumed with that indescribable pain of loss.

Exhausted, Juliet wiped her eyes and thought it was time to return downstairs and help out; there would be people calling, a lot of phone calls to make.

However, when she walked into the kitchen, she found her mother sat quietly, cuddling Rosalind who was scrolling through her phone.

Cassie sat holding their mother's mobile to her ear with one hand and with the other, a pen, which she held over a piece of paper.

'Hi, I'm ringing around the family for my mum,' Cassie was saying, speaking in a quiet but efficient way. 'I am so sorry to have to tell you my father died today.' She added a few more polite sentences and rang off, then wrote down the name on the paper and gave it a tick. 'Shirley next?' she asked, and her mother nodded. Cassie picked up the phone again, pressed the number.

Juliet was a bit put out. 'Would you like me to ring some people as well?' she asked.

'I've got it under control,' said Cassie.

'I could start getting a meal ready then,' said Juliet.

'There's no need. People have started calling with food.' Cassie pointed at a casserole dish. 'It's the way things work here,' she added, as if Juliet was some stranger, unfamiliar with their ways.

The house phone rang and her mother answered it. Incongruously, Juliet heard her comforting someone on the other end.

Then the doorbell rang, but before Juliet could move, Cassie had put down the phone and gone to answer. She returned with a bunch of flowers. As she started to fill a vase with water, she said to Juliet, 'You could go and talk to Mira; she's on her own.'

'Are you sure there is nothing I can do to help?' asked Juliet.

Her mother glanced towards Cassie, and then said to Juliet, 'No, love. We're okay here.'

Feeling like a child being sent to play, Juliet left the kitchen through the patio door and went to find Mira who was sat with Lola.

Mira signed, 'I thought I'd let Cassie and Mum have some time together.'

Juliet turned to Mira. 'I offered to help, but Cassie has taken over.'

'Maybe Cassie wants to play her part as the eldest sister for once.'

'She's never wanted to before; she always hid away in her music room when anything needed doing.'

Mira gave her a gentle smile. 'I know, but Cassie is still very close to Mum. I used to think they had their own language, like me and you, except they communicated with looks instead of signs.'

Juliet shrugged. 'Maybe you're right.'

'You must be tired after all the travelling. I am glad you were able to say goodbye to Dad.'

'And me, although it felt a bit fraught.'

'Really?'

'Yes, he said some weird things.'

'He had a pretty long talk with Rhys. Rhys seemed stunned but he wouldn't tell me what Dad had said. Have you any idea?'

Juliet paused. 'No... I think he told Rhys a lot more than me.' Then Juliet remembered something. 'There was one thing that Dad said, it was something about a key? He said he'd given you one? He didn't want anyone else to have it. Do you know what he meant?'

Mira frowned. 'Oh, he gave me one on Monday, on his birthday. He was late home, and I was in the garden. He thrust this key into my hand and told me to hide it in your drawer in the workshop.'

'What was the key for?'

'It was an old car ignition key, I think. Anyway, I put it in your drawer.'

Juliet looked around at the workshop, a tatty wooden building with large windows that looked out onto the garden. 'I feel like he should be in there now, working. All the hours we spent in there together, me drawing, him making some beautiful tray or box.'

Mira glanced at Juliet. 'I don't understand him drinking like that and then driving. He was never usually reckless. I keep going over the day of his birthday, trying to work out if I'd missed something, but he seemed normal. A bit quiet but that is all.'

Juliet put her hand on Mira's arm. 'None of this is your fault. I'm glad you were there for Dad when he was in hospital. I am sure you were a real comfort to him.'

'I wanted to be there more, but Rhys thought I should keep to my other commitments, going into the care homes and things.'

Juliet looked up at the house. 'Do you think Mum will sell the house, downsize?'

'I hope not. I always dreamed of bringing my children here for tea and to play. I thought Rhys would feel the same but lately he's started to talk about moving...' Mira paused.

'Rhys wants to leave? I thought he loved living on the island.'

'He's been talking a lot to his uncle who is working on some mission in Wales. You give up all your possessions and spend your days serving the poor and disadvantaged apparently.'

'Wow. That sounds, um, radical.'

'I know I shouldn't say this, but it sounds a nightmare to me. Rhys says we are living too comfortably. I think he feels guilty because we have that money he inherited from his parents.'

'He's not going to give it away, is he?'

'I don't think he would do that.'

Juliet remembered her father's words about Mira. 'You have to look after yourself, not just everyone else.'

'That's what everyone says isn't it.' She lent down and stroked Lola. 'At least I have her now, she gives me an excuse to escape. The vicarage is always so hectic with people calling in all the time. Rhys is up at the church a lot; he goes every Saturday night now, always at about half eleven and stays till about one. He calls it praying one day out and the next one in. He thinks it's important preparation for a Sunday.'

'Blimey, he wasn't doing that before. I wouldn't fancy being up there on my own at night either – it's completely deserted.'

'I don't like him being up there at that time to be honest. I've heard of kids going up there, smoking and drinking – but he says this is what he feels God has called him to do. I don't understand a lot of what he says about his beliefs to be honest.' Mira gave a half-smile. 'I can't believe I hadn't figured out that having a faith would be so important to being a vicar's wife. Stupid, eh?'

'But you share Rhys's passion for caring, looking after people.'

'I know, but it's not enough, is it? Also, having the vicarage as a kind of open house twenty-four seven is driving me a bit mad. Rhys says we should always be available, which I understand, but it's exhausting.'

'Rhys should think about how tiring socialising can be for you. You need a break.'

Mira wrapped a long strand of hair tightly around her finger, something she would do when she was little.

Juliet was concerned for her. 'Mira, you need to talk to Rhys, make changes.'

'I know, but it's not all his fault. I have made some pretty awful mistakes—'

'No way.'

'Oh yes.'

Juliet was surprised at how serious her sister looked. 'Has something happened? You can tell me anything, you know that.'

'No, not this. I have to sort this out in my own way.'

Juliet was worried about Mira but also hurt that she wouldn't tell her; she felt a wall between them that had not been there when she'd left.

At that moment, Rosalind came out, tutted as the heels of her shoes dug into the lawn. 'I don't know what to do with myself. Cassie said not to put the TV on. She told me off for being on my phone. What the hell am I supposed to do?'

'What about a walk to the beach?' Juliet suggested.

'Okay, I need to change though.'

'I assume my car is over in the field?' Juliet said to Mira. The field was next to the main car park at the beach and, as parking at the back of the house was so limited, the farmer had given them permission to park over there.

'Oh yes. Thanks so much. We really appreciated having the use of it while you were away. I have my own now. Hang on, I brought the car keys for you.'

From her bag, Mira took out a small bunch of keys and handed them to Juliet.

Juliet looked down. She touched the smooth heart-shaped stone on the key ring, then held it to her nose, smelt the sea, memories, watching the sunset. She smiled. 'Thanks.'

'It's got petrol in and Dad MOT'd it a month ago.'

They looked at each other, not daring to speak.

Juliet turned to Rosalind. 'So, are you ready?'

'I'll go and put something better on my feet.' Rosalind went back into the house.

'Are you coming?' Juliet asked Mira.

'I would rather stay here. Could you take Lola with you, though? She's not had a good run today.'

'Of course. Hang on, I'll go and get my handbag.'

Juliet went inside, found her bag on the dresser and returned to find Mira attaching Lola's lead to her collar. Lola was standing up, wagging her tail excitedly.

'You can let her off once you're down the beach,' said Mira. 'Oh, and you'll need poo bags.'

Juliet screwed up her face but smiled and put the bags with her car keys into her handbag. Rosalind returned in a whole new outfit; hair tied in a high ponytail, jeans, top, and smart flip-flops.

Rosalind gave a look of mock horror when she saw Juliet's handbag. 'You've still got that old bag? Tell me you have better ones in your case.'

'Nope, still the one handbag.'

'You take that when you go out?'

'Yup. I bought a cheap one that looked posher, and it drove me mad. I kept having my phone and keys in the wrong place. I gave the cheap one to a charity shop and kept this. I like it. I have the zipped bit for keys. A pouch bit for my phone. The front pocket is for my diary. Inside, plenty of space for my purse, tissues, and all that. It's perfect. I am a one-handbag woman.' She smiled.

'You must be the only one then.'

Juliet took Lola from Mira and left the garden with Rosalind. As they walked down the road, Juliet asked Rosalind how her job was going.

'Good. I've been doing a lot of extra hours down in Cowes.'

'I saw the crowds when I got off the Red Jet. Things are hotting up down there.'

'They are, and mainlanders pay proper tips. They seemed surprised that I can do anything beyond a basic manicure. I guess they think we've just come out of caves. They look genuinely shocked when I tell them I have people that come regularly from the mainland to see me.'

Juliet smiled. 'That's brilliant.'

'I need to get money together. I'm going to travel.'

'You're really planning to leave the island, leave Mum?' Juliet wasn't sure why the thought shocked her so much; they had all left at some point.

'It'll be good for me to get away. I never went to uni like the rest of you.'

'No, of course not. What will you do? Go on a cruise liner or something?'

'No, not that. The hours are crazy. I've spoken to some girls who've done it and they've had dreadful times. No. I want to go and work in some upmarket beauty salon or spa. I have a really good portfolio. Maybe I'll go to Dubai or America, I'm not sure.'

They crossed the military road, walked through the car park where Juliet was surprised to see several campervans. Some looked settled in.

Rosalind nodded over at them. 'They're not meant to be here overnight. There've been a lot of complaints. It's getting a bit druggy around here. Not sure I'd let my kids come down here at night like Mum and Dad always used to let us.'

'The police ought to do something.'

The path down to the beach had always been rough and steep, but Juliet was surprised at how much it had deteriorated.

'There were bad storms. The path is horrendous,' said Rosalind. 'I think they'll have to do something, maybe even put in steps.'

Suddenly, Juliet's feet slipped. 'You're right,' she said, and laughed as her sister grabbed her hand.

'Be careful, old lady,' Rosalind joked.

'Wow, this is worse than ever. I think I'll let Lola off. I need my hands free.'

Lola ran straight down onto the beach, running, sniffing, but always with one eye on them.

The tide was far out, and so Juliet suggested they walked to the right, adding, 'We can walk around the point to Compton if we feel like it.'

And so they started the walk. Despite the crowded car park, it wasn't densely packed as most holiday beaches would be on a day like this. They both took off their sandals and flip flops. Juliet rolled up her jeans as they walked in the shallow waters where the sea met the land. Juliet felt her feet sink into the sand, leave their print as the cold water washed away the dirt and dust of her journey.

'So, it sounded like you had a good time in China,' said Rosalind. 'But you were very vague when I asked you about men. There must have been someone.' Before Juliet could answer, Rosalind grabbed her hand and scrutinised her nails. 'I see you've not done anything to your hands or feet, I'll give you a free manicure and pedicure now you're back. Anyway, tell me everything, who did you meet?'

'There wasn't anyone.'

'Come on, it's got to be better over there than on the island.'

Juliet smiled and shrugged. 'Honestly, there wasn't anyone.'

'I despair of you. You're thirty. Tick tock and all that. So, have

you come back to pick up where you left off with Gabriel? I think
he's still single. Someone in this family has to make a decent
marriage.'

Juliet's cheeks were burning as she leant down and picked up a
shell. 'You're forgetting Mira is married to Rhys.'

'We can't forget that, can we?'

Juliet was surprised at the bitterness of Rosalind's tone. 'I
thought you liked Rhys.'

'I've gone off him. Honestly, he's become a real pain. He's always
butting in, telling me how to live my life—'

'I'm surprised you see much of him, it's not like you go to
church.'

'Unfortunately, you can meet people in the strangest places,'
said Rosalind.

Juliet was about to ask Rosalind what she meant by that when
she realised they'd reached the point where they could walk onto
the next bay.

'Shall we just go round the point?' asked Juliet.

They clambered over a few rocks and then she saw it: miles of
sand, the beautiful expanse of Compton Bay. Where Brook was
snug, homely, Compton was wild and free.

'Come on, let's find the footprint,' said Rosalind and suddenly
they were children again.

They ran, and there it was, the fossil of a dinosaur footprint
that had been there for the last 120 million years. Juliet ran her
hands over its cold, bumpy surface; it still filled her with a sense
of awe.

'Amazing,' she said, 'it makes my two years away seem like nothing. I can still remember the first time Dad brought me here.' She
blinked the tears away and looked up at Rosalind. 'Dad said the
island never forgets. That's good, isn't it? It means it won't forget
Dad; it won't forget any of us.'

Rosalind shrugged. 'Although not all memories are good, there must be some things we'd rather it forgot.'

Juliet stood up, wiped the sand off her knees. 'You're right. I guess the trick is for some memories to be held more lightly than others.'

They started to walk back around the point to Brook.

Juliet looked at the cliff line. 'I've only just noticed, it's not just the path that's been crumbling, the cliffs look very different.' She smiled at Rosalind. 'See, the island can change, it's not just about the past.'

'It seems so slow though; I want to see more, see different places,' said Rosalind. 'I don't blame you going off travelling. Seeing the world, going somewhere people don't know you.'

'I admit it was fun, you know, at first, living anonymously in China. After being here where everyone knows what colour socks you've put on, no one knew me, no one asked me what I was doing. We all disappeared behind identical doors in this huge block of flats.'

'I'd really like that.'

'Yes, it was good for a bit, but I missed home in the end, I missed the island.' Juliet held out her right arm. 'It's why I had this done.'

'Shit!' exclaimed Rosalind. 'I can't believe it!'

Juliet touched the small black island outline tattooed on her arm. 'I had to give the tattooist a drawing of the island. Obviously she had no idea where the island was or even that it existed.'

'I really like it. Has Mum seen it?'

'Not yet.' Juliet grinned. 'She's still taking in the hair.'

They were back on Brook beach when Rosalind surprised Juliet by asking, 'Did Dad say anything special to you when you spoke to him in the hospital?'

Juliet hesitated. 'He said a few things. Did you get to speak to him on your own?'

She nodded. 'He told me he loved me, and to be careful. I had this feeling there was something else he wanted to say. He kept looking at me but not speaking. I've felt it before, you know, that there is something that we are not being told, you must have noticed it.'

Juliet shook her head. 'No, not really. But in the hospital Dad did talk about keeping secrets. He said there had been something he was going to tell you when you turned twenty-one, but something happened the day of his accident that made him change his mind.'

Rosalind swung around to face her. 'Did he give you a hint as to what it might have been?'

'No, nothing, but I know he had a long talk with Rhys; I have a feeling he might have told him more about it all.'

'Oh God, of all the people to tell.'

'I think Rhys is very concerned whether he should tell us or not.'

Juliet saw Rosalind clench her fists, give a tiny stamp of her right foot on the sand, gestures she'd seen her sister make since she was a toddler. 'If it's to do with me, I have a right to know.'

Juliet instinctively adopted a conciliatory tone. 'I think it's more complicated than that. Look, I know it's frustrating, but we are going to have to let Rhys take his time on this.' Juliet looked around, desperate to change the subject. 'Anyway, you look even more glamorous than when I left. Is there someone new on the scene that you've not been telling me about?'

'Not really.'

'Come on, who's the Prince Charming?' Juliet gave her an encouraging smile, but Rosalind scowled.

'I'm not a kid any more, Juliet. I've joined the real world now. No more princesses with love stories and happy endings. It's sad that fairy tales are bullshit, but it's the way it is.'

Juliet stared at her sister. There was a hardness in her voice reflected in her eyes.

Rosalind threw a pebble out to sea. It flew through the air, much further than Juliet could have imagined.

Juliet watched as Rosalind continued to throw pebbles with force. It wasn't a game; it was an expression of frustration and disappointment. Clearly Rosalind had been hurt, but Juliet had no idea how. When Juliet had told her father she'd look after them all, it hadn't seemed anything out of the ordinary. It was what she always did, act the mini-mum, the substitute elder sister, but everything seemed to have changed. She felt distant from them, as lost as those pebbles Rosalind was throwing out to sea. She was meant to have answers and yet she felt even more confused, more in the dark that anyone else.

She looked around and saw Lola pulling at some seaweed. 'I need to call Lola back. Hang on.'

Lola came back as soon as she was called. Juliet made a fuss of her, and they all walked back up the path.

'You were going to check your car – I would if I were you. There's been a few problems at the car park, break ins, that kind of thing,' said Rosalind.

Juliet walked over to her little blue car and touched it with fondness. She had driven it to the school where she taught every day for those years at home between uni and going to China. The first car she had owned; it had seemed very grown-up and independent, as well as rescuing her from the tyranny of an ever-decreasing bus service.

She took her car keys out of her bag, opened the driver's door, sat inside, and blinked at the acrid smell of fake lavender from the air freshener she guessed Mira had put up. Juliet opened the driver's door wide to try and get some of the smell out.

'It may stink,' she shouted to Rosalind, 'but I have never seen it so clean. No crisp packets or wrappers from diet bars on the back seats. I think they've hoovered it out or paid someone to do it. I'll never keep it to this standard!'

Juliet got out, slammed the door, relocked it and zipped her car keys in her bag. It was good to have the car. It would give her independence for however long she was back home.

Out of excuses for staying away, they headed back to the house.

The evening dragged on. Rosalind, ignoring Cassie, put the television on and they all drifted in and out of the living room between answering the phone, putting flowers in vases or opening cards that had been pushed through the letter box.

Eventually, Juliet felt she could go to bed. In her room, she opened her window wide and heard the familiar noises of crickets, chirping, a robin still singing long after most of the other birds were silent. There were lights over in the car park, voices, the occasional car on the main road. Only in August would there be so much happening out there. Usually, it was black and silent.

It seemed to Juliet that she had returned to a family far less at ease with itself than the one she left. Of course, they were all devastated by the loss of her father, but there was more, nuances not conveyed in emails, texts and the very occasional video call.

Mira was unhappy; her father had been right, and what was this mistake Mira had said she'd made? Why wouldn't she tell her? Juliet's mind drifted to Rosalind, pictured her throwing those pebbles into the sea. She was clearly hurting and angry, but not just with grief. And then there was Cassie. She was even more uptight than usual. What had Dad said about her? That it was so lonely being forced to keep secrets. It had never occurred to Juliet that Cassie might be keeping secrets, be lonely. It had always seemed Cassie's choice to cut herself off from them all, shut the door of the music room and never come out. Surely Cassie's life had been exemplary: the gifted, the exceptional, never putting a foot wrong.

Juliet stared into the darkness and shivered. Underneath all the grief and sadness, the anxiety over her sisters, she recognised another emotion – fear. It had taken root when her father had spoken to her in the hospital. And that fear was telling her something was very wrong, that ahead lay uncertainty and danger.

4

Early the next morning, Juliet went for a long walk on her own down on the beach. She had that feeling of walking in a cloud of cotton wool, numbing the pain of loss. The anxiety of travelling, the grief, it had all left her exhausted.

She sat down on the pebbles at the top of the beach and watched two young men with their surfboards running into the sea.

Juliet closed her eyes, let the sun rest on her cheeks, felt the breeze in her hair. She needed to spend a few moments alone thinking about what she would do next. As she'd told her mum, she didn't want to go back to teaching. What she longed to do was get back to her art and a possibility, that she hadn't told the family about yet, had opened up. A friend from university, Alistair, had started an online business taking commissions for portraits. This was getting to be so successful that he'd asked Juliet to share the work with him. He'd handed her a commission for her to see if it was the kind of thing she'd enjoy doing.

However, there was another proposition from Alistair that she was more torn about. Although the commissions could be done remotely, he had suggested she work in a studio with him in Edinburgh. Although this sounded exciting to Juliet, she was unsure about the move.

Firstly, there was her love of the island and the fact her mum might need her to stay with her. There was also the question of Gabriel. He was the son of the local vineyard owner, Maddie, and after years of just being friends, Juliet had had a brief but intense fling with him before she left for China. She'd hoped he'd visit her out there, but he'd never made it and now she felt she had to find out just how serious this relationship was.

Juliet opened her eyes, took a deep breath of sea air, and then reluctantly stood up. She ought to go back to the house.

She walked over the pebbles and up the steep path, smiling at the families excitedly making their way to the beach.

When Juliet returned, she saw her mother's car and concluded that her mother and Cassie had returned from the hospital.

She found them in the kitchen, along with Mira. Cassie was reading texts, Mira was making coffee, and her mother was arranging yet more flowers in a jug.

'Some more came this morning and I've run out of vases,' her mother explained.

'A lot of people loved Dad and they care about you. How are you this morning? How did things go at the hospital?'

'As well as they could have. They had everything ready for me.'

'Did you get any sleep?'

'Not really. How about you?'

'No, I didn't either. It's hard to believe yesterday wasn't all a horrible dream, isn't it?'

Just then, Rosalind came in.

'You look dressed up,' Juliet said.

'I'm going down to Cowes, to work. I had a lot of appointments booked, so I thought I'd better go and do them.' She looked over at their mother. 'Mum doesn't mind, do you Mum? You know you can phone me any time.'

'Of course, you go now,' said their mum.

Rosalind picked up her bag and left through the patio doors.

Juliet was shocked. 'Rosalind shouldn't be going to work.'

'Why ever not? She's best kept busy,' her mother said firmly. 'Some people, like Mira, find their own thoughts comforting, but Rosalind will just get depressed. She needs people, she needs to talk. At least if she's in work, people will be kind, give her attention. She can always come home if she finds it too much.'

It still seemed odd to Juliet, but she didn't say any more.

Mira poured coffee, and they all sat at the kitchen table in silence.

'So, on the whole, you enjoyed your time in China?' Cassie asked finally.

'Yes, it was good, the children were lovely, but as I said, some of the days were long, as I was expected to teach adults in the evenings as well.'

'The language school got their money's worth out of you then?'

'I guess, but I was working those hours over here at school anyway, and at least in China I didn't have the paperwork. Everyone is so keen to learn English that my students were all very attentive.'

'I thought the flat you were living in looked a bit bleak.'

'Yes, it was a bit, but everywhere was very clean and the transport and shops were good.'

'But you wanted to come home?'

'I missed everyone and, like I told mum, I want a break from teaching.'

'I'd not realised. So what will you do?' Cassie asked.

Juliet took a deep breath. 'I've a few ideas; I want to go back to doing my own art.'

'But it's very hard to earn a living that way. Teaching is safe, pays the bills,' said her mother, the words boringly familiar.

Juliet didn't reply, refusing to be drawn into the same old argument.

'You've always loved drawing and painting; if that's what you want to do full time, I don't see why you shouldn't at least give it a go,' said Cassie.

Juliet blinked with surprise; her sister hadn't been interested in her art before. 'You do?'

'Yes, now is the time in your life to try something new. You've no mortgage or kids. Have you any ideas how you might go about it?'

Juliet tugged at a short strand of hair, avoided looking at her mother. 'A friend, Alistair, has offered me some work which I am considering,' she said nervously.

'What is it?' asked Cassie.

'Apparently, people are starting to want to have real drawings again, pencil portraits. I think they are fed up with selfies and photographs.'

'But you can't earn a living doing that, unless you charge a fortune, surely?' said Cassie.

'It's not the old idea of people sitting for portraits. People send you photos, and you use them. I know it's not exactly the kind of thing my tutors would have raved about, but it means you can charge very reasonable rates for what is actually a decent portrait and people love them. Alistair has so many commissions he can't cope, and that's why he's asked me to work with him. He's sent me a commission to have a go, see if I enjoy it.'

'I have to admit, it sounds like you've given it a real thought through. Maybe you should give it a go,' conceded her mother.

Juliet smiled, relieved her mother seemed to at least accept the idea, and decided the discussion about the move to Edinburgh could wait for another day.

Seemingly placated, her mother turned the conversation to Mira. 'Has Mira told you about her new venture?'

Juliet shook her head. 'No, what's that?'

'Mira has organised a very successful retreat up at Gabriel's new lodges, haven't you?'

Juliet turned to Mira. 'You didn't say,' she signed.

'It was for Deaf adults, just a week earlier in the summer, it went very well. Gabriel joined in as well, he even learned some signing,' Mira signed back. 'Everyone had a good time, the lodges they have built on that land by the vineyard are lovely. There are not many, but they are beautifully set out. The evenings were the best, having barbeques, watching the sunsets.'

'You stayed up there?'

'Yes, but just for a few nights. Gabriel organised things very well, it was... special.'

Mira looked down, but through the curtain of hair Juliet could see her blushing, winding her wedding ring round and round her finger. What was going on?

Oblivious to Mira's discomfort, Cassie said, 'I was surprised you decided to go to China in the end, Juliet... you and Gabriel were together before you left, weren't you?'

'Well, we went out a few times...'

'I like him, he's been such a support to Maddie. It's good to see a young man look after his mother,' said her mother.

'You really know how to sell someone, Mum,' Cassie laughed, and Juliet was suddenly aware of how seldom she'd seen her sister laugh.

'How a child treats their parents matters,' said her mother. 'Juliet could do a lot worse. She isn't getting any younger, all this jetting around has to stop sometime.'

'I was teaching English, not backpacking around the

Himalayas.' Juliet tutted and then turned to Cassie. 'So how is orchestra? Any tours coming up?'

'I have a few weeks off now,' Cassie replied and then pressed her lips firmly together.

The conversation felt like a maze where Juliet kept reaching dead ends.

She tried again. 'Rosalind was talking about travelling or at least working abroad.'

Her mother's reply surprised her. 'I think that would be good for her actually. She could do with getting away.'

'I thought you'd want to keep your last baby at home for ever,' Juliet said with a smile.

'Even I realise Rosalind has to fly the nest sometime. She needs to get money together first though. She's working hard, and she even does some restaurant work over in Southampton occasionally, which seems to pay very well.'

'Restaurant work that pays well?' queried Juliet.

'I don't know exactly what it is,' her mother said quickly.

Cassie and Mira both seemed to avoid eye contact with Juliet, and she wondered what was going on.

Without warning, her mother put down her mug, placed her hands over her face and started to silently sob. Juliet moved next to her and put her arm around her.

Her mother, eyes still covered, shook her head. 'I can't cope with all this... how do I manage everything without him?' She put down her hands but still didn't look at Juliet.

'Mum, you have me, you have all of us, you're not on your own.'

Her mother finally turned to face her, her eyes wide, deep, dark, impossible to read. 'You don't understand, you can't.'

'Rhys is coming later to talk about the funeral... we can all help, Mum, you'll see, we're all here for you,' said Mira.

Cassie reached over to their mother, squeezed her hand. 'I'll sit with Mum now and sort some of the paperwork out,' said Cassie. 'Have you work to do, Juliet?'

Cassie sat upright, business-like and Juliet sensed she was being pushed away again.

'I suppose I could have a go at this commission Alistair sent me.'

'Yes, best get on with that then. You go upstairs, it'll be quieter up there,' said her mother.

Juliet felt hurt. Her mother clearly wanted Cassie. She looked out in the garden and saw the workshop.

'Do you mind if I work out there?'

'Of course, not, it should be used.'

'Right, okay, Mum. If you need anything though, get me, okay?'

'Of course.'

Juliet went upstairs to find her drawing equipment and her laptop, and then went out into the garden.

She opened the door of the long rectangular building. It was hot and dusty inside, the familiar smell of wood, shavings and dust almost overwhelming her. Along one side was the main workbench with her father's tools still set out, all very neat and clean. At the end was an old armchair where she'd often sat and done her sketching.

She perched on one of the stools at the workbench and looked out of the large window. To the left, the house and kitchen leading to the gate; to her right, the rest of the garden leading down to the hedge that separated them from the main road that ran along the side of the beach, and in front of the oak tree.

Her father had always loved the ancient tree, and together they'd imagined it growing up from the young sapling planted over a hundred years ago.

Juliet left the workshop and went over to touch the bark of the tree. If she could feel her father anywhere, it would be here. A vertical white line ran down one side of the trunk, from the night it was struck by lightning. At the bottom was a small wooden plaque she had made with her father. *Sunday 20 August 1995, 10.30 p.m., I was struck by lightning, but I survived, and now I am standing tall.*

Juliet sat on the grass in front of the tree, her hand still on the bark.

'Remember that night, Dad? It had been such an exciting day. I remember seeing Mum and Cassie arrive home, Mum carrying Rosalind – she was so tiny wasn't she! It must have been so emotional for you, seeing your Rosalind for the first time. Mira and I had spent the morning making that banner. I remember being so desperate for the sun to shine for Mum. And it did for a short time. But then, much later, after we went to bed, the storm came in. I remember how scared I was. The thunder seemed to shake everything in my room and then as I looked out, I saw a flash of light and a crackling sound as it hit the tree. I was terrified and crept out of the bedroom and looked down the stairs, saw the light on in the kitchen and went to find you. "Our tree, Daddy – it's been struck by lightning," I said. You looked out of the window and said, "You're right."

'"We have to go and save it."

'"No, it's too dangerous out there, but it's not on fire."

'"On fire?"

'And then you told me all about what happens when lightning strikes a tree. You told me that because it was struck on the side, you were confident it would survive, and you were right.'

Juliet took her hand away from the tree, closed her eyes, remembered the warmth of her father's hand as he held her, and she'd sat with him, talking. Eventually he'd said it was time to go back to bed, and as a treat he'd heated up some milk and given her a biscuit and taken her back to bed just as the grandfather clock chimed eleven.

Juliet remembered the feeling of being warm and feeling safe, and then like that flash of lightening the realisation shot through her that all the reassurance, that feeling of life making sense had now been snatched away. Her father had gone. She'd known it as a fact yesterday but it was only slowly sinking in. Was this how nature helped you cope with losing someone? They took them away from you piece by piece?

Juliet returned to the workshop and walked around, touching things lightly, smelling them. One large drawer had been hers, and when she opened it, she saw spare sketchbooks, a range of sketching pencils, and other equipment still there safely. However, there was also a key that she didn't recognise. It was an ignition key with a beautiful old Volkswagen fob, the VW logo, silver on black leather... odd. This must be the key her father gave to Mira. What on earth was it all about?

Juliet chewed on her thumb and, confused, returned the car key before shutting the drawer. Then she remembered Rosalind's musical box and opened the cupboard where she guessed her father would have put it for safekeeping. There it was, like the others, a polished walnut box, with exquisite marquetry on the top. On the sides were slots for photographs just like on hers, except here there were photos of Rosalind as a baby, when she was ten, fifteen, an adult. Juliet turned it around in her hands, why had her father wanted to keep this from Rosalind? The box was clearly finished, it was beautiful; her father would have been happy with it, she was sure. So why didn't he want Rosalind to have it?

She opened it and read the inscription on the inside of the lid, 'To our darling daughter Rosalind, born 14 August 1995'. Carefully she closed the lid, turned the box over and wound the small key. Turning it back, she opened the lid again. The tune her father had chosen for Rosalind was 'Somewhere Over the Rainbow'. As Juliet listened, the tune filled the workshop and, as always, music had a way of reaching raw emotion inside her. There was a deep sadness but also a feeling of things not finished, questions not answered. All those cryptic messages about boxes and keys, the warnings. She was sure she should have understood them, that she was letting her father down by not knowing what they meant. Somehow, she had to find out.

_____

5

The funeral for their father was to be on Monday 15 August.

In the week before, Juliet spent a lot of time in the workshop drawing. The commission turned out to be much more all-consuming than she expected. The portrait was of someone's daughter; it was to be her eighteenth birthday present. The daughter knew about it and had chosen a number of photos to send and even made a short video of herself talking about things she enjoyed, her hobbies and the like. Juliet felt she was really starting to know the girl, and as she started to compose the portrait, it seemed to absorb some of those impressions. Juliet was soon lost in the work. It wasn't only the work that consoled her, however. In here, she felt closer to her father than anywhere else and in a way that warmed rather than saddened her.

Mira returned to sleep at the vicarage. Cassie stayed close to their mum, seldom

leaving her side, while, in contrast, Rosalind seemed to stay out of the house as much

as she could.

Juliet gave a cursory thought to clothes for the funeral, before realising she needed something more than jeans and T-shirts. Her sisters had never been much good for borrowing clothes from; Mira had so few, it never seemed fair to take them, Rosalind's were too fashionable and uncomfortable, and she could never imagine borrowing clothes from Cassie, even though she had plenty of black clothes as she often wore black and white for concerts. And so, Juliet drove into Newport, picked up some black trousers and a conservative top. She guessed these would always be the clothes she wore to her father's funeral; they would never be worn again.

The day before the funeral was Rosalind's birthday, but, as they had a family meal planned for the following weekend, Rosalind spent the day with friends.

The morning of the funeral finally dawned, far too sunny and bright. The service was at eleven, and Juliet, her sisters, and their mother had decided against cars to get to the church and so walked together up through the village.

The day before it had finally rained, washing down the dusty roads, freeing the scent of the wild roses that weaved themselves among the hedges. Juliet was touched by the respect of the villagers, some of whom walked quietly behind them, some who stopped their gardening and stood solemnly as they passed. There were of course holidaymakers walking in the opposite direction, with bodyboards and picnics, but they walked quickly past, avoiding eye contact.

When they arrived at the church, Juliet walked to the front with her family. The coffin was already in place. She glanced around, recognised Anwen, Rhys's sister. She had toned down her Goth look from the last time Juliet had seen her, but she still had the black hair and eye make-up and was wearing a black leather jacket with badges pinned down each arm. There was a hard sadness about her, her red lips pressed together, a refusal to exchange glances with anyone.

Rhys came in from the vestry at the side of the church with a few members of the choir, numbers depleted by the summer holidays. He had the same stunned, tense look he had had since the day her father had died, and an uncustomary nervousness about him. Juliet saw the tips of his fingers tremble as he turned the pages of the service book; in some of the hymns, she saw him stare blankly at the floor.

When they came to the eulogy, Rhys placed his notes on a small lectern, spoke and also signed. He opened with a summation of their father's life, the kind you hear at funerals. He did add warmth and colour, however, by mentioning her father's delight in his wife and family, his love of nature and the island where he had spent all his life.

When this part was finished, Rhys removed his glasses, gave them an unnecessary wipe, paused a few seconds too long, implying a searching for words rather than respectful silence. Even when he signed, his hands and fingers seemed uncertain.

'I had the privilege of sitting with my father-in-law on his final days on earth. In my work, I have sat with many people as they have passed. Some are at peace with their life, some have sadness and regret. Ian had so many good memories of life with his family, with Helena, and his daughters, Cassie, Juliet, Mira and Rosalind.' He looked over at them. 'You were his life, his world. He talked about you all with such love and devotion. He also shared more private matters. Even if he made mistakes in some of the things that had been withheld, you can be sure that whatever choices he made were done in love.'

Rhys turned to the whole congregation. 'It is both a privilege and a responsibility for someone to confide in you, but when what you learn affects others, we can be faced with a dilemma. Do we keep silent, respecting the wishes of the person who has confided in you? Do we reason that these things are best left in the past, buried, forgotten? But what if a person has committed wrongdoing, should we expose that? Surely sin should be punished. But what about those around them? We have no idea how it will affect those close to them, their family, our whole community.' Rhys was speaking very fast now, his eyes wide, wild. His words echoed around the church, as the congregation held their breath. No one dared move, not even a twitch of a service sheet, sniff, or cough; there was silence.

Rhys suddenly looked down, blinked as if he had forgotten they were there. He wiped his glasses again, took a breath. 'But enough, that is for another day.' He caught his breath, steadied his voice. 'This morning we are here to remember Ian. He showed and spoke a great deal about his love and devotion to his wife and four daughters. Everything he said, or did not say, was because of the love he had for them. Ian left this world at peace, surrounded by his family. We thank God this morning for his life and for the wonderful gift he was to each of us.'

Rhys stood back from the lectern and bowed his head. He had finished.

Juliet felt the congregation breathe again. It had been a bizarre eulogy. The few words of comfort at the end were lost in the tension that had preceded them.

Juliet then noticed the organ was playing, and people were slowly coming to, standing up and starting to sing the final hymn.

Even for a funeral, it was a very subdued congregation who left the church. Juliet spotted Gabriel sat with his mother. It was strange to see him in a suit and she was shocked to see he'd grown a beard. It was short, neatly trimmed and suited him. It made his brown eyes shine with greater confidence. Juliet felt guilty at the ray of warmth that forced its way through the sadness. She quickly gathered her feelings and walked on.

The immediate family gathered around the grave that had been dug, waiting for her father's coffin. Juliet stood next to Mira and they held hands, while Rosalind clung to their mother. Cassie stood alone; head bowed.

After the short service, Juliet went to speak to some of the neighbours. Rosalind, she noticed, was knelt by a grave reading the headstone earnestly. Juliet knew whose grave it was and was not surprised to see Gabriel and his mother go over to her.

Juliet knew Gabriel had always called his mother Maddie, a kind of combination of her first name Madeline and Mamon. After her conversation with her own mother about shortening names, Juliet thought it was a shame that everyone had adopted Maddie when Madeline was such a pretty name.

When she was able, Juliet walked over to join them. Rosalind stood up, smiled at Juliet. 'I'll just go and see how Mum is,' she said and quietly left them.

Maddie stepped forward, held out her arms and kissed Juliet on both cheeks. 'Juliet,' she said, her voice heavy with French accent, 'I am so sorry for the passing of your father. We were devastated to hear what had happened. We were all so fond of him; we shall miss him.'

Maddie was wearing a sleeveless black linen shift dress and a small black hat. She looked, as always, very chic, younger and more fashionable than Juliet's mother, even though Juliet was pretty sure they were the same age.

'Thank you, Maddie, and thank you so much for coming.'

'Your mum said you were back in time to see your father in the hospital,' said Gabriel.

Gabriel, having been born and grown up on the island, had no trace of his mother's accent. Juliet felt her cheeks burning; it felt a long time since she'd heard his voice and she'd not been prepared for how it would affect her.

'Yes, at least we had some time to talk.'

'He was such a good father,' said Maddie. 'You girls were his life.'

'We had some wonderful times growing up.'

'You girls, like my boys, were very lucky to grow up here. I often think about those early days, innocent times. We used to have barbeques together on the beach, didn't we? We provided the wine; your dad did the cooking and you kids would play on the beach. I always imagined we'd grow old together, you children would have the next generation. It goes to show you never know, do you, which way life will go.'

Juliet saw Maddie glance down, flinch with pain. These were the graves of her husband, Clarence, and son, Harry.

'Dad mentioned Harry when we were talking in the hospital actually. Your son died so young, didn't he, and so soon after your husband. What a terrible time for you.'

'It was. I lost my Harry the same day your mother brought home your new sister Rosalind from the maternity hospital. Your parents gained a child the day I lost my son. That is the way of life, I suppose.' Maddie frowned. 'It seems to me odd that your father should remember my Harry on his death bed.'

'His mind wandered a lot, flipping between the past and the present.'

'Rhys gave a very unusual eulogy. Your father's words seem to have unsettled him.'

'I know, but I have no idea what they talked about,' Juliet acknowledged.

'It seemed very odd to talk about sin and punishment at a funeral.'

'Um, yes,' said Juliet, not sure how she should reply.

'But he did speak about your father's love for you all,' said Gabriel, clearly trying to lighten the mood.

'Yes, he did.' Juliet shot him a grateful smile.

Maddie, however, was not ready to move onto easier things. 'I was surprised to hear your father had been drinking while driving; it seems very... out of his character.' For all her apparent softness, there was occasionally a piercing directness from Maddie.

'It was a shock to us too. He'd had a bit of an issue with drink years ago, but we thought it was well in the past. Apparently, something upset him on the day of his accident – you know it was his birthday.' Juliet swallowed hard. 'I don't know what was wrong, but I hate to think of him up there on the Downs on his own so unhappy.' She looked away, blinking fast.

Maddie sighed deeply. 'I expect he was trying to silence ghosts.'

Juliet frowned. 'What do you mean?'

'It happens as you age, the ghosts seem more real, they speak more clearly. You will learn that one day.' Maddie paused and then added, 'But that is of no importance today. I hope your father found peace at the end, that is what matters.'

Juliet saw Maddie shoot a glance at Gabriel and was struck by how much it reminded her of the looks between Cassie and her mother.

'Of course,' said Gabriel, in a slightly over-bright, rather embarrassed voice. 'I have wonderful memories of your father, Juliet.'

Juliet put her hand up to twirl her hair around her finger out of habit, but it was too short now.

Gabriel continued, 'Yes, your father was very kind, he took me under his wing when I was in my teens. I'm sorry I'd not seen him lately.'

'He was fond of you too. You enjoyed working with him in the garage, didn't you?'

'I did. He trusted me enough to give me responsibility, although he always checked my work of course. You know, he would let me go in and open up on the weekends? That was good for me.'

'What will happen to the garage now?' asked Maddie. 'I hope

the land is used well. The garage may be a bit ugly, but your father was a quiet neighbour. It would be good if a smart house was built there, I think.'

'I've no idea, but Mum will sort it out.'

'Well, I for one will be sorry to see it go,' said Gabriel. 'I have good memories from those times.'

'None of us girls were interested in cars, poor Dad, so it's good you were. You were like the son he never had,' Juliet said, smiling.

'It was good Gabriel had someone else to be a kind of father figure to him,' Maddie interjected. 'I am glad he didn't take up working with cars though, I don't know how I would run the vineyard and now the lodges without him.' She smiled proudly at her son.

'How are the lodges?' asked Juliet, relieved to move away from talking about her father for a moment. She was speaking to Gabriel, but Maddie replied.

'Up and running, and what a wonderful sight they are. The vineyard is making good money, but a few lodges have made a welcome addition; Gabriel has done very well.'

Gabriel shuffled from foot to foot, looking uncomfortable now. 'You should come and see them sometime,' he said to Juliet.

Before Juliet could answer, Maddie asked, 'So now you are home, are you going to settle back into teaching?'

'I don't know yet,' Juliet replied.

'It's a good steady job, allows a woman to take care of her husband and family,' said Maddie.

Juliet saw Gabriel redden, but at that moment she noticed that most people were leaving the cemetery. 'I need to join the family... Are you coming to the wake? It's only up the road at the pub.'

'Thank you, yes, but I don't think we will stay long,' said Gabriel. 'How long are you home for?'

'A few weeks at least, maybe longer.'

Juliet walked away, caught up with her mother and Cassie and headed to the pub where the wake was to be held.

The pub was far busier than they expected, the car park full, cars and motorbikes parked up along the road.

Ed, a friend of Gabriel's who was now part owner in the pub, came out to meet them in the garden. 'I'm so sorry, I had no idea we would have numbers like this. I hope you don't mind; I have set you up out here. It's chaos inside and I was able to cordon off this end of the garden. I have set the teas and refreshments on a table over there.'

'Thank you, that's lovely, it will be even better to be outside,' said Juliet's mother.

They went and joined the others, who, in their formal wear, were in stark contrast to most of the customers, who were in very casual, summer wear. They could hear loud shouts coming from inside the pub, and the sounds of people happily enjoying themselves.

Juliet grabbed a cup of tea and looked out over the Downs and to the sea. She breathed it in, tired from so much emotion. She saw Gabriel and Maddie arrive and went over to them. 'It's so busy, did you walk up?' she asked.

'Luckily, I found somewhere to park outside,' said Gabriel. 'It's too far for Maddie to walk back from here.'

'Let me get you a cup of tea,' Juliet said and found a chair for Maddie before she settled them in the shade.

'I just need to catch Cassie,' Gabriel said and went over to Juliet's sister.

'It's so hot isn't it,' Juliet sighed.

'Unbearable. And due to continue,' agreed Maddie. 'I see some of the wheat harvest is in already, but it's a few weeks before we can harvest the vines. I have been out there most days tasting the grapes, taking then to the winery for testing, choosing exactly the right time to harvest. You would find it very interesting, I'm sure.'

Juliet tactfully replied, 'I think you have done an amazing job up there. You and Gabriel have put so much work in, you deserve it to be a success.'

'Thank you, yes. I am fortunate that Gabriel is also committed to it.'

'I was sorry he couldn't come out to China though; I'd have liked to show him round.'

'Not everyone can take extended holidays,' Maddie replied, her tone sharp.

Juliet scowled. 'I was working, I was teaching.'

Maddie patted her knee. 'Of course, forgive me. Tell me about your time there.'

Juliet started to tell Maddie and was pleasantly surprised by what seemed genuine interest, Maddie even recalled a friend who had lived in the area where Juliet had been teaching.

Eventually Maddie said she needed to use the 'facilities'. As she left, Juliet saw Gabriel coming over to her.

'Has Maddie gone inside?' He asked Juliet, glancing at the pub.

'Yes, she just went in.'

'It's chaos in there, hopefully they will take pity on someone older. It was good to catch up with Cassie,' he said. 'I went up to hear her playing at Wigmore Hall recently, she was the soloist.'

'You went to a concert in town?'

'Why not? She's very talented, you know.'

'Of course I know that, but to go to London for a concert is so much hassle... you must have had to stay the night.'

'I did, but it was worth it. I've done it a few times.'

Juliet shrugged. 'Well, I hope she appreciated it. Mum gets up to the odd concert, but the rest of us haven't heard her perform for years.'

'Well, you should! She's amazing.' He gave a smile. 'You know, I had quite a crush on her in my teens, she was always a bit out of my league though.' He threw away the words with a laugh and then looked around. 'It's gone well today. It's not easy having a funeral in August when the island is so packed.'

'It's all a bit crazy. I was surprised how crowded it was down at Brook. I suppose it's good for the tourist industry.'

'Yes, the weather has been brilliant.' He moved closer, spoke in a quieter, more intimate way, 'I love your hair by the way, it suits you short.'

Her cheeks burned. 'Thanks, like your beard as well.'

At that moment, Ed, who had been collecting glasses, came over to them.

'Wotcha, Gabriel,' he said, slapping Gabriel on the back. 'When this crazy month is over, me and you need to go and have a decent night out.'

'I think I'm getting too old for all that now,' Gabriel replied.

'I refuse to go under, but you know I've not got down to Cowes once this year.'

'It's time you settled down, Ed.'

'I could say the same to you. Still, you must be raking it in up there now.' Ed grinned at Juliet. 'Good to see you home, even at such a sad time. Have you been enjoying your travels? I can barely get over to the Rose Bowl to watch the cricket, let alone get all the way to China.'

'It's been great thanks,' said Juliet, 'but it's always good to come home.'

Juliet glanced over at the pub and noticed Anwen entering.

Following her gaze, Ed said, 'I've seen a fair bit of *her* here lately; she has some strange friends, not that I'm including Cassie in that of course. I know they're quite close. You really wouldn't know she was related to Rhys would you.'

Before Juliet could reply, she saw Maddie come out of the pub and start making her way back to join them.

'Goodness, the queue for the ladies!' she complained when she reached them.

Ed smiled at her. 'It's good for business though. Right, best get back to work.'

As he left them, Maddie said to Gabriel, 'I saw the chap from the bakers inside. Didn't you want to speak to him about the delivery?'

'I do, but I'm not going in there, I can't stand the crowds. I'll give him a ring.'

Juliet's mother came over to them. 'Thank you so much for coming, Maddie.'

'It is a privilege,' replied Maddie. 'We are fortunate to have such wonderful children to stay by our side. If you need anything, please ask, you know how much I admired Ian, we shall all miss him.'

'Thank you, Maddie, that is very kind.'

Maddie put her hand on Gabriel's arm. 'I wonder if we could go soon, I am finding this heat quite exhausting.'

'Of course,' he replied.

Maddie smiled at Helena. 'I am sorry to have to leave a bit early but thank you so much for inviting us and remember, we are always here if you need us.' She kissed Juliet's mother on the cheek.

Gabriel smiled at Juliet. 'I'll be in touch then?'

She gave a shy smile and watched them walk away.

'Maddie really would be lost without Gabriel, wouldn't she?' Juliet's mother said.

'You're right. But I can't help feeling he's rather allowed her to take over his life. He has always wanted to travel, explore, experience life, and yet he is stuck here, and as far as I can see, he will never be able to leave.'

'I think Gabriel is very content with his lot,' replied her mother.

'He loves it up there just as much as Maddie, and they are running a very successful business.'

Before Juliet could respond, Barbara, the woman who ran the local shop, came over to speak to her mother.

'It was a lovely service, Helena. How are you keeping? I know it's difficult but do try to get out for the odd walk, and make sure you eat regular meals, even if they are small.' Barbara glanced at Juliet 'Are any of the girls going to be with you?'

Juliet's mother nodded. 'Cassie, Rosalind and Juliet are all with me at the moment, and of course Mira is never far away.'

'Of course, it's lovely when they stay on the island, isn't it? I am glad our Ed stayed. Us mothers and our children, eh! Your Mira is doing a good job here. Her and Rhys work hard; people in the shop say how kind he is, how he's always there for them. I'm glad they settled here and, let's face it, there are worse places to live. Now, let me know if there is anything we can do. If you can't face the super-market, give me a ring and me or Hubby will pop round some groceries.'

'Thank you, Barbara.'

'Remember, and I mean this, I'd like to help. Right, I'd better get back, it'll be busy at the shop. Take care, Helena.'

Barbara bustled off.

'Barbara is amazing, she has enough energy for an army,' said Juliet's mother fondly.

'She must have been a great nurse before she gave up to help her husband at the shop.'

Juliet's mother looked out into the distance. 'She's right though, there are far worse places to live. It's just too perfect a day for a funeral, isn't it? Remember going for early-morning swims with your dad?'

'I do, me and Dad were talking about it in the hospital. I'd take a packet of crisps, play on the beach while he swam. I loved that. It's a good memory.'

'Ah memories. And yet I feel he's still here. I don't mean like a ghost; I feel him everywhere. Is that wrong?'

'Of course not, Mum. I feel him as well, particularly in the workshop.'

'I'm glad you do...' Her mother paused.

Juliet could see the exhaustion on her face. 'Listen, it's been a long day. I think we should go home, don't you?'

As most people had left already, and the few that remained had moved onto alcoholic drinks and looked set for the rest of the afternoon, her mother agreed. Juliet found Cassie and Rosalind and, together with Mira and Rhys they left.

Juliet put her arm though her mother's as they walked along the road. At the junction, Mira and Rhys turned right and walked back to the vicarage while the others walked down towards the village.

They walked along in silence, and Juliet reflected on the day. She had always believed funerals were a rite of passage, a time to say goodbye, to lay things to rest. However, Rhys's eulogy had been disturbing. He was clearly still very upset and burdened by what her father had told him.

Juliet's mind went back to her own conversation with her father. She'd been shocked at his insistence that, given the right motive, anyone could kill. The words seemed so unlike her father, usually so gentle, so forgiving. But then he'd said he was warning her. Why would he think he needed to do that?

The only person who could give her any answers had to be Rhys. She had to know the truth now, she had to find out what her father had said.

6

After they had returned home, Cassie and her mum went into the living room and sat reading through cards, but Juliet could see Rosalind was restless and suggested they go for a walk.

They were planning to go down on the beach, but as the tide was in, they walked along the cliff tops. There was at least a breeze up there and fewer people. You could also see the coastline, the meeting of land and sea. It reminded Juliet that the island had boundaries; if it wanted to it could keep them all captive.

Rosalind's mind was clearly on other things. 'Funerals are weird aren't they – like sad weddings. And the wake always feels so awkward, doesn't it? I didn't know how to behave, people kept asking me how work is going, have I been to Cowes, things like that.'

'People don't know what to say half the time.'

'Gabriel was looking well though.' Rosalind gave Juliet a knowing grin.

'I didn't notice,' joked Juliet.

Rosalind picked her lip. 'So, Mum still wants to do the coming home meal next Saturday – I was surprised, it always seemed more Dad's thing than hers.'

'I know, but it matters to her as well.'

'To be honest, it always seemed odd to me when I was a child that Mum and Dad made such a fuss about a date a week after my birthday. None of my friends had a celebration for the day they came home from the hospital.'

Juliet put her head to one side. 'That's because their dads were probably with their mum's when they were born or would have seen the baby within hours. Our dad had to wait a whole week.'

'I know. It seems to me Mum took quite a risk going off with Cassie when she was so heavily pregnant.'

'Cassie had really wanted Mum to go up with her, it was more than a course wasn't it, there were auditions and things. Anyway, you did come early.' Juliet laughed. 'You always were in a rush.'

Rosalind grinned. 'I guess I was.'

The main thing is to make sure you keep next Saturday free,' said Juliet. 'After all, it is your twenty-first as well, you need to celebrate it with family as well as your friends.'

'Okay, okay, don't worry, I'll be here. I'll make sure I've next Saturday free, no going out with friends, no working.'

Juliet frowned. 'Oh, yes, Mum said you worked some Saturday evenings now, waitressing or something? She said it paid well which surprised me – where is that then?'

'Oh, some posh hotels, that's all.' Rosalind looked away.

'I didn't think anywhere paid much for waitressing.'

'For God's sake, Juliet, it doesn't matter. Anyway, I think we need to get back, we shouldn't leave Mum for too long.'

Juliet was shocked and hurt; she wasn't used to being pushed away by Rosalind.

They walked back in silence.

* * *

Later that evening, they sat down to a simple tea of cold chicken and salad. They were all quiet, and Juliet was aware of how much of their time over the past few days had been spent talking about the funeral. The passing of the day seemed to mark the end of one stage of mourning, as if now they had to start to find ways to join the world again.

'Maddie was asking me what would happen to the garage, Mum,' said Juliet.

'She wouldn't want to buy the land, would she?' said her mother. 'I know it's close to them, but she always wanted to expand the other way. But the vineyard is such a huge business now, it's her life.'

'It's so impressive what she has achieved up there,' agreed Rosalind.

'I think Harry and Gabriel's father would have preferred it to stay the farm he grew up on,' said Cassie.

'I was surprised he allowed it to be transformed into the vineyard,' replied their mother. 'Clarence loved the farm; it had some beautiful old woodland back then. I used to play up there when I was a child.'

'So, you knew the family when you were young?' asked Juliet.

'Oh yes, I was good friends with Clarence when we were in our teens. Of course, he went off to boarding school, but we went out a few times when he came home. Then I met your dad, and Clarence married this lovely girl from over in Ventnor. It was so sad when she died so young. Poor Harry was only about six I think.'

'Hang on, Maddie wasn't Harry's mother?' questioned Juliet.

'Oh no,' replied their mother. 'Not long after his first wife died, Clarence went to France on holiday, met Maddie and she came back with him. She had Gabriel and created Laurent Vineyard.

When you see what she accomplished, the vineyard, the winery, the shop and everything, all from scratch, well it's very impressive.'

'What an amazing woman,' said Rosalind.

'Depends how you look at it,' said Cassie. 'I happen to know Maddie's family was broke. So, to my mind, she snapped up a grieving, rich man and came back and turned his farm into a vineyard.'

Juliet was startled at the venom in Cassie's words and looked at her questioningly, but it was their mother who replied.

'Whatever the truth if it,' continued their mother, 'Maddie has done miracles up there and she's been incredibly successful.' Their mother moved deftly onto a change of subject. 'Now, about the garage, I guess I will have to go up and check out the fridge and things, there must be milk going off in there.'

'I can do that, Mum,' said Juliet. 'I could go up this evening if you'd like?'

'Oh, you don't want to do that after such a long day.'

'It's okay, the walk will do me good.'

'Let me run you up there then, but I'll not come in.'

'I can walk, it's not far.'

'No, I think it would be good for me to face it. The road to the garage leads on up to the Downs where Dad had his accident. I'm going to have to drive up it at some point, and I'd appreciate the company.'

'But you don't have to do it today.'

'I'd like to.'

Juliet could see this was something her mother really wanted to do and gave in.

Her mother smiled gratefully. 'Good, we'll go after tea.'

* * *

After they'd finished eating and cleared up, Juliet's mother fished a bunch of door keys from the dresser drawer.

'This big old rusty one is for the front door, if you can call it that. See that brass key ring? It has your grandpa's initials on it; your dad used the same key as his own father.' She handed them to Juliet, and they went out to her mother's car.

The garage wasn't far. They drove down their road, turned right onto the main military road and then, as they approached the entrance to the car park at Compton Bay they turned into a steep narrow country road.

As they drove, her mother spoke softly. 'I'll need to speak to someone about the garage. It's so run-down; I don't think anything in there has changed since your dad's father ran it. I went into a garage in town the other day to pick up a part for Dad and I couldn't believe it. The reception was like a hotel! Marble floor, coffee machine, comfy chairs. They had a window where you could watch someone mending your car.'

Juliet laughed. 'Dad would have hated that.'

'He would, but it made me realise how old-fashioned your dad's place was.'

'But it didn't matter. He was working on his own, and he just had his regulars.'

'I know, but he was a clever man. He should have done more.'

They passed the turning for the vineyard on their right, and then a little further on they reached the garage on the left.

'Do you mind if we carry on up the road, please?' asked her mother.

'Of course not,' Juliet replied.

They drove on; the road became increasingly bumpy, and her mother went slowly, trying to avoid huge potholes and thick tracks of mud left by tractors. Without warning, she pulled into a passing place and Juliet instantly knew why.

She looked over at a stone barn on her right, set back off the road. There were no flowers, no signs of what had happened there.

'He had driven down here,' said her mother, 'and then lost control. I hate driving around here. If you don't drive carefully, it can catch you out.'

Together they got out of the car and went over to the barn. Juliet held her mother's hand. They saw a rabbit chewing grass, a buzzard swooping over the field. Nature carried on. In the hedge, Juliet saw a few red poppies which she picked and laid against the wall of the barn. They stood together in silence for a short time, and then quietly got back in the car.

Her mother smiled at Juliet. 'Thank you, love, I was dreading that, but it wasn't as bad as I expected. It's odd, isn't it, you'd never know anything had happened there. Come on, I'll take you to the garage now.'

They drove to the top of the road, turned around and back down towards the garage. It looked even more dilapidated than before.

'Are you sure you don't want to come in?' said Juliet.

'No, not today love.'

Juliet saw a flash of pain on her mother's face. 'I understand. Leave me then, I'll enjoy the walk home.'

'You sure?'

'Of course, it'll do me good.'

Juliet's heart was racing and it surprised her – she hadn't expected to feel nervous. She opened the front door and went in. The garage was dark and cold, functional. She put on the lights, which flickered to life.

To one side of the main garage, she saw a small blue Fiat Panda parked alone.

She waited until she knew her mother would have time to drive home and then rang her.

'Oh gosh, yes, Dad told me when he came home the day of the accident that Walter had left his car with him. It needed an MOT, and they were off on holiday, Dad was going to see to it, but of course he never did. I know he said they'd gone until September or something, so there was no rush. Anyway, it's probably best just left in there for now, isn't it?'

'I think so; I was just checking.' Juliet rang off and went into the tiny room her father called his office.

In there was one scruffy, oil-stained chair, some paperwork but no laptop on the desk – her father must have taken it home. On the wall was a small pegboard with one set of car keys hanging up, with a luggage label on. Those must be the keys to the blue Fiat.

Behind her, there was a small fridge, and she took out a carton of milk, poured the remainder down the sink. There were a few mugs, a jar of coffee, but her father's old flask that he refused to update was missing, and then she remembered he had taken it to the Downs the night of his accident. She saw a new box of choco-late beans and the biscuit tin, old and tatty now, but it still had the vague outline of owls painted on it. Juliet had made it for her father when she was in her teens. She remembered drawing the birds, painting them, and then wrapping the picture around the tin. She had carefully covered it and her father had taken good care of it. She picked it up, put it in her bag.

Glancing in the bin, she saw the usual debris: the wrapper from the packet of biscuits, paper and bit of string, an old envelope with writing on it and something green sticking out. She'd need to come up with a bin liner sometime, sort this out.

Suddenly she felt and heard a cold, whistling breeze from the corrugated roof. In her head she knew it was just one of the many draughts in this place, but she shivered nonetheless and looked around nervously. She couldn't help remembering Maddie's words about ghosts whispering. She wondered what the ghosts would be saying now.

She walked around the building but there was nothing to see here, and once outside she was glad to lock the door and walk away. Out here the sun shone, warming her face, and the ghosts were silent.

7

SATURDAY 20 AUGUST

Juliet woke early on the Saturday of Rosalind's coming home meal. Today's wasn't a pleasant heat; it clawed at her, and even at this time, the air was too thick. Despite having all the windows open and sleeping on top of her duvet, she'd been too hot, and she was relieved to get up and have a shower. Today was too warm even for her to wear jeans and she reluctantly found a plain cotton skirt, knowing Rosalind was going to tease about her white legs.

She went downstairs to find her mother already up.

'Oh, Lola's here,' said Juliet, spotting the dog in her basket.

'Yes, Mira dropped her off first thing. Rhys has meetings and she's meant to be visiting people. I have to say she looked done in, and I wanted her to go back and rest. I'm glad she's staying here tonight after the meal. I hope she'll have a lie-in in the morning.'

'Is Rhys staying as well?'

'Mira wasn't sure. He doesn't have any services tomorrow, but he has this routine of praying up at the church at midnight on a Saturday night. If he decides to keep to that he will probably go back to the vicarage after to sleep so as not to disturb us. By the way, I have invited Anwen to stay as well seeing as she is cooking for us.'

'Oh right, does she want to sleep in the spare bed in my room?' Juliet offered.

'Thank you, but Cassie has already offered for her to sleep in her room as they are quite good friends now. There is that fold up bed in there which is very comfy, Cassie said she could use that.'

'Oh, okay, if you're sure?'

'Yes, I think that should work out. Now, I wonder, could you walk Lola for me? I'm going to the supermarket in Newport with Cassie. Anwen has given me a very comprehensive list.'

'You're lucky she's free on a Saturday night. Where does she work?'

'In a pub in Newport. She's working from early this morning until teatime. Lots of lunch covers apparently, but she wangled tonight off. Oh, I forgot, we're dropping some things off at the charity shops as well, so we'll be a while.'

'I'll get out now with Lola before it gets too hot.'

'Good, and then I've made a list of things that need doing...'

Juliet glanced down at the list. 'Good grief, Mum, it's only family!'

'I know, but I want the house to look perfect.'

Juliet smiled at her mother, pleased she was able to get lost in something for a few hours at least. 'Of course, it'll be lovely. Right, I'm off.'

Lola came running over, tail wagging madly.

To Juliet's surprise, Rosalind was up early and offered to go with her.

Only a few other dog walkers were on the beach at that time in the morning. Lola had a wonderful time running, rolling in seaweed.

On the way back, Juliet's phone alerted her to a text. She felt her heart beat faster when she saw that it was from Gabriel.

If you are free, can you come to meet me this evening?

I have the family meal for Rosalind.

After? Please. Nothing heavy.

Okay I'll text you when the meal is over.

Bring my heart...

She smiled.

'Who's that?' asked Rosalind.

'Nobody.'

'You're blushing... is it Gabriel? He's not bad-looking, and that hint of a French accent is very sexy. They must be minted owning the vineyard and the lodges up there, all very posh. I'm surprised he hasn't been snapped up. How old is he?'

'Thirty-nine, same as Cassie.'

'So, is he asking you out then?'

'I don't think it's a date, no, he just wants a chat.'

Rosalind grabbed the phone. 'Tonight... eek! Bring my heart!'

Juliet laughed, opened her bag and unzipped the inner pocket. 'That's the heart he means. It was a little gift.'

'A heart and it means nothing? Sorry, I don't buy that!'

Juliet zipped the set of car keys carefully back in her bag, saying, 'Let's get back, Mum has a load of things to be done.'

When they arrived back home, Juliet found her mother had returned and started to work her way through the list of housework. Rosalind, she noticed, quietly disappeared, and so did Cassie.

Soon, she heard the sound of the piano drifting from the music room and realised Cassie had escaped into the music room. Usually, she would be frustrated at her sister not helping, but today there was something about her sister's playing that grabbed hold of Juliet and made her listen.

Juliet walked quietly to the music room, stood in the doorway and listened to her sister's playing, transfixed. Cassie was sat at the piano, her eyes closed, at one with her music. Cassie's first instrument was the violin, but her piano playing was just as beautiful. Maybe for the first time in her life, Juliet stood truly in awe at her sister's ability. She felt a wave of guilt, how had she missed this? Was it the case that in the eyes of family you could remain a caterpillar and only the world saw the butterfly?

Suddenly, Juliet saw Cassie's face crease with pain, and she snatched hands away from the piano. The room for a second was silent and then with a violent crash as Cassie slammed down the lid.

She looked over at Juliet and their eyes met. Juliet was shocked at the pain and sadness she saw in her sister's eyes, but there was something else there that stopped her going over to her. There was anger at being exposed and it felt voyeuristic rather than empathetic to stay. Juliet turned away.

Her mother's voice cut through the awkwardness telling them lunch was ready.

Rosalind was already there, and they sat together at the kitchen table in an awkward silence.

Juliet picked up a cheese sandwich. 'You know, the day you came home from the maternity hospital, Dad made these for everyone,' Juliet said to Rosalind to try to lift the mood. 'Mira and I drew a huge a banner and coloured it in. I guess it kept us out of Dad's hair for the morning. People from the village kept coming round with cards and food.'

Her mum smiled. 'I remember coming back, gosh, we were so tired, weren't we, Cassie? But it was so exciting to see everyone.'

Juliet glanced over at Cassie, but she made no attempt to

respond. Instead, Cassie had pushed her chair slightly back from the table and was staring down at her sandwich as if she'd, mentally at least, stepped away from the conversation.

'It felt like you'd been away a long time,' said Juliet said.

'Well, I'm sure it did.'

'Do you know where the photos of the day are?' asked Rosalind. 'I don't think we've looked at them for years.'

'Yes, they're upstairs, but I'd need to move the cases on top of the wardrobe,' said her mother, sounding weary.

'I can do that, just show me where they are,' said Juliet.

They went into her mother's bedroom; Juliet noticed a kind of woody, sweet smell.

'Have you got a new perfume?' she asked.

Her mother shook her head and picked up a small bottle of oil. 'It's frankincense.'

'Like the three kings.'

'Well, sort of, but it's helpful for all kinds of things. I use it for my arthritis – it's so good, I've recommended it to a few people. I mentioned it to Cassie, I think she gets a few aches and pains, and she has told Anwen about it for her hands. I should have shares in it! Now, I put some of the older albums behind there, you'll need to stand on a chair.'

Juliet got up and handed her mother the cases. There were two large cardboard boxes with lids, which she handed down next.

Her mother took the lid off one. 'Oh, this is all your father's bits; you know how he was for collecting things.'

Juliet picked up a small pile of photographs held together in an elastic band.

'Your father never got round to putting those in the albums. They're mainly of the barbeques we had on the beach.'

'Oh, Maddie was talking about those after the funeral.' Juliet took the band off and flicked through. 'That must be Gabriel and

Harry playing football with Cassie, and who is that good-looking chap giving you a glass of wine?'

Her mother smiled. 'That's Clarence, Maddie's husband. He was very good-looking wasn't he and very charming.'

Juliet grinned. 'You look so happy, Mum, and look at your hair, it's gorgeous.'

Her mother put the photographs back in the box, laughing. 'That was a long time ago.' She took out some old, yellowed albums. 'These are cigarette cards; Dad has a whole set of kings and queens.'

'Do you think they're valuable?'

'I shouldn't think so.' Her mother opened a stamp album. 'Do you remember these? They're your dad's collection of first day covers.'

'I do. He collected them for a few years, didn't he?'

'Yes, he started a few years before Rosalind was born. He would buy every set. Actually, the year she was born was a good year, look, January was cats, then these were my favourite, the pictures of the Globe theatre in London, weren't they beautiful?'

Juliet looked down and laughed at the stamps that featured a group of grey haired older men. 'I remember saying to Dad how boring these ones were, and he told me that the men had all been very important. One had invented the wireless and I remember he said that this chap, Rowland someone, had started up the post office. Dad was interested in so many things, wasn't he? Now these I did like.' Juliet pointed to the row of Christmas robins. 'They are so pretty. How long did he keep collecting?' She turned over the pages.

'Another, what, five or so years?'

'That's impressive. Can I look at the cigarette cards again?'

'Of course. Take the box and you can look at them all properly. Now, this is the box we need, so we might as well take them all down. Can you put everything back on top of the wardrobe for me?'

Juliet took the box to her room, put the cases back on top of the wardrobe, then followed her mother downstairs.

'Here we are,' her mother said breathlessly, holding out a pile of albums. 'I found a few that I've always meant to put on the computer, but never got round to it. This album is your actual coming home party.'

Juliet sat next to Rosalind as she went through the album. It showed them all sitting in the garden, chairs arranged in a horse-shoe. Her father was stood at the front, and her mother stood holding Rosalind.

'I'd arranged for someone to make a cake, and you girls all gave Rosalind little presents to welcome her to the family.'

'Who is that holding me?' asked Rosalind as she picked through the photographs.

Juliet took the photo. 'That's Gabriel.'

Rosalind laughed. 'Sorry, but he looks awful in that backwards cap and baggy T-shirt! Glad he's sorted a few things out since then.'

'He was very clever, but I think I was the only girl he spoke to back then,' said Cassie. 'He went round with a group of boys like him who pretended to be into heavy rock music and played on Game Boys.'

'Game Boys?'

'Old-fashioned, handheld games things – this was before games consoles and even computers took off.'

'Sounds lame!' Rosalind picked out another photo. 'And who is this holding me?'

'That's Harry, Gabriel's brother,' said their mother.

'Wow, he was hot.'

Juliet took the photo for a closer look. Harry was holding Rosalind, Maddie was stood next to him, looking slightly away, her face serious.

'Maddie looks unhappy,' Juliet said. 'I suppose it wasn't long since she'd lost her husband.'

'No, only a matter of months. It must have made family things hard for her. I remember feeling sorry for her that day. She stood apart, never held Rosalind, but she brought a very special gift. A white French lace dress, Rosalind looked so beautiful in it.'

'And to think that evening she was going to lose her son as well,' said Rosalind. 'That's terrible.' She paused. 'Oh look, here's one of you holding me, Mum. You were so pretty, how old were you there?'

Her mother laughed. 'Thirty-nine years young but thank you. I was so tired that day, well, for weeks after that, new babies are exhausting. I was glad I'd stopped my full-time work at the school. Supply work was more than enough for me those first few years when you came to us. Still, Cassie was very good, weren't you, when Rosalind first arrived. Do you remember that you used help me out with the night feeds sometimes before you went away, and even came home for weekends when you could? And you two younger girls were great as well.'

Juliet saw photos of herself with Mira on the garden seat. Rosalind had been carefully placed into her arms. She thought what very young ten- and eight-year-olds they looked in simple cotton shorts and T-shirts.

'So how old were you here, Cassie?' asked Rosalind, looking at a different photograph.

'Eighteen.'

'What on earth's going on with your hair?' asked Rosalind, laughing.

'Oh, I wanted it shorter than that... We all wanted to look like Rachel in *Friends*. I managed to persuade Mum to let me have the front layered, but to do the look properly I'd have had to have it cut much shorter and she said no. We had a few rows about that... hard to imagine it mattered so much now.'

'You do look older.'

'I guess I was mixing a lot with older people at orchestra or at work up on the vineyard, not just mucking about like some people,' she glanced at Juliet.

'When I got to sixteen, I worked at the pub in the food area,' said Juliet, glaring at Cassie. 'And I did a lot with Mira and Rosalind. I even took Mira to some of her hospital appointments... you never did any of that.'

'But you never played in London concert halls. I couldn't just turn up for them. It was one long round of exams, auditions, concerts...'

'But you enjoyed it, didn't you?' There was a pleading edge to her mother's voice.

'Of course, I am defending myself against the charge of opting out that's all.'

'Right, that's enough,' said their mother firmly. 'You were all wonderful children; your dad and I were very proud of you all. And that reminds me, Rosalind, your musical box. We forgot it on your birthday. It's in the workshop.'

'Oh, but Dad said...' Juliet paused, not wanting to finish the sentence. On her actual birthday Rosalind had been out most of the day and it had been easy to shelve the problem of whether to give her the musical box, but now she had to confront it. One part of her felt, like her mother, that Rosalind had a right to it. On the other hand, her father had seemed very insistent that Rosalind wasn't given the box and maybe she should respect his wishes.

'I know what your dad said, but he was unwell. I am sure he would want Rosalind to have it,' said her mother.

'Don't worry, I'll get it later,' said Rosalind and then looked back at their mother. 'I was thinking about the age gap between me and my sisters, I must have been a bit of a shock. You must have thought you'd finished having children.'

'Of course not.' Her mother smiled. 'You were a wonderful gift. Now, I think we should get on, come on, let's finish tidying up. Get this kitchen fit for Anwen.'

'She's cooking this evening?'

'She is, and I asked her to do duck as I know that's your favourite.'

Rosalind grinned. 'Good stuff. She's a very good chef, bit wasted in pubs, isn't she?'

'She'd like her own place one day,' said Cassie.

'It's a risky business opening up a restaurant.'

'You need to know what you're doing, that's all,' said Cassie.

'Now, girls, I know it's going to be difficult tonight,' said their mother, 'but I hope we can have some family time, celebrate Rosalind's home coming – that's what Dad would have wanted. No drama, just a quiet evening together.'

8

By the end of the day, the house was shining. The heat had eased and there was a slight breeze. It was an idyllic evening to eat outside. They had decided to find the old garden furniture and had covered the shabby table with a beautiful lace cloth which they decorated with candles and flowers from the garden.

'It looks perfect,' said Juliet and her mum smiled. 'Are those new earrings?'

Her mother fingered one of the small, silver, moon-shaped earrings. 'Mira gave them to me.' Her mother paused, looked Juliet up and down and smiled. 'It makes a change to see you in a skirt.'

'Yup, it's too hot for jeans. I've even put my best top on and, look, Rosalind has done my nails.'

Before her mother could answer, however, they were both distracted by the sight of Cassie. She was wearing a long red cotton dress, her hair hung loose and on her feet were flat brown sandals – very 'boho' and very different to her normal, formal black and white attire.

'You look great,' Juliet said to Cassie.

'Oh, um, thanks.'

'Very pretty,' said their mother. 'I've not seen that dress before, it suits you.'

Despite the positive words, their mother looked puzzled, and Juliet understood why. It seemed Cassie was making some kind of statement with her change of appearance, like a teenager trying out a new, more rebellious look.

Before she could ask any more, Anwen arrived. Unlike Cassie, she was dressed more conservatively than usual, in black trousers and a polo shirt, more business-like.

'I parked over in the field. Is that okay?'

'Of course,' said Cassie.

'Thanks so much for this,' Juliet said. 'It feels very posh having our own chef in to cook for us.'

'You're welcome. I like cooking like this, it's better than churning out pie and chips in a pub,' said Anwen. Her voice was a surprisingly soft lilting Welsh.

'How are you finding life on the island? You've been over since Mira and Rhys's wedding, haven't you?' Juliet asked her.

'Yes. It's taking some getting used to. I miss the gigs and nightlife on the mainland, but it's cool being close to the sea. I have been getting some fantastic fish from Ventnor, the lobster is amazing, and the farms over here are really great for supplying meat and fresh produce. I can see why food is taking off here.'

'Do you have a flat?'

'Yeah, in Newport; it's handy.' A phone pinged in Anwen's bag. She took out a very basic mobile and read the text. She quickly replied and then gave Juliet a quick smile. 'Right, I'd better get on.'

Anwen put her chef's apron on and very efficiently set to work. Her mother, Juliet noticed, seemed slightly at a loss without her usual role in the kitchen.

Rhys and Mira, accompanied by Lola, arrived at seven. Mira

brought a small overnight case and wore the usual denim skirt, this time with a blouse, and to Juliet's surprise, a thick cardigan.

'You must be baking,' said Juliet.

Mira shrugged but pulled the cardigan even more tightly around herself.

'Are you feeling okay?' Juliet signed.

Mira replied with a quick smile and then said, 'Sorry we're late. Rhys had yet more visits to make, Maddie up at the vineyard and then others, and then sorting out cover for the various rotas in the churches – it's a nightmare in August.'

'And what about you? Will you be going away anywhere?'

'We've not booked anything; we don't need a break,' said Rhys. He put his arm around Mira, but she closed her eyes in a grimace and gently pulled away.

Cassie came into the hall. 'I've made cocktails,' she proclaimed.

They followed her through to the kitchen, where Anwen was hard at work, her back to them, and they went out into the garden.

Outside, Rhys stayed very close to Mira. Juliet watched her sister, sipping her drink nervously, small sips like a bird, and wondered again what was wrong.

Her mum handed around sophisticated snacks that Anwen had made in advance. They were like fairy-sized portions of proper meals – a tiny bit of black pudding with bacon and eggs, and beef and Yorkshire pudding. They all tasted wonderful.

Rosalind joined them all, in a clinging strappy gold dress. Her blonde hair highlighted; her face professionally made up. Everyone seemed taken aback. They were used to Rosalind's sophisticated looks, but tonight there was a kind of red-carpet glamour, totally foreign to them and way beyond what would normally be worn at a family meal. Juliet decided it wasn't only Cassie making a statement this evening; she thought maybe Rosalind was making the point that she was not a child, not the baby any more.

'Are you staying? You look too glam for us,' asked Juliet.

Rosalind laughed in a slightly self-conscious way. 'Someone had to make an effort.'

Juliet took another of the gorgeous canapés, felt the breeze on her face and started to relax. Her mother was right, they needed a family evening together.

Rosalind spilt off from them soon after and headed down to the bottom of the garden. Juliet noticed Rhys finally leave Mira's side and walk quickly away to join Rosalind.

Mira put her drink down and signed to Juliet, 'Have you been busy?'

Juliet blinked; the question seemed very formal.

'Um, yes, I've finished one piece of work and I'm pleased with it.'

'Great. You mentioned about this friend Alistair in Edinburgh, do you think you will go up there then?'

'Maybe, but I don't want to rush anything. I think Mum needs an eye kept on her.'

'I'm here and Rosalind is for the time being.'

'But Rosalind wants to travel, and you said Rhys wanted to move.'

'I don't know what we'll be doing now,' Mira said and picked up her glass, this time taking a long drink.

Juliet could see her fingers trembling and she reached out, grabbed Mira's arm. 'Mira, are you okay?'

'Aah,' Mira exclaimed, her face flinching in pain as she pulled her arm away.

'What's wrong? Has something happened to your arm?'

Mira put down her glass, rubbed her arm gently. 'No, nothing.' Mira glanced down the garden. 'Things look a bit heated over there.'

Juliet looked over. Rhys was wagging a finger and Rosalind was glaring at him. Juliet was about to go and intervene when Rosalind left Rhys and strode towards her and Mira.

'What on earth is wrong?' Juliet asked, seeing the fire in Rosalind's eyes.

Rosalind signed and spoke angrily to Mira. 'I know he's your husband, but Rhys is a sanctimonious prick.'

'Rosalind, stop it, you can't say that,' interrupted Juliet.

'But he is. I don't know how you can bear him, Mira. He wants to destroy my life; I won't let him.'

Juliet couldn't imagine what Rhys had said but could see Rosalind was very upset. However, she was aware of her mother frowning in their direction.

'Shush, calm down. We'll talk about it later, but try and forget for now, Mum needs this evening to go well,' Juliet said.

'He needs to butt out of my life. I swear if he doesn't, I'll kill him,' Rosalind said.

Juliet was shocked at how angry Rosalind sounded, but before she had a chance to delve deeper into the issue, their mother called them all to the table.

Rosalind appeared to take a deep breath and put on a fixed smile. Relieved, Juliet went to sit opposite Mira at the end. Lola, who hadn't left Mira's side, now lay down and rested her head on Mira's feet.

Rhys sat between Mira and Juliet at the head of the table. He sat very still, stern, fiddled with the stem of his wine glass with one hand, drummed his fingers with the other. Rosalind sat on the other side of Juliet, Cassie opposite, with their mother at the head of the other end.

Juliet knew that Mira could get left out of large group chats, although at least with family everyone would sign and remember to cue Mira into a change of conversation. The bulk of the conversation was led by Rosalind, peppered with questions from her mother and Juliet. Rosalind spoke loudly, with a forced cheerfulness which Juliet guessed was partly in defiance of Rhys, but Rosalind loved being the centre of attention, and this was her night.

The meal started with a light fish mousse followed by the duck. Anwen and their mother had worked so hard, and Juliet felt sorry that the mood was so forced. She tried to help jolly things along, took some photos, related some anecdotes.

In the distance, the sun was making its final dramatic farewell, spreading orange and yellow streaks across the sky. Juliet watched; like autumn leaves there was a very narrow window to catch the colours of a sunset at their very brightest and best. There it was, the final burst of colour. Usually, Juliet felt exhilarated by the sight, but tonight the atmosphere was heavy and as she saw dark clouds replace the light across the sky; she felt that now all there was ahead of them was a gathering darkness.

A hard laugh made her refocus on the table; Cassie was drinking far more than usual. Occasionally, she would throw her head back in a rather self-conscious way. What really surprised Juliet, however, was seeing Cassie push back her seat and light a cigarette. She had always been obsessively anti-smoking, avoiding smoky places. Juliet saw her mother glance nervously at Cassie, obviously also stunned by her behaviour. Cassie was clearly avoiding eye contact, and Juliet knew neither of them dared confront her. Juliet, however, was even more certain that something was going on with her eldest sister.

When they reached chocolates at the end of the meal, her mother invited Anwen to sit with them. Anwen, apparently unaware of the strained atmosphere, sat back, looking happy and relaxed, and poured herself a large glass of wine.

'I'd like to thank Anwen for this exceptional meal,' said Juliet's mother.

'Hear, hear,' shouted Cassie, raising her glass.

Tentatively, the others raised their glasses too.

'To the best chef on the island,' Cassie continued, her words slurred, 'and my future business partner.'

An uneasy hush fell over the table.

'Cassie not now,' Anwen said.

But Juliet's mother picked up on it immediately. 'What do you mean, business partner?'

Cassie flapped a hand in Anwen's direction. 'We might as well tell them all, I'm so tired of keeping everything a bloody secret. Anwen and I are setting up a restaurant here on the island.'

'A restaurant?' said Juliet, stunned.

'Yup. It's very early days but this is the next stage in my life, and it's very, very exciting.'

Juliet's mother's voice shook as she said, 'But what about your music? What about orchestra? I don't understand.'

Her words seemed to sober Cassie up slightly. 'We don't have all the details worked out yet... and, well, orchestra is something we need to discuss.' She glanced nervously at her mother. 'But let's celebrate fresh starts, shall we.'

Cassie raised her glass, but this time no one else joined in.

Rhys coughed loudly. 'Anwen, have you told Cassie everything she needs to know about her future business partner? I assume you are both putting a lot of money into this venture, you should both know what you are getting into.'

Anwen groaned. 'For God's sake, Rhys.'

'Cassie has a right to know and so does her family.'

Anwen scowled. 'This is nothing to do with you, keep the hell out of my life.'

'You should be honest, that is all.' Rhys looked around the table.

Mira sat with her hands tightly clasped together in front of her, her mouth pinched, alert, clearly taking in everyone's reactions, not wanting to miss anything that was said.

Rhys coughed, took his glasses off and rubbed them. 'You all know your father told me things in the hospital and that I have been struggling with them ever since. Well, after a lot of thought and prayer, I have decided that I shall share with you what your father told me. In fact, I have no choice now, this all coming out very soon.'

'Hang on,' blurted out Cassie. 'At the funeral you said you didn't know how these things were going to affect people, and anyway, you promised Dad you'd keep the things he said to yourself.'

'I know, but I can't do that now; I promise you I don't take this decision lightly.'

'You can't say anything,' said their mother, panic in her voice. 'I forbid it. As a vicar, I would have expected you to show a great deal more discretion than this.'

'Don't expect any kindness from him,' spat Rosalind. 'He thinks he is God Almighty, that he can threaten and control people, it's pathetic.'

Rhys shook his head. 'You're wrong. I would love to bury all this, forget. But my calling is to lead people into the light, not leave them stranded in the darkness.' He put his head in his hands. 'I haven't slept for days, I have prayed and agonised over what I should do.'

Juliet's heart was racing, her mouth dry in anticipation. Was she finally going to discover what her father had said?

However, before Rhys could continue, Mira reached out, touched his arm, and signed, 'Are you sure this is the right time for this? This is meant to be a celebration for Rosalind.'

Rhys looked at her, his eyes filled with tears. 'I know, and I am not going to say anything more tonight.'

Juliet clenched her fists in frustration. 'If you have decided to tell us, why not get on with it?'

Ignoring Juliet, he looked directly at her mother. 'Helena, I am going to give you this evening to talk to your family. You know what you need to tell them. I know you will find it hard, but you need to do this.' He glanced around the table. 'In fact, you all have things you need to share. I know it's not the way in this family, but you really need to start talking to each other.' Rhys stood up. 'You must be brave, have courage. You must speak tonight.'

Cassie leapt to her feet. 'You can't go around giving ultimatums like this, and you have no right to break your word to my father.'

'I told you, it's out of my hands now. Either you speak this evening, or I will share everything I know tomorrow. I will go to the church now, pray for you all.' He kissed Mira lightly on the head and said, 'I will sleep at the vicarage, so I don't disturb you when I return.'

As he walked away, the silence was broken by the sound of a phone – Anwen's. She quickly took her iPhone out of her pocket, glanced at the screen, got up and made her way to the bottom of her garden, standing with her back to them.

They sat in silence, no one sure what to do next. Anwen's call was short and she soon returned. 'I'm sorry, I have to leave,' she said with a trembling voice and hurried into the house. Cassie ran after her.

'I think I'll clear up and then we can all have a drink, maybe a cold one would be better than more coffee this evening. You can all go and watch TV or something,' her mother said.

Juliet was shocked at the instant recovery of her mother; it was as if nothing had happened. She had a sudden and vivid flashback to a time when she'd once made a sponge that had cracked badly down the centre. Her mother had spread thick icing over the cake, saying, 'There we are, Juliet, no one will ever know.'

'Stop, Mum. Rhys asked us to talk to each other, I think he's right. You know things we should be told, we're not children,' Juliet demanded.

'Rhys doesn't dictate how we deal with things. We are a family, we decide, and I'm telling you, we don't need to talk about this now,' her mother replied and there was challenge in her eyes as she slowly looked around the table.

Rosalind stood up without saying a word and went into the house. Mira followed, but a few steps behind her. Juliet groaned; her mother had won. She wanted to scream with frustration, but instead, she ran out of the garden after Rhys.

She could see him walking up the road, lit up by tight beams of light from the new streetlamps. It was too quiet, with trees looming silently, silhouetted against a cloudy black sky. There were tiny pinprick stars, the moon a slither of light.

Juliet ran after him and grabbed his arm. 'Rhys, you have to give Mum time. She's not going to have some great heart-to-heart with us this evening.'

'Then I shall take charge tomorrow. I have to do this, Juliet.'

Juliet bit her lip. 'I'm scared. What did Dad tell you?'

'We'll talk tomorrow,' he said, and she knew he would not say any more to her that night.

Juliet stepped back, the darkness seemed to press in on her, she felt it suffocating her.

'You feel it too, don't you,' said Rhys, 'you can feel evil. It's close to us tonight.'

'Don't say that,' Juliet pleaded.

'Denying it won't make it disappear. You have to be brave, Juliet.'

'Dad said that, he told me to look after everyone, but I'm not strong. I'm scared.'

He put his head to one side. 'Being brave doesn't mean you're not scared; it means you act despite the fear inside you. And if you are going to look after them all you will need to be brave. There are darker things than you imagine here.' He looked up the road leading to the church. 'Usually, I enjoy walking through the village in the evening. Not tonight. I know I have put myself in danger. I shall go to my church. Maybe there I will find peace. Take care, Juliet, and, if anything should happen to me, take care of Mira for me. I do love her.' With that, he walked away.

Stunned and still confused, Juliet turned and went back down the road.

As she was opening the gate, Anwen was coming out. She had changed into a black dress.

'Is my brother still there?' she said, not looking at Juliet but up the road. 'Oh yes, I can see him; I'm going to sort this out.' Pushing past Juliet, she marched off towards Rhys.

Juliet went into the garden where she saw her mother was still outside, clearing the table.

'Have you been speaking to Rhys?' her mother asked.

'Yes.' She paused. 'I'm so sorry the evening has been ruined, but we ought to talk, Mum.'

'I think enough has been said for one evening. Now, there's not much clearing up for me to do; Anwen is a very neat worker. Everyone has gone in to watch TV or rest.'

'How can they all rest? What about Rhys—'

'Enough, Juliet. Everything just needs to be left alone. I will talk to Rhys; explain why.'

'If you think he's not going to tell us, you're wrong.'

Her mother shook her head and spoke quietly but with a hardness Juliet had never heard before. 'Trust me, whatever happens, he won't be saying anything else on the subject.' Her mother looked down at the table. 'Leave this to me, Juliet, I shall see to everything.'

9

At that moment, Juliet's phone alerted her to a text – it was from Gabriel.

Are you still able to meet up?

Juliet looked up at her mother. 'Do you want me to help?'
'Not at all. If that is someone wanting to meet up, you can go.'
Juliet answered the text.

I'm free now, any good?

Perfect, I'm out cycling, see you at the car park in ten minutes.

Juliet looked over at her mother. 'I'm just popping out for a walk then.'
'Okay, be careful.' Her mother replied.
'I won't be long. Shall I take the front door key?'
'No, I'll be up for a while yet, and I don't lock the patio doors

until I go to bed. But don't go hanging about. There are all sorts around now, make sure you have your phone.'

Juliet closed her eyes in frustration. Thirty years old, she had lived in China for two years, and yet her mother was talking to her as if she were thirteen. Did mothers ever stop worrying?

Juliet ran into her bedroom, grabbed something from her case, went back downstairs and then took her bag from the dresser. Without speaking to her sisters, she left the house.

After closing the garden gate, she was surprised to see Anwen still talking to Rhys. She'd expected him to be in the church by now. He certainly looked uncomfortable, and he was backing away as Anwen shouted and jabbed her finger at him, but their confrontation appeared to be coming to an end.

'Keep the hell out of my life... I'm warning you...' Juliet heard Anwen shout, and then she saw her throw her hands up, walk away from Rhys, and come back down the road.

Juliet, unsure what she should do, waited.

'Are you okay?' she asked Anwen when she was close enough to hear.

'I'm fine, and he can't say I haven't warned him. He's not going to ruin this.'

Juliet went to open the gate for her, but Anwen said, 'I'm not going in, I'm late already.' She pushed past Juliet and ran down the road, swinging a carrier bag before disappearing around the corner.

Juliet had been shocked at the level of threat and anger in Anwen's voice when she had been speaking to Rhys and glanced up the road. She was surprised to see Rhys still there. He stood as if in a daze, and then, shaking his head he continued his walk up the road to the church, disappearing into the darkness. He looked very vulnerable and alone, a saint walking into the flames. Juliet shook her head, she had to stop her mind racing away like this. Tomorrow

Rhys would explain everything, no more mysteries or secrets. She just had to be patient and wait.

Juliet turned away, marched quickly down the road. Ahead of her lights flickered, voices, laughter, even shouting echoed in the distance. It was not the constant background noise of a bustling seaside town, but for a place normally deserted and silent, it felt busy.

As she walked along, Juliet started to focus on her meeting with Gabriel and realised she was actually quite nervous. She'd handled bumping into Gabriel at the funeral quite well, but this was different. Whatever she had said to Rosalind, she knew this was a lot more than just old friends catching up.

Juliet went to the car park. She saw several campervans and vans parked up, youngsters drinking.

At the top of the path leading to the beach, she saw Gabriel. There were the new downlighting lamps that only lit a small area of ground and Gabriel was stood directly under the light so she could see him quite clearly. She felt the warmth of familiarity flood over her. This was Gabriel as she remembered him. Relaxed in his sports trousers and T-shirt, although of course the beard was new.

'I'm glad you came.' His voice was soft, caressing. He held out his arms and she walked into them, felt the stress and pressure of the evening start to slip away. Eventually she stood back and smiled.

Gabriel lifted up the canvas bag in his hand. 'I brought a picnic. Well, a drink anyway. There's a lovely breeze down on the beach. What do you think?'

She smiled in reply. Glancing over to a fence, she saw a bike chained to it. 'You've still got the same bike?'

'Yup. Have you still got your car?'

'It's sitting in the field waiting for me.'

'And have you brought my heart?' he said softly.

'Of course.' Her hands shook as she opened her bag, unzipped the pocket, and showed him the key ring.

'You still have it,' he said, and she was surprised but touched that it meant so much to him.

'I'm keeping it safe,' she said, zipping it back into the pocket again and closing her bag.

They turned to go down the path. 'Let's use my torch,' said Gabriel, switching it on.

He gently held her arm, but once on the beach, he turned off his torch and slowly their eyes adjusted to the darkness. To their left, they could make out a small group of people sat around a small fire and so they walked to the right which was completely deserted.

Juliet felt the sand and pebbles dig through her sandals. The tiny pinprick stars were the only thing that distinguished the blue-black sea from the sky. Eventually they stopped. Gabriel opened the bag, took out a blanket, a bottle of wine and two picnic glasses. Without speaking, he opened the wine, and she held the glasses as he poured.

'You seem quiet, are you okay?' he asked. 'I suppose the meal was bound to be difficult without your dad there.'

'Actually, it was terrible. And far worse than anything I imagined, and not just because we were missing Dad.'

He took his glass and touched the edge of hers; it felt very close, intimate. They both sipped their drinks and, as they did, she started to tell him about the evening. Her words were coated by the sound of waves kissing the shore, as if the island was listening.

'Do you remember how Rhys was at the funeral?'

'I do; very intense.'

'Well, he was talking about his conversation with Dad in the hospital again.'

'That seems a strange thing to bring up at Rosalind's meal.'

'I know but it's really playing on his mind. He's decided he wants to tell us all what Dad said.'

'Gosh, what did he say?'

'Nothing in the end. Mum got really upset and he stopped, went off to his Saturday night prayers at the church – he stays up there till one in the morning apparently.'

'I heard he does that. Maddie said he's invited members of the congregation to join him, but I don't think anyone has yet.'

'I'm not surprised. Anyway, he told us we had to bare our souls to each other and then he would talk to us all tomorrow. Of course, after he left, no one wanted to talk.'

'Not much of a celebration for poor Rosalind then.'

'Certainly not. The atmosphere was awful. I'll be relieved tomorrow when everything is out in the open. I was glad to get away and come out here to be honest.'

He put his arm around her. 'It will all be okay. You'll see. Rhys is a sensible man, he is a good vicar, very caring.'

'So, everyone tells me. Mira said he came to see Maddie today?'

'Yes, he always sees her on the anniversary of Harry's death; he never forgets.'

'Oh Gabriel, I'm so sorry. I should have remembered the date with it being Rosalind's meal as well.'

'That's okay. You must have all missed your dad this evening?'

'It still doesn't feel completely real, but it was lovely hearing your memories of him after the funeral, to be reminded that Dad was loved by so many people outside of the family.'

'Well, he helped me a lot. Our special thing was having hot chocolate together. Do you remember that I always bought him a special brand on his birthday? It was my way of saying thank you.'

'Yes, I think it's lovely.'

'I've always thought how lucky you are to be such a close family, don't ever forget that.'

'I don't feel as close now; they've all changed a lot since I've been away.'

'I don't expect it's as much as you think. I'm sure they missed you. I know I did.'

She heard the intensity in his voice, her heart raced. 'Did you? You never came to see me.'

'I'm sorry, I really wanted to, you know that. I had everything planned and then, as I told you, things got so complicated with the lodges, I had to stay and supervise them.'

'I was thinking about that. Surely Maddie had taken on people to do that, and it's not like it's that many lodges is it?'

'I know, but Maddie depends on me and, I really felt I needed to keep an eye on it all. You know how important this place is to me. My future is here, and...' he smiled, 'I hope yours is as well.'

'I'll be staying, for a while at least,' she said shyly.

'That's great. So, are you looking for a teaching post? You'll need to get on, term will start soon.'

'Actually, I'm not going back to teaching.' Juliet told him about the drawing commission.

'Surely you could do that as a side-line; you need a proper job.'

Juliet swallowed the annoyance she felt at her plans being dismissed. 'No, I think I can make a proper living out of it, this is something I really want to do.' Aware of the strain building up between them she decided to change the subject. 'Anyway, let's not worry about that tonight. I've just remembered something.' Juliet took a small parcel from her pocket and handed it to him.

He opened it and inside was a bright red velvet fish, covered in sequins and with a loop at the top.

'They sell them everywhere in China; they are meant to guarantee wealth. You should hang them at the doorway to your house.'

'I shall do that. It's very sweet, thank you. It will have to go next to my bed for now until I put a hook up, but I am sure it will be just as effective.' He laughed. 'So anyway, you know what I've been doing. Tell me about China and I can travel vicariously through you.' He sat back.

'I don't quite know where to start.'

'Well, for example, is there anyone special in China who is going to miss you?'

'No, definitely not.'

His face relaxed. 'That's all I need to know.' He looked down at the frothy shallows of the sea. 'Fancy a paddle?'

Juliet hesitated. Paddling at night seemed so much more daring than in daylight. The sea seemed less friendly somehow. However, she took off her sandals and walked down to the water's edge with Gabriel and she noticed a sliver of moon escape from behind a cloud. Its brightness glistened on the tar black surface of the sea.

It was wonderful to feel the cold water on her feet and legs, the cool breeze on her face, not to be hot and sticky.

'Hang on,' said Gabriel. 'Let me take a photo.'

He ran back up the beach to get his phone, while Juliet threw pebbles, hearing the satisfying plop as they landed in the water.

Gabriel returned and held the camera to take a selfie of them. Their faces were very close, and she could feel his cheek on hers, warm, soft. He lowered the phone, and it was the most natural thing in the world for him to kiss her. At first, she relaxed into it, but then she pulled away.

'Listen, come and have breakfast with me tomorrow. It's lovely up at the lodges first thing, and I can grab a quiet few minutes before the day kicks in,' Gabriel suggested.

She smiled. 'I'd like to, yes, thanks.'

He held up his phone. 'Have you got WhatsApp?'

'I have. I put it on a few days ago because, of course, I couldn't use it in China.'

'Great. Hang on, I'm forming a WhatsApp group, just me and

you. Phone signal up at the lodges can be a bit iffy.' He typed away on his phone and then said, 'Done. I have invited you to join me in "Gabriel and Juliet"!' He grinned. 'Sounds good, doesn't it?' He sighed and then said, 'I could stay here all night, but I ought to get back. I'm on duty, it's not fair to leave it all to Joe, our new chap.'

When they'd collected their stuff, they walked up the path from the beach. Gabriel had started to walk across the road with her when she stopped. 'What about your bike?'

'Oh, I'll come back for it.'

Slowly they walked back to the house, his arm automatically falling around her shoulder, and when he kissed her at the gate, she didn't pull away.

'You know I have my own lodge. One night you must come back with me; we can eat under the stars. It's amazing. I can stare out and all I see is the sea. I can leave the world behind.'

'Sounds heavenly. So, you're not living up at the house with Maddie?'

'The lodge is my slice of independence. Right, I really have to tear myself away. I'll come and pick you up in the morning.'

'Oh, I can walk.'

'But I've not said what time I have breakfast. I'll need to come for you about half six.'

'Half six?'

'Please.'

She smiled and he grinned. He knew he'd won.

10

After Gabriel had left her, Juliet pushed open the gate, went back into the house through the patio doors and found her mother sitting drinking coffee in the kitchen.

'Ah good.' Her mother got up from the kitchen table where she'd been flicking through a magazine.

'You've not been waiting up for me I hope?'

'Of course not.' But her mother didn't sound very convincing.

Juliet saw Lola lying in her bed. 'I thought she'd go up with Mira.'

'She does usually head upstairs, but she seems content to be down here at the moment. Right, I'm ready for bed. Now that everyone's in, I can lock up properly.'

Juliet smiled. So her mother had been waiting up for her.

'Is Anwen back?' Juliet asked.

'I'd assumed she was, but actually I haven't seen her since the meal. I'll check.'

Juliet's mother went upstairs and she heard her knock gently on Cassie's door.

She came back down, pushed the old bolt across the front door, then came back to the kitchen.

'Cassie said not to go in. Apparently Anwen is asleep, so I must have missed her coming in. Anyway, it means I can definitely shut up the house now. There's only one door key to these patio doors by the way, and I hang it here in case you ever need it. I must ring the company and get some spares some time.'

Juliet could see her mother's hands were shaking. 'Thanks, Mum. It was a difficult meal this evening wasn't it, so I hope you're okay.'

'You'd think Rhys would have learned to be more careful in what he said by now.'

Juliet saw her mother double-checking the locks. 'It's okay, you did it already.'

'Silly me, I just feel more on edge at night now without your dad. I know it's stupid, it's not as if he'd have been any good chasing off burglars.' Her mother looked out into the darkness of the garden. 'I can't remember the last time I slept here without him before he died, he was always here...'

'We're here for you now, Mum.'

'Thank you, love, but I know you all have your own lives. I don't want to be one of those mothers who everyone feels responsible for, you know – *are you going to do Mum this Christmas or is it my turn?* I'd hate that.'

'When we spend Christmas with you, it will be because we want to. We do love you, Mum.'

'And I am very lucky to have my four girls.' Her mother seemed to shake herself. 'Right, I'd better get on up.'

'I'll make myself a drink and follow you up.'

'I hope you sleep well; everything will be better in the morning.'

Her mother left her, and Juliet poured herself a long, cold drink of water, adding ice cubes from the fridge. She was about to leave the kitchen when Mira came in still wearing the dress she'd worn to the meal.

'I came down for Lola,' she said. Mira sat down next to Lola, but didn't move, instead she sat there staring.

Juliet went over to her and sat next to her. 'It's been an awful evening, hasn't it?' she signed. 'Are you okay?'

Mira shook her head.

Juliet saw the anguish in her eyes. 'How are things with you and Rhys?'

'Not good; we had a row last night. I honestly don't know what's going to happen.'

'Tell me about it.'

'Not now, Juliet. I need time to think. I'll go up to bed. Today has been long enough already.'

'Okay, well talk to me when you are ready. Sleep well.'

Mira left the kitchen with Lola and went upstairs.

Juliet took her phone out of her handbag and, after turning off the lights in the kitchen, went upstairs to her own room. Once she'd got ready for bed, she took out a novel; she needed to escape, go somewhere else in her head. But she found it impossible to concentrate.

Her heart was racing with so many emotions from the evening. The meal had been so stressful, with Cassie talking about some kind of business venture with Anwen, and Rhys anxious about the things her father had told him. What on earth was he going to come out with tomorrow? If only her mother would talk to them – what was she so afraid of? What secrets was she keeping from her? And not only her, what about Rhys, Cassie, Rosalind, Anwen and even Mira? They all had secrets, but then everyone kept secrets, didn't they? What was different here was the intensity that surrounded them, the sense of desperation to keep things hidden.

Juliet lay listening to the strange sounds a summer night let into her room: the crickets, the snuffling of nocturnal wildlife, and felt the breeze, the breath of the sea. It was impossible to know if she was hearing or imagining the sound of waves, the smell of sand and wet pebbles. Then, she heard a creaking sound. But it wasn't outside, no, it was the top step on the landing. Someone going downstairs, probably one of her sisters needing a drink. Normally she wouldn't have taken any notice but after such a stressful evening, Juliet was on edge and felt the need to check what was happening. She went out onto the landing, peered down the stairs, heard rustling from the dark kitchen, the shush of the patio door opening. That surprised her, why would someone be going outside? She pushed away the feeling of apprehension, there would be some simple explanation. It was late, she needed to go back to bed.

However, back in her room she decided to check out of her window, see who was out there. Down below, she could see a shadowy figure pulling the gate open, but there were no streetlights by the gate, and she couldn't make out who it was. The person was moving quickly, and soon they were out of sight. It was only then she noticed there was a light coming from the workshop, she could see shadows, someone was in there... Why would anyone be there at this time?

Juliet sat down on the edge of her bed; she needed to stop fretting. She checked her phone, just gone half twelve, time to try and rest. However, just as she was about to lie down, a WhatsApp video call came through on her phone.

She pressed receive and saw Gabriel smiling back at her.

'Hiya,' he said and scanned his phone around the room, 'like the lodge?'

Seeing the chandeliers and rich patterned carpet, she was confused until she figured out that, of course, this wasn't a lodge. For some reason Gabriel was at the main house on the vineyard where Maddie lived.

He tried to smile, but his eyes were screwed up and anxious. 'I came back to the house because Maddie phoned to say she didn't feel too good. I will stay up here; they can phone me if anything crops up at the lodges.'

'Oh dear, what's the matter?'

He shook his head. 'She's got a really upset stomach. She looks so pale and keeps being sick. I'm hopeless when people are ill.'

'Do you need to get a doctor?'

'I don't know. Maddie hates them. I rang Barbara, you know, who runs the shop, did you know she used to be a nurse?'

'Of course. She's a good person to speak to.'

'Well, she had a FaceTime with Maddie, and just told me to make sure she doesn't get dehydrated.'

'Good, I'm sure your mum is grateful you're there.'

Gabriel held up the red fish she'd given him earlier. 'I shall put it on my bedside table later.'

'Lovely. It's so hot, isn't it? I have all the windows open. I think someone here has just gone out for a walk, so I think we're all struggling to get cool.'

'No one can sleep in this, can they? It's not helping mum.' He paused. 'Sorry, she's just called out. I was only ringing to say goodnight, see you very soon.'

'Night. Hope your mum is okay.'

'Thanks... see you then.'

He rang off and Juliet lay down on the bed. She heard the sound of the gate banging; whoever had gone out couldn't have shut it properly. Too hot to move, Juliet picked up her phone again. She lay scrolling, looking at emails, pictures, playing a mind-numbing game. But nothing seemed to lull her off to sleep.

As the grandfather clock chimed one, another WhatsApp video call came in from Gabriel.

'Sorry, I hope you weren't asleep. I just needed someone to talk to.'

His face was creased with anxiety this time.

'Are you okay?' Juliet asked, concerned.

'I'm a bit worried now to be honest. Maddie is still being sick.'

'Could you ring Barbara again?'

'I don't like disturbing her when it's so late.'

Juliet heard the ring of the house phone at Gabriel's house and his face lit up.

'That might be her, sorry, I need to go,' he said.

'Okay, but get the doctor if you need to.'

Almost as soon as she'd put her phone down, a text came through from Alistair in Edinburgh. She'd let him know she'd left China, but she hadn't spoken to him since. She guessed he was wondering how the commission was going and if she had any decisions about moving up there. Juliet decided to phone him, and, despite the late hour, he answered. She explained everything that had happened since she'd returned, and as she did so she realised just how extraordinary the past few weeks had been. Alistair was very sympathetic and told her to take her time. They left it that, with her saying she would be in touch once she had a better idea of what she would be doing next.

Juliet was exhausted at the end of the conversation, and before finally closing her eyes, she got up and peered out of the window again. The light was off in the workshop; whoever had been there had come back in. There was an unease about the night. She'd be relieved when dawn came, the light of a new day.

11

Juliet woke the next morning from a deep sleep. She looked at her phone – it was twenty-five past six. 'Shit – Gabriel.'

She threw on some clothes, dragged a brush through her hair, dashed to the bathroom to brush her teeth. *What a state*, she thought glancing in the mirror, but there was no time to do anything else. She rushed back to her room, grabbed her phone and ran downstairs.

Juliet put her phone into her handbag and then reached up for the patio door key, but it wasn't there, and as she pulled the door, she found it unlocked. Whoever went out through the gate or to the workshop had forgotten to lock up when they returned. She pulled the door closed behind her, there was nothing else she could do; it was light now, her mother would be up soon.

She saw Gabriel's car at the gate and waved to him. She ran down the path, through the gate and had just started to get into the car, when she saw Anwen coming up the road. Juliet was puzzled to notice that Anwen was wearing the same black dress as the night before and yet Cassie had said Anwen was safely in bed. Perhaps she had been the person who went out at half twelve?

'Hang on,' she said to Gabriel and she ran down the road to check on Anwen.

'Morning, Anwen, you're out early. Are you okay?'

'What?' asked Anwen crossly.

'I asked you if you are okay?'

'Of course.'

Anwen went to walk on, but Juliet frowned. 'You didn't get locked out, did you?'

'Of course, not.'

'Oh sorry, you're in the same dress as last night.'

'I came out for a walk.' Again, she tried to walk away, but Juliet persisted.

'Did you open the patio doors then, have you got the door key?'

'Listen, Juliet, I don't have any shitting door key.' Her voice was raised now. 'For God's sake, I just want to go back to bed.'

Juliet blinked, rather taken aback by Anwen's brusqueness. 'Of course. Um... the patio door is open.'

Anwen scowled and walked past her, pushing open the gate.

Juliet stepped back, shocked at how rude Anwen had been and then went back to Gabriel.

'Everything okay?' he asked.

'Just had a bit of a set to with Anwen. God she is so prickly. What on earth is she doing up at this time?'

'Maybe she just couldn't sleep in this heat and went for a walk to cool down.'

Juliet noticed then how tired he looked. 'I suppose so. Anyway, how is Maddie?'

'A lot better thanks, although she got really rough. Barbara came round in the end, thank God. She rang III and a doctor spoke to Maddie at about three. She had started to settle down by then and so he said to see how she went. Barbara was brilliant, I was so glad she was there.'

'What a night. You should have cancelled me this morning.'

'Oh, it's okay.' Gabriel looked at her and his face relaxed into a smile. 'It's good to see you and anyway I have to be up, the lodges are fully booked. I know it's not that many but there is always lots to do.'

They drove down onto the main military road. Juliet looked over at the light blue sea, the white chalky cliffs in the distance; it was a beautiful morning. As they turned into the road that led to the vineyard, she saw a van ahead of them driving into Compton car park, no doubt some early morning surfers.

They reached the vineyard quickly, a large, smart sign welcoming them to 'Laurent Vineyard'. Juliet remembered what Cassie had said about Maddie adopting her family name here. It certainly looked impressive, with a list of opening times, tours, a site map with directions to the winery, shop, and restaurant. The small site with the lodges was to the right and set slightly apart.

'Can we drive up and just check Maddie's okay?'

'Of course,' Juliet replied.

They drove along a well-maintained road which was lined with poplar trees. With the sun and the vineyards sloping down the hill, it was like stepping into a slice of the South of France.

The beautiful old house was a large, stone building, styled as a manor, with ivy creeping over the walls and around the windows. It looked out over the tidy rows of vines, and even from here Juliet could see the grapes weighing down the branches. Next to the house was a small field of lavender, a sea of lilac, the scent thick in the air. In the distance, the sea sparkled – it was idyllic.

The restaurant and winery were further on. Juliet could see cars parked there already and tractors driving between the vines, as well as people on foot working.

'It's so busy here, so early in the day.'

'Yes, not long until harvest,' said Gabriel. 'There'll be a tour later, and of course the restaurant and shop will be open. It's all quite small-scale but still a tremendous amount of work.'

'Cassie was saying this used to just be farmland, but it's hard to imagine. It's like being in France now.'

'I know, and I think people around here were a bit shocked by the changes here all those years ago. My father and his family had done very little work themselves here, the farming was by tenants. My father wanted to live the life of the landed gentry, hunting and riding, that kind of thing.'

'Did he resent what Maddie did?'

'He would grumble sometimes but he also knew things had to change; they weren't making any money and yet he kept spending it, sending Harry to an expensive prep school, and things like that. It was Maddie who saved this place.'

'Hang on, so Harry went away to school, but you didn't? You stayed local and went to school with Cassie.'

'Maddie would never have let me be sent away.' He opened the car door. 'Right, just hold on a tick, I'll be quick.'

Gabriel jumped out of the car, ran into the house, and returned a few minutes later.

'Do you fancy coming in and saying hi to Maddie?'

'Are you sure she's up to a visitor?'

'Yes. Come on in, it will cheer her up.'

As they went into the house, Juliet glanced into the sumptuous room to her right, the one Gabriel had spoken to her from the night before. She knew Gabriel's home was very different to her own, with rich embroidered rugs, gold gilded frames and mirrors, white satin chairs with gold surrounds. At either end of the room hung crystal chandeliers, reminding her of a chateau she had visited on holiday.

When they reached Maddie's bedroom Juliet saw it was also very ornate and dominated by a four-poster bed with lace hangings and rich flocked wallpaper. Maddie was propped up, her head resting on crisp white pillowcases.

'*Bonjour*, Juliet.' She looked pale and exhausted, her voice quiet and a little shaky.

'I am sorry you were so poorly last night.'

Maddie flapped a hand in the air. 'It was only sickness; Gabriel worries about me too much.' She smiled at him. 'But I know I am lucky to have a son who cares.'

'I would have been useless without Barbara,' said Gabriel. 'She's coming round later when things are quieter in the shop.'

'I told her not to worry, but she has always been such a good friend.'

'She's bringing you some clear beef soup; she said it would be good for you. I'll pop down and put a tray ready for her.'

Maddie gave her son an adoring look. 'You spoil me.'

As Gabriel left the room, Juliet went to look out the window. The contrasts between the lilac of the lavender and the green fields of vines was spectacular.

'The vines look good,' Juliet said, not really having any idea how they should look.

Maddie sat up and pointed to the window. 'I am very pleased with the vines this year. If the weather holds, it will be a good year for our white sparkling wine. Have you ever tried it?'

'Yes, I think Dad bought it for Mira's wedding.'

'Oh yes, that's right, he did. Could you pour me some water please?'

'Of course.' Juliet poured some water from a neat carafe by the bed into the drinking glass next to it. She pointed to a family photograph next to Maddie's bed. 'We were looking through Mum and Dad's old photos yesterday. There was one of both of our families on the beach. Your husband was so handsome, wasn't he?'

'I remember when I first saw Clarence, he looked like some

Greek god. Women were always attracted to him; I had to fight them off when we came back here. I knew all the women in the village had been after him. I remember your mother seemed quite sweet on him too.' She gave Juliet a knowing grin.

Juliet laughed. 'Cassie was telling us about how he came over to France and rescued you from your run-down vineyard. What a love story.'

The sweetness on Maddie's face melted away. She pushed herself to sit even more upright in the bed and her eyes flashed with fury. 'My parents' vineyard may have hit bad times, but we were very proud of what my father had accomplished. I learned all my skills there, I would like to think this is the vineyard my father would have built if things had worked out differently for him.'

Juliet stepped back from the bed. 'I'm so sorry. I didn't mean to upset you.'

'No, people never know the trials we go through. The truth was Clarence was charming but hopeless, he'd have probably ended up having to sell this land, frittered it away. I was devastated of course when he died, but all of this has come from my hard work.'

Maddie rested back on her pillow.

Gabriel came in and seemed to immediately pick up on the strained atmosphere.

'Is something wrong?' he asked Maddie.

'I'm so sorry,' said Juliet. 'I made an insensitive remark about Maddie's family vineyard in France.'

'You are not to worry,' said Maddie with a sigh. 'This is such a difficult time for me. I am, as you say, oversensitive.'

'Last night was the anniversary of my brother Harry's death,' Gabriel explained.

'I'm so sorry, of course, you mentioned it,' said Juliet and turned to Maddie. 'We had Rosalind's meal last night and I saw photos of you all at the party the day she came home as a baby. It reminded me how grey it had been that day. Did you know the oak tree in our garden was struck by lightning that night?'

'Your father told me. It was struck at the same time as my boy was killed; nature knew something monumental was happening. What a night. So often I think, if only we had stopped Harry going out, but he was determined to train for some marathon. He was out there every night, even when it was late.' She looked out of the window.

'It was a tragedy,' said Juliet.

'It is a terrible thing to lose a son. Nothing prepares you for it. It was awful losing Clarence only six months before to cancer, but Harry's death was devastating. He went out and never came back. I was here with Gabriel and his friend Ed, Barbara's boy. We were so cosy in the house, no idea of what was happening. It was fortunate Barbara had just come round to pick Ed up when the police came. I don't know how I would have coped without her. It was awful and you know Harry was due to move to France the very next day to start a wonderful new job. I think sometimes if he'd just left a day earlier, well, he would still be alive.' She paused and then added, her voice quiet, broken, 'They never found out who was driving the car you know. I try not to be angry but, it's not right is it, someone out there, living their life when my Harry's life was snatched away from him.'

'It was awful, Maddie, but as you say, a long time ago now. You should rest,' said Gabriel.

'I am sorry I am such a burden to you. I am just a tired old lady that is all,' Maddie said weakly, and Gabriel patted her hand.

'There is nothing remotely tired or old about you. You rest now, and you'll be back at work tomorrow running rings round us all. Now let me move your phone within reach.'

Gabriel moved the phone next to the bed and glanced at the carafe of water.

'I'll go and fetch you some fresh iced water.'

Juliet decided it was time to leave Maddie to recover.

'I hope you feel a lot better soon,' she said and headed downstairs with Gabriel. She followed him into the kitchen. It was a beautiful room, just like the pictures she'd seen in magazines of French country kitchens, although this was clearly not for show – this was the real thing. There were strings of onions, bunches of herbs drying. No tiny jars of herbs on a flimsy spice rack, but large jars of basil, and opened packets of mustard and coriander. Juliet breathed in the most wonderful aroma of garlic and fresh fruit.

Gabriel ran back upstairs. She heard him shout, 'I'll be back in an hour, phone me if you need anything,' as he came down.

Once back outside, Juliet could feel the warmth strengthening in the sun. There were more cars now over at the winery, and more tractors driving between the vines.

'You and Maddie have every right to be proud of this place, you know,' Juliet said. 'I was surprised just now when Maddie said Harry had been planning to go and work in France. Wasn't he interested in making a life here?'

'No, this wasn't the life Harry wanted. And he was lost when Dad died; they had been so close, they both loved to go hunting and shooting together. Harry was also pretty wild, drinking and things. As much as I didn't want him to go away, even I could see he needed to make a fresh start somewhere else.' Gabriel smiled.

'But if he was going to France... wasn't that to work in a vineyard?'

'God no. Dad had connections with a chateau in France where they organised game shooting. He'd taken Harry out a few times. Harry loved it over there, and his plan was to sell his portion of the land here to us and use that money to buy into the business over there.

'Oh I see, I assumed all this land would have belonged to Maddie when your father died.'

'It's very complicated but basically the land was passed down to me and Harry, with the vineyard profits going to Maddie. Anyway, all that was left was for Harry to sort out a few things in France, sign the papers to finalise the sale of his land here and he'd have been set up in his new life over there. It was really tragic; he was so close to living his dream.'

'I'm very sorry, it's all so sad.'

Gabriel looked around, gave a sigh then a smile. 'It was tragic, but, well, it's all in the past now. Let us go and have breakfast, I'm starving.'

Gabriel drove them to the reception block and parked outside.

'Morning,' shouted a young man, also far too awake for Juliet's taste.

'Hi Joe, this is Juliet.'

Joe looked about eighteen to Juliet, but of course he was probably older.

'Hi Juliet, nice to meet you.' He turned to Gabriel. 'How's Maddie? I hear she's had a rough night.'

'She's much better now thank you. Has the delivery from the bakery come?'

'Yes, it's all in the trays.'

'Great, I had a word. It's been late a few times now but looks like they've sorted things.'

Gabriel found a bag, took some pastries from one of the trays, and poured two take away coffees from the machine on the side. Turning to Juliet he said, 'Come on. I'm ready for this.'

As they walked along, Juliet was impressed. Although no more than seven or eight lodges and pods, everything was tidy and well set out.

'It's very smart; I'm not surprised you're fully booked.'

'We could have taken double the number if we'd had the accommodation,' said Gabriel, 'but neither Maddie nor I wanted to give over any more land to this. The main business here is the vineyard, and it will always take priority.'

'So, where is the ubiquitous bathroom block?' she asked.

'There's nothing like that here. Each lodge or pod has their own facilities. Obviously, the pods are more basic, but still, they have their own loo and shower. Of course, it means a tonne more work, but people like it and will pay a lot more for it. We have a small shop here just for basics... well, locally sourced meats, jams, honey, fresh bread, pastries, and our wine of course, but also milk, toilet roll and ketchup, that kind of thing. Then there is the restaurant over at the vineyard where our guests can have lunch or an evening meal.'

Juliet looked out at the fields and the sea, and on a morning like this it was magical.

She followed Gabriel past the buildings to a lodge closer to the cliff edge, facing the sea. Like all the others, it had a small wooden patio area complete with a table and chairs.

Gabriel placed the bag on the table.

'This one is mine. Maddie thought I was mad, but it's my escape. See, I have it facing away from the rest and I look out to sea and pretend I am far away from here.' Gabriel's bike propped up at the side.

He took out the coffee and pastries and laid them out on the small table. Next to them she spotted his binoculars.

'Ah I remember these. Are you still using them?'

'Always. I remember you not liking them, but it's amazing sitting here looking out. We get falcons and buzzards, all sorts.'

He handed her a cup of coffee and pastry and they chose to sit on the grass that was crispy dry and already feeling warm.

Gabriel nodded back towards reception. 'I am so glad I took Joe on; I wasn't sure he'd be any good, he had hardly any paper qualifications, but he works hard, and I need that. This place is twenty-four seven.' He looked towards the door of the lodge with a smile. 'However, it's very quiet and discreet out here, any time you fancy a night away...'

She grinned, more tempted than she wanted to let on. 'Noted... Now, tell me about these lodges.'

They chatted and the time flew, but at eight Gabriel stood up.

'Well, I'd better give you a lift back. I need to get working and I'd better check on Maddie to be on the safe side.'

Juliet sat up and stretched. 'I have to say this was a very relaxing way to start the day. Don't worry about the lift, I can walk.'

She left the site and headed down the road, breathed in the unique smell of sand and sea that bundled together all those memories of sandcastles, dipping her toes into cold water, eating sandwiches with a slight crunch of sand that always managed to get in the food. She smiled to herself.

Once on the main road she saw cars heading to Compton Bay car park; families were already heading onto the beach, not that they would be jostling for places even in August, but Juliet could understand people who didn't have the luxury of a beach within minutes' walk making the most of their holiday.

When she reached home she was welcomed by the fabulous smell of cooked bacon. Her mother raised an eyebrow as Juliet came in through the patio doors.

'You were out early.'

'It's a lovely morning,' Juliet said, reluctant to share who she had been with.

'Did you take the patio key then?' her mother asked.

'No, it was already open when I left.'

'Oh, that's odd,' her mother said. 'I know I locked it last night before we all went to bed.'

'I saw the light on in the workshop in the night, do you know who went out there?'

Her mother shook her head. 'No idea. Now, do you want a bacon sandwich?'

'I'm okay, I've had some pastries.'

'Oh, have you?'

Thankfully, Juliet was saved from offering her an explanation because Mira came into the kitchen. 'Morning. I can't get hold of Rhys this morning. His phone just goes to voicemail when I try.'

'Maybe the signal is down, you know how it is around here.'

'I suppose so. He sent me a text last night to say he was about to leave the church at one, but nothing this morning. I'd have expected him to say hi by now... Maybe he's been called out somewhere. Mmm, that smells good.'

Mira sat down to a sandwich while Juliet drank some coffee. Occasionally Mira tried Rhys's phone again, but still there was no reply. Juliet's mind kept drifting back to the lodge, the sea, Gabriel... she smiled at the thought of going back.

She was shaken from her daydream by Mira poking her and giving her a mock frown. She signed without speaking. 'What's up with you? I know that smile and you're dressed. Where have you been?'

Juliet grinned, returned a quick sign of, 'Mind your own business,' before her mother returned to the table. The sisters swapped a conspiratorial grin.

Once she'd finished her breakfast, Mira rang the house phone at the vicarage, but still there was no answer. 'It is a bit strange, maybe I'll pop up and check everything is all right. Fancy a walk?' she asked Juliet. 'I need to take Lola out anyway.'

'Of course. It is a lovely morning,' Juliet said before adding, 'Are you really worried about Rhys?'

Mira shrugged. 'It's silly, I know. It's just a feeling that's all.'

Juliet thought back to seeing Rhys leave last night. He had seemed a bit scared, a bit unnerved, but that felt rather melodramatic on such a lovely morning. Nothing awful could happen on a day like this.

Juliet and Mira got their things together and left. It was very quiet walking through the village. Through August there was only one Sunday morning service among the three churches, instead of Rhys having to space out three individual ones, and today the service was in the next village. They walked past the small stream, which, despite looking seriously depleted of water following the days of sunshine, was being enjoyed by ducks quacking contentedly as they tugged at the grasses along the bank with their beaks. Mira greeted a solitary dog walker.

The vicarage was a further climb up the hill, past the church.

'I have my church key,' said Mira. 'We might as well check the church as we go past. He could have been taken ill, couldn't he?'

'I doubt it, but we'll check to keep you happy.'

There were two paths up to the church door. The one through the lychgate was narrow, made from muddy gravel and hardly used. The second, much wider one was a steep incline that split at the top, the right to a car park, the left to the church door.

Juliet and Mira walked up the wider path. It was steep and winding, and overhanging trees meant it was always in the shadows. Mira, familiar with the path, was looking over at the church, but Juliet kept her gaze fixed to the ground, making sure she didn't trip. And that was the reason she saw the body before Mira.

12

Juliet rushed over and knelt down next to Rhys's body. He lay staring up at the sky with unseeing, unblinking eyes. She grabbed his wrist but could feel no pulse. Mira fell down next to her and gave a heart-rending scream.

'No, not Rhys.' Mira collapsed onto his body, her own convulsing with pain. 'I'm sorry. Come back, please come back.'

Juliet took hold of Mira firmly, eased her away, and Mira curled up, foetus-like in her lap, gulping tears.

'I have to phone for an ambulance,' she signed to Mira.

Mira sat up. 'Tell them they have to be quick,' Mira signed back urgently.

Juliet's eyes were blurred with tears and her fingers were shaking, making it hard to pick out even the simplest of three-digit numbers.

The voice that answered was calm and listened carefully as she explained what had happened, and Juliet heard the compassion and warmth flood into the woman's voice.

'Someone will be with you as soon as they can, but please don't hang up.'

Juliet answered incoherently a barrage of questions that seemed irrelevant, but which she later understood was the woman making sure she was safe as well.

The sisters sat together on the ground waiting. Juliet couldn't take her eyes off Rhys, the large gash on his forehead, his bloodied legs that lay at an unnatural angle. Nothing about this looked like a 'natural' death. Her mind flashed to stories of kids in cars up here, drinking, taking drugs. Had they been responsible for this? Or had something darker and more sinister happened here?

Juliet shivered. Rhys had talked of evil; he'd been afraid. He'd been on the brink of revealing what her father had told him, difficult things he knew would affect the family. But death had intervened, Rhys would take what he knew to the grave. A terrible idea came to Juliet. Was it possible that this accident had been a deliberate act by someone to silence Rhys? Was it even possible that this person was someone she knew? Juliet shook her head. No, no one she knew would so anything so wicked. However, her father's words came back to her. 'You think you know them but you don't... Anyone who has the motive can kill.'

Her heart thumped so hard in her chest it hurt. Fear and terror threatened to suffocate her.

She heard Mira sobbing beside her. She had to be brave, she had to take care of Mira.

Juliet checked around, there was no one here. Then she heard the sound of children walking down the road to the beach. She panicked, what if they were to come up here, see Rhys? But of course, they didn't, they walked on by, unaware of the horror they'd passed.

Juliet's eyes were drawn again to Rhys, and it was as if one tiny space cleared in her head, helping her to focus, to think. Something was missing... She touched Rhys's neck. 'His crucifix has gone. I saw it on him last night. Has it fallen off?' As soon as she'd said the words, she regretted them.

Mira uncurled and reached out to touch Rhys's neck. 'Where is it?' she stammered.

'Sorry it doesn't matter,' Juliet said quickly.

'He always wore it; it had a safety chain. Where is it?' said Mira and she started to scrape and scrabble at the mud around Rhys.

Juliet gently took hold of her, and this time they stood up and she managed to guide Mira to a wooden seat close to the body. It had been put there because it was a slightly raised area that allowed you to look downland to the sea. Today it seemed wrong that the sea sparkled, that the sky was cloudless.

At that moment, Juliet heard the sirens.

'Wait here,' she signed to Mira and she walked down to the edge of the road, waving to a police car and ambulance.

A police officer and paramedics followed her to where Rhys lay. They formed a circle around Rhys's body, so Juliet stepped back and went back to look after Mira. Soon a female police officer came over to them.

'You said on the phone that this man is the vicar here. I believe you said his name was Rhys?'

'That's right,' replied Juliet. Mira had her head in her hands. 'He's my sister's husband.'

The police officer spoke to Mira. 'I am so sorry—'

Juliet interrupted, 'My sister is Deaf, she needs to read your lips.'

Juliet tapped her sister on the knee and Mira looked up into the police officer's face.

'I am PC Wendy Gregg,' she said and lent down to touch Mira's hand. 'I am sorry to tell you, it appears your husband died some hours ago.' The officer glanced at Juliet. 'Has she understood?'

Juliet usually hated it when people bypassed Mira, asked

things like that, but maybe it was a valid question to ask of anyone frozen in shock. However, Mira's expression changed, as she allowed the words to at least skim across the surface of her mind.

Juliet nodded to the officer.

The officer went to speak to Mira again, but Mira shook her head.

'Talk to her,' Mira said, pointing to Juliet.

The officer appeared relieved. 'We need to try to ascertain what happened. Do you know what Rhys was doing up here?'

'He came up here very late to pray,' said Juliet, she signed as she spoke. 'He sent my sister a text at about one in the morning to say he was leaving—'

'Was that unusual, did he do that often?'

'Yes, every Saturday evening, he usually came up here at about half past eleven and left about one, but he came earlier last night, more like half past ten.'

'Thank you, that's useful to know. Now, I'm afraid this area will need to be cordoned off; can we give you and your sister a lift somewhere, are you able to stay with her?'

'Our mum lives down the road and I am staying with her. It's best Mira comes there.'

'Good, we'll take you there, and someone will come to speak to you very soon. We'll need your contact details too so we can keep in touch.'

Juliet signed to Mira, but Mira shook her head, tears running down her face now.

'No, I can't leave. I have to stay with him.'

'I'm sorry, but you can't, not now,' said the officer sympathetically.

Juliet put her arm around a reluctant Mira, walked her to the police car, and the sisters were taken home.

They arrived as Rosalind was leaving the house, and her eyes shot from them to the police car that was now driving away.

'What the hell?' she asked, looking first at a tearful Mira and then at Juliet.

'It's Rhys, he's had an accident. He's dead.'

'Oh God! No! Mira, I'm so sorry.' Rosalind turned and walked back to the house behind them.

Once inside, Juliet called her mother and, as calmly as she could manage, explained what had happened. After a moment of stunned silence, her mother's lips trembled, and she flew to Mira.

'My darling girl,' she signed, and Mira fell into her mother's arms.

Just then, Juliet remembered Anwen. One of them would have to tell her the news about her brother.

'Where are Cassie and Anwen?' she asked her mother.

'Cassie said Anwen was sleeping in. Cassie is reading up there, I think.'

'Well, I'd better go and tell her, hadn't I.'

Juliet went upstairs and gently knocked on Cassie's door before going in. Anwen was tucked up in bed, fast asleep, and Cassie was on her own bed, dressed, reading.

'What's up?' Cassie asked, scowling.

'It's Rhys, there's been a bad accident,' Juliet replied quietly.

Cassie threw her book down, got out of bed and went and shook Anwen awake.

Startled and half-asleep, Anwen looked confused. 'What's the matter? What's happening?' Anwen asked.

'It's your brother, Anwen. It's Rhys, you need to wake up.'

Anwen sat up, confused, annoyed at being woken. 'What's my brother done now?'

Juliet broke the news as gently as possible but could see Anwen was struggling to comprehend what she was saying.

'Rhys is dead?' repeated Anwen.

'I'm so sorry,' said Juliet.

'Rhys can't be dead.'

'The police are with him now; we found him at the church.'

'He's dead? Are you sure?' Anwen was stumbling over her words.

'I'm so sorry. I'm afraid so.'

Anwen shook her head slowly, numbly. 'That's not right. Not Rhys. It doesn't make any sense.'

Cassie went over and put her arm around Anwen.

'How is Mira?' asked Anwen and Juliet was touched that her thoughts went to her sister.

'She's downstairs with Mum. She's in shock, I think.'

'And she found him? God, how awful.'

Anwen got out of bed, pulled on jumper and trousers over her pyjamas, but then stood helplessly.

'I don't know what to do. I wish my last time with Rhys hadn't been so awful.' She paused. 'I know me and him weren't close, but he was still my brother. I've not got Mum or Dad; he was the only one left.' She burst into tears, sobbing into her hands.

'Is there anyone I should ring?' Juliet asked her gently.

'No, there isn't anyone close. There are my aunts – I'll phone them, I suppose. I can't believe this.'

Anwen sat back down on the bed.

'Juliet, you go back to Mira. We'll come down in a minute,' said Cassie, putting her arm around Anwen again.

As Juliet walked downstairs, she heard a knock at the front door, and she went to answer it. It was the PC who had brought them back, now accompanied by another officer who she introduced.

'This is your family liaison officer, DC Adam Smith. Could we have a word with your sister?'

DC Smith was a tall, grey-haired older man, with a quietly self-assured and serious manner.

'Of course, come in,' said Juliet.

Her mother was out in the hallway now and Juliet explained that their visitors needed to see Mira.

'I don't think Mira is in any state to talk to anyone at the moment,' said her mother, but Mira appeared close behind her.

'It's all right, Mum.'

The new officer introduced himself directly to Mira, adding, 'Now, PC Greggs has explained that you can lipread. Is that correct?'

Mira nodded. 'Yes, but if we are to talk, I would like my sister Juliet to come.'

'Of course, and in future we can arrange an interpreter if you wish.'

They went into the lounge, where Juliet sat on the sofa with Mira, and the police officers sat opposite them.

It was clear from the start that DC Adam Smith would be leading this conversation.

'Firstly, I'd like to offer you my sincere condolences. I know you will all be in a state of shock. A large team will be working to find out what has happened. My role is to act as a liaison between you and that team of people. It might be easier for us to use first names; I am certainly very happy for you to call me Adam.'

Mira glanced at Juliet, who finger-spelled Adam.

Adam sat forward. 'Now, I need to find out certain details which I know can feel very intrusive, but the more we know as soon as possible, the quicker we can get on with the investigation. Of course, you must also ask me any questions you want.'

He paused, looked first at Mira, and then glanced at Juliet.

'Is it possible to tell me what happened to my husband? Was he attacked?' Mira asked.

'Well, we are only starting to form a picture. At the moment, it would appear a vehicle was involved.'

Mira frowned at Juliet. 'A vehicle was involved?' Juliet nodded and Mira looked back at Adam. 'But that's not a roadway.'

'No, but the path leads to a car park and we think the vehicle had been parked up there, and perhaps hit your husband on the way down.'

Juliet could picture it. Coming up the path, you would pass where they'd found Rhys and either go left along the path to the church or branch off right where the rough track led to the small church car park, not visible from the lane.

'There have been youngsters hanging about there, drinking,' said Mira.

'Yes, we found a smashed bottle of vodka in the car park.'

'So maybe someone was drunk-driving and hit Rhys by accident? But why wouldn't they stop?'

'Well, it's of course possible they stopped their vehicle but didn't report the incident.'

'And you have no idea who it was?'

'No, not yet I'm afraid, but of course it's very early days. We have secured the area; the forensic team and an investigation team will be working on the case. Now, I know you told PC Greggs a few things, but I wonder if we could go over the whole evening to give me an idea of your husband's movements, his state of mind.'

'Of course. Well, we had a family meal here and then Rhys left at about half past ten to go up to the church.'

'That was very late, would he usually do that?'

'Yes, he goes every Saturday evening, he feels... he felt, it prepared him for the Sunday. He believed in praying out one day and praying in the next. Usually, he would leave to come home at about one.'

'And would many people have known about your husband's habit of going up to the church late at night?'

'I would think so, after all, he talked about it in his sermons and even encouraged others to join him, but I don't think anyone ever did...'

'When was the last time you spoke to him?'

'When he left here... oh and he sent me a text just before he left the church.'

'Great, do you have your phone here please?'

Mira nodded and took her phone out of her pocket.

'Thank you. And this is the last time you heard from your husband?'

Mira nodded again.

'And when did you realise that he'd not returned to the vicarage.'

'Not until this morning as I stayed here last night. Rhys wasn't answering his mobile or the vicarage phone, which was strange.'

'Was there a reason you were particularly concerned; I assume he gets called out all the time without warning?'

Juliet picked up a subtle change in the police officer's tone, less sympathetic, more accusatory.

Mira looked at Juliet and shrugged, and Juliet signed what the officer had said.

'It had been a difficult evening; I was worried about him.'

Adam raised his head in interest. 'In what way was it difficult?'

Mira gave a glance of appeal at Juliet.

'It's only a couple of weeks since we lost my father. I expect you heard about it. He was driving down from the Downs and crashed into a barn. He died after he'd been in hospital for a few days.'

'Of course, yes, I'm sorry, I'd not made the connection. I am so sorry; you are having such a hard time as a family. So, the meal was difficult. Who was there?'

Mira nodded to Juliet to take over. 'Well, there was me and my three sisters, Cassie, Mira and Rosalind. Also, my mum, Rhys, and his sister Anwen, who was cooking the meal for us. She's a chef.'

'I see. And were there arguments? Disagreements? It was a very emotional time for your family after all.'

'No big rows, no.' Juliet scratched the back of her hand, how much should she be saying? That wasn't actually a lie.

'So, you had the meal, and then what?'

'Rhys said he was going to the church to pray, as Mira said.'

'I see. So, did everyone leave at about the same time as Rhys?'

'Oh no, we were all staying here except Rhys.'

'So, you were all here. Did anyone go out that night at all?

Juliet chewed on her thumb. 'Um, I went to meet someone for an hour or so, but I was back here by about half past eleven.'

'Did anyone else go out?'

Juliet hesitated. Should she mention the banging gate, the light in the workshop? She glanced at Mira, deadly white, in shock; no, she didn't need to string this interview out, none of those things probably mattered.

'No one has told me they did.'

'I see. Well, I think that is enough for now.' He turned to Mira. 'I will be back in touch with you very soon.'

'Oh, one thing I meant to mention is that we noticed Rhys's crucifix was missing,' interrupted Juliet. 'We are sure he was wearing it when he left the meal last night. He always wore it. Mira gave it to him, but it wasn't on him when we found him.'

Adam jotted this down. 'I will ask about that, thank you.' From his bag, he took a large booklet. 'This is full of information about procedures, people involved, and the like. You won't be wanting to look at it now, but it might come in useful. This is my card with my mobile number and email. Do you have any questions?'

'When can I see my husband?' asked Mira.

'I'm afraid it won't be possible today, but I'll organise it as soon as I can. Now, are there any other family members we should be in contact with?'

'Rhys's sister Anwen is here, I can tell her what you told me.'

'Of course, and I'll go and see her myself in a minute.'

'You will find who did this, won't you?' pleaded Mira.

'Mira, I can promise you we will do everything we can. It may take some time though as there has been a lot of traffic coming and going since early this morning – all the car and passenger ferries have been packed since first thing. Then there was the motorbike rally and vintage car show yesterday, we also have the big cycle race today, as well as some kind of moped show, so the island is pretty chaotic.' He ran his hand through his hair. 'Of course, everything will be on CCTV, so if someone has tried to leave the island, they should be on there, and we will look through everything. And if the people who did this are still on the island, we will be going around the holiday accommodation as well as to talking to residents.'

'Goodness, that's a huge job,' said Juliet, feeling overwhelmed on their behalf.

'It is, but as I said we will of course be taking this very seriously, and we have every confidence of catching whoever is responsible.'

They sat in silence for a minute and then, as the conversation seemed to have reached its natural conclusion, Adam and PC Greggs stood up.

'Thank you for all your help, and again, please accept my condolences. I will be back tomorrow. Now, could I see Anwen?'

They left the room and Juliet went to find Anwen, who then went into the living room with the officers.

Juliet had a horrible feeling that even though the police seemed confident, far from being over, their nightmare had only just begun.

13

While the police spoke to Anwen, Juliet and Mira went into the kitchen to talk to Cassie, Rosalind, and their mother.

Cassie looked over at Mira. 'I'm so sorry,' she signed and then reached out and touched her hand tenderly.

Juliet watched her sisters and saw the invisible bond as their eyes met. If you hadn't known they were related by looking at their faces, their two hands that were so similar would have given them away. Both of them had long, slender fingers that moved gracefully, and they seemed to use their hands to sign in the same way. It was something Juliet had never noticed before.

They heard the front door shut, and then a tearful-looking Anwen joined them in the kitchen.

'It's all wrong, a hit-and-run, up there of all places. It's crazy. He'd only gone to pray,' Anwen stammered.

'It seems unbelievable, I agree,' said Juliet.

'They think it must have happened at about one in the morning,' said Anwen, 'but you didn't find him until, what, about ten? Whoever did this could be miles away already.'

'Maybe, but it's not that easy to get off the island, certainly in the early hours.'

'I hope you're right, but they could lay low and then leave any time,' insisted Anwen.

'But the car would be spotted, wouldn't it? I wonder if it would be damaged.'

'The police didn't say much about the car, did they, so I don't know if they had any clues about it. It'll be the best chance of catching the bastard, find the car and you should have the driver.'

Cassie went over to Anwen. 'I think you should stay here with us for a few days.' She glanced over at their mother. 'That's alright with you Mum isn't it?'

'Of course, yes, you must stay here Anwen.' Their mother nodded and then wandered over to the patio doors, reached up to the empty hook. 'It's still not here,' she said quietly and then looked around. 'Which one of you has the patio door key?'

The question seemed so petty and out of the blue that they all looked a bit taken aback.

'Mum why are you fussing about the patio door key?' asked Cassie impatiently.

'Because Juliet said it was missing when she went out this morning at half past six, but I know it was there at about half past eleven when I locked up. Someone has been out in the night, and I'd like the door key back.' She looked anxiously around.

Everyone looked blank.

'Why on earth would anyone be going out in the middle of the night?' asked Cassie.

'I don't know, and I don't particularly care, but we only have one key, and I will need it to lock up tonight.'

Juliet could hear a rising hysteria in her mother's voice.

'Okay, Mum needs the door key, so let's help her find it,' she said to the others. 'Think, someone must have it. Anwen, are you sure you didn't go out last night?'

'No, of course not.'

'But I saw someone leave at about half past twelve. Oh, and the light was on in the workshop. So come on guys, who went out and where is the door key?'

Juliet's eyes travelled from face to face. Cassie and Anwen looked at her blankly as if she'd gone mad, Mira was hugging herself, in her own bubble of grief, not following anything that was said. For a moment, her eyes rested on Rosalind. It was the first time she'd looked at her properly that morning and she was shocked by what she saw. Rosalind's appearance was always perfect – immaculate make-up, styled hair – but this morning, her hair had been scrunched back roughly and, although she wore make-up, it had been applied quickly. There were smudges of mascara, and her eyebrows, normally thickly painted on, were uneven. She was pulling on the scruffy ponytail in a distracted way, with one hand, while she scrolled aimlessly through her phone with the other.

Juliet returned to her question. 'So, who went out? I'm not imagining things. Someone definitely went out,' she repeated and then she turned to Anwen. 'Are you sure you didn't come home and go back out again? You looked like you'd been out most of the night when I saw you this morning.'

Anwen glared at her, but Cassie interrupted, 'Anwen was in all night as I told Mum. Leave her alone, Juliet.'

Juliet was sure Cassie was lying. She knew the defiant stance, the locked jaw, but she had no idea why she was protecting Anwen.

Cassie tutted. 'Mum, the patio door key will turn up, don't panic. After all that's happened, it's not important, is it.'

Her mother frowned. 'I need to find it. I don't like the thought we were all in bed with the house unlocked. I shan't be able to sleep tonight with it like this.' She sounded desperate.

'Look, Mum, I know it's Sunday,' Juliet said, 'but I can ring the people who put the doors in. I assume they are on the island?'

'Oh yes, it was a friend of your dads in Sandown.'

'Right, well give me his name and I'll ring him. I can drive over and get a spare patio door key today hopefully.'

'Oh, thank you, that would certainly put my mind at rest.' Her mother sat picking at the quicks of her nails distractedly.

The kitchen was silent. They all seemed at a loss as to what to say or do.

Rosalind had started pacing up and down, still looking at her phone.

'Rosalind, did you have appointments today, do you need to go to work?'

Rosalind looked up, but she stared blankly at her mother. 'What?'

'I asked if you needed to go to work.'

'Ha, how can I do that?' She gave a strange, hard laugh. 'Nothing makes sense any more.'

Her mother went over to her. 'It's been a shock, hasn't it?'

Rosalind nodded, and then in a calmer voice said, 'Maybe I should go in. Maybe you're right.' She looked over at Mira and signed, 'I'm sorry, do you mind, I need to get out of here.'

'It's all right,' Mira replied.

'No, it's not all right. She should stay,' said Juliet. She remembered how Rosalind had gone to work so soon after her father died, and felt it was time she stayed and played her part in supporting the family.

However, Mira shook her head. 'No, it's really okay. There's nothing to be done.' Her eyes filled with tears, and she sobbed quietly, as if her heart was breaking.

'I've got my phone,' Rosalind signed, 'text me if there is any news.' She picked up her bags and slipped out of the house.

Juliet watched her go; how could Rosalind leave at a moment like this?

Her mother was preoccupied with Mira and had her arms around her. 'I can make some calls for you, don't worry about any of that, you stay there.'

Mira nodded, and their mother quietly left the kitchen. Cassie and Juliet stayed behind with Anwen. Juliet's mother had given her the card of the man who'd fitted the patio doors, so she called the mobile number, and it was answered immediately. Juliet explained who she was, and the man offered her condolences for the loss of her father. She told him about the key, and she was relieved when he was instantly helpful.

'I tell you what, I have to come over that way later anyway, I'll pick up the spares from the office and drop them in, shall I?'

Juliet thanked him.

Later in the afternoon, Juliet asked Mira if she needed anything from the vicarage.

'Oh, um, I don't know.' Mira's eyes were full of panic as they had been at lunchtime when Juliet had asked her if she wanted ham or cheese in her sandwich. Mira's mind had closed down to the simplest choices and her signs had become just wisps of movement.

'Don't worry, just give me the key to the vicarage and I'll pick you up a few things. You stay here with Mum,' said Juliet more decisively.

But Mira stood up slowly. 'No, I want to come.'

'Okay, then I tell you what, I'll take the car and we can pick up as much as you need. Then we don't have to go back again too soon.'

Juliet went to find her bag, opened it, but despite rummaging couldn't find her set of car keys.

'Has anyone used my car, Mum?'

'Why would anyone do that? Everyone has their own.'

'I know, but my set of car keys are gone. I had them yesterday, I know I did. I showed them to someone because of the key ring,' she felt herself blush, 'and I haven't driven anywhere since. They were zipped in here, I'm sure of it.' A picture of Gabriel, 'my heart is safe', she had shown him the heart and she was sure she hadn't dropped them...

'Actually Juliet, I'd rather walk. I'd like to see what's happening at the church, and a walk will help clear my mind too, I think,' Mira said suddenly. 'We could take Lola with us.'

'Of course, if you think it would help... I could check the car park at the same time. I may have dropped my set of car keys there.'

'But can we go to the vicarage first?'

Juliet could see this was something Mira was steeling herself for and needed to get over and done with.

As they walked through the village, Juliet saw a curtain twitch in an upstairs window. She usually liked that people watched through leaded windows, listened behind hedges pretending to garden, but today it felt unsettling. Last night there had been a murder here, a few weeks ago her father had been so desperate that he'd drunk heavily, had a fatal accident.

As they approached the entrance to the church, they could see police cars parked. Mira insisted they stop at the bottom of the path. There seemed to be police and people in overalls everywhere, the area was sealed off with a tent-like structure. Juliet wondered if Rhys's body was still there.

Mira stood, frozen, staring over. 'It's not right,' she signed, 'they have him now, my husband, it's like he belongs to them, not me. I should be looking after him. He's nothing to them.'

'But they have to find out what's happened,' signed Juliet. 'You need to know, don't you?'

'Do I?'

'Of course, even if it doesn't feel like it matters now, it will do in time. They have to find who did this.'

'But the person could be miles away on the mainland by now... carrying on as if nothing has happened.'

'The police will be looking everywhere to find them.'

Mira just shrugged, looking broken and blank.

'Come on, let's go and find your things,' said Juliet.

They carried on and Juliet was aware of Mira looking back over her shoulder.

Finally, they arrived at the vicarage.

* * *

Mira looked up at the house. Modern, soulless, one of a few new builds in the village. She had vague memories of the original vicarage; an old rambling building, dark wood furniture, a wild, overgrown garden. But it had been in desperate need of repair and the church had decided to sell it and purchase this new house. Despite being far more practical, easy to maintain and heat, Mira would have preferred the old house, but she knew that went with a very dated picture of church life. Everything had changed.

The job of the vicar now was all-consuming, and Mira understood why many partners found separate work. Maybe she should have done that, done some maths tutoring online or something. However, that, she knew, would only have been pushing the main problems aside.

Mira looked at the house. She may have been allowed to choose the paint for the walls, but the building belonged to the church, the parish. Their pictures hung on the walls, the cheap sofa and supermarket mugs belonged to them, but it had never felt like their home.

On the driveway stood two cars, both second-hand, tidy,

sensible cars. She'd have to sort Rhys's soon, sell it or something. There was so much 'business' when someone died, so many times you had to keep telling different people someone was dead. She remembered the advice Rhys would often give: get a few copies of the death certificate – no one prepares you for how often you must prove your spouse has died.

Over the doorway hung a sign – 'God, the silent visitor in every home' – Rhys had put it there. He loved it but she always felt it was creepy. As she opened the door, she brushed against one of Rhys's coats hanging in the hallway and she turned and buried her nose in it, in the smell of Rhys. She let Lola off her lead, and she ran excitedly around the house, on into the kitchen, and Mira could see her slurping stale water from her bowl. Coming here was too normal; it really was as if nothing had happened.

Mira stared at the silent phone, especially adapted for her with a screen to show messages. She saw there were four. Reading them she found, 'I'm so sorry, Mira, anything we can do. We are all praying for you.' She stopped reading after that.

She went into the kitchen and opened the fridge. 'I ought to clear this,' she signed to Juliet, but she looked back, frightened to touch the contents. It seemed too soon, too final to throw away Rhys's cheese, his chocolate mousse, and yet...

'Leave it,' signed Juliet, 'you or I can do it another day. Let's just get some clothes and go.'

Mira shook her head. 'No, please, you do the fridge, I'll go upstairs. Put the rubbish in a black bag, we can put it out.'

Mira ran upstairs into her bedroom and closed the door. Part of her would like to stay here, be alone. Back at her mother's house she felt on show, another woman who has lost her husband. She wasn't sure what people expected to see, was she meant to cry all the time? She felt numb, lost; maybe they had the right idea in the past when she would have worn black for months. That would have been easier than people always looking at your face.

Still, that wasn't an option. To distract her from her racing thoughts, she reached up to the top of the wardrobe, and took a down tatty case, which she lay on the bed. She started to pack clothes. The good thing about having so few possessions meant it was very easy to pack. She packed some books, including her books on research into prime numbers. She didn't know when she last seriously sat down and read any of them, but she carried them round like a talisman, a sign she had not given up that part of her life. From the top drawer of her bedside table, she took her box of hearing aid bits and pieces. Spare batteries, ear mould cleaners and the like. Finally, she took a draw key out of a pot on the windowsill and opened the next drawer down – her drawer. The only place in the whole house she felt was truly hers, and hers alone.

The first thing she saw was the cracked photograph, taken seven years ago. It was one of the few professional photos she had of their wedding day. They'd only paid someone for the most basic package. The dress she'd bought second-hand from a charity shop, the flowers had been given to her by a member of the congregation. She'd not minded any of that and seeing herself smiling out at the camera she knew she'd been happy that day. How had it gone so wrong?

At that moment, she saw Juliet standing in the doorway. She'd seen the photo.

'I dropped it,' Mira said quickly and tucked it under a top in her case. Aware of Juliet standing there still, she slipped out a washbag. She could feel the box in there and stuffed it to the bottom of her case, which she started to zip up. 'Okay, ready to go.'

They left the room and as they passed, Juliet glancing in the spare bedroom. It had clearly been used recently; on the bedside table, a bible and a clock, some pyjamas lay on top of the duvet, a dressing gown hung on the door. Mira noticed Juliet looking in and explained. 'When he got back late or something, Rhys would sleep in there.'

They went downstairs and Mira bustled them straight out of the front door. She noticed a neighbour, who looked over at her nervously, but hurried back into the house. It hurt, but it told her news had spread. Everyone knew – the vicar was dead.

They walked back down the hill, back past the church, back home. Relieved to be away from prying eyes, Mira went straight in, but Juliet carried on down across the road to the car park.

* * *

There were less cars today, the tide was well in, and most of the campervans seemed to have moved on.

Juliet went to where she had met Gabriel. She searched all over the car park, but she could not find the set of keys and then went into the field to look around her car. But as she entered the field, she stopped short, she couldn't believe what she was seeing.

14

Juliet stared at the empty spot where her car had been. *That's madness*, she thought. Where was it?

She knew she had to tell the DC her car was missing and so she ran home and rang him. He was formal, polite and took the details.

Juliet then went into the kitchen and told her mother what had happened.

'That's awful,' said her mother. 'We've never had trouble down there before this year. The police should be coming out on the weekends, moving people on.'

'I still haven't found my set of car keys. I wonder if I could have dropped them down there, it would have made it a lot easier to steal my car.'

'But you seemed pretty sure they were in your handbag; I should think they are in the house somewhere. These youngsters don't need keys to get into a car.'

'I suppose not.' Juliet paused. 'You don't think my car was the one used in Rhys's death do you, Mum?' She was pleading for reassurance.

'Of course not. There have been some rough crowds down

there. Someone has probably been off joyriding, or whatever they call it. It will turn up somewhere on the island. You've done your bit, told this liaison officer, that is all you can do. Now, how was Mira at the vicarage?'

'She picked up a few things. I don't think any of it has sunk in yet.'

'No, I don't suppose it has. It's hard to believe much of what we've been through lately.' Her mother put her head to one side. 'I was wondering, do you think Mira would like to share your room again?'

'I'd not thought about it. You think I should ask her?'

'I do. You two were always close; I think she might appreciate it.'

And so Juliet went and asked Mira. It turned out her mother was right, and that night Mira and Juliet went up to their room together.

* * *

It was strange to be in the same room. Juliet turned on the night light, which to her amazement still worked. They turned away from each other as they changed into their night things, but Juliet turned just as Mira was pulling on her dressing gown. It was then that Juliet saw Mira's arm and gasped.

'My God,' she said, 'what have you done?'

Juliet looked more closely. Mira had deep red and purple bruising covering much of the top half of her arm.

'Oh, it's nothing,' said Mira, quickly tying her dressing gown tightly. 'I fell on Friday evening when I took Lola to the beach.'

The way her sister stumbled over the words, the panic in her eyes, sent a shiver through Juliet. 'How did you fall? Were you with someone?'

'No, of course not, just forget it. It doesn't matter any more.'

Mira got into bed and took her hearing aids off, sending a clear signal she would not be speaking to Juliet again that night.

Juliet got into bed and remembered how Mira had been when they'd arrived at the meal, how she'd pulled away from Rhys, how she'd looked so pale and tired. She thought of the broken photograph, the separate bedrooms. Had Rhys been abusing her sister? A picture pushed its way uninvited into her head. Mira leaning over Rhys's body asking for forgiveness.

Juliet turned over, pushing the thought aside. There was the business with her set of car keys, where were they? She'd sworn they had been in her bag. Her mind flew quickly back to Anwen. She had had that row with Rhys, maybe she'd sneaked back out without Cassie knowing. But was she really prepared to suspect Anwen or even Mira of murder? If only her father and Rhys hadn't spoken of danger, hadn't seemed to almost expect something terrible to happen, then she could have accepted this as a random accident. *Dear God, please let it be that.*

* * *

Juliet woke the next morning, her head thumping. It had been one of those nights when sleep had been more exhausting than being awake.

To Juliet's surprise, Mira had already got up and she assumed she must be out with Lola. Juliet checked her phone, saw a text from Gabriel.

I am so sorry to hear about Rhys, please give my condolences to your family. If there is anything I can do, please let me know. If you want to chat anytime, I am here xxx

How odd it was to think this time yesterday she'd been having breakfast at the vineyard. How could she have been so completely unaware of the tragedy that had occurred the night before, that Rhys's body lay cold by the church?

Juliet went downstairs, where she found Rosalind still in her dressing gown, sitting stirring her cereal with her spoon, but not actually eating anything.

'Morning, Rosalind. Was work busy?' Juliet asked her.

Rosalind gave her the blank look she'd given her mother yesterday. 'What?'

'How was work?'

'Oh that, it went okay. I've taken the week off now though, cancelled my appointments. I need a break.'

'Of course, it's been a terrible time, losing Dad and then Rhys. We all need some time to come to terms with it all.'

'Nothing makes sense, does it?'

Juliet noticed it was the phrase she'd used the day before.

'No,' said Juliet, 'none of it does, but we have to look after Mum and Mira now.' She went and put her arms around her little sister. 'They need us to be strong.'

When Mira returned with Lola, Juliet made her breakfast and stayed close to her for the morning.

As promised, the family liaison officer, DC Adam Smith, returned. He was with a different officer this time, who introduced herself as Detective Inspector Ann Rolf.

The new officer was short and had a cuddly appearance until she spoke in sharp, clipped sentences, giving an impression she viewed everyone with suspicion.

'I would like to speak to you all together,' she said on the doorstep, and then, without waiting to be invited in, she led the way into the house. Glancing into the living room, she announced, 'We'll use this room, please gather everyone together.'

Juliet was annoyed, but a flicker of a smile indicating a silent apology from Adam helped calm her down.

They all assembled: the four sisters, their mother and Anwen.

'I wanted to come and meet you,' said the detective. 'I am the officer in charge of this case, but Adam will still be your point of contact. Now, we have some significant updates for you.' The detective spoke directly to Mira and for the first time Juliet was impressed with her professionalism. 'I understand you are Deaf, so you must tell me at any point if you need me to clarify what I am saying. Are you happy at this point to use your family to support you?'

Mira nodded.

'Good, but if that should change, just let me know. Now, you have been told we suspected your husband had been hit by a car that had been parked in the church car park. We are sure about that now. Based on your information and the preliminary examinations of the body, we estimate the incident occurred not long after one o'clock on the morning of Sunday, 21 August.' She paused, checked that Mira was understanding, and then continued. 'Rhys was hit by the car from behind. We can tell from tyre prints that the driver stopped afterwards. We think they walked back to Rhys and moved the body, rolled it over, then returned to the car and drove away from the scene. We have not found anything as helpful as footprints, but we do have a scraping of paint from the car.'

Juliet clasped her hands together. 'You have identified the make of car?'

'Actually, we are pretty sure we have found the car that was used.'

'You've found the car?' said Mira, wide-eyed.

'Yes, the paint and tyre prints match.'

'So, you know who the driver was?' asked Mira, her lips trembling, tears forming in her eyes once more.

The inspector paused, looking as if she was choosing her words carefully. 'As always, it's more complicated than that. We found the car, abandoned in the woods near the church. Someone had made a good attempt at setting light to it.' The detective shifted her gaze back to Juliet. 'I understand you reported your car missing yesterday?' the detective asked.

Juliet frowned. 'Yes, but...' The detective kept staring at her and slowly the horror of what was being said started to sink in. *Oh god, no*, Juliet thought, *not my car. I can't bear it, please don't let it be my car that was used to kill Rhys.* She felt hot, the room was spinning, the voice of the detective sounded far away as she continued.

'We believe it was your car that was used and then abandoned. We were able to identify it from the registration number.'

Juliet clasped her hand over her mouth; she was going to be sick.

Ann Rolf held out a photograph. Juliet's hands shook uncontrollably as she stared at the blackened, windowless remains of her car. Most of the damage was to the front part, the driver's seat completely destroyed.

Mira pulled Juliet's arm, shaking her. 'She's right. It's your car!'

Tears burned Juliet's eyes as the full horror of what she was looking at sank in. 'My car was used to kill Rhys?'

'I'm afraid it would appear so.'

Juliet turned to Mira, her voice shaking. 'I'm sorry. I'm so sorry.' She turned back to the police, signed as she spoke. 'You are sure?'

'Yes. Of course, it needs to go through many tests, but, yes, we are sure. I am sorry, this must be a shock.'

Juliet nodded, breathed deeply, tried to think straight. She looked again at the photograph. 'Why set fire to it?'

'The damage from the fire will make it very hard for us to use DNA to identify the driver. However, some things survived which may be of use.'

'Such as?'

'There were drugs, other illegal substances, both found in the church car park and in the car – all of which will be analysed. The drugs we found were in pill form, they are a kind of ecstasy we have not seen on the island before, so it will be interesting to see if we can source them.'

Juliet could feel the heat of the inspector's eyes on her again, but Mira seemed oblivious. Instead, she said, 'So you're saying the people who killed Rhys were stoned, high?'

Juliet saw the anger and dismay on Mira's face.

'Well, that's definitely a possibility.'

Juliet stared once more at the photograph of her car. It had taken her on so many innocuous trips and yet it had been the weapon used to kill her sister's husband.

'This must be very upsetting,' the detective said, 'but, Juliet, maybe you could fill us in on a few things. To start with, when did you last see your car?'

'Um, I suppose it was when I checked it with Rosalind when I first came home, that was the day after Dad died… 6 August.'

'You hadn't seen it or used it since then?'

'No, after Dad died, we haven't been anywhere. I didn't even think about it until I went to use it yesterday… I wanted to take Mira to the vicarage to get her things, but I couldn't find my set of car keys. They are always zipped in my bag, but they were not there, so we walked to the vicarage instead. I went to check if I had dropped my keys down at the beach car park, and that's when I found my car was missing. I came straight home and rang you.'

'So, it is a couple of weeks since you actually saw your car. Why was it down there, not parked here at the house?'

'We are short of parking here. I've always parked down there in the field, we had permission.'

'I see. So your car had been sitting there, unattended. And then yesterday you looked for your set of car keys but could not find them?'

'That's right.'

'So, had you seen your car keys since you checked your car a couple of weeks ago?'

'Um, I did see them on Saturday evening, I took them out of my bag down in the car park, but I didn't use them.'

'So, you could have dropped them then?'

'I thought I'd zipped them back in my bag, but I suppose I could have dropped them. Is that what happened? Someone found my set of car keys and then used them to steal my car?'

'Unfortunately, there is no way of knowing whether your car was started with keys or they managed to bypass the ignition switch some other way. The fire damage was considerable. But if your set of keys are missing, that suggests they were used. And we need to find out how they got from your bag where you say they were, into the hands of whoever drove the car.' The detective sat more upright, her voice more formal. 'We will need to take individual statements of all the members of the family as to your movements on Saturday night.'

'Why do you need to do that?' asked Cassie, her voice shaking with anger. 'This was obviously the act of some drunken thug; we don't need you insinuating anything else. My sister has been through enough.'

For the first time in the conversation, Adam spoke. 'It's just procedure. It is important we eliminate people from the inquiry so that we can get on with finding the real culprits. Also, it may be that you are holding on to useful information without realising it. We do know how distressing this can be, but please understand we need to tick the boxes.'

His words seemed to pacify Cassie.

The inspector flashed a hard smile at him, and then turned

back to the family. 'For the time being let us just check a few more facts, shall we? Let's just go through all your movements on that Saturday evening, Juliet.'

The use of her name was unnerving, she felt singled out. She was acutely aware of the notebook, the eyes, slightly screwed up, alert, taking in everything she said, her manner, judging her. Juliet tried to relax, to breathe more slowly, but she had a feeling she was just making herself look more guilty.

She started going through the evening, the meal, who had been there.

'I understand the meal was tense, difficult?' said the detective.

Juliet glanced at Adam, feeling betrayed for some silly reason.

'Well, yes, but I explained to Adam why that was.'

'And you went out after the meal? Who did you meet?'

'I met with my friend Gabriel...'

Mira signed, 'You saw Gabriel?'

Juliet nodded. 'Only for a chat,' she signed and then continued. 'We talked for some time, and then I returned home. I showed him the key ring on my keys, so I definitely had them then.' She could see the questioning look on the detective's face, inwardly cringed, and knew she was going to have to explain. 'You see, Gabriel had given me a stone heart-shaped key ring, and when I met him, I showed it to him, so he knew I still had it.'

'Can you give me Gabriel's details?'

Juliet told them his address.

'Ah the vineyard, yes, I know it,' said the detective. 'And what is the nature of your relationship with Gabriel?'

'We are just friends.'

'I see. And after you saw Gabriel, what time did you return to the house on Saturday evening?'

'At about half past eleven.' She signed to Mira, 'It was about half eleven, wasn't it? You came down for Lola.'

Mira nodded.

She saw the police officers shoot each other a glance.

'Mum checked everyone was in and then locked up...' Juliet paused, she thought of Anwen, the sounds of people leaving, but how could she mention that? It was all supposition and they'd all denied going out. Maybe she'd got it all wrong.

Suddenly she was aware of the detective watching her again. 'And then?' she asked.

'And then I went to bed.'

'And did you leave the house again at all that night?'

'No, why should I? I went to bed, had some calls.'

'Ah that could be helpful. Who called you?'

'Well, I video called on WhatsApp with Gabriel at about half twelve... and again at about one... his mother wasn't well, he was worried... oh and then I chatted to a friend in Edinburgh.'

'And you said you noticed your set of keys were gone yesterday. Had someone in the house borrowed them, used your car?'

'No, I asked everyone, no one knew where they were.'

'But if you are right, they were in your bag on Saturday night. Where did you put your bag when you came home?'

'Down here on the dresser.'

'So, anyone in the house could have taken the keys without you knowing?'

'Well yes. But—'

'So, if I've got it right, the people who stayed in this house the night of the accident, were yourself, your sisters Mira, Rosalind and Cassie, and also Rhys's sister Anwen and your mother.' Her eyes scanned the room. 'No one left the house all night?'

Her question was met with a stony silence.

'Right, and, Mira, your husband Rhys was meant to be going back to the vicarage after he'd been to the church?'

'That's right. He didn't want to disturb me, and he liked to be close to the phone at the vicarage in case anyone needed him.'

'I see,' the detective said. She closed her notebook and looked around. 'Thank you for answering my questions. One more thing, we would like to have access to the vicarage; I assume your husband's computer and personal effects are there?'

'Yes, his computer is in his study. The wardens have spare keys, I can give you their numbers, or of course, you can have mine.'

'The numbers of the wardens would be ideal, thank you.'

After Mira had given these, the detective asked, 'Now, do you have anything you would like to ask me?'

'I asked yesterday about seeing my husband,' said Mira. 'Adam said he'd try and organise something.'

'I'd like to see my brother as well,' said Anwen quietly.

Adam spoke. 'I have arranged things. If you could come up to the hospital at about two this afternoon. Um, go to the main entrance. Someone will meet you there. Is that convenient?'

'Yes, thank you,' said Mira.

Their business apparently concluded, the police officers rose to say goodbye to them all. Juliet rose too to show them out.

When they'd gone, Juliet went back to the living room, but no one seemed to know what to do next.

'I'm really sorry they used your car,' Cassie said, 'but you have to be careful about this business with your lost set of car keys. You need to reassure the police that no one in the house took them out of your bag, you must see how it looks otherwise.'

'But I don't know what happened to them, so how can I reassure the police?'

'Well, you must have lost them outside, and you need to say that to them.'

'But I don't know that for sure, do I?' insisted Juliet.

'Well, no one here took them out of your bag. You know that,' said Cassie.

The two sisters stared at each other, neither giving way.

In the end, Juliet spoke. 'Look, I think we ought to start being open about the meal on Saturday night. The police are going to interview us all. I am not saying anyone here had anything to do with Rhys's death, of course I'm not. But we need to tell the truth. For example, someone still has the original key to the patio doors, someone left the house in the middle of the night, someone was in the workshop, I saw the light on, the shadows.'

'Well, if you're so sure, why didn't you say anything to the police just now?' asked Rosalind.

Juliet was surprised at the confrontational tone in her sister's voice. 'Because I hoped and expected whoever it was would own up. I don't want to go around accusing you all, do I, but there is no point in hiding things. The police will find out and it will look worse in the end. Like my set of cars keys, I am sure they were in my bag, so if anyone knows anything, please tell me.'

No one would meet her eye, and no one spoke.

Juliet threw her hands up in despair.

'Listen. This is all supposition. You think you heard or saw someone; you think someone took your set of car keys. Maybe you are just letting your imagination run away with you,' said Cassie.

'No, I don't think I am. I'm sure I saw someone go out of the gate, I saw the light in the workshop, I didn't imagine them,' said Juliet.

Cassie interrupted crossly, 'People don't have to explain themselves to you.'

The defensiveness in her tone was clear and Juliet couldn't help wondering just where it came from.

Her mother, however, agreed with Cassie. 'Juliet, whatever we were all up to that night had nothing to do with Rhys's death. The people who did this wicked thing were strangers from the mainland.'

'Of course they were,' said Cassie, and Anwen nodded in agreement.

Juliet longed to join in their certainty, but she was uneasy. Of course, she wanted this horrible deed to have been done by strangers. Even better, strangers from the mainland. If only it didn't feel so personal to her – it was her car after all, her set of car keys with her special key ring. And it was her who knew Rhys was scared, who her father had warned.

'We must trust the police to catch these people, I am sure they will,' her mother continued with confidence.

'Are you? Are you really?' asked Rosalind, her voice quiet, but strangely cutting.

'Of course, why wouldn't I be?'

'Well, they never caught the person who killed Maddie's son Harry, did they?'

'Oh, that was completely different, and it was years ago. I'm sure the police are more effective these days,' said her mother sharply.

'It was exactly twenty-one years ago to the day of our meal,' said Rosalind, 'and Rhys's accident, it makes you think, doesn't it?'

Juliet wondered about her sister, saw the dark circles make-up had failed to cover up. Rosalind had been so strange since Rhys's accident. It was more than grief; it was more than that hardness and frustration she'd noticed when she first came home. Why had she kept saying she didn't understand, that nothing made sense? Now she was bringing up Harry's death. Why? Like her mother said, that was years ago.

Juliet shook her head; she had no idea what was going on with Rosalind. She did know that there were a lot of questions that needed answers, and of all the people present on Saturday evening, Anwen had been acting the most suspiciously. It was time to find out what she was hiding.

15

Juliet had been listening to Mira tossing and turning all night. It had been heart-breaking seeing her sister's face when she returned from the mortuary with Anwen yesterday afternoon. It reminded Juliet of the grief, the shock they were feeling, and made her question her suspicion of Anwen. Her pain had seemed so raw and real; surely, she couldn't be putting that on.

Juliet got up and saw Mira was finally sound asleep, her arm on top of the duvet. Juliet tried to avoid looking at the bruising. Lola appeared to be asleep next to Mira, but as soon as she saw Juliet move, she was up.

Lola followed Juliet out of the bedroom, clearly hoping for an early walk and breakfast, but just as Juliet was about to go downstairs, she heard a voice coming from the bathroom. Juliet crept closer to the door, bent over, and listened.

'You need to understand, this is something I need to do.' There was a brief pause as presumably the person on the other end spoke and then Juliet heard Cassie speak again. 'I can see doctors here; you are not to worry but I have to stay here. I'm sorry, of course I miss you, you just have to try and see this from my point of view.'

The phone call must have ended abruptly, because before Juliet had time to move, the bathroom door opened, and she was caught red-handed by Cassie.

Cassie's eyebrows shot up. 'You were waiting?'

Juliet looked up. Cassie was in her towel dressing gown and drying her hair, but there was something about the way she was behaving that made Juliet's heart race. Inexplicably Juliet felt a burning sensation in her hand. She looked at it but there was no mark, nothing.

'Um, yes.'

Lola ignored them both and carried on downstairs alone, but Juliet felt she had no option but to carry on the pretence and so she walked past Cassie and into the bathroom. She could feel her cheeks burning with shame at being caught listening at a door, but she couldn't work out what she'd found so unnerving. It was odd that Cassie should be making secret phone calls in the toilet, wasn't it, and the conversation sounded rather intense and cryptic. It had been someone Cassie was obviously close to, in a relationship with perhaps? The mention of doctors frightened Juliet, what was wrong with her sister? Juliet completed the pantomime by pulling the flush and turning the taps. She came out to an empty landing and went downstairs.

In the kitchen, Juliet found Lola philosophically lying in her bed and went over to stroke her, but noises behind her made her stop. Looking over her shoulder, she saw Rosalind reaching up to the hook where the new patio door key was hanging.

'Morning,' Juliet said.

Rosalind turned, startled, and demanded, 'What are you doing up so early?'

Juliet was shocked. Her sister looked so dishevelled again. It was so unlike Rosalind to come down without her hair done and at least a smattering of make-up.

'Are you okay?' Juliet asked.

Rosalind pulled her silky wrap tightly around herself; she was breathing fast. 'Of course.'

Juliet could see her hand clenched, something metal sticking out.

'What's that?' she asked, pointing to Rosalind's hand.

Rosalind opened her hand slowly, shrugged. 'It's just a spare key for the patio door.'

'But that's the original patio door key, isn't it? The one mum was looking for.' Juliet stared at Rosalind. 'How long have you had this?'

Rosalind tossed her head back. 'For God's sake, it's only a door key. I found it in my pocket, I must have put it in there by mistake.'

'But you must have taken it after we went to bed on Saturday night, why didn't you say? You knew we were looking for it.'

'Oh God. Look, there's no great mystery. I just came down because I wanted to look in Dad's workshop for something without everyone asking a load of questions.'

'So, it was you in the workshop on Saturday night? What time did you go out there?'

'About half twelve, I guess. I unlocked the doors and took the key.'

'And when did you come back in?'

'Oh, a few hours later, so it was about two, I think.'

'You were out there all that time? Did you see anyone leave the garden?'

Rosalind shrugged and then her face brightened. 'Oh, I did see someone going out now you mention it.'

'Who?'

Rosalind looked away. 'It was dark...'

'Well, what time then?'

'About half past twelve maybe, but I was busy... I didn't think about it.'

'Did anyone else go out while you were in the workshop?'

'No idea, I settled down in the old armchair and put my headphones on after that. I wasn't looking out of the window.'

'So that's all you saw? Someone going out at about half past twelve?'

'That's right, and eventually I came back inside and went to bed.'

Juliet paused. She'd been bludgeoning her sister with questions and hadn't asked her the most important one.

'Why did you go out there at that time of night?'

Rosalind sighed. 'I wanted to look for my musical box and I wanted to look at it on my own.'

'But I could have got it for you anytime. You just had to ask.'

'But you kept forgetting and I heard what you said... you don't think Dad wanted me to have it, do you?'

Juliet shrugged. 'He might have been confused.'

'That's not what you really think, is it?'

'Okay, so Dad did say not to give it to you, but I've no idea why.' Juliet saw the distress on her sister's face.

'I know now,' said Rosalind. She spat the words out, her face white-hot with anger.

Juliet felt her heart racing. 'You do?'

'Yes, he'd hidden a letter behind one of the photographs.'

Juliet shook her head in confusion. 'A letter?'

'Yes.' Rosalind's hands began to shake. 'He'd written it, thinking we'd spoken. You know he was going to tell me something on my twenty-first? I'm sure this was it.'

Juliet's eyes widened. 'Hang on. So, he didn't want you to have the box because he remembered the letter. He must have written it before whatever happened the day of his accident to change his mind.'

Rosalind nodded. 'Exactly.'

Juliet walked over to her sister. 'What was it? What was this big secret?'

Rosalind started to sob. 'I can't tell you; I can't bear it. It's so horrible, but I wish he'd at least had the courage to tell me himself.'

'I don't think it was cowardice that stopped him, I think he genuinely thought it was safer for you not to know,' Juliet reassured her.

Rosalind shrugged. 'I don't see how that makes sense.'

'What does it say? Let me see it.'

'No, once you see it everything will change, nothing will be the same again.'

'But this is too much for you to cope with on your own, you've not looked right since Saturday evening.'

'No, I feel rubbish. I don't know what to do. When I first read it, I knew Dad had told Rhys.' Rosalind stood clenching her fists, her long nails digging into her palms. 'How dare he do that, tell him and not me.'

'Did you go and speak to Rhys after reading the letter?' Juliet asked quietly.

Rosalind glared at her. 'No, but I wish I had, and I'll tell you this, I'm glad he's dead.'

She stormed out of the room. Juliet had seen Rosalind have many outbursts over the years. But Rosalind was no longer a child, she was an adult. Those words of frustration and anger with Rhys had not been thrown out like a toy across the room, they had been cold, considered. Rosalind had meant every word.

16

Juliet took her coffee out into the garden and sat on the bench in desperate need of a way to shut down the thoughts pinballing around her head. She looked around; the birds were quieter now it was coming to the end of August. She noticed blackberries ripening on the bushes, the borders looking scruffy. Looking ahead, she could see a mist hanging over the sea. Schools would be back soon; the holidaymakers would all leave the island. Life would be getting back to normal.

But, of course, nothing would be back to normal for them. Her mother would have to learn to live without her father, Mira without Rhys. And there would be more questions, more police, coroners, and inquests. There was a long road ahead.

Today, the police would be coming to take their statements so Juliet was determined to see if she could find her set of car keys. At least that would then be one mystery solved. She was going to have a good search for them.

Inside, she went through her bag, looked around the dresser, and then moved out to the workshop. It had been shut up for days and there was a strange, acrid smell in there, so Juliet opened the window. She searched high and low, but her keys weren't there. She left the workshop, feeling even more sure now that she wouldn't find them.

When the police arrived, it was Adam Smith and a constable they hadn't yet met. They were all asked to sit in the music room, so they could be called in individually, and then shown to the kitchen afterwards. They were asked not to chat to one another between interviews.

Juliet was first. Adam explained what was involved and suddenly the process felt more serious, more official. This statement was something she was going to have to sign; she would have to agree she had told the truth.

She was happy to go through her own movements the evening Rhys died – the fact Gabriel had been able to see that she was in her bedroom when he called her had given her an alibi. She gave her phone to Adam to check the record of the calls.

The problem came when he asked her about everyone else, and whether they had stayed in all night.

'Well, it wasn't quite that straightforward. Mum checked everyone was in and locked up at about half past eleven. However, I know my sister Rosalind went out to the workshop. She unlocked the patio doors with the key, and I saw a shadow in the workshop, which I now know was Rosalind.'

'I see, so that is a different account to the one we have been given. What time did she go out?'

'She told me it was about half past twelve, and she was out there for quite a while. When she did finally return to the house, she forgot to lock the patio door and went straight to bed.'

Adam was looking more serious now. 'Okay, I will need to talk to her about that. Has anything else come to mind since we last spoke?'

'Well, I remembered I saw someone leave the garden at about half past twelve and Rosalind said she saw someone go out as well.'

He sat up and fixed her with a stare. 'I see, and who was it?'

'I really have no idea, and nor has Rosalind. It was a very hot night, so it could have been someone going out for fresh air.'

'Of course, but no one has admitted to that, have they. It would help if people told us these things from the outset. Is there anything else?'

Juliet bit her lip. 'Just one thing. I saw Anwen the next morning, very early, at about half past six, and I did notice that she was wearing the same clothes as the night before. She looked like she might have been out all night, so it struck me as a bit odd.'

Andy did a strong intake of breath. 'I see. So, she could be the person who you saw leave at half past twelve. If I've understood properly, by then Rosalind had unlocked the patio doors, so Anwen could have gone out of that way. When you saw Anwen the next morning you had the impression she had been our all night and so if she had left the house at half twelve, you are pretty sure she did not return.'

'I suppose it's all possible, although, as I say, I can't be sure the person who went out at half twelve was Anwen.'

'Interesting. Well, it would have been much better if you'd told me this before but thank you for telling me now, it's very helpful. By the way, have you found your car keys with that special key ring yet?'

'No, they are still missing. I had another look for them this morning, but I can't find them. I must have dropped them outside somewhere.'

'Hmm, it would appear so. We did comb through the car park, but they weren't found there. All I can suggest is you keep searching, and if you find them let us know. We talked to Gabriel and he can remember you showing him the keys, and he seemed sure you put them away. I assume no one in the house has admitted to taking them?'

'No, no one.'

'Okay, well thank you for your help. That's all for now.'

Juliet left the room.

Because she had been first in, it seemed a long wait until everyone had finished giving their statements.

Finally, the officers took their leave after politely thanking everyone for their cooperation, and they all sat in the kitchen together, stunned into silence for a while until their mother suggested coffee.

'I don't know about coffee; I could do with something stronger after that,' said Cassie. 'Talk about the third degree. I almost wondered if I should have had a solicitor with me, I'm sure we would have had the right to one.'

'I think they wanted to keep it informal,' said their mother.

'But everything we said was written down.' She turned on Juliet. 'They said you told them about someone going out. What the hell? They went through my night in minute detail.'

'I was forced to explain my evening to the police as well.' Anwen looked at Cassie. 'Thank you for telling everyone I was in; I appreciate you supporting me. However, I've been forced now to tell them the whole story of why I was out all evening, and that I never came back after talking to Rhys.' She glared at Juliet. 'The police know where I was now, and I can promise you I wasn't up the church killing my brother.'

Juliet could feel her cheeks burning, but she was curious as to where Anwen had been and why she was being so secretive. Her mind went back to her set of car keys. If she was right and she'd not dropped them, someone in the house had taken them. It had to be after she'd seen Gabriel, and if Anwen had not come back, then she couldn't have taken the keys out of her bag. Of course, all that depended on whether Anwen was telling the truth.

Anwen continued, 'Cassie, I don't want to tell anyone else, but I think you have a right to know where I was that evening, and I will tell you privately. If you no longer want to go into business with me, I will understand.'

Rosalind turned to Juliet, spoke quietly. 'By the way, I told the police about being out there,' she said, gesturing out of the window. She stopped when she noticed her mother was listening.

'You were out in the workshop?' interrupted her mother. 'Why on earth did you go out there at that time?'

'I just needed some time to myself. And I was the person who unlocked the patio doors and had the key. I'd forgotten it was in my pocket, but it's back where it's meant to be now.'

'I wish you'd told me; you knew how worried I was, but I suppose at least we have two keys now.' She turned to Mira. 'And you, love, how did you get on with the police? I could have come in with you.'

'Adam offered for me to have an interpreter, but he spoke very clearly, I was fine. I read through my statement, and I was perfectly happy with it.'

'Good.' Her mother put the kettle on but sat straight back down. No one had the energy to actually make a drink.

Juliet was aware of Anwen glaring at her, and then had a thought. 'Hang on, if Anwen really didn't come home at all, then who was the person I saw go out of the gate? Both Rosalind and I saw someone, who was it?'

She was answered with silence.

'They asked me about my set of car keys as well. Are you all sure you've not seen them?'

The continuing silence that followed was frustrating.

'If you won't answer me, what am I meant to think?'

Cassie tutted at her. 'Look, your stupid car keys will turn up and the rest is just your overactive imagination.' She took a deep breath. 'Now, after all that unpleasantness, Anwen and I would like you to make time to come and see something with us tomorrow afternoon. Some good news to cheer us all up.'

'But I need to explain things to you first,' said Anwen to Cassie, looking worried.

'Whatever it is you have to tell me, we are going to do this.'

'You don't know what it is yet.'

'I am certain nothing you can tell me will change my mind. So, everyone should meet here at three tomorrow, okay? This is very important to me. I need you all to come.'

Juliet watched Cassie get up and leave, with Anwen following her. She was guessing whatever Cassie had to show them was to do with the business Cassie and Anwen were setting up, and she glanced at her mother. She was holding onto the edge of the table, her face white. Maybe she'd been hoping Cassie's plans were some kind of momentary blip, but it was suddenly becoming a reality.

When they'd left, Mira said to Juliet, 'I'm going up to the vicarage now, just to do some sorting.'

'Okay, I can come with you, we can walk up together.'

'Thanks, but I'd like to go on my own. I was thinking, Rhys's car is sitting up there unused.'

'Oh yes, you'll need to sort things out so you can sell it. I can help with that if you want.'

'No, I don't want to sell it. What I thought was, why don't you have it?'

'You mean for me to buy it off you? That would be great as long as you don't mind the thought of me driving Rhys's car. I am going to have to replace my old one.'

'I'd like to give it to you; we used yours for two years, he wouldn't have wanted me to take money for it.'

'Wow, are you sure?'

'Of course. I was thinking if I get you put on the insurance today, you can start using it. We can sort out making it formally yours another time.'

'Gosh, thank you.'

'You're welcome. I'll drive it back down, park it over in the field.'

After Mira left, Juliet felt at a loss as to what to do next. Her mind was still buzzing. Who had gone out that night? Where were her car keys? What had Anwen really been doing that night? All these questions but no answers. She left the kitchen, wandered out to the workshop alone.

In the evening, they all decided to make the most of the weather and went to sit outside. They had the air of people who knew they were stringing out the summer. Anwen prepared a meal for them, marinated chicken with salad and new potatoes, and a chocolate cake for pudding, which Juliet ate far too much of.

With pangs of indigestion, Juliet went to the bathroom and had the last tablets in the packet. So as not to offend Anwen, she buried the packet in the bathroom bin, but as she did, so she uncovered something far more interesting.

There, right at the bottom, looking as if it had been hastily hidden, was a white plastic stick, with a small window on one side.

A positive pregnancy test.

Who had put it there?

She remembered Cassie that morning hanging about in the toilet... could she be pregnant? More likely it was Mira. Or, of course, it could be Rosalind or Anwen. If anyone would know, it was her mother, but whether she would tell Juliet was another matter.

Juliet went downstairs. The house seemed very quiet, and she wondered where everyone was. Looking out in the garden she saw her mother sat on the bench and went out to join her.

'I was just looking at the horse chestnut,' said her mother. 'Remember how Dad would put the conkers on strings for you?'

'Dad used to fix it so Rosalind won.'

Her mother smiled. 'It's years since you all played that, but Dad would still gather up a few, put them on the kitchen windowsill for me...' She paused. 'It's the little things that really bring home how much I miss him. The big things, like the money, I can sort out; I've always been on top of all that. I feel sorry for women who have never looked at a bank statement. No, it's the things that quietly build up over years of marriage. You look around and wish you'd appreciated them more at the time.'

'Dad knew how much you loved him.'

'I hope so. How is Mira doing? I am pleased to see her sharing your room, that will be a comfort to her.'

'Actually, there was something I wanted to ask you about, it was something I saw.' Juliet told her mother about the bruising on Mira's arm. 'She said she fell, but I don't think she was telling me the truth.'

'I can't see why she should lie about something like that.'

'Maybe, but, Mum, I know when Mira is hiding something.'

'So, what do you think happened?'

'To be honest, I wondered if Rhys had been abusing her in some way. You've seen her all the time I've been away, what do you think? Is that possible?'

Her mother blinked in surprise. 'Goodness no. I know life could be stressful for them both, but I was always certain he loved her. I think he may have been torn between the huge commitment he felt towards the parish and his work and giving time to Mira. I was wondering if they'd been planning a family, it might have brought them together.'

'Well, it's funny you should say that. I just found a positive pregnancy test in the bathroom.'

'Goodness...'

'I wondered about Mira, could she be pregnant and not have told us yet? Of course, there's Anwen... Cassie...'

'Cassie? I suppose she's not too old. I'd had a hysterectomy when I was two years younger than her. I'm not sure they'd do it so readily nowadays. Anyhow, Cassie could still have children, but I don't think she has a partner at the moment. I think Mira seems more likely...'

'Yes, I guess it must be Mira... Maybe that's why she was looking so exhausted when I came home, but there's Rosalind of course.'

'Oh no, I hope not. She's not ready for that. I suppose we'll have to wait and see; we will know soon enough. Whoever it is clearly isn't ready to tell us yet.'

* * *

It was late when Mira stirred that night. She'd arranged the meeting for very late so that she could be sure Juliet was asleep, or at least so Juliet would be so dozy she'd not register that her absence was a lot longer than a bathroom visit.

She'd left her hearing aids in and put her clothes in a neat bundle under the bed ready to be pulled out swiftly.

Lola looked up as soon as she moved, so Mira quietly picked the clothes up and, together, they left the room.

Downstairs, she dressed quickly, put on her coat, settled Lola in her basket with a treat, then she took down one of the patio door keys and left. In her coat pocket she had a torch, but there was a full moon and her eyes soon adjusted to the light. Carefully, she unlatched the gate, shutting it quietly behind her.

It was deadly quiet as she walked down the road, but she looked around, dreading meeting anyone, dreading the whole village talking the next day of her wandering the streets alone. She crossed the road, walked into the deserted car park, and finally felt she could relax. The place was empty except for one person – the person she had come to meet.

17

The next morning when Juliet woke up, she looked over at Mira, who was asleep, and noticed that Lola was missing. And then she remembered seeing Mira leaving the bedroom with a bundle of clothes – what had that been about?

Mira stirred, sat up, and Juliet noticed she was still wearing her hearing aids.

'Are you all right?' she signed to Mira.

'Of course. Why?'

'I saw you leave the room with Lola; you were carrying clothes. Was something wrong?'

'Of course not, why would I go out of the house at that time?'

Juliet blinked; she'd not suggested Mira had gone out but now she was pretty sure she had. It was odd, but why lie about it?

Mira clearly didn't intend explaining further because she turned over and at least made an appearance of trying to go back to sleep. Juliet gave up and went downstairs. Here her mother told her that Adam had phoned very early to say he would be coming soon to talk to them all again. Apparently, he had some news to share.

When Adam arrived at about ten, he was definitely more relaxed than the day before.

Once they'd all gathered in the living room, he opened his notebook and began to speak.

'Thank you for your coming together again. I wanted to keep you updated. I was given some more news yesterday afternoon. Firstly, we have the initial post-mortem results.' He looked over at Mira, and Juliet signed post-mortem.

Mira nodded.

'This confirms that Rhys died as a result of the injuries he sustained when the car hit him. It would seem he was knocked unconscious and then died of internal bleeding. What I am trying to say is that Rhys did not appear to have a prolonged period of suffering, he was unconscious when he died.' Adam paused.

Mira gave a nod of comprehension and said, 'I'm grateful he didn't suffer too long.'

Adam continued. 'Now, obviously, the car is undergoing meticulous forensic analysis. As we thought, the fire destroyed a lot of the DNA evidence. However, we did find a few objects in the rear of the car that survived the fire and I need you, Juliet, to look at these and tell me if these belong to you or if you recognise them.'

He held out the photos.

'Mira had better look as well; her and Rhys have been using my car for the past two years.'

Together they looked through the photos. There was a generic travel card, unnamed. Some crumpled theatre tickets, a London souvenir cigarette lighter and a leather wallet. All were dirty and singed.

Juliet shook her head decisively. 'No, none of these are mine. I don't recognise them. Do you, Mira?'

Mira shook her head.

'Good, thank you. I will feed that back to the team,' said

Adam and he was smiling now, looked excited. 'This travel card may not have a name on it, but it has been used and we can trace the journeys it was used for. The theatre tickets should be even more helpful. The lighter, which we found close by and we believe was used to start the fire, had clearly been discarded carelessly.'

'And what about the wallet?'

'That was empty, but there were initials on it, so that will help with tracing our suspects too.' He looked around at them all. 'Well, I just wanted to bring you up to date. Obviously, there is a lot of work to do, but these could be very helpful leads, I'm sure you'll agree.'

Juliet glanced at Mira to check she was following, and Mira nodded quickly.

'So, do you think the person who did this was someone who didn't live on the island?'

'That is a possibility, yes,' said Adam.

'Did you ever find my husband's crucifix?' asked Mira.

'No, and there is no evidence of a chain being removed, although we do know the body was rolled over. It may have been removed carefully, even fallen off at one point, or, of course, it may never have been worn. It's so easy to add things into a memory, it's not done deliberately. If it was something he normally wore, it's easy to imagine he had it on that night too.'

Mira looked sceptical but didn't reply.

'Now, do any of you have any other questions?'

'Do you know when we will be able to hold the funeral?' asked Mira.

'I'm so sorry, these things take time, but I promise you as soon as the coroner is prepared to release the body, I will get in touch. It shouldn't be long now.' He stood up. 'I'll be back soon, please phone me if you need to know anything at all.'

After Adam had left, they all headed for the kitchen.

'That all sounded like good news,' said Cassie. 'It certainly sounds like they are going to find the person who did this.'

Mira nodded but didn't speak.

'Don't forget, everyone, meet here at three this afternoon,' continued Cassie. 'I'm sorry if this is a lot to take on, but once you see this place, you'll see why we are so excited. It will be good to plan something new, look ahead.'

Juliet went outside to the garden. So, could the answer to all the mysteries just be the easy one – a stranger stole her car, got drunk in the car park and the killing of Rhys was accidental? And yet, she had her doubts – her missing set of car keys, the missing crucifix, they raised questions that had not been answered.

* * *

Juliet reluctantly went to the kitchen at three.

Cassie smiled nervously at them all. 'Look, I know this is not ideal timing, but I want to show you this, and it's important to me to have your thoughts before we go any further.'

'With what? What's the big mystery?' asked their mother.

'I need everyone to come to the old café on the military road, meet us there will you.'

Without any further explanation, Cassie left with Anwen. The rest of them travelled with Juliet's mother.

The drive was short, and they parked alongside Cassie's car. The site had been a few single-storey shops and a café, but they were all shut down now. They followed Cassie behind the buildings, where there was a large grassy field that led to a fence and cliff. Today the sea twinkled in the distance.

'What are we doing here?' asked Juliet.

'Well,' said Cassie nervously, 'Anwen and I are thinking of putting an offer in on this site.'

'You are going to buy it? Why?'

Juliet looked around, speechless.

'I know it seems mad, particularly with all that has happened, and it's still just the seed of an idea. When I came home to be with Dad, what I hadn't told any of you was that I had been working out my notice with the orchestra.'

'You've actually left orchestra?' Her mother stepped forward. 'You can't have—'

'It's complicated, Mum. I'm sorry, but I knew if I'd talked to you about it, I'd never have had the nerve to leave. But for lots of reasons it wasn't the right place to be any more. I knew I had to find a new direction in my life. Since I met Anwen at Mira and Rhys's wedding, we have got together a few times for a drink and we shared our dreams for the future. She told me about her dream of starting her own restaurant here on the island, but she was worried about doing it on her own. Anyway, as I say, I was looking for a new direction and so when I came home, I suggested we go into business together.' She paused. 'Anwen has explained where she was the evening Rhys died. I understand why she'd lied to me, and that is all cleared up now.'

'Why on earth haven't you talked to me about it?' said her mother.

'Because you'd try to change my mind. Mum, this is the end of my music. I always said if I felt my music wasn't at the highest possible standard, I would stop. I know I am not playing as well as I used to. I don't want to teach; I want to start something completely new.'

'But your playing is still wonderful. Not so long ago you made that recording, it did so well.'

'I know, and I'm grateful for the money that has made me. But my playing is slipping, I know it is.'

'You mentioned something about some aches and pains, has it

got worse? Oh God, is this all my fault, did I make you practise too hard?' cried her mother.

'No Mum, you didn't do anything wrong. The point is it's time to move on.'

Her mother threw her hands up, and her words were laced with pain and frustration. 'You can't. You have to use your gift; you could be passing on your passion for music to students. You can't give it all up to run a restaurant, it's such a waste, and anyway, you know nothing about hospitality, you'll hate it.'

'No, Mum, this is my decision. You won't change my mind.'

'I can't believe you are saying this, and now of all times. How could you, Cassie? After everything I have done, sacrificed. You have no idea.' Her mother burst into desperate tears.

Juliet went over to her mother, put her arm around and looked at her sister accusingly. 'Cassie, you really should have broken this to Mum more gently; this is unfair, putting her on the spot like this.'

Anwen spoke now. 'But there was no gentle way to do this. You have to respect Cassie's choice. She has every right to make changes in her life.'

Rosalind pointed over to the buildings. 'But all this must be very expensive, how can you both afford it? And what if it goes wrong? Restaurants fail all the time; you would lose everything.'

'Between us, my inheritance, Cassie's money from her flat, and with loans, we can do this, and failure, as they say, is not an option,' said Anwen confidently.

'It's a huge gamble,' said Juliet.

'I wish someone could say something positive,' said Cassie, beginning to sound angry now.

'It's such a shock,' Juliet replied, 'that's all. It's too much to take in out of the blue, and we all know how much Mum sacrificed for your music.'

'I thought you of all people would understand how much I want to do something for me.'

Juliet bristled. 'Something for you?'

'Yes, for me.'

'But your whole life, our whole lives, have been about you. All Mum's time and money went into you and your music. Everything else took second place.'

'That's not fair and you know it,' said Cassie. 'You have all achieved things you wanted, just without the pressure of having to be the best. I know what you think, Juliet. You stayed here like some Cinderella, while I spent my days being given cups and awards and being showered with applause. But in reality, every minute of my life was timetabled. I couldn't play picnics in the garden when I was little or hang about on the beach on a Saturday night smoking, no, I was always practising, rehearsing. Over and over again, alone, in the music room, in empty halls.'

The picture was bleak, and Juliet felt sure she had to be exaggerating, but Cassie's voice held a pain that was real.

'You see what you've done to Cassie?' said Anwen. 'And not one of you can be pleased for her now.'

'Anwen, you have no idea of Cassie's talent. Her life might have been hard, but she has lived a life you could only dream about.' Juliet could hear the bubbles of fury rising in her mother's voice now.

'It was your dream,' said Anwen. 'Cassie has her own dreams now and so do I. We don't care what you lot think, we will succeed. We can achieve this and there is nothing you can do to stop us.'

Juliet gasped at the rage Anwen was spitting at them all, a frustration that had clearly been building up for years before she'd met them.

Her mother stood tall now, her face red and angry. 'Your dream may be to run a scrubby little café on the seafront, but that is not worthy of Cassie. You are trying to use her, but I won't let you.'

Anwen walked over to their mother and spoke right into her face. 'You won't stop me, no one will.' The words shot out individually like bullets.

Juliet saw her mother step back in horror and felt the fear spread around the group.

Cassie stood, clearly shocked at Anwen's outburst too. She went over to her, pulled her away, her voice shaking as she spoke. 'Leave it, Anwen.'

Anwen turned around, her fist clenched, but Cassie stood her ground. Slowly Anwen's arms relaxed and, still breathing heavily, she walked away.

'I'm sorry,' said Cassie. 'It was never meant to get nasty like this. Mum, me and you will talk later. Anwen and I need to give you time to catch up.'

Juliet was both impressed with Cassie's handling of the situation but also very anxious about her plans, particularly the fact she would be working with Anwen. Cassie had obviously completely accepted Anwen's explanation of where she was the night her brother died, but how could she be sure Anwen was telling her the truth? Rhys had insinuated there was a lot in Anwen's past and Juliet was not at all convinced Anwen had told Cassie the whole story. Listening to her now, it seemed to Juliet that Anwen was a very volatile woman, with frustration and rage simmering away inside her.

'It's not just about me and Anwen,' Cassie continued, her voice calm, conciliatory now. 'The premises here are huge, we would like to use part of it to extend the purpose of the building. We were thinking, Rosalind, a nail bar or beauticians, we weren't sure. It would mean people could come and have their nails done, then come into the restaurant for a meal.'

Rosalind blinked, clearly shocked at the mention of her name. 'You want me to be involved?'

'We do,' said Cassie, smiling.

'Good God! Wow!' Rosalind looked around the room as if seeing it for the first time. 'It would be exciting in some ways but like the restaurant, starting up anything in nails is a huge gamble. There are a lot of nail bars, beauticians and spas on the island now, if you want to stand out you have to provide something special. To do that would be very expensive, I don't know how long it would take you to start making money.'

'I know,' said Cassie, 'but it could work, and if you came on board, you could run it.'

'But the money?' repeated Rosalind.

'Well yes, we would have to look into that, think about a loan or a franchise, I'm not sure. But we would find a way.'

Rosalind shrugged. 'I don't know. I was going to travel, or at least get away. Life is getting so complicated; I just can't make any big decisions at the moment.'

'But you could think about it?' Cassie was pleading now.

'I'll think about it.'

Juliet saw the desperation in Cassie's face, and surprised herself by feeling sorry for her sister. 'I think you have run ahead of everyone on this Cassie. It's not that we are all trying to be negative, we just need time to take it all in.'

'I'd hoped you'd all be pleased for me,' said Cassie mournfully.

'How can we be?' said her mother. 'You have such a special gift and you're just throwing it all away, and why? For what reason? I don't understand.'

Juliet could see tears in her mother's eyes; her face was lined with pain in a rare display of vulnerability.

Mira went over to her, spoke and signed gently, 'I have that appointment with the archdeacon. You don't need to come; you've had enough for one day.'

'No, no, of course I'll come. I'm sorry, I'd forgotten. Let's go and do that.'

Mira, Juliet and her mother left, leaving Rosalind to stay behind with Anwen and Cassie.

When they arrived at the car, her mother asked Juliet if she was okay to walk back home.

'Of course, if you can give me the front door key. I'll see you later.'

Truth be told, Juliet was glad to get away from everyone. What had got into Cassie? Dad had said she was vulnerable, and Juliet had seen that today. Along with excitement, there was stress in Cassie's eyes. It wasn't like her to be this impetuous. And that violent anger she'd seen in Anwen frightened her.

Juliet stopped and looked out to sea, saw the white tips on the waves as they rolled over the shore. What was happening to them all? She felt her life and the people in it had become completely unpredictable.

Her phone rang – it was Gabriel.

Gabriel told Juliet he was out running so they arranged to meet at the car park. When she got there, she saw there were a number of cars and vans parked up, full of families and surfers. It was busy, the last fling of the holidays before schools went back next week.

She could see Gabriel heading her way and was impressed at his speed. Heaven knew when she last did any proper exercise... One day she would. But she allowed the thought to snuggle in the back of her mind, like a hedgehog hibernating for the winter.

Gabriel ran up to her, stopped and did a few stretches, then grinned.

'I should be running a lot further than this, but I'd rather talk to you.' He caught his breath with his hands on his hips and his head to one side. 'Let's go over on the grass and talk.'

They went into the field where her car had been parked, and she grimaced as she saw the empty space where her car had been.

They sat together, taking in the view and the cool breeze.

'So, how are things? What a terrible time it's been,' he said sympathetically.

'It's been a nightmare to be honest. First Dad's accident, and then for Rhys to die in such a horrible way. I keep getting waves of guilt that I'm not properly grieving for Dad... Everything keeps changing, things keep happening. And yet I miss him so much.'

'Of course you do. I'd be devastated if anything happened to Maddie.'

'How is she by the way?'

'She's fine now thanks, completely over the sickness, obviously very upset about Rhys though. How is Mira coping? She has lost her father and her husband in such a short time.'

Juliet shook her head. 'In shock, stunned... We found Rhys, you know.'

'That must have been really traumatic. The whole village is very upset. Things like that don't happen here, do they.'

'No, although of course you lost Harry in a hit-and-run, so you know something about how it feels.'

'That was twenty-one years ago, a freak accident. It was dark, raining. I suppose there were some dangers inherent in what he was doing. But Rhys was up at the church. It's not like he was even on a road or anything. Rumour has it that it was visitors from London, taking drugs or something?'

'Wow, word gets round! The police have hinted at that, but they are checking everyone out. We all had to give statements about what we were doing on Saturday evening.'

'They can't suspect any of you. That's ridiculous.'

'Of course, but they said they have to check on everyone.'

'I suppose so. They came and asked me about meeting up with you and whether I'd seen your set of car keys, and they checked about the video calls too.'

'It's so frustrating. I can't find the keys anywhere and now my car has been used in a hit-and-run. I am so upset about it all.'

'So, do they think someone found your set of car keys and then used them to steal your car? Where might you have dropped them?'

'That's the problem, I don't think I did. I was sure they were in my bag. I came back from the beach from seeing you and then my bag was on the dresser all night. When I said that to the police, of course they then asked who in the house could have got hold of them. That's ridiculous of course, but I don't understand what has happened.'

'Have you asked if anyone in the house touched them?'

'I did, but no one has owned up to going in my bag. The police are asking loads of questions about everything. Anwen is angry because I told them I thought she'd been out all night, but it turns out I was right, but I've no idea what she was doing. There is so much I can't explain. Someone left the house, but they won't own up, and where the hell are my car keys?' She was close to tears now.

Gabriel put his arm around her. 'Hey. It'll be all right.'

She shook her head. 'No, everything is so messed up and of course now there's all this business with Cassie.'

'Oh, what's wrong with Cassie?'

Juliet told him all about Cassie leaving the orchestra and setting up the restaurant.

'So that is what the text was about,' he said, grinning, and then explained, 'Cassie sent me a mysterious text this morning saying she wanted some business advice.'

Juliet frowned at him, frustrated at the grin on his face. 'Mum is devastated.'

He quickly put on a more serious expression. 'Of course, she has always been so involved with Cassie and her music and this would be a completely new life for Cassie, that's for sure. I always thought she'd meet some rich type up in London, stay in the music scene forever.'

'Yes, it seems odd to me. She's asked Rosalind to be part of it too, doing nails in one part of the complex or something.'

'I suppose it would mean she is back on the island for your mum. What about you, will you be involved?'

'I can't see me and Cassie getting on in business, can you! No, I'll do my own thing.'

Gabriel reached out and stroked her hair. 'There are plenty of other things to occupy you here though.'

She looked up at him, the feeling of warmth and safety she craved flooded her.

He kissed her gently, and she sank into his arms.

They sat together, time slipping away.

'Fancy going out soon? You know, like on a proper date?' said Gabriel. 'I finally have a night off a week on Saturday – gosh, it'll be September then – we could go mad, go over to Southampton even... What do you think?'

Juliet nodded. 'Do you know what, that would be good.'

'Great, and what we do is your choice, just tell me where.'

'Okay, thanks, sounds perfect. It'll be good to have something to look forward to... Sorry I know that sounds selfish, but there has been such a lot of sadness around.'

'Not selfish at all; I understand. We'll go out and have fun. Oh, and while I think about it, I brought you a present.'

'A present? Really?'

'It's not much. I was in town and saw it. Now, I know you don't like binoculars...'

'No, not really. I can never adjust them to both eyes.'

'I know, I remember you saying that, and then I saw these!'

From the bag he had strapped around his waist, he pulled a small black case and gave it to her.

'Don't worry if you don't want to use it,' he said, looking embarrassed now.

She opened the case and found what looked like a mini telescope.

'It's a monocular... much easier to use – you only have to focus with one eye.'

'That's so clever.' She lifted it to her eye and adjusted it slightly. 'Wow it works – it's so much easier!'

'Look out there, over the cliffs, there's a kestrel hovering. Go and have a good look.'

She got up and walked a few paces forward and lifted the monocular up to her to eye.

'It's amazing, Gabriel, I can see the colours, so rich... How on earth does the kestrel stay still like that in the breeze.' She stood for a minute or two watching it, totally entranced, and then she turned back to Gabriel. 'Thank you so much, what a beautiful present. It's really thoughtful.'

He shrugged but had the slightly smug look of a person who knows they have bought a good present. 'I'm glad you like it.'

She sat next to him and kissed him. 'Thank you.'

'Sometimes looking out at nature can take your mind off things. Right,' he said, sitting up, 'I'd better do a proper run now. I think I'll stay up the top.'

'Be careful, there was a major slip the other day; honestly they are going to need to move the main road over soon.'

'I'll be careful. Text me if you fancy a chat or anything. I'm not far.'

Juliet left him feeling a lot better. That little taste of normality had given her back some sense of perspective.

When she returned to the house, she was surprised to find it empty. She sat down, glad of the space to think. She was still very worried about Anwen – Juliet had seen an unpleasant side to her today. There had been ruthlessness, violence even, in her manner. Juliet remembered seeing her with Rhys that night and she was sure now that Anwen had threatened him. Thinking logically now, Juliet realised that if Anwen had killed her brother, she may have taken the car keys from Juliet's bag to use. What if she had held onto them?

Juliet looked up the stairs. Now was the chance to find out.

Quickly she went upstairs. As she crept into Cassie's room, she knew, like someone checking their partner's phone, she was crossing a line, but she didn't turn back.

In one corner of Cassie's room sat three violin cases and it struck Juliet that she'd not heard Cassie play the violin since she'd come home. She opened each of the cases in turn, the familiar smell of wood, resin, leaping out at her. Funny how she'd never even known she was aware of that smell and yet it was another piece of the puzzle of her childhood. There were the familiar little red cloths, the blocks of resin all used to carefully tend and nurture the instruments.

Juliet closed the cases and then looked around the room again. She realised how little she'd been in here; like the music room, Cassie had always had a well-defined territory. There was an unfamiliar smell in here, something sweet, and she traced it to a small bottle of oil on Cassie's bedside table. It was a bottle of frankincense – the same as she'd smelt in her mother's room.

Next to Anwen's bed, she saw a rucksack and case. It felt wrong to be doing this, but she told herself this was for Cassie and for Rhys, and so Juliet started to rummage through them.

Her heart sank at first – there was no sign of her car keys. But as she was searching through, a letter dropped open on the floor. It was on plain white paper, not expensive but matching the envelope, and was written with an ink pen – Juliet guessed it was from an older person. The address of Anwen's flat was written neatly at the top and it was dated Saturday 20 August.

Dear Anwen,

I am sorry to hear things are so bad. I am planning to come

*over again on Sunday (28th). I enclose the card of where I'll be
staying. I would like to come with you to visit Euan. I am not sure
how things will stand then, but if you meet me at my hotel we
should know by then where we have to visit him. Either way, we
could visit him at two o'clock, and so could you come to me
about half past one? I will travel over early that morning but will
stay overnight as it is too far to return again that day.*

*Time is running out and I would like to see him again; it is
good to mend some bridges. I admire that you have stuck by him
when so many would have abandoned him after what he did.*

*Any problems ring me at home. One day I'll have to get a
mobile phone!*

Best wishes,

Aunt Jean.

The card was for the Travelodge in Newport.

Juliet took out her phone and noted the date and time on her
calendar and started to replace everything carefully. However, as
she was doing this, she saw a large zipped-up toilet bag tucked
underneath everything. She took it out, it was very full, the zip
strained. She started to unzip it and stared at the contents. There
was a wad of notes. She flicked through it – a couple of hundred
pounds maybe. What on earth was Anwen doing with that kind of
money loose in her bag? She had said about working in different
places, maybe some of it was cash in hand. Juliet carefully replaced
it.

She got up then and started to walk around the bedroom. She
tentatively opened drawers, but they were all very tidy, their
contents unremarkable. She glanced at Cassie's iPad, opened it. It
was still on and unlocked which wasn't like Cassie. Juliet was in too
deep now to stop and so, after taking a big breath, she went to the
emails. There were only a few in her inbox, but she noticed there

were a number of files. That was Cassie: each email put in its place. One was labelled 'restaurant', one 'orchestra', one 'holidays', and then, right at the bottom, a file which was called 'boring stuff'.

Juliet, of course, clicked on it and the first thing she saw was an email from someone called Tim. She'd never heard Cassie mention a Tim. She read the email. 'Please come back, Cass, the doctors up here have to be better. I don't understand why you have to go back there to live. There are so many more opportunities for you up here.'

Juliet re-read the email. Why the talk of doctors? What was wrong with Cassie? She also noticed that this person Tim had called her sister Cass; it seemed to emphasise that Cassie had led a life separate to them in London, almost as if she'd taken on a different identity.

Juliet read on. Cassie had replied, 'There is no point going over this any more, I'm staying.'

There were previous emails, all from Tim. It seemed he'd been writing at least once a day since Cassie had come back to the island. A number of times, Tim had asked Cassie to return, and lines such as 'you know how I feel about you' and 'I miss you so much' made it clear this was a romantic relationship. Juliet was sure this was the person Cassie had been talking to on the phone in the bathroom. What was less clear was the meaning of phrases such as 'we can get help for you' and 'I will pay for you to see someone privately'. Was illness the real reason for Cassie leaving the orchestra, and if so, why not tell them? It would make it so much easier for Mum to come to terms with Cassie giving up music, and they would all want to support her. As always, Juliet was aware that of the four sisters, Cassie was the one she understood least.

Juliet took out her phone and noted down Tim's email address. If she had the nerve, she would write to him, see if she could find out what was the matter with Cassie. She looked in one or two more drawers, but there were no more clues, although she did find an old-fashioned pager and wondered why Cassie would have held onto that.

Juliet left the room, feeling a mixture of guilt for what she had done, relief to be out of there, disappointment at not finding her car keys, but also a sense of accomplishment. She had found out about this meeting of Anwen's, and she'd found out about Tim.

She was about to go downstairs when she saw Rosalind's door ajar, and so pushed it open. The letter in the music box – would it be awful to try and find it too? After all, if she knew what it said wouldn't it mean she could help Rosalind? Without daring to delve any further into her motives, she went in.

19

Rosalind's room couldn't have been more different to Cassie's. Despite the window being open, there was an acrid smell, not quite drowned out by the rich mixture of perfumes, scents and hair products.

The dressing table was crammed with beautiful bottles of perfume, oils and jewellery. There was a separate trolley of make-up, brushes and nail varnish, small cloths of all colours. There was a bin overflowing with used make-up wipes and tissues. Clothes were strewn everywhere.

The idea of trying to find anything useful amongst all this seemed rather overwhelming, but Juliet started to open drawers anyway. Clothes spilled out of them and it was the same in the large wardrobe, where clothes draped off hangers onto the shoes below. However, next to this was a smaller wardrobe. Juliet opened it, expecting the same jumble of clothes but, to her surprise, it was organised and tidy. The dresses and tops were carefully hung on padded hangers, some were even in covers. They were glamorous, sophisticated dresses; the labels were designers Juliet had only seen in magazines. There were several pairs of shoes lined up. The one pair of Jimmy Choos she recognised, having teased Rosalind about them before, but there was half a dozen more pairs Juliet had never seen. She slid open the drawer below. In there was silk underwear and a couple of handbags. Everything was expensive, stylish.

Juliet stood back. How on earth could Rosalind afford this stuff? She was always talking about saving up to travel and yet she was paying out for these kinds of clothes. Where would she be wearing such things anyway?

Juliet was startled by what she thought was a door banging downstairs. She got up quickly, opened the bedroom door and listened. No, she must have imagined it, all she could hear now was the steady ticking of the grandfather clock. She went back into Rosalind's room.

Juliet picked up one handbag that was bulging slightly and opened it. There was a small, zipped compartment and she could see that inside was a smart, gold cigarette lighter. She was surprised Rosalind was smoking. In the main compartment, Juliet found a small, beautiful, leather notebook and she couldn't resist flicking through it. The notes appeared to be recording dates, which, at first, she thought must be Rosalind's dates for working at the restaurant over in Southampton. However, what surprised Juliet was that there were various locations mentioned. Sometimes hotels, sometimes restaurants. She wondered if Rosalind was working for some kind of catering agency, but she couldn't ignore the other idea that had started to creep into her mind. Rosalind couldn't be working as an escort or something, could she? Only the other day she'd seen something on YouTube about sugar daddies; young girls, Rosalind's age, students, and the like, being paid to go out with older, rich men, for companionship and more. Juliet blanched. Was it possible Rosalind would do that? If Rhys knew about it, no wonder she was frantic for him not to tell anyone.

Juliet glanced through the diary and recognised the name of the

Sea Walls Hotel, which she knew was a very smart hotel in the centre of Southampton. Rosalind appeared to be working there Saturday, 3 September.

Juliet had an idea. She took out her phone and sent a text to Gabriel.

Found the perfect place for our meal out.

Conscious of the amount of time she'd been in there, she went back to the door and listened. It was still quiet down there and so she continued her search.

Finally, she found the musical box buried deep inside a small case under Rosalind's bed. She noticed the photographs had all been removed and with a shaking hand opened the box, expecting to find the letter inside.

Unnervingly the music started to play, and the sound of 'Somewhere Over the Rainbow' echoed around the room.

There was no letter inside, but at that moment she heard voices downstairs. Quickly, she returned the box, pushed it under the bed and went to the bedroom door.

She heard Rosalind shouting, 'I'll just get a cardigan, I'm cold.' Juliet was closing the door behind her when Rosalind appeared at the top of the stairs.

'What were you doing in my room?' Rosalind demanded.

'I was just seeing if you were back, um, and here you are. I hope everything went okay?'

Rosalind screwed her eyes up sceptically but said, 'I think so, yes, but there is a lot to think about.'

'Of course, well, I just need to sort a few things out in my room,' said Juliet and quickly made her escape.

* * *

That evening, they all ate in the kitchen. Anwen was still taking on the cooking duties, and rather tactfully cooked comforting rather than flashy food, presumably to lighten the mood. Juliet looked out at the darkness, and there was a slight chill to the air. Autumn evenings would soon quietly be taking over from the bright summer nights.

'How about we take our pudding into the living room and watch TV,' her mother suggested.

They all looked a bit stunned; their mother had always insisted on them sitting at a table to eat, and the idea of eating in front of the TV was anathema. However, sitting together this evening was far from comfortable.

'I think that's a good idea,' said Cassie. Taking her lead, they all started to gather their things.

'If you don't mind, I'll go out to the workshop and finish some drawing,' Juliet said.

She took her dish out to the workshop, put the light on and sat in the armchair. She leaned back and closed her eyes; it was so quiet, and she remembered why she and her father escaped out here as often as they could.

Juliet felt uncomfortable, guilty about what she'd been doing. It was hard to believe she'd been creeping around the house, looking through other people's things. It was something she wouldn't normally have done, but nothing was normal any more.

She wandered over to her drawer, opened it and saw the old ignition key with the VW fob that her father had got Mira to hide in here. Examining it more closely this time she saw a piece of string through the ring and attached to it the remnants of a torn cardboard label with 'Tho' scribbled on it. She had no idea what it meant and still didn't have any idea why this ignition key was important.

Juliet did some sketching and eventually went back into the

house. She could hear the noise of the TV and glanced in to see them all quietly staring at the screen. That any of them were taking in much was doubtful, but at least it gave them space to think.

A wave of exhaustion washed over her, she wasn't up to sitting with them all, she needed to go to bed. In the kitchen, she poured some water into a glass, and then went to get her phone out of her bag, but as she was taking it out, her hand brushed against something hard in the inside zipped pocket.

Juliet's heart skipped a beat as she held her car keys in one hand, touched them lightly with the fingers of her other, felt the cold of the stone heart. Had someone been waiting for a chance to return them? Maybe this was some kind of mind game, trying to make Juliet doubt herself.

But she didn't. Juliet knew the set of keys had not been in her bag earlier. It had been on the dresser most of the day and this evening when she'd been out in the workshop. Anwen could have put the keys in at any time... so could anyone else in the house.

Juliet stared at the keys and suddenly the situation felt shockingly real. Someone else here had taken her car keys the night Rhys had been killed and now they had returned them. That person had not owned up to it and for the life of her Juliet could think of no reason other than they had been involved somehow in Rhys's death.

She let the enormity of that sink in.

Before Juliet had a chance to compose herself, Mira came bustling into the kitchen with Lola. Silently, Juliet held up her set of keys, the hard stone heart keyring jangling the keys. Her hands were shaking, and Mira frowned, looking confused.

'These are my car keys,' signed Juliet. 'Someone put them back in my bag...' She paused. She knew she had to ask everyone in the house the question, even Mira. 'Did you put them in my bag? Please, Mira, tell me the truth, I won't judge you, I just need to know.'

Mira shook her head. 'Of course not. Could they be different keys? A spare set?'

'No, only these had this key ring on.'

Mira signed and spoke clearly, precisely. 'I promise you I did not take your car keys.'

Juliet felt her face burning. 'I'm so sorry to ask. I just don't know what I'm meant to think. I went through my bag only this morning, and they definitely weren't there.'

'I don't understand it either,' signed Mira. Juliet was relieved that at least Mira believed that she'd not had them in her bag the whole time. 'Have you asked the others?'

'No, not yet... Mira, you promise me it wasn't you? I won't tell anyone.'

'If I had a bible, I'd swear on that,' signed Mira. 'And you are really sure they haven't been there all the time?'

Juliet reached out to Mira. 'There's no way.'

'But why would anyone take them?' Mira signed, but when their eyes met, Mira shuddered. 'Please no, you can't think that. No one in our family would have used your car to kill my Rhys, that's madness.'

'Mira, I don't want it to be that, but why did someone in this house take my keys? I can't stop thinking about it. Anwen has admitted now she was out all night. I don't know what she told the police, but it has to be possible she was up at the church, and she was so angry with Rhys...'

Mira's eyes widened. 'But to kill her brother!'

'I know, I know. But someone took my set of car keys. People are lying, Mira, someone went out the night Rhys died... I heard them; I saw them going out.'

'Juliet, listen, it's the police's job to find out what happened to Rhys. Please leave it to them, please, leave it alone. You'll drive yourself crazy.'

Juliet saw the desperation in Mira's eyes, she heard what she was saying, but it wasn't enough. 'I'm so sorry Mira but finding my set of car keys has made me realise I have to start taking seriously the possibility that someone in this house killed Rhys. It's been going in and out of my head since the day we found Rhys, and now this proves it.'

Mira shook her head. 'You're wrong, Juliet. No one we know could kill.'

'That's not what Dad said.'

'What do you mean?'

'When he talked to me in the hospital, he said anyone who has a motive can kill.'

'Why on earth was Dad talking about things like that?'

'I don't know, he said some odd things but I think he was warning me for some reason. I am sure he said a lot more to Rhys and that Rhys knew something really important about our family. Rhys may not be able to tell us what Dad said, but I am determined to find out what it was. I can't take it any more. I can't stand all the lies and the secrets, it's time we all told each other the truth.'

'You need to be careful, Juliet; you're sounding like Rhys now,' said Mira.

Juliet wondered how many times she'd been told to be careful. 'I will, but I'm still going to talk to the others about these car keys. I've had enough of their silence.'

20

Clutching the car keys, Juliet went into the living room, picked up the remote and turned off the TV. They all looked at her, bemused.

'I've just found these in my bag, zipped in the pocket that was empty. They are my car keys. The set I lost.'

'Great news. They must have been there all the time,' said her mother cheerfully. 'It's easily done with those bags with all the zips.'

'No, you're wrong.' Juliet spoke slowly, trying not to shout. 'They weren't there this morning and they weren't there yesterday. So, who put them there? I'd like you to tell me now.'

There was silence.

'Juliet, you can't be sure. Now, this is not the way to behave, stop bullying everyone,' said her mother, cross now.

'I just want to know the truth. I've had enough of this silence.'

'Why don't you just come out and say it then. You think one of us sneaked out of the house, having nicked your car keys, stole your car and killed Rhys... that's the truth of it, isn't it, Juliet?' said Cassie her face hard, cold.

Juliet swallowed hard. 'I don't want to believe that, of course I don't. But if no one will admit to going out, to taking my keys, I don't know what I am meant to think.'

'But the police think it was someone from London, they found all that stuff,' said Rosalind.

Juliet flapped her hand in despair. 'I suppose someone could have flung a few things in there to confuse matters, I don't know. The point is, the business of my car keys needs explaining. One of you took them and then returned them and if you won't tell me what you were doing with them, I can only assume the worst.'

'That's an awful thing to say,' said Cassie. 'Why on earth would one of us want to kill Rhys anyway? I know he was a bit harsh that night with all his talk of secrets, but people like us don't kill to shut others up, for goodness' sake. We're not the Mafia or something.' Cassie flipped her hand into the air, giving a false laugh.

'Dad said to me that anyone can kill given the right motive,' Juliet replied.

It seemed to Juliet as if the whole room froze; no one dared move, breathe.

'Yes, he said that,' said Juliet quietly. 'He was warning me about someone, and I think every one of you here had things you were desperate for Rhys to keep silent about.'

Still, no one spoke, and so she continued.

'Firstly, any of you could have stolen my car keys and gone up to the church, but then we come to why. What possible motive could one of you have that would make you want to attack Rhys?'

She turned to Anwen, who sat with her arms crossed, glaring at her.

'Anwen, I don't know what you told the police, but you were out there all night and I saw you argue with your brother. Whatever you have done in the past, you were sure Cassie would pull out of the restaurant if she knew, you were frantic to shut him up—'

Cassie interrupted. 'Leave Anwen alone. She has talked to me, there is no reason why I should not work with her. She had no reason to kill Rhys, he was her brother for God's sake.'

Juliet ignored her sister, turned back to her mother. 'Mum, why wouldn't you talk to us all when Rhys left us at the meal?'

She saw her mother grasp the arms of her chair, but she didn't answer.

'What are you so scared of?' Juliet asked, exasperated.

Her mother was chewing her lip so hard it went white where her teeth ground into it.

'Well, Mum?' Juliet pressed, more gently now.

'Stop badgering Mum,' snapped Cassie.

'You are desperate to cover everything up, aren't you,' Juliet said to Cassie. 'What's the matter? Why all the secrets?'

Cassie crossed her arms. They all stared at her in silence. But it wasn't an empty silence, it was thick, heavy with suspicion and unspoken words.

'No one is going to say anything, really? Don't you see the walls around all the secrets are slowly crumbling? Everything is going to come out. There are ghosts everywhere, they will speak. Rosalind has already had a message, a letter from Dad.'

'What letter?' said her mother, panic screaming in her voice.

'Leave it,' Rosalind shouted. She stood up. 'What's the matter with you, Juliet? Leave everyone alone.'

'I can't and I will find out the truth.'

Mira had been standing in the doorway with Lola, watching, following what had been said. Apart from Anwen, they had all automatically been signing as they spoke.

'Juliet, Rosalind is right, it's not fair to throw all this at people. I want to know as much as you who killed my Rhys. I think the car key business is odd, but you can't go accusing our family of killing someone, that's not right. I am not asking you; I am telling you to stop.'

Juliet walked over to her sister. 'No, Mira, I'm not stopping. I know you have your own secrets, but I'm not going to give up now.'

'Me?' Mira looked horrified.

'Yes, Mira, what was Rhys doing to you? Those bruises? If you were desperate to find a way out of your marriage, how far would you go?'

'You actually think I am capable of taking the life of my own husband?'

Juliet paused, blinked, unable to speak.

Mira shook her head and looked away.

'For God's sake, Juliet, listen to yourself,' said Cassie. 'I think you have lost your mind. If it wasn't so dangerous, it would be laughable.'

'Dangerous?' Juliet caught the word. 'Yes, this is a dangerous world now, isn't it? But ignoring it won't make it any safer. I don't care what any of you think, I *will* find out the truth.'

Juliet left the room and went into the kitchen. She zipped the car keys back in her bag, took out her phone and went out into the garden, shaking with frustration and anger. It was dark, quiet, and she took out her phone and composed an email. She was going to act and would start by sending an email to this Tim, see if she could get some answers from him at least. Juliet composed the email on her phone.

Dear Tim,

This will take you by surprise. I am Cassie's sister, Juliet. I accidentally saw an email from you saying Cassie was unwell. I am concerned about her. She appears to be giving up her life in London and has not explained why. I am sorry to ask you to break a confidence, but please, if you are able, could you tell me why she has been going to see the doctor. If you need any more information from me before you feel able to

confide in me, I quite understand. I am able to come to London any time if you would like to speak to me face to face.
Best wishes,
Juliet

Without giving herself time to think, she pressed send.

A few moments later her phone flashed back a response from Tim – that was quick.

I think it would be better to talk face to face if that is okay with you. I can meet you either on Friday this week or Wednesday next, Tim.

She replied that Friday would be fine; it was time to act, not to think.

* * *

In the morning, Juliet went out to the workshop with her breakfast and sat deliberating whether she should ring the police and report that she had found her set of car keys. Part of her felt she had a duty to tell them – in fact, they had asked her to let them know if she did. On the other hand, despite all her heated words the evening before, she knew it was a huge thing to put her family through a fresh round of suspicion and questioning.

What was she to do? She didn't honestly feel it was an option not to tell the police at all. Maybe she could find a compromise. If she worded things carefully, then she could leave it to the police to decide whether or not to follow it up.

Nervously, she rang DC Adam Smith. He answered quickly and she told him that her keys had 'turned up in her bag'.

'That's surprising, isn't it?' he said. 'You seemed very sure they weren't there before.'

'I know, but I suppose life has hardly been easy around here, my head is all over the place.'

'I see...' She heard him hesitate and then he continued, 'Are you saying you now believe there is a possibility the keys have been in your possession all this time?'

She swallowed. 'It has to be possible, doesn't it?'

'I guess it does, but I have to remind you that if you have any information that you think might be relevant to this case, you have a duty to share it with us.'

Juliet took a deep breath; her mind was racing. Surely everything she had was supposition, there was no solid proof. Maybe after she'd been to London, she might have more to go on, but she had to be careful.

'Of course,' she said, trying to steady her voice. 'If I have anything else to tell you, I will get straight back to you.'

'Okay, well make sure you do and thank you for letting us know.'

Juliet ended the call with an immense sense of relief. Tomorrow she would go to London and do some investigation on her own.

* * *

Juliet managed to keep out of everyone's way the rest of that day. It was late when she crept into the house and up to her bedroom. She had expected to find Mira in bed but instead she was knelt by the side of her bed, Lola lying beside her.

A wave of guilt flooded her. Of all the people she had accused the evening before, it was Mira she felt the most awkward about. Her and Mira had a special bond, how could she really have believed her capable of murder?

Juliet went to her, touched her shoulder, and Mira looked up, startled.

'Sorry, I didn't mean to creep up on you,' Juliet signed quickly and then saw an empty box in Mira's hands and suddenly the events of the evening before were pushed away...

'Are you pregnant?' Juliet asked.

Mira gave a sad smile. 'I hope so.'

Juliet sat down next to her, put her arm around her. 'That's wonderful.'

Mira pulled back and shook her head. 'I don't know for certain.'

'You must know, I saw the used stick in the bathroom – it was positive.'

'You found it? I thought I'd done a better job at hiding it. The problem is I had bleeding last Friday, the night before Rosalind's meal, the night before Rhys died.'

Juliet saw the tears and distress deep in Mira's eyes and as she remembered those awful bruises, a terrible thought occurred to her. Was the bleeding the result of an attack by Rhys? Had that attack led to Mira killing Rhys in anger?

Juliet screwed her eyes up. 'Mira, you can tell me everything, you know that. Did Rhys hurt you? I will stand by you whatever has happened.'

Mira shook her head in frustration. 'No, it wasn't like that, of course not. I've told you before, Rhys never physically abused me, and I had no reason to kill him. You really have to stop throwing these accusations around now.'

Juliet sighed, not knowing what to believe. 'Well, what happened then? Tell me.'

Mira took a deep breath. 'All that happened was that I had the fall on the beach, as I said, and then later, I had some bleeding. When I came to stay at Mum's the night of Rosalind's meal, I took the pregnancy test to see if I was still pregnant, and it said I was. I was worried though and so I have a scan tomorrow, then I'll know for certain how things are.'

'I see.' Juliet paused, looked at her sister. She knew there was more to this; what was Mira hiding? She leant forward, asked gently, 'Did you get the chance to tell Rhys you were pregnant?'

Mira scratched the back of her hand so hard that the white trace marks quickly turned red. 'No. I'm only about six weeks in and I had been going to tell him over the weekend. Then, well, we had a difficult talk that night, it didn't seem the time. So no, he never knew.'

'Oh, Mira, that's awful. I'm sorry.'

'I have a lot to work out in my head, and I want to have this scan first. Please don't tell anyone will you.' Mira spoke calmly, but there was no spark of joy. 'And what about you? You sounded so angry last night; I don't think anyone means any harm, you know. You have to leave the police to do their job, Juliet. This is making you ill.'

'But I have to find answers, Mira. Don't you understand? It was my car that killed Rhys, I feel like I'm responsible in some way.'

'You are not responsible; you didn't kill Rhys,' Mira replied firmly.

'No, I suppose not, but I have to find out who did.'

Mira looked at her earnestly.

'Don't worry about me, I have a few things planned.'

'Be careful, Juliet, this isn't a game you know.'

21

Juliet got up early the next morning. She told her mother that she was having a day out in London.

Mira had given her the keys to Rhys's car, insured it for her to drive and it was parked over in the field. Although Juliet was nervous about driving a strange car, she had decided it was much easier to drive herself to the Red Jet than wait around for a bus.

Juliet got into the car, which was a lot less tidy than Mira had left hers. There was also the same awful smell of fake lavender that had invaded her own car – Mira must have bought a job lot of the air fresheners. She took down the one hanging off the mirror and put it in the dashboard drawer, which she noticed was jam-packed with paperwork – Juliet would need to go through that at some point.

Juliet found the handbook and flicked through it, checked she knew all the basics and finally took the keys out of her bag. She noticed her old car keys were still in there, touched the smooth heart key ring; she needed to put them in the house, stop carrying them around. She pushed Rhys's car key into the ignition. With a slight jolt, she drove the car out of the car park and over to Cowes.

After parking close by, she walked to the Red Jet terminal. It was a very different Cowes to the one she'd arrived at. The bunting was still there, but the crowds had gone. There was still the odd tourist come out early to buy a paper, but most families were holidaying over the other side of the island.

As she queued for her ticket, Juliet thought how much more significant getting away was when you lived on an island. It wasn't something you just did, it had to be planned, it depended on weather, the tides, the number of people who also wanted to leave at the same time as you.

Fortunately, today, everything was running to time and she bought her ticket just as the Red Jet arrived, walked down the gangway and boarded straight away.

It wasn't until she was getting off that she noticed Anwen had been on board. She was walking fast and didn't look back. Juliet wondered if she was also going over to the train station but Anwen walked straight on, ignoring the connecting bus.

Once she was at the station Juliet treated herself to a large cappuccino and a croissant and sat on the train with a slight air of someone on holiday.

As the train notched off numerous stops, however, the novelty started to wear off, and by the time she arrived in London, she felt unaccountably weary for someone who had just sat down for the past hour and a half.

Juliet stood on the platform at Waterloo station, nudged by strangers, wrapped in a thick blanket of noise. Feeling very much the country mouse, she made her way to the ticket barrier, pushed and shoved on all sides, not unkindly, but everyone seemed to be in a rush.

She knew where the clock was and went straight there. She saw a man in a black leather jacket, reading *the Guardian*, and felt pretty sure this must be Tim, but she took a moment to scrutinise him before he saw her. He was tall, with black hair and thick glasses and older than she expected.

As if sensing she was there, the man looked up, grinned, and tucked his paper under his arm.

'You must be Juliet?'

'Um yes, you're Tim?'

'That's me. Let's go to the Embankment and get a coffee.'

Juliet felt swept along. She had been expecting some meek, quiet man, not someone so assertive, and she was walking quickly to keep up.

'I'm not usually free now, it's lucky it's a later rehearsal today,' Tim was saying, not in the slightest bit out of breath.

'You are in the same orchestra as Cassie?'

'Oh no, I am a composer, the rehearsals are for a new piece I've written.'

'Oh right.'

Once they were at the café, she was relieved to sit, and when a waitress came over, Tim said, 'I'll have a flat white please. Same for you, Juliet?'

Feeling annoyed at him for taking over, she said, 'No, an Americano please.'

He sat back and looked her up and down. 'I can see you and Cass are sisters,' he said.

She had the same feeling of discomfort she'd had when Tim called her sister Cass in the emails. It wasn't right; her name was Cassie, and it was like he was claiming a special intimacy with her sister by giving her a different name.

'Well, we both have brown hair, I think that is where the likeness ends.'

He shook his head. 'No, there is far more than that. I can see from the way you pursed your mouth when I tried to order coffee for you. That is exactly how Cass would have reacted.'

'Cassie and I like to speak for ourselves, that's all. All us sisters are like that.'

'I've heard about you four sisters, it reminded me of *Little Women*.'

She groaned. 'That's not very original, although I've not heard it for a while. If Cassie has told you the truth about us, you'd have understood we are nothing like them. Cassie was no Meg, fussing over us all – in fact, we didn't see much of Cassie at all.'

Tim put his head to one side. 'I know Cass felt left out in a lot of ways, it's an odd childhood for the gifted. Some may say it's no childhood at all.'

'Was it like that for you?'

'A bit. Although I was an only child, so I had no brothers or sisters to feel cut off from. I was aware of being different; I wasn't involved in the social lives of most of my friends at school. My own son has no musical inclinations in the slightest and I have to say I'm rather pleased.'

'You have a child?'

He grinned. 'I should have brought a CV with me... you would like a quick resumé of my life, wouldn't you, which I understand. Yes, I have two children, both at university now.'

'Sorry if you feel I'm interrogating you.'

'Don't apologise. It seems only fair. I know a lot about you after all. I was fifty last year, I'm a composer – a title that sounds a lot more impressive than it is in reality. I was married for fifteen years. I am on good terms with my wife. My children have met Cass. My daughter gets on particularly well with her, they read the same books.'

'I don't even know what Cassie reads nowadays.'

'They both like high-brow literary stuff. Me, I like science fiction, which they think is hysterical, but then they are both very superstitious.'

'Cassie is the only one of us like that. I blamed it on being a performer – you know, you hear of actors having all these rituals.'

'It's so illogical, isn't it? I bought Cass this beautiful green bag to keep her resin in, showed it to my daughter and she went mad, "you can't give her something green, it's unlucky, Cass will go mad." I changed it to red and all was well.'

Juliet listened to this other life of Cassie's and had to admit to feeling hurt that she had created and kept secret a world apart from them all.

'How long have you and Cassie been together?'

'We've known each other for about five years but got together about two years ago now. Still, as my daughter would say, we're not really an item now.' The bantering tone slipped, and he suddenly looked older. 'It was all so sudden, the break-up, I didn't see it coming... she seemed fine even after her diagnosis.'

Juliet's heart thumped. 'What's the matter with her?'

'Well, I don't see why you shouldn't know. Cass has arthritis in both her hands. It has been getting worse, even though she's seen specialists. All the exercise and playing from a young age has caught up with her. She can't play her violin for long periods now; the rehearsals were killing her.'

Juliet remembered Cassie's bottle of frankincense that her mother also used for arthritis. 'But she told Mum she just had some aches and pains, she told mum they were nothing to do with why she was leaving music. Is it really that bad?'

'It feels that way to Cass at the moment.'

Juliet gave herself a minute to try and take in the implications of what Tim had told her. 'So that is why she's not played her violin since she came home. She was playing the piano and it was wonderful. In fact, it might be one of the few times I've really appreciated how exceptional she is. You don't with family, do you, we got so used to hearing her practising.'

'It seems to me that Cass's life was very separate from the rest of yours.'

'It was in a lot of ways. But we're all older now, and it hurts that she didn't tell us about her arthritis or why she was really leaving the orchestra.'

'She said she didn't want your mum to go blaming herself; you see, it could be partly from over practising when she was young.'

'Gosh, Mum asked if that had caused a problem, but Cassie denied it. I can see she was trying to protect Mum, but it would be better to have talked about it; Mum is so confused.'

'I tend to agree, and I hope Cass will talk to her but it's all been so heart-breaking for her, she's kind of lost.'

'When she was talking to us, she sounded almost relieved though to be getting away from it all. She talked about being a kind of slave to all the practising, never having time to have fun.'

Tim smiled. 'Ah, that's the huge paradox. Can't live with it, can't live without it. Musicians are not easy people to understand. Very driven perfectionists who moan about missing out on the real world but at the same time are completely lost without their music. So, tell me, what is this restaurant Cass is talking about?'

'She's thinking of going into business with someone called Anwen on the island. She showed us a site – well, part of a site – they are thinking of buying. I think Anwen has money to put in and she is a chef.'

'I see. But it seems so odd to me. Why would Cass be interested in a restaurant of all things?'

'It seemed odd to us as well.'

'The trouble with Cass is she is so secretive. She seems to have real problems trusting anyone...' His voice broke. 'I always knew there was a history with Cass, things she's not told me. Did something happen to her in her teens?'

Juliet scowled and said defensively, 'No, nothing. Her home life was wonderful; she was so loved, Mum and Dad did everything for her.'

'Sorry, I didn't mean to offend you. I'm confused that's all, I can't make her out. She has this problem with trust and the way she closes down, and yet she seems drawn to go back to the island all the time. I know it's your home, but you must admit it's a bit weird to live on an island miles from everywhere.'

'Oh, it's not that far. I came up this morning, I'll be back this evening. Add an hour on from Southampton. It just happens to be on a boat instead of a car.'

He grinned. 'You make it sound so normal.'

'That's because it is a lot of the time... unless the weather changes or the ferries break down. Then it goes a bit crazy. Have you ever been to the Isle of Wight?'

'No, never. I've always gone to Cornwall or Devon for holidays.'

'You should come, it's beautiful. Fabulous beaches and downland, it's lovely.'

'Cass has never invited me over.'

Juliet looked down. 'I can't think why not, but then I don't understand a lot of what Cassie does. Me and her have never been close, it's hard to know what she thinks of any of us.'

'But she admires your art and was impressed you went to China.'

'She told you that?'

'Yes, and about Mira. You're so dedicated as a family, what with you all learning to sign, it's special.'

'Of course we all sign!'

'Not of course. But most people can't. I love it, I ask Cass to sign as she speaks to me sometimes, it's like a beautiful language that most people don't even know exists. Like music. It expresses things in a way words can't.'

Juliet fiddled with the teaspoon next to her mug. 'I suppose Cassie told you that Mira's husband, Rhys, was killed in a hit-and-run?'

'Oh yes, how tragic. I didn't think things like that happened over there. Up here, well, we have guns, knives, the lot, but I imagined your island to be cut off from all that... Cass was obviously very upset, although she did say he was interfering with her plans. To be honest, she said that, as awful as it was that he'd died, it could be a blessing for some people.'

'She said that?'

'I don't think she was thinking straight, she was in shock, in fact I offered again to come and be with her, but, as always, she turned me down.'

'I can see you still really care about her.'

'I do, but I don't see how I can help her if she keeps pushing me away. I'd be very grateful if you could persuade her to come and talk to me sometime.'

'I'm not sure she'll listen to me. In fact, I'm not sure I'm brave enough to tell her I came to meet you!'

'But you're her sister, you should be able to talk to her.'

'That's the theory...'

Tim looked at his watch. 'I'm sorry but I've got rehearsal, I'll have to go. I don't know where that hour went.'

'Thank you for taking the time to see me. It's been helpful to talk to you. At least I can understand a bit more now about why Cassie has left the orchestra.'

'Good, and maybe we could send each other the odd email, I'd like to know how Cass is doing.'

'Of course.'

They said goodbye and Juliet realised there was no rush for her to get back. She walked over the bridge and up to the National Gallery and then round to the National Portrait Gallery.

After a couple of hours wandering the halls of the gallery Juliet found something to eat before reluctantly returning to the station.

On the train home, Juliet thought about Cassie. As awful as it was about her arthritis, Juliet couldn't help being annoyed with her for keeping it a secret, particularly from their mother. Her phone rang and Juliet saw it was Cassie.

'What the hell?' Cassie shouted.

Juliet held the phone away from her ear.

'Tim told me you've been talking to him.'

Juliet cringed; she'd not expected Cassie to find out so quickly.

'How do you even know about him?' demanded Cassie.

Juliet panicked, there was no way of dressing this up. 'Cassie, I'm so sorry. I read the email on your laptop.'

'You did what? How dare you.'

'Look, I'm sorry, I know I shouldn't have done it, but no one would give me any answers. I needed to find out what is going on.'

'And you think everyone has to answer to you?'

Juliet could feel the heat of Cassie's anger down the phone.

'I'm sorry I snooped, but why didn't you tell me about your arthritis, or about Tim for that matter?'

'Why should I?'

'Well, not me maybe, but Mum at least, she is heartbroken about you leaving the orchestra, you should have explained.'

'My relationship with Mum is none of your business, my life is nothing to do with you. You have no idea what I've been through.'

'Well tell me then.'

'I can't, I won't. All you're doing is messing up everyone's lives. Just get off the island – go back to China for all I care – no one wants you here any more.'

The line went quiet; Cassie had ended the call. Juliet stared at the table in front of her, stunned. She'd had plenty of arguments with her elder sister over the years, but none had been this bitter and venomous. 'No one wants you here any more' – was that true? Juliet knew she'd upset people but surely they wanted the truth as much as her. Yet even she knew she'd overstepped the mark looking through their things. She wanted to throw all her anger at Cassie and yet she felt Cassie had a point. Maybe all she was doing was making everyone more unhappy; she wasn't solving anything was she? Should she just pack up her bags and leave?

Juliet crossed her arms and hugged herself. There was no one sitting opposite her fortunately, but she caught the eye of the young woman across the aisle, who threw her a sympathetic smile. Juliet tried to smile back but her lips were trembling. Instead, she turned away and looked at her reflection in the window, fighting back tears.

The train pulled into Southampton and Juliet made her way to the Red Jet. Usually when she came back to the island, even if she'd only been gone for a day, she felt those flutters of excitement, breathed in the familiar sights and smells of home. But today she felt she'd become the enemy, neither the island nor her family wanted her here.

* * *

Juliet walked to the car park and then drove to the village and parked in the field. She wanted to stay here, sit in the car, have time to think, but she knew she couldn't stay out all night. She had to get this over with. Juliet walked up the road, pushed open the gate and entered the house as quietly as she could, hoping not to see anyone. However, as she ran up the stairs and turned onto the landing she nearly collided with Cassie, who was dressed but wrapping her long hair in a towel. Juliet saw a flash of anger on Cassie's face, but she didn't speak to her, just pushed past her and went downstairs. Close to tears now Juliet threw her bag down on her bed and decided to go back out to try and sort out her head.

She went downstairs, glanced in the living room and saw everyone in there, including Anwen. But before she could run away, her mother caught sight of her.

'Oh, you're back.' Her mother said, and the calm normality of her voice was comforting.

'Um, yes.'

Cassie continued to stare steadfastly at the television, but Anwen glanced her way.

'I saw you on the Red Jet this morning,' Juliet said, feeling she should at least try and say something. 'You looked in a rush.'

'No, you were mistaken, I didn't go anywhere today,' said Anwen quickly and looked away.

Juliet sighed. She was sure she'd seen Anwen but why bother arguing again? Instead, she said, 'I'm going to the beach to get some fresh air,' and then left the house.

She went straight down to the beach car park and was relieved to see there was no one around tonight, perhaps because there was a chill in the breeze. She stood at the top of the rough path that led to the beach. It was hard to associate the dark, bottomless, endless sea which merged so easily with the black sky, with the innocuous blue twinkling sea of the day time. The tide was in and waves crashed noisily below. Juliet closed her eyes and breathed in the smell of the sea, salt, shingle, and sand. But then she paused, what was that other strange smell, and was that a whisper of warmth?

Her heart beat faster as she opened her eyes, and a voice hissed in her ear. 'You need to stop. Remember Rhys.'

Juliet went to turn, but before she could, she felt a hefty push from behind. She was propelled forward, helpless to stop herself tumbling down.

Once she managed to stop, Juliet rolled herself to sit upright, wiped her hands, felt pinpricks of pain where small stones had stuck into the palms of her hands. There were holes in the knees of her jeans, and the grazes stung. She was sat uncomfortably on the sandy mud; the beach was only a matter of feet away now.

She got up, shaking, looked around, but she was alone. Her ankle was sore, but she stumbled back up the path. She nervously scanned the car park, but there was no one there either.

Quickly she crossed the road and made her way to the house but paused by the gate. In the same way she'd felt uneasy coming back to the island, now she felt scared of going into the house. The island, her home, once places of retreat and safety, had become threatening, unknown, dark.

She pushed open the gate and knew there was one place she was happy to go. She walked across the garden and opened the door to the workshop, put the light on and eased herself into the old armchair.

Slowly, the truth of what had happened began to sink in. Someone had purposefully pushed her, threatened her. There was nothing playful or light-hearted about this, there had been hatred behind that push. It hadn't been an attempt to kill her, no, it was a warning – this time.

That voice, who was it? They'd spoken gruffly, but there was something familiar about it. 'Remember Rhys,' they'd said. The implication was clear: if she didn't stop interfering, she could die as well. Did this mean the person who pushed her was the person who killed Rhys? It might do, or maybe it was someone using it as a threat.

But who was it? Had they found her there by accident? No, that was not likely. Someone had known she would be there; she'd only told the people in the house, which meant it had been one of them. That would mean Cassie, Mira, Rosalind, her mother or Anwen. To

Juliet's mind Anwen seemed more than capable of physical violence. However, Cassie was also very angry with her. If she'd thought Cassie capable of killing Rhys, surely she must also be able to imagine Cassie pushing and threatening her. It may have been one of them, but it could have been one of the others in the house. The threat from a faceless enemy was somehow even more terrifying that one who was known.

Juliet covered her face with her hands; whoever it was, someone she knew had done this. Suddenly she was aware of warm blood seeping through the knees of her trousers. She was desperate for someone to take care of her, someone to put their arm around her and tell her everything would be all right. But who? She would normally go to her mum, her sisters, but one of them could have been the person who did this. Her father had said you never knew anyone, and for the first time she believed it.

She was getting cold; she couldn't stay out here all night, and so she dragged herself out of the chair and over to the house.

There was no one in the kitchen, and Juliet could see they were all still in the living room. No one looked her way and so she crept upstairs to the bathroom.

She took off her clothes and examined the grazes, some deeper than others. Before attending to them, she got in the shower and stood there, letting the hot water and steam engulf her. Who had done this, who had crept up behind her in the dark? She remembered the voice with a shiver, but she couldn't identify it, it may have been Anwen or Cassie, she had no idea. She closed her eyes. What about the strange, slightly sweet smell – it was familiar, but where had she smelt it before?

She had no answers at that moment and so she got out of the shower and wrapped herself in a towel, before putting antiseptic on the grazes, plasters on her knees and elbows, and then retreating to her room.

Juliet climbed into her bed and wrapped her duvet around her, still shaking. She was lying in the bed she'd slept in since a child, surrounded by family who'd she known all her life, but she was terrified, frightened by what this person had done, petrified of what they might do to her in the future.

22

Juliet woke stiff and exhausted the next morning. Blood had seeped through some of the plasters, bruises were creeping to the surface of her skin. Every part of her ached. She crept around, got dressed, made a strong coffee in the kitchen and went out to the workshop.

She should have been sketching but she couldn't even lift her pencil; she sat wrapped in a black blanket of misery.

'What am I going to do, Dad? You told me to look after them all, but I've failed, they don't even want me here any more.' She allowed herself to cry; she curled up and cuddled herself. She had noticed in films how often someone found a crying person and comforted them, but she also knew it didn't happen so often in real life. She was alone, no one was going to pick her up.

Juliet remembered the times she went down to the beach when she felt like this, but that wasn't for her today, and then she knew what she had to do.

Grabbing her pad and pencils, Juliet left the workshop and walked out of the garden. Turning left, she headed past the houses and on past the junction that led to the pub. Instead of stopping, she walked straight on until she reached the church.

There were no signs of the police any more. A blackbird was shuffling in the undergrowth; a robin sang from a branch. It was like at the site of her father's crash, nature carried on. On one level, it felt wrong – surely places where people had died violently should feel sad, different? And yet, at the same time, it was strangely comforting.

Juliet quickly reached the place where they'd found Rhys. How long was it since they'd found him? A week ago already. In fact, this time last week, they were cleaning the house ready for the meal. It reminded Juliet of when Maddie talked about being at their house for Rosalind's coming home party, having no idea of the tragedy that would befall Harry that night. Maybe it's a good thing we don't always know what is ahead.

There were some bunches of flowers, cards of sympathy starting to shrivel and fade in the sunlight. One memorial, however, stood out. It was a large cross of woven sticks which had been pushed into the hard, sun-scorched ground. That had to have taken effort, in the same way the cross itself had taken time and effort to construct; someone had gathered sticks, probably had to soak them after all this dry weather to make them pliable enough to weave. It was a work of art and had clearly been made by someone who cared, but there was no note, nothing to identify who had put it there.

Juliet walked on and reached her destination, her father's grave. She saw fresh flowers had been placed, and she recognised them as the roses from their garden and guessed her mother had been quietly coming up here to visit. It was a lovely spot to sit, high up, looking over downland and the woods behind her. She'd come to talk to her father, tell him everything that had happened, but now she was here, she was too tired to talk, to work through anything. Instead, she did what she'd done for so many years with her father, she took out her sketchbook and sat drawing the landscape in front of her. And then that magical thing happened when she drew here, the landscape, the sea came closer and closer, and she became absorbed in them. That was when she knew the island was claiming her, wanted her to be here. However much she might feel threatened by the person who had pushed her the night before, at least she had the assurance she should be here, this was still her home. No one had the right to push her away; she would stay, she would carry on digging for answers.

Juliet had no idea how long she sat there, but eventually she stood to leave. The family had to be faced. Before she left, she went over to Harry's grave to pay her respects and she read the inscription on the headstone – 'a time to be born, a time to die'. The choice was surprising, but she was sure this sense of acceptance would have been of greater comfort to Maddie and Gabriel when Harry died than empty platitudes.

She was about to leave the graveyard when she saw Barbara from the shop, closing the church door and walking towards her.

'Good morning, Juliet,' she said.

'Hi,' Juliet replied, not really in the mood for a chat, but Barbara didn't pick that up.

'Rhys had asked me to take on the cleaning for August. It's not a big job, it's not been used for any meeting or services since the night poor Rhys died. I was just giving it a quick going over before the next service.'

Juliet forced a smile. 'That's very good of you.'

'It was so terrible what happened to Rhys, we are all still in shock. What a time your family is having.' Barbara looked at her more closely. 'Are you all right? I hope you don't mind me saying, but you look shattered.'

'It's been difficult.' Juliet swallowed, realising how close to tears she was.

'Of course,' said Barbara gently, 'and you have been looking after them all. You must take time to rest as well now. It's hit a lot of people hard. That's the thing about a village, we don't all go about our separate lives, we are a community. People have been coming into the shop in tears. It's the shock, you know. To have another hit-and-run here. We don't expect it, do we.'

'So, even after all this time, people still talk about Harry's accident?'

'Oh yes. I know people will say it was years ago, but in a village like this, well, it's like yesterday. I was with Maddie, you know, when the police came around to tell her Harry had been found dead on the military road.'

'Yes. Only the other day Maddie was telling me about it. She told me how grateful she was that you were there.'

'It was lucky. I was working in a nursing home at that point and went to pick up Ed after my shift. Usually, I'd have left him to walk back but the weather was so bad that night, the storm frightened me. I know Maddie blamed herself for letting Harry go out, but he wasn't a child and anyway, she never had any control over him.' Barbara put her head to one side. 'I had more sympathy for Harry than some. I know he had a reputation for being a bit of a tearaway; it's a great shame he didn't channel more of his energy into sport. He had a real gift, you know. Harry was a member of the Wight Arrows, the running club where my husband coached. Him and Zac, the other coach, worked with him. Harry had been training so hard until he got these ideas of going to France. He stopped for a few weeks. But the fact he'd been out training the night he died made me think he must have decided to stay.'

'But Maddie was sure he was going.'

'I know, and she told me after he died that Harry had bought his ticket and everything, so there we are.'

'It does feel a tragedy that he was killed so suddenly, and they never caught who did it.'

'I know. How is anyone meant to come to terms with the death of their son when you don't even know who to blame, don't see them punished. You know everyone in the village feels the same, still we all wonder about this person who killed Harry. Who are they? What are they doing? Are they living happily over on the mainland, maybe have children, grandchildren of their own? We still need answers.'

Juliet heard the passion and anger in Barbara's voice and knew she was speaking from the heart of this community. They had all lost a family member; they were all still grieving.

'I just hope for your Mira's and all our sakes they find the person who killed Rhys. We can't go through that again.'

Barbara looked away and then sighed, smiled at Juliet.

'I'm sorry, but these things are hard to deal with, aren't they? Tell me, how is your mum? To have lost her husband and then her son-in-law, it's so much for her to cope with.'

'You know Mum, she keeps a lot of her feelings inside, but she carries on.'

'Yes, she hides a lot, but that's not always healthy. Oh, I've just remembered.' Barbara took something out of her pocket. 'I found this on one of the pews... I don't know if it might be Mira's, I wondered if she'd been up there on her own since Rhys died.' Barbara held out a piece of jewellery in her hand.

Juliet saw the moon-shaped earring, and it looked familiar, but she couldn't put her finger on why. 'Hmm, I don't think it's Mira's, but I'll take it and ask her.'

'Okay, thanks,' said Barbara. 'I'll be thinking of you all.'

'Thank you,' said Juliet and she slowly walked away from the church. As she did, she received a text from Gabriel.

I'm on duty but wondered if you fancied coming up to the lodge this evening for a meal?

Juliet replied without hesitation.

I'd love to.

And she meant it, an evening away from her family was exactly what she needed.

* * *

As she got ready that evening, Juliet decided to keep things casual, so put on her usual jeans and T-shirt, but wore a light jumper, not sure if they would be sitting outside.

She walked down the road, crossed over, glanced into Brook car park. The sun was still warm, it was quieter now most of the tourists had gone. Despite that, she shuddered when she looked in and remembered the events of the evening before and was glad to walk on.

There was no pavement along the military road and so she walked on the grassy verge. To her left there was grassland that led to the cliff edge, there was no easy way down to the beach now until you reached the next car park at Compton Bay. The walk would take her about twenty minutes, and it was one she'd loved, with beautiful views of the white cliffs of Tennyson Down in the distance. Before arriving at Compton she turned up the country road and up the steep hill that led to the vineyard entrance. Once there she made her way towards Gabriel's lodge. She saw Gabriel sat on the patio outside. He was wearing jeans and a polo shirt, glass of wine in hand. When he saw her, he got up and went to greet her.

'You made it. Thank God, I've got so much food here!'

When she saw the beautiful laid table, the bottle of wine, Juliet wished she'd made more of an effort. 'I'm sorry, I feel a mess, this looks beautiful.'

'You look perfect,' he said and smiled. 'Come and have a look around.'

Like a Tardis, the lodge seemed much bigger inside than it appeared on the outside. There was one main living room, with beautiful warm wooden walls and a sloping ceiling, comfy sofas, a TV and a log burner. To one side was a kitchen area and the smell of casserole was wafting from the oven.

They went back outside and Juliet sat down, looking out at the view. It was still light enough to just make out the sea and the horizon.

Gabriel poured her a glass of wine.

'Wow, this is wonderful,' Juliet said, feeling herself relaxing for the first time in days.

Gabriel disappeared inside again and returned with a tray with some dishes of hors d'oeuvres.

'These are fancy,' she said, 'been to Marks and Spencer?'

'Not at all,' he said in mock horror. 'These are from the restaurant. Freshly prepared by the chef.'

'Gosh, I'm honoured.' She laughed.

He leant down, kissed her and she smiled.

'I love sitting here in the evening. I can pretend I am anywhere in the world.'

'But would you really want to be anywhere else?' she asked.

He smiled the warm, gentle smile she had loved so much.

'You've got me there, probably not. This place is part of me. I have been making some decisions though about changes I want to make.'

'Really?'

'Yes, I'm impressed with Joe. I want to extend his responsibili-

ties; he can take over the day to day running here. I want to get back
to being fully involved with the vineyard.'

'I thought you enjoyed all this.'

'I do, but it's such a waste of all the knowledge I have about
running the vineyard. Maddie has been teaching me the ropes since
I could walk. I know everything about growing the vines, the
harvest, the winery, everything. She's not getting any younger, she
will need me to start taking on the work there – this will be my life.'

She could hear the passion in his voice. 'It's lovely you feel so
committed. Maddie is very lucky.'

'Thank you, now, enough of all that. Have a read of this.'

He handed her a typed menu of the food that had been
prepared for them.

'We have a tasting menu, devised by me, cooked by our chef. I
have chosen a wine to go with each course.'

'This evening just gets better and better.'

Juliet read down the list:

Prawns and soda bread.
Tiny tomato tarts.
Sole.
Duck and miniature rosti.
Crackers with cheese.
Lemon sorbet with lavender.
Cherry tart and chocolate truffles.

'We can't eat all that!' Juliet said, laughing.

'Just you wait and see.'

They sat eating, each plate of food, each glass of wine, comple-
menting the other.

'You really know what you are doing with food, don't you,' Juliet
said, impressed.

'I have a French mother, so of course I do. I may not be able to cook it, but I know what it should taste like!'

'And do many lucky women get this treatment?'

'Only you... I am not the lothario of the island,' Gabriel said with mock horror.

'Come on, there aren't many good-looking single blokes around... you have lodges, a chateau, a vineyard. What more could a girl want!'

'Well maybe, but the only person I want to have sitting here is you...' He leant forward and touched her hand.

They were onto their sixth course now. She was losing track of the wine as they had glasses from various bottles. Gabriel gave her the lemon sorbet.

'This is gorgeous... I've never eaten anything with lavender in it, I can smell it.'

'It's freshly picked from our field... the real thing, not like the air freshener in your car.' Then he moved very close to her and put his arms around her, drawing her in close.

She laughed but suddenly he looked at her arm and seemingly for the first time noticed the plasters.

'What's happened to you?'

Juliet paused. Should she tell him? No, not tonight, it was too fresh, the fear too real. In a crazy way, she was scared the person who had done this might be watching her, listening to her.

'It was nothing, I fell,' she said.

'You need to be careful,' he said lightly. 'So, what have you been up to over the past few days?'

Maybe it was the drink, but soon Juliet found herself telling Gabriel everything that had happened.

'Good God, Juliet, you accused the family of stealing your set of car keys, killing Rhys and then, let me get this right, went to see this Tim in London?'

She nodded, looking sheepish.

'Come on, you can't suspect anyone you know of killing Rhys, surely. The keys were probably in your bag all the time.'

'They were not.' The alcohol was making her anger surface too quickly. 'I don't need you accusing me of imagining things. I know what I saw.'

Gabriel held his hands up. 'Hey, okay, I'm just saying. If you're wrong, I can see why your sisters would be upset. No one wants to be accused of something so awful, and the police said it was someone from off the island anyway, didn't they?'

'Yes, but I think they're wrong.' She looked away.

'Enough of all this heavy talk, eh, me and you don't need to fall out,' Gabriel said gently. 'Another glass of wine I think.'

Juliet could see the disappointment on his face. 'I'm sorry, I didn't mean to spoil this lovely evening. I'm just scared.'

He put his arm around her. 'You need to stop all this. Leave the investigation to the police. The past is behind us now.'

'Is it? How can we just ignore things that have happened?'

'Because if we keep digging over the past, we miss the good things that are happening right now. Look, let's take our tart and truffles down on the grass. I'll get a rug; we can eat under the stars.'

He went and found a rug and lay it down by the edge of the cliff.

They sat nibbling their puddings, but Juliet was more than full now. She rested back on her hands, closed her eyes, and let the sound of the sea below soothe her. She felt Gabriel put his arm around her and pull her close.

'You need to let your mind stop running away with you. You are exhausted, you need to rest.'

His words seemed to match the rhythm of the waves below, soothing her, slowing her breathing. He stroked her hair and she looked up as he kissed her. The kiss became more intense, and the need she felt for him deepened. Without speaking, they stood up and went into the lodge.

Later that night, she lay in his bed. The lodge was very quiet and cosy inside. She was close to the bedside cabinet and reached out to touch the soft velvet of the red fish she'd given him. She crept out of bed and found her phone. It crossed her mind that her mother might wonder where she was, but it was too late to ring her. Instead, she sent a text to Mira.

I'm staying round a friend's, if Mum is worried xx

Then she crept back into bed and curled up next to Gabriel and fell asleep.

23

Juliet woke early the next morning. Her head was heavy from the drink and she wasn't sure she wanted to stay any longer. She didn't exactly regret the evening, but she worried things were moving too fast. Quietly, she got dressed and Gabriel was still asleep when she left the lodge.

She walked quickly through the site. The walk down the steep road was easy, and once she'd reached the main road, she crossed over to walk along the cliff top. She saw a single dog walker but no one else.

She tried to figure out how she felt about Gabriel. He was certainly attractive, and attentive; she'd appreciated the warmth and care he'd shown her and was sure he wanted more from their relationship. He seemed to be offering something safe, predictable, but it would all be about her fitting into his life, and was that what she wanted?

Juliet reached the car park at Brook and she felt a kind of dread at the thought of going in. It annoyed rather than frightened her. No, she would not let whoever had pushed her ruin one of the most important places in her life.

Resolutely she went into the car park, glanced at where she'd stood and then turned into the field where her car was parked. She went over and sat close to the cliff edge.

As it was still very early, the light was just breaking on a new day. The sky was shades of pale blue, with pink tufts nearer the horizon, the cliffs slowly emerging from the silhouettes. It was if the island was reminding her that despite everything that had happened it still held onto its magic.

Eventually she knew it was time to go home. As she left the field, she glanced at the top of the footpath down to the beach. The sea was sliding its way inland, not as bright blue as it had been, but there was a grey peacefulness there. She looked over to where she'd been pushed, and the fear started to return. There may be great beauty here, but people could still do ugly cruel things.

She hurried home.

It wasn't until she reached the gate to the garden, that it dawned on her how early it still was – half past six in fact – and she had no house key.

She wandered over into the workshop and once more saw the comfy chair and sat down, closed her eyes.

Her phone pinged, and taking it out of her bag, she read a text from Gabriel.

You left?

Sorry, I needed to get back and didn't want to wake you, thank you for a lovely evening.

Miss you.

Juliet paused then quickly typed back.

Miss you too x

She started to scroll through the photos on her phone as something to do while she waited until the house woke up. Soon she was at the ones she'd taken at Rosalind's meal.

It was interesting to pick up on the faces of people at the edges of the snaps. She was shocked to see the look of anger on Mira's face as she watched Rhys speak, and Juliet wondered where it had come from. Then there was one of her mother caught off guard, the anxiety showing through the mask that had slipped. However, it wasn't the expression that caught Juliet's eye, it was the earrings her mother was wearing – the moon-shaped earrings. As far as she knew, her mother hadn't been up to the church since her father's funeral.

The enormity of what she was looking at slowly sank in, a memory of her mother determinedly saying she would talk to Rhys, sort things out.

It could have been her leaving the house at half twelve; she'd have had time to get Juliet's car, drive up to the church and wait. But, no, the earring meant she'd been inside the church. It was horrible to think about, but she had to try and face this. What did Rhys know that was such a threat to her mother?

Juliet looked over at the house. Her mother was in the kitchen in her dressing gown putting on the kettle. Juliet was cold, she needed to go in, but she dreaded it now. She couldn't talk to her mother about any of this, not yet, she had to have time to think. To her annoyance, her phone had fallen down the side of the cushion and as she reached down to retrieve it, she noticed the usual accumulation of pens and biscuit crumbs. She wiped the phone clean with her hand and walked to the house.

Her mother looked over; her eyebrows shot up.

'Oh, um, good morning...' said Juliet and kept walking, desperate to get away.

Her mother, chin down, gave her a mock look of disapproval. 'Mira told me you were at a friend's.'

'Sorry, I should have sent the text earlier. You didn't wait up for me, did you?'

'Oh no, I was reading. I can't seem to sleep lately, and you know how I am with locking up now. I checked with Mira before I pulled the bolt across.'

Juliet swallowed, once again feeling very much the teenager, caught in her mother's web. 'I lost track of time...'

Her mother waited.

'I had a meal with a friend and stayed over.'

'And is this friend Gabriel? Are you and he—'

'I don't know, Mum.'

Her mother smiled. 'I know everyone says it was Harry who was so like his father Clarence, but Gabriel reminds me of him in his loyalty to Maddie. Clarence was like that. He might not have understood what Maddie was doing up there, but he always supported her. He was a special man.' Her mother looked dreamily out of the window and then, as if bringing herself back to the present stood up saying, 'Well, I've made coffee.' Her mother handed her a steaming mug and Juliet realised her mother had prepared this already and had probably seen her lurking in the workshop.

Juliet took her mug, sipped the hot coffee, but it was hard to swallow. Her mother said something inconsequential about the weather, but her voice seemed muffled, far away.

'Mum.' The word shot out of her mouth, too loud, too frantic.

'What, Juliet, whatever is the matter?'

'I have to ask you about something. Did you go up to see Rhys the night of his accident, was it you who left the house? Please, Mum, tell me the truth?'

Her mother reached over and gently placed her hand on Juliet's cheek. 'Oh, Juliet, of course not, you really need to stop worrying about all that. Tell me more about Gabriel.'

Juliet for a moment relished the warmth of her mother's hand, but then something made her stomach lurch, it was the smell. She pulled her face away.

'What's that perfume?' she asked, her voice shaking.

'It's that oil, the frankincense.'

Juliet stared at her mother. That was the perfume she'd smelt on the person who'd pushed her. Had it been her own mother? Of all the things she'd imagined her mother capable of, this somehow upset her more than anything. She paused. Hang on, it wasn't only her mother who used this oil, Cassie had had it in her room as well.

She was aware her mother was talking. 'It would be nice for you to settle down with someone like Gabriel, and what a wonderful place to live.'

Juliet stood up, holding the edge of the table to steady herself. 'I need to go upstairs,' she said quietly. 'I need to think.'

Her mother looked at her quizzically but let her go.

Juliet was aiming straight for her own room. However, before got there, she heard a noise from Rosalind's room. The door was ajar, and Rosalind was not in bed. She was stood staring out of the window.

'Morning,' Juliet said.

Rosalind spun round and Juliet thought how pale and exhausted she looked.

'Are you okay?'

Rosalind shook her head.

Juliet went into Rosalind's bedroom. 'I'm sorry about the row, I hope you're not too upset with me. I shouldn't have mentioned the letter.'

Rosalind shrugged. 'I'd be a bit pissed off if I thought my car keys had been nicked and no one owned up.' Rosalind frowned, looked her up and down. 'You look like a woman who has been out all night.'

'Maybe,' Juliet replied, feeling herself blush.

'Gabriel?'

'Yes, but I'm not sure it wasn't a mistake.'

They stood in an awkward silence until Rosalind coughed, fiddled with her hair.

'Actually, I've been wanting to talk to you. I think, you know, I should show you this letter. I keep going over and over it in my head, but I'm not getting anywhere.'

'I'd like that, Rosalind. I'd like to help.'

Juliet held her breath. At last she was going to see the letter. She sat down on the bed as Rosalind went to her drawer. She took out the photograph of Rosalind as a baby that had been on the side of the musical box and with it she held a very creased piece of paper that had been folded many times.

Rosalind thrust the letter towards Juliet.

Juliet carefully flattened the piece of paper and started to read the letter.

My darling Rosalind,

I slipped this in behind the photo of me and you because I wanted to put in writing how much you mean to me. The day you came home was one of the best, happiest days of my life. I know, now we have talked, you will have lots of questions, but hold onto this note. You were always loved, always wanted. Your mother is a beautiful woman, and you must love her and forgive her.

As for your father, I am genuinely sorry you never got to know him. It is tragic he died. You sometimes remind me of him. You

*have his charm and good looks. He would have been so proud
of you.*

*Remember this, if you had been my own, I could not have
loved you any more.*

With all my love,

Dad

Juliet put the letter on her lap, stunned, then picked it up and
read it again.

Eventually she said, 'This is incredible. Did Dad really write
this?'

'Of course he did. You must recognise his awful writing.'

'Yes, I suppose I do. Goodness, what a letter, Rosalind, it
means... oh it must mean... oh I don't know.' Juliet found herself
gabbling, her eyes wide in disbelief.

'It means Dad was not my father,' said Rosalind. Her voice was
white hot with rage and hurt. She spat out the next words. 'He says
to forgive Mum; you do realise what that means, don't you? He's
saying our mother had an affair.'

The words came crashing over Juliet like a giant wave. This had
to be what her mother had been so frantic to keep secret. Her father
had wanted Rosalind to know, but something had made him
change his mind. He must have told Rhys and now Juliet knew her
mother had been to talk to Rhys the night he died. It was as if
piecing together a picture of her mother but someone very different
was emerging, someone she hardly recognised.

Juliet was aware of Rosalind watching her. 'I'm so sorry
Rosalind, I don't know what to say. I never dreamed of such a
thing. You do know, whatever the truth of this, it makes no difference to the way I feel about you. You are, and always will be, my
sister.'

Rosalind started to shake; she lifted her knees to her body, making herself as small as she could. Deeply moved, Juliet reached out and put her arms around her, stroked her hair.

'We need to speak to Mum,' she said quietly.

Rosalind shook her head. 'How can I? I'll have to accuse her of having an affair; I don't want to do that. I mean, we know Mum would never have done anything like this without a reason. What had Dad done to make her so desperate to find someone else? Maybe it was the drink problem. Maybe Mum has been covering up all this time... maybe he was abusive, and we never knew... she might have had a terrible life with him—'

Juliet sat back. 'No, stop, no. Dad was never anything but loving to Mum.'

'We don't know that... It can't have been Mum's fault. I know her, she's my mum.'

Juliet guessed that Rosalind's attempts to blame her father were a kind of self-preservation. She still had her mother and she desperately needed someone who she could still trust.

They sat, both breathing heavily as if they'd been climbing a steep hill.

'I can't believe Dad treated her so badly that she chose to have an affair or a fling, or whatever it was,' Juliet said gently to Rosalind, 'but marriages go through difficult patches, it might have been the briefest of flings.'

'Maybe,' spat out Rosalind, 'but why?'

'You need to speak to Mum, you need to know the truth about this, Rosalind, you deserve to know,' said Juliet and, in her heart, she knew now she needed to know the truth as well.

'I can't say anything to Mum; I don't want to ruin my relationship with her.'

'But you can't unknow something, you can't block it out.'

'I can. I'm good at that, acting a part.'

Juliet put her arms around her sister, and Rosalind sobbed

quietly.

'It's not fair, it's not fair, I want to be normal. I want to be like you,' shouted Rosalind suddenly.

'But you are, Rosalind.'

'No, I'm not, I'm some dirty little secret.'

'Hey, you're not that, you are our beautiful Rosalind who we all love very much, this doesn't change anything, you will always be my little sister.'

'Your half-sister.'

'No half. Look, biology and all that doesn't matter, you are my sister. Full stop.' And as Juliet spoke, she knew she meant it. No one, no act by her mother, would spoil her relationship with her sister. 'Promise me you will never call yourself that again.'

Rosalind nodded, sniffed.

'I am here, I will look after you.'

'I do feel a bit better now I've told someone. I can see why Rhys said it should have been talked about before now.'

'Yes, I agree, but we still don't know what changed Dad's mind about telling you.'

'The big question of course is who is my real father?' said Rosalind. 'Dad says he was good-looking, charming... but he's dead.'

A thought came to Juliet. She grabbed the letter, read it again. A picture came into her mind, her mother at that barbeque smiling up at Maddie's husband. 'Women were always attracted to him – your mother seemed quite sweet on him.' Maddie had given her a knowing grin. And, of course, he'd died, around the Christmas before Rosalind had been born.

'What is it, Juliet, what have you thought of?' asked Rosalind.

Juliet realised how frantic Rosalind was, but she held back. What if she was wrong? She needed to talk to their mother. They all had the right to know the truth.

24

After leaving Rosalind, Juliet had to go and rest; she was exhausted and the revelations about Rosalind and her mother felt overwhelming. She also remembered that she had been planning to follow Anwen that afternoon.

She was very tempted to leave it, the fear from Friday night hadn't left her. Like the night before with Gabriel, she had this horrible feeling someone was watching her.

She shook herself; she couldn't let herself be scared off. In any case, it was broad daylight, she would be among lots of people. It would be good to get out.

Juliet drove into Newport, arrived at the Travelodge at about half past one. It was down a side street off the high street. The town itself was small and not particularly pretty. There were some smaller independent shops but mainly it was phone and charity shops, and less and less brand-name chain stores each year. There were, however, plenty of coffee shops.

Juliet parked her car and then stood on the corner, watching the hotel, not knowing what else to do. Before long though she started to feel rather foolish as she watched everyone going about their normal business, shopping, dashing out for a sandwich for lunch. What was she doing here, waiting to follow someone? What on earth had got into her?

She was close to the point of leaving when she saw Anwen's car pull up outside the hotel and a small dark-haired woman in an old-fashioned floral summer dress and cardigan, who Juliet assumed was Jean, come out of the hotel and get into the car. Juliet ran back to her car, jumped in and was just about fast enough to be able to follow. She had no idea where they were going. They were soon on the dual carriageway, heading in the direction of Cowes until they abruptly turned off. They were at the hospital.

Juliet managed to park not far from them and followed as discreetly as she could. She had a moment of panic when she thought they may get into the lift. She could not get in with them... but, no, they went up the stairs. She followed them at a safe distance and then paused. They were going into a ward, what was she going to do now?

Juliet stood at the end of the corridor and watched as they went into a side room.

Glancing over her shoulder, she tried to walk in a way that looked like she should be there and slowed as she passed the room they had just entered.

Anwen was sat by Jean, and they were both looking at a man lying very still, machines all around him. Suddenly, Juliet was taken back to her last visit, sitting next to her father. The smell, the haze of cleaning products, the stuffy air. On the walls were cheerful pictures of the countryside, but none of it took away from the fact that this was a place where people were ill, many very ill.

Certainly, the man lying in the bed, presumably the Euan that Jean had referred to in the letter, looked extremely unwell, his eyes closed, arms motionless next to his body. Jean started to cry, but Juliet found herself staring at Anwen's face. It was the first time she had seen her with no mask, no exaggerated expression. Her eyes were wide, her lips thin, pressed together, her whole body rigid. Then Juliet saw noticed someone sitting on this side of the bed.

It was a uniformed man, and he had one had lying on the bed, joined to the patient with a handcuff. Juliet's first reaction was to think how ridiculous and unnecessary the handcuff was, but she had lived on the island with its prison and workers for long enough to know what a prison warder looked like. So, the man was a prisoner... what relation was he to Anwen? What was going on in there?

Her gaze switched back to Anwen.

'Can I help you?' a voice said behind her.

Juliet swung around on her heels to face the nurse talking to her.

'Um, sorry, I think I've come to the wrong place.' Juliet could feel her cheeks redden. She glanced back into the room and for a millisecond she was sure her gaze met Anwen's.

Juliet was glad to get away but resisted the temptation to run like hell out of the hospital. She had to find out more and so, although she'd left the ward, she waited just inside the short corridor that led to the next ward. She took out her phone and tried to look like she was studying it but kept glancing up at the entrance to the ward she'd just left.

Finally, she saw Anwen, and Jean come out, and walked slowly behind them at a distance. She watched them get in the lift and so ran to the stairs, where she was able to catch sight of them coming out, but what to do next?

She decided to take a gamble and walk in their direction. She tried to casually greet them, saying in as surprised a voice as she could, 'Oh goodness, hi Anwen.'

Anwen screwed her eyes up with suspicion. 'What are you doing here, Juliet?'

'I could say the same to you,' said Juliet, laughing too loudly, and casting a questioning look at Jean.

'I'm Jean,' the woman introduced herself, holding out her hand to shake Juliet's.

'I have been visiting an old friend with my aunt,' said Anwen and then as Jean was clearly expecting it said, 'Jean, this is Juliet, one of the sisters of my friend Cassie.'

'How lovely to meet you,' said Jean in a warm, Welsh, maternal way.

'Ah, you have Anwen's lovely accent, you must be from Wales as well?' said Juliet, trying to keep things light and ignoring the glare from Anwen.

'I am. I travelled up this morning. The journey's not as bad as you think is it, although I shall stay here overnight, too far to do both ways in a day.'

'So, what are you doing here, Juliet?' asked Anwen.

'Oh, I'm visiting a girl I was at school with,' said Juliet, thinking quickly. 'She's in for a minor op, just thought I'd pop and say hello.'

'That's kind,' said Jean. 'I like this hospital, not as big as some of the places back home. The staff are very friendly, they are getting to know me now.'

'So, you've been coming over a lot?'

'Just a few times, I don't visit as often as Anwen of course, but I shall come again next week.' She glanced at Anwen. 'I'll make it Friday, all being well.'

'I think I'm working then.'

'Never mind, I can visit alone.'

'I hope you are staying somewhere nice,' Juliet said, trying to sound normal and chatty, and ignore the continued glare from Anwen.

'Oh, just a Travelodge, but it's a good price, very clean. They do a good meal deal in the evenings. Anwen is taking me somewhere fancy tonight, but I am very happy staying there.'

'Anyway, we ought to get going,' said Anwen. 'Good luck with your visit, although the visiting time must be nearly up now. Funny, I thought I saw you up on our ward.'

'I must have a double,' said Juliet, but her laugh was forced. 'Right, lovely to meet you, Jean.'

She left them and headed for the lift, which came annoyingly fast. She had to go up to the next floor, and then walk back down to maintain her cover story.

Once back at the car, she took some deep breaths. She'd managed to follow Anwen, but she wasn't too sure what she'd learned. Who was Euan? Clearly a prisoner, and Juliet couldn't help but wonder what he'd done. What was his relationship to Anwen? Husband or partner were her best guesses, but clearly someone she kept very quiet about. Juliet wondered how much she had told Cassie. He must be part of the reason she'd been staying on the island, but he looked very ill.

It was a shame Jean was seeing Anwen that evening, Juliet would like to have talked more to her. Juliet decided to put off returning home and drove over to the other side of the island. It was a place Juliet normally avoided in August, but today it was exactly where she wanted to be.

She was lucky and found a parking space along Sandown seafront. She got out of her car and was immediately hit by that aroma of chips and burgers mingled with the sea and salt, the sound of disgruntled children tired after a long day on the beach, the shouts of teenagers carrying bottles of beer.

She walked along the pier, with its noisy arcade games, the racket of clashing music from slot machines and the speakers. For Juliet, a few minutes was enough. She bought herself an ice cream and went to sit on a bench. In front of her, parents were paying for their children to go on trampolines, an attempt to tire them out before bedtime. It did Juliet good to be over here among a different kind of normal life. Her village was wonderful but could be claustrophobic. It showed that even on this small island she could find somewhere where no one knew her, no one was gossiping about her father's accident or Rhys's death.

Her mind went over the past few days. Finding her set of car keys, the trip to London, the push, the night with Gabriel, the earring, Anwen, but what rose to the surface was the revelations about Rosalind. Her sister had a different father to her. It was so hard to take in, and if she was finding it difficult, how must it be for Rosalind? The lengths her mother might have gone to cover this up were almost too frightening to contemplate. Is that what had stopped her father saying anything to Rosalind? If it was, what had happened on the day of his accident to make him realise this?

Juliet closed her eyes, tried to shut out the people around her shouting, the seagulls above her, their beaks wide, screaming for food. She went through what she knew of the day. And then it came to her – that old VW ignition key. Her father had come home from work, given that key to Mira, the key he'd been so keen for her to get rid of. She had to find out more about it.

25

The next morning, Juliet woke with fresh determination. Today she would give a lot more thought to this VW ignition key, ask the family, maybe ask Gabriel, he'd worked in the garage and the key was old, he might know why it was significant.

The more difficult task, however, would be to talk to her mother, but Rosalind and the whole family deserved to know the truth. Juliet found the earring, put it in her pocket; her mother would have to at least explain that.

She left her room and could hear Rosalind talking to Cassie in her room. It seemed odd; Rosalind usually liked to go through her complicated make-up regime before work uninterrupted.

When she reached the kitchen, she found her mother dressed and tidying up.

'I am going to have a big sort out today,' said her mother. 'The house has become such a mess over the past few weeks. It's time these cards came down,' she added, taking the birthday and condolence cards off the dresser.

Juliet went to make herself coffee and looked over at her mother.

'It's Cassie's birthday next, she's nearly the big 4-0,' said Juliet.

'That's no age,' replied her mother with a smile.

Juliet frowned. 'Hang on.' Juliet went over to her mother, lowered her voice, 'You said you were younger than Cassie when you had your hysterectomy? I think you said you were two years younger, so thirty-seven.'

'Yes, that's right, why?'

Her mother froze; Juliet knew she was doing the same maths as her in her head.

'I might have said the wrong age,' her mother said quickly.

'No, I don't think you did. Mum, you are sixty now, Rosalind is twenty-one, that means you had her when you were thirty-nine. However, if you had your hysterectomy at thirty-seven then you couldn't have given birth two years later and that means you couldn't possibly be Rosalind's birth mother.'

'Juliet, you're being ridiculous. Where is this all coming from?'

Juliet took a deep breath. 'It comes from something Rosalind told me. She found a letter from Dad in her musical box.'

Her mother went white and began swaying, and Juliet grabbed her and helped her to a chair. She quickly got her a glass of water and sat down next to her.

'The letter Dad left Rosalind told her he wasn't her father,' Juliet added.

'No...' Her mother covered her face with her hands.

'Yes, Rosalind showed it to me.' Juliet kept her voice as calm and measured as she could.

Her mother lowered her hands, tried to lift the glass, but her hand was shaking. She slowly let go of the glass and raised her trembling fingertips to her lips. 'Oh God, what is going to happen now?'

'Rosalind thinks you had an affair.'

Her mother stared up at her. 'She thinks that?'

'If you won't explain, Mum, what else is she meant to think?'

Her mother shook her head, tears filled her eyes. 'I can't, I don't know what to do.'

At that moment Cassie and Rosalind came into the kitchen. Rosalind was in old jeans, looked pale and fragile.

'Where's Mira?' Cassie asked.

'Out with Lola,' said their mother.

Cassie shot a look at Juliet.

'You want me to fetch her?' Juliet asked.

Cassie nodded and Juliet, knowing something significant was about to happen, ran out of the house.

Mira was ambling up the road with Lola, Juliet waved frantically and signed to her to come home quickly.

Mira walked quickly back with her, and they went into the kitchen.

Her mother was sitting, staring at the table, Rosalind and Cassie sat opposite. Mira fed Lola, then they all sat together.

Cassie led the conversation, signing as she spoke. 'Rosalind and I have been talking. Juliet knows and now Mira you must. The letter from Dad told Rosalind that our dad wasn't her birth father.'

Mira was the only person now who looked stunned. 'Dad is not your dad?' she signed to Rosalind.

Rosalind nodded. 'No. Dad left a letter in my musical box.'

'But I don't understand,' said Mira. She shot a look at their mother.

Cassie looked over at Mira. 'This is going to be a lot to take in. Rosalind and I have been talking most of the night.' She turned to Juliet. 'I heard her telling you about the letter and knew then it was time.'

'No, Cassie.' Their mother's voice was weak.

'Yes, Mum. Dad knew there would come a time and he was

right. The fact is...' She swallowed hard. 'Rosalind's father is Harry, Maddie's son.'

Juliet gasped. 'Harry?'

'Yes, it was Harry.'

Juliet thought of the photographs, Harry with his father's good looks, and of course poor Harry who died.

'When I stood by his grave, I felt something,' said Rosalind, 'a kind of shiver, and then the date he died, the day I came home.' She wiped her eyes.

'So, if Harry is Rosalind's father...?' said Mira, and she looked at their mother in horror now.

'No, it's not Mum,' said Juliet. Her mind was rushing – the trip away, Cassie sleeping in with her mother to look after Rosalind, it all added up. Her eyes met Cassie's.

'Yes, Juliet. I am Rosalind's mother.'

Rosalind spoke slowly. 'When Dad said in the letter to love and forgive my mother, he was talking about Cassie.'

They all sat stunned. Juliet stared at Cassie. Cassie had given birth to Rosalind, so, Rosalind was... well, Rosalind was her niece!

As if reading her mind, Rosalind spoke directly to Mira and Juliet. 'I don't want this to change things with you. I don't want to be anything other than your sister.'

Mira grasped her hand. 'Of course not. Nothing will change.'

Juliet understood why Mira said this, she'd had the same instinctive reaction when Rosalind had told her. However, on another level, she knew everything had changed. Cassie was not Rosalind's sister; she was her mother.

Cassie didn't move, she sat, as she always did, slightly apart. Her father had said how lonely it was keeping secrets, and that is how Cassie's last twenty-one years must have been. No wonder she had seemed distant, it must have been the only way to survive. How had it felt, watching her own daughter run to someone else? For her own daughter never to know who she really was?

Tim had been right, something traumatic had happened to Cassie in her teens. She'd been pregnant, given birth secretly, come home and then the father of her daughter had died. She had the early years with Rosalind, but then weeks at a time away from her because of her music. No wonder she kept wanting to come back, no wonder she said her heart was here.

'So, what happened?' It was Mira who spoke and signed.

Cassie replied, 'I slept with Harry on my eighteenth birthday in November 1994, Rosalind was born the following August. Mum and I went away for a month, I really did do a music course, but I was also heavily pregnant. We timed it so Rosalind would be born while we were away.'

'So, Rosalind didn't come early?' Juliet said.

'No, she was bang on time.' Cassie smiled over at Rosalind. 'But it wasn't an easy delivery, it was touch-and-go.'

'I thought I would lose both of you,' said her mother, looking broken. 'It was only once we came back here to the island, I felt you were both really safe. When we came back, the plan had always been that we would adopt you so that Cassie could carry on with her music. You see, Cassie had completed the course and auditions and at the end had been approached by the virtuoso Matties. She was off to a conservatoire and he was going to give her individual sessions. I was so proud of you.' Her mother's face glowed at the memory as she looked over at Cassie.

'But,' said Cassie, 'I had been prepared to give it all up. You see, when I came back, and Harry saw Rosalind at the party that afternoon everything changed. Harry knew he wanted to stay here, marry me; we were going to be a family. I would give up my music and he would turn down the partnership in France. We would live on Harry's portion of the land up there, and we would build our own house, plant woodland for Rosalind to play in, keep animals, sheep, hens and goats. Everything would have been perfect.'

Juliet watched her sister, her eyes dreamy and far away. She was that eighteen-year-old girl, in love for the first time, a girl who believed in happy endings. And then Juliet saw Cassie's face slowly crack, the dream crumble, her hands clasped at her chest as she said, 'I have never felt anything like that love, before or since. The kind of love that drives you insane, that makes you feel that if you can't have them, then no one else can. The only thing that matters is you being together, you need them to breathe, to live.' She paused and then added, very quietly, 'I knew people had said he was going away, but I knew he couldn't ever leave. He had to stay here with me forever.' She paused, looked up as if remembering they were all still there. 'We never got the happy ever after, did we.'

Juliet saw pain suffuse Cassie's face, as her heart splintered again.

'I'm so sorry,' Juliet said the simple words, trying to encompass so much. Sorry that her sister had been through such agony, but also sorry she'd never tried, not even in her adulthood to look behind that self-sufficient mask and find the source of her pain.

They looked at each other, Cassie's eyes warm, finally a bridge of understanding between them.

'I didn't know what to do when they told me about Harry. I was in pieces and when Mum and Dad suggested we go back to the original plan for them to bring up Rosalind, well I was so numb and shocked that I agreed.'

'So, you regret it?' asked Rosalind.

'I really believed it was the best thing for you. You had a lovely home, Mum and Dad here and sisters. I couldn't bear you to go away from me but it gave you a very stable life, a happy childhood. Dad went to register your birth – Mum and Dad are the named parents on your birth certificate. Dad only had to take the letters from the hospital, it was easy to lie, but, at the same time it was incredibly hard for Dad. Lying on the form was contrary to everything he stood for, but he did it for Rosalind, he really believed it was best for her. His one consolation was that he would be telling her the truth when she was twenty-one.' Cassie hesitated, looked over at Rosalind. 'I admit I was not happy about that. I wondered how you would cope knowing I'd lied to you. I was so scared that I would lose everything, that you might not want any more to do with me. I don't know how I would have coped with that.' She paused. 'But you have taken it so well, I feel so grateful.' She smiled at Rosalind, who gave a whisper of a smile back. To Juliet's mind Rosalind looked in complete shock.

'You sound so calm, Cassie,' said Mira, 'but it must have been very hard. To hear Rosalind call someone else Mum, and also leaving her so much.'

The mask slipped again, and Cassie's eyes screwed up in pain. 'There were many times I cried on my own, I felt my heart would break; the only way I coped was building a wall around myself. I had to keep telling myself not to be selfish, this was best for Rosalind.'

'And do *you* think it was?' Mira asked Rosalind.

'I don't know. I may have been saved a lot of tears and tantrums, but I'm not sure now how I am meant to rebuild my life.'

Juliet's mother looked over at her. 'You were always loved, nothing has to change, you can still call me Mum if you want to – you can call me and Cassie whatever you want.'

Rosalind blinked; Juliet guessed she wasn't ready to even think about that yet. Instead, she said quietly, 'I wonder how much Dad told Rhys.'

'I would guess he must have told Rhys about Harry and Cassie,' said their mother.

'But you are not just guessing are you, Mum? You spoke to Rhys at the church,' said Juliet and she took the earring out of her pocket. 'Barbara found this in there when she was cleaning; you were wearing it the night of Rosalind's meal, I have a photograph to prove it.'

Her mother went to protest and then sighed. 'Okay yes, I did slip up to speak to Rhys. I was desperate for him not to say anything about Cassie and Harry, that was for Cassie and me to do if we ever thought the time was right.'

'So, it was you who went out at half twelve that night?'

Her mother shook her head. 'Oh no, I went earlier than that. It was while you were out with Gabriel, I wasn't long. It was obvious Rhys would not be persuaded by me. If I'd gone later, then I'd have known about the missing door key, I'd not have left you all in bed with the patio doors unlocked.'

Juliet had to concede what her mother said made sense, that was if she was telling the truth.

As if reading her mind her mother added, 'I know after what has happened you must wonder if you can still trust me. Of all the people in the world you should be able to believe your mum. All I can tell you is that when your father and I made this decision, we were doing what we thought was best for Cassie and Rosalind.' She hesitated and looked over at Rosalind. 'I don't want you to get the impression we felt forced into this. We loved you so much; the moment I saw you, I knew I couldn't have borne to let you go to anyone else.'

'I suppose you were really my grandparents,' said Rosalind quietly.

'In title yes, but any grandparent can tell you the love they feel when they see their grandchild can be as overwhelming as seeing their own child. That love is very, very special.'

'Of course, Maddie is my grandmother. How did she feel about me?'

Their mother shook her head. 'That is harder to tell. She was in mourning for her husband, and of course she lost Harry so suddenly, she seemed content to stay away. I did talk to her about it, I never wanted her to feel left out, but she chose to keep out of things. As far as she was concerned, she said she was happy for you to always consider me and Dad your parents.'

'But Dad was going to tell me when I turned twenty-one. Cassie explained she'd not wanted Dad to say anything because she was scared of how I'd feel towards her. I can understand that, but she also said you'd not wanted him to say anything either. Why was that?' The words shot out and Rosalind did nothing to soften the accusation in her voice.

Her mother shot a glance at Cassie. 'I felt it was too much for you to take on. Why upset you? As long as Cassie was happy, I believed it was better to leave things be.' She pressed her lips together tightly, clasped her hands. Juliet knew there was more, something their mother wasn't telling them.

Rosalind didn't seem to notice however and asked, 'Why did Dad change his mind about telling me? Why did he think it was dangerous for me to know?'

Her mother looked away. 'I have no idea.'

She'd answered too quickly, and again Juliet was sure she was hiding something. What was the real reason she'd not wanted Rosalind to know about her parents? Was it the same thing that her father had discovered the day of his accident? Juliet knew her mother was quite capable of keeping secrets for years even from her father. Why was it dangerous for Rosalind to know Cassie was her mother and Harry was her father? Juliet's mind went to Harry. Her father had talked about Harry in the hospital, talked about his death. Was that where the fear lay? Was this all something to do with Harry's death?

Juliet frowned and she knew in her heart that the revelations this morning were not the end, it was just a new layer being unwrapped, a pass-the-parcel of lies.

The room was very quiet. The enormity of the news had overwhelmed everyone and what was needed now was time alone, the questions could wait.

Juliet was grateful when they started to leave, there was something she urgently needed to do.

26

Juliet went out into the garden. Her laptop was in the workshop and she desperately had to look something up.

Juliet googled 'Isle of Wight news August 1995'.

It took a few duff searches, but finally she found what she was looking for.

Tragic Hit-and-Run Death in West Wight

Late last Sunday evening, 20 August, the body of Harry Durand age 26, was discovered on the military road on West Wight. He was found by a member of the public out walking their dog. An ambulance was called but he was declared dead at the scene. Harry was seen running soon after 11.00 p.m. and it is understood the accident happened between 11.10 p.m. and when the body was found at 11.30 p.m. The detective in charge of the investigation said that it appears that Harry was hit by a car from behind while running. The car was abandoned, without the ignition key, further down the road. The police are very keen to locate the key and are asking for people to look out for them. They have a fob on them for a VW, and possibly have the label attached by the garage owner, which would have the name of the car owner, Mrs. Thornton.

While the car belongs to Mrs Thornton, who lives in Elmstone, the car itself had been left at Ian Lacey's garage, which appears to have been broken into. The car was stolen and was then involved in the fatal accident.

The police are anxious to speak to anyone who might have been travelling or in the area of the accident at the time.

Harry was a well-loved member of the Brookstone community. His mother owns Laurent Vineyard, where Harry was working. He is well known for his sporting prowess, being a member of the Wight Arrows, and having competed in the Island Games in 1993. The family are in shock and are very grateful for the support of their community at this distressing time.

If you have any information at all that may help the police, please ring the station, you can leave information anonymously if you wish.

Juliet read and reread the article. There was a photo of the car on the military road, at night in the rain. There was also a photograph of the site two days later. Juliet could just make out a large woven cross in the grainy picture – was that the same as the one that she'd seen at the site of Rhys's accident? She wasn't sure but there was something else she really had to check.

She rushed over to her drawer and took out the old ignition key. The fob was for a VW. She turned it over in her hand and looked again at the piece of cardboard with 'Tho' on it, of course this was the part of the name Thornton. Her hand trembled. This was the ignition key to the car that had killed Harry.

So how did her father come to have it? Why hadn't he given it to the police if he'd found it all those years ago? Even if he'd not discovered it until the day of his accident, what scared him about it?

Her mind went back to the article about Harry's death. The police had wanted this found; to them it had been an important clue to the driver of the car that killed Harry.

Suddenly the room began to spin. Juliet sat down. She had entered a cold, dark room, terrified to move. And yet she had to keep going, keep thinking.

Her father had the ignition key to the car that killed Harry. It was the link to the driver. She closed her eyes, breathed deeply before she could even let the words be heard in her head. What if her father had been the driver of the car that killed Harry?

Juliet fell back in the chair, shook her head.

No way would her father have killed anyone. And yet, argued a cold logical voice, maybe he had seen it as the only way he could protect his daughter and her unborn child. Whatever Harry planned, Cassie was clearly infatuated with him. She could easily have given up everything either to wait for him or follow him to France. And she would be putting her life and that of her child in the hands of a man her father must have been angry with, a man he may have been convinced would ruin the life of his daughter and her child.

Juliet took a deep breath and had to admit all of this had to give her father a motive to kill Harry that evening, ensure he would never have the chance to ruin the life of his daughter and grandchild.

And who would have suspected her father? As far as most people were concerned, he didn't have any motive. Very few people knew that Harry was Rosalind's father and as the truth had never seeped out, Juliet assumed Maddie had kept it to herself.

After he'd killed Harry maybe he'd promised himself that one day Rosalind would at least be told the truth about her parents.

Twenty-one years on no one would make that fatal link between Harry's death and the motive for Cassie's family. His death would be ancient history, forgotten.

However, had it been that the day her father had found the old ignition key in his garage a few weeks before Rosalind's birthday he'd realised that actually, twenty-one years was no time at all?

The memory of Harry's death was still raw; no one had forgotten. Barbara had reflected the grief and anger the whole village still felt, and in particular about the fact no one had been brought to justice for the crime. People still wanted, needed, to know who it was. When they heard about Rosalind, how long would it take for people to start putting the pieces together? It was then her father realised it would never be safe to tell Rosalind the truth about her parents and it had broken his heart. He'd drunk, had the accident, but then remembered the old key he'd given to Mira. He'd never had time to get rid of it properly and so he'd asked Juliet.

Juliet's mind went to her mother. Had she known or suspected what her father had done? She might even have been grateful; she was as invested in Cassie's music, knew just as much about Harry's reputation as her father. She'd have also known that it would never be safe for her father to tell Rosalind the truth. Juliet's thoughts turned to Rhys. How much of all this had her father told him? How far would her mother have gone to silence Rhys, stop him telling the world about Rosalind, possibly even telling the world about who killed Harry?

Suddenly Juliet was brought back to the present by her phone pinging and she looked down to see she had received a text from Gabriel.

Fancy a drink at the pub?

What was she to do? Her mind was in turmoil. How was she meant to face Gabriel suspecting her father had killed his brother?

She took a deep breath; she had to calm down. This was guess work, she didn't know anything for definite. In any case, if anyone could tell her more about the night Harry died it would be Gabriel. She'd take the old key and see what he made of it. Hopefully, Gabriel could tell her something to dispel her fears.

* * *

When Juliet arrived at the pub, she found Gabriel waiting. 'I've ordered drinks. Ed has to put another barrel on, so I have to wait for my pint. You okay? You look in need of a stiff drink,' he said.

She gave a thin smile.

'That bad?' asked Gabriel. 'Look, I'm sorry if you felt I was moving things on too quickly.'

'Oh, it's not that,' she said, but seeing him flinch she realised she'd been a bit insensitive. 'A lot has happened at home since then, that's all.' She sighed. 'There is no easy way to tell you this. I found out today that your brother Harry was Rosalind's father, that Cassie is her mother.'

She was watching him carefully, waiting for his reaction, but his face was composed, accepting.

'You knew?' she asked.

'Yes.'

'But how long have you known? Why didn't you say anything to me?'

'I knew Cassie and your parents were keeping it a secret from you all, it wasn't for me to say anything.'

'When did you find out about Harry and Cassie?'

'Maddie and I knew before Rosalind was born. Cassie rang Harry from that course she was on. Harry told us.'

'How old were you then?'

'Eighteen.'

'Of course, sorry, you're the same age as Cassie. Harry was twenty-six, wasn't he? That means he was quite a bit older than her,' she said, an edge to her voice.

Gabriel raised his eyebrows. 'He was, but Harry enjoyed flirting and, in any case, Cassie always found boys her age irritating.'

'You and Maddie must have been very shocked?'

Gabriel rubbed his lips. 'I know we should have been, but it was more complicated than that.'

'Why?'

'Like Dad, Harry was good-looking. Girls fell for him, but even I knew he didn't treat them well. He literally made notches on his bedpost. He told Mum it was to do with sport, but I knew what they really were. He liked to brag to me. When Dad died, he got worse if anything. I was the quiet, nerdy one. I watched as all the girls, even ones my age, looked through me and up to him.'

'So, Cassie was only one of a string of girls?' Juliet could feel the anger rising. 'She was eighteen and very naïve when he slept with her.'

Gabriel cringed. 'I know, I was very upset about it. I thought a lot of Cassie and yet she fell for him like everyone else.'

'Cassie believed Harry loved her, believed that he would give up the partnership in France and stay here. She was prepared to give up everything to be with him and raise Rosalind together.'

Gabriel sighed. 'I know that's the line he spun at that party. He might even have meant it for a minute. She told me after the party and I tried to warn her to be careful, not to rely on him, not to give up everything for him.'

'But she didn't listen?'

'I think she was surprised when I told her he'd had other girl-friends; she was quite naïve, her life had been a lot more sheltered than most eighteen-year-olds. But still she talked of marriage and happy-ever-afters. He'd said things to her, promised her the world, but I knew he was leaving the next day. I told Cassie but she didn't believe me. She knew he went out for his run at about 10.30 and so she said she'd go out to meet him and talk to him. I said if I got a chance, I would tell Harry to look out for her.'

Juliet gasped. 'Did she go, do you think?'

'Yes, I'm sure she did.'

'There was the terrible storm. I was surprised Harry went out in weather like that.' Juliet tried to encourage Gabriel to talk.

'He went every night. Maddie had tried to stop him, but he was insistent about going. She still feels guilty that she didn't try harder, even I do sometimes. I was eighteen, not a child, but I was too caught up with what I was doing.'

Juliet looked up and saw Ed had come over with their drinks.

'There we are, one red wine, one best bitter.' He smiled at Juliet. 'I was sorry it was so hectic here the day of your dad's wake, I hope it didn't spoil it for you.'

'Oh no, thanks, it went very well. I think it was rather nice to be outside.'

'I am so sorry to hear about Rhys. Terrible to think of there being another hit-and-run in the village. I know Harry's was a while back, but it makes it feel like yesterday, doesn't it?'

Juliet nodded; there it was again. It felt like it was only yesterday.

'We were just talking about the night Harry died actually,' said Gabriel. 'I was saying I should have supported Maddie more in stopping him going out.'

'I do remember Maddie and him arguing about going out, but then of course he went. Harry always did what he wanted, and anyway, you and I were so busy, weren't we?' Ed grinned at Juliet. 'Do you remember Game Boys?'

She nodded. 'I do. I didn't have one but lots of my friends did.'

'We may have been eighteen, but we were so excited, back then. I'd just got mine for my birthday and I went round that evening. Gosh what an evening that was. It's weird, although it was years ago, because of what happened to Harry so much of it is still really clear in my mind. Like the weather. I remember that storm, it was terrible. Didn't you have a tree struck by lightning, Juliet?'

'We did.'

'Didn't you lose some vines as well, Gabriel? I seem to remember you'd been out in the rain before I arrived?'

'That's right, I got soaked.'

'I got soaked as well. I'd walked up from the church.' He grinned at Juliet. 'I was very religious in those days and helped lead a Bible group on a Sunday evening.'

'I can't imagine that,' said Juliet, grinning. 'Do you remember much else of the night?'

Ed sat down, ignoring the customers who were waiting at the bar. 'Well, I did, and I remember walking in the rain to Gabriel's after church. The meetings finished about quarter to eight, so I must have got to you about eight. Then we played games, I think we watched *The Young Ones*, and later Harry went out for his run. I didn't take much notice, but I did think he was mad going out in the rain. We listened to some music. Maddie gave us great food, I remember that. Pastries, cheeses, so much. It's terrible, isn't it, to think we were just carrying on as normal.'

Gabriel screwed up his face as if trying to picture the evening.

'Mum had just come to collect me when the police came. It was so awful. I remember Maddie apologising for being in her dressing gown and having a towel around her head – I couldn't understand why she was worrying about that, why it mattered. Now I understand she was probably in shock, the poor woman.'

'It must have been a nightmare for you all,' said Juliet.

Ed was distracted by the sound of a fist on the bar. He tutted. 'Sorry, best go and see to that lot.' He got up and sauntered over to the bar, shouting, 'So who's next?'

Gabriel took a long drag of his beer.

'I'm sorry, it's not fair raking all this up for you,' Juliet said.

'It's okay. You're bound to be full of questions. I've had years to take it in. But with Rosalind... she doesn't need to know about Harry, not everything. Let her think he was going to stay and be a great dad, what harm does it do?'

'But how do you know Harry hadn't really changed his mind when he saw Rosalind? Cassie seemed very convinced.'

'I think that's Cassie remembering what she wants to remember. He spoke to me after and was in a panic. Told me he'd promised things to Cassie to keep her happy. He was glad he'd be off first thing.'

'So, he wasn't going to tell her himself?'

'I'm sorry, my brother was a bit of a coward like that.'

Juliet put her head to one side. 'I've not thought much about your mum in all this. It must have been so difficult for her seeing her only grandchild growing up but never being able to acknowledge her, never having a relationship with her?'

'Maddie is very pragmatic. She knew Harry was going away, in her mind he was never going to do "the right thing" and so she felt the arrangement your parents made was best for Rosalind, she didn't want to rock the boat.'

'I've seen the photos and couldn't help but notice how much Rosalind looks like Harry. Has that been upsetting or a comfort for Maddie?'

'She never talks about it, I don't know.'

'But, of course, she could spend as much time as she wants with Rosalind now.'

'Oh, she won't do that. If Rosalind wants to talk to her, of course she'll be fine, but no, she won't be pushing anything, I'm sure of it.'

'That's as well, I don't think any of it has really sunk in with Rosalind yet, and when it does, I'm not sure how she will react. She needs time to think.'

'I'm sure you all do.'

Juliet sipped her wine. Her mind went back to that damn old car key, and her suspicions about her father.

'You've gone very quiet, are you okay?' Gabriel said.

'Sorry, it's all so overwhelming. I just don't know what to think.'

'Let's start making some plans, working out our next dates. You know you could come and stay up at my place as much as you like. It would be a break for you.'

Juliet knew then she had to say something. Slowly she took the key out of her pocket and handed it to Gabriel and he took it, looking completely mystified.

'What's this?'

'I think it came from Dad's garage.'

'It's pretty old, must be a spare of some sort, the fob is for a Volkswagen. Why have you got it on you?'

'Look at this scrap of the label, those letters. I am sure this is the old ignition key for the car that killed Harry.'

'It can't be.'

'It has to be, it is exactly like the one described in the paper, it even has part of the name of the owner still attached.'

'Good grief, I suppose you could be right. Where did you find it?'

'In the workshop. Dad brought it back from the garage the day he died, gave it to Mira to hide in there.'

'How odd.'

'It's more than odd. Why was dad so worried about this old key? Why did he have it?'

Gabriel shrugged his shoulders. 'I don't know, it could have been lying around there for years.'

'But if it was used to drive away the car the night Harry died...'

Gabriel frowned. 'I don't think they knew how the car had been started, it could have just been left and got buried under stuff.'

Juliet shook her head. 'I don't think so. Dad was definitely worried about this key. In the hospital he asked me to get rid of it. He wouldn't have done that if he'd not thought there was something significant about it.'

Gabriel sipped his beer. 'And what would that be?'

'I think this old key was used to drive the car down to the main road. Harry was killed and then the driver for some reason brought the key back to the garage.' She bit her lip. 'And the thing I'm really scared about is, well, what if my father had been the driver of the car?'

He looked at her carefully. 'That's crazy. There could be any number of reasons your dad had the key, it's madness to start speculating about your father being involved in Harry's death. I don't think the key is significant at all.'

'But I think it was, why else would Dad have been so worried about it? And the police specifically asked people to look out for it, so they must have believed it to be important.'

'Even if they were right, maybe the person who stole the car took the key by mistake and then thought the garage was a good place to hide it. The garage was always such a terrible mess, it could have taken your dad ages to find it.'

'I suppose so.'

Gabriel stared at her. 'You can't be seriously suspect your father. Granted, your father may have been upset with the way Harry treated Cassie, but your father would never have killed him. Honestly, you've let this get way out of perspective. No way would your father have had anything to do with Harry's death. You must never think that.'

She smiled weakly. Gabriel sounded so certain, and she desperately wanted to believe him. 'I hope you're right. Thank you.'

'By the way, talking of keys, could you give this to Mira for me? I've been carrying it around for ages and forgetting to give it to you. It's the spare key to the filing cabinet in the office. I think she wants to check on the costs and things of the retreats; she's been hoping to plan another one for Christmas.'

'Has she?'

'She only mentioned it the other evening. I know she's only just lost Rhys, but I thought it was good that she was able to think about something in the future.'

'Yes, I suppose it is.' Juliet took the envelope, with 'spare key for Mira' written on it. 'Your handwriting is really fancy, look at all those loops on the p, k, y and f. I've inherited my dad's awful writing. People think because I'm arty I can write neatly, but that's rubbish.'

Gabriel grinned. 'I've got to have some gifts. Fancy anything to eat? The roast smells good.'

Juliet screwed up her nose. 'It does, but I think I'd better get on home.'

'Of course. I'll be in touch,' he said tenderly.

Juliet walked slowly home. Her mind went back to that night, the rain, the storm, the tree and suddenly she thought of something. If she was right, then maybe, just maybe, everything would be all right.

27

Juliet ran into the garden and over to the old oak tree, with the vertical white line running down one side of the trunk.

She read the small wooden plaque she had made with her father – *Sunday 20 August 1995, 10.30 p.m.*

She closed her eyes, went back to that night, standing looking out of the window at the storm, and then hearing the horrific splintering as the lighting struck the tree. She'd run down to her father and he'd comforted her, made her some hot milk. He'd taken her back to bed, and she remembered hearing the grandfather clock strike. She'd laid in bed, had some milk, slept and at one point had gone out to wash her hand after spilling it. But all the time she'd been aware of her father downstairs, heard his footsteps in the kitchen, the TV being turned on and off. Her father hadn't gone out, she was sure of it.

With a crashing wave of relief, she knew it meant her father was innocent. She reached out and touched the bark of the tree. 'I'm so sorry, Dad, forgive me for doubting you.'

Her mind went back to the old ignition key. It had frightened her father. If he'd only found it the day of his accident while clearing out maybe he'd been unaware all these years that someone close to him was implicated in Harry's death. Had finding it made him realise that they had and because of that he'd known he couldn't tell Rosalind the truth? Had he suspected her mother? Or, of course, it could have been someone else in the family.

Juliet stared in horror at the thoughts going through her mind. And then she turned to Cassie. She denied going out the night Harry died, and yet something about Cassie and that night didn't feel right. What was it?

Juliet went through the night again in her head. Her dad had taken her back to bed, she'd drifted off to sleep and then it must have been much later, she'd woken up, and decided to have another sip of her milk, she'd misjudged it in the dark and spilt some on her hand. Juliet flinched at the memory and remembered thinking she should tell her dad. But she hadn't. What had happened? That was it; she'd left her room and then she'd seen Cassie. Just as she had the other night, drying her hair; that was the memory that kept slipping away from her. As a child she'd assumed Cassie had been in the shower but thinking back, something had been wrong about the picture.

Juliet screwed up her eyes. Yes... Cassie's was wearing trousers; they were wet. Why was she wearing clothes if she'd had a shower? And now of course she knew. Cassie hadn't been showering, she'd come in from the rain. Cassie had been out.

Of course, Cassie would say she went to meet Harry, to make plans for their future together. But Gabriel was very insistent that Harry was going away.

What if Cassie had known that in her heart? What if that night all her dreams had been shattered and that all-consuming infatuation had turned to hate? The line could be so fine; had she crossed it? Cassie had said, 'He had to stay with me forever.' Is this how she'd made sure he would never leave? Had Cassie gone to her father's garage and stolen the car and run Harry over? A kind of *if she couldn't have him no one else could*. Is that how she'd felt?

Juliet held the old car key in her hand. So, was it possible that when her father found this key, he'd known, or suspected, a link between Harry's death and Cassie? He might well have known Cassie had gone out, maybe she had even given him the key, confessed everything.

And what about Rhys? Had Cassie been the person who left the house at half twelve, had she driven up to the church and killed Rhys to silence him? Had she pretended Anwen was with her to give herself an alibi? Juliet thought of that person who'd pushed her, the threats of doing what they'd done to Rhys to her – had that been Cassie?

Juliet shook her head. To think of her sister being responsible for a crime of passion was horrendous enough but to kill in cold blood like that. '*You must be very careful. Anyone can kill,*' her father had said.

Juliet went to the workshop and put the old key away. She'd walked into somewhere very dark and frightening, but she had no idea what she could do next. She hid away with her thoughts for the rest of the day and crept into bed that night, still struggling to make sense of everything.

* * *

In what seemed a strangely welcome intrusion, Adam Smith came to see them the next day. He told them investigations were carrying on. The Met in London were working with them now. He also told Mira the coroner was prepared to release Rhys's body and so the family could plan his funeral.

Planning the funeral seemed to give everyone a new focus. The date was set quickly, and they were fortunate to get a slot the following Monday. The preparations were made with the archdeacon who was to take the service.

It wasn't until they were planning the funeral that Juliet could see how much Mira and they all needed this. It was a kind of milestone to pass. With her father's funeral, she'd not liked the feeling of being under pressure to move on, but with Rhys it felt different. It signalled that a normality had returned to the grieving process, a proper time to say goodbye and maybe a glimmer of hope in moving on.

Maybe it was that sense that moved Mira to share her news on the Wednesday evening. It was the end of the meal, and she tapped her spoon on the table. Lola, who had been resting under the table, pricked up her ears and they all looked at Mira expectantly.

'I know it's been a difficult few weeks, but I think it's time I told you all my news. I was going to wait until after the funeral, but, well, to be frank, I'm not going to be able to hide this much longer. I am not going to be one of those women who don't show for months.'

'Oh my God,' screamed Rosalind.

'Yes, I'm pregnant.'

A warm smile spread over their mother's face, like she was feeling the first touch of the sun's rays after a long hard winter. She went and hugged Mira and gave her a kiss.

'That's the most wonderful news, it's like a miracle,' she signed, and she wiped a tear from the corner of her eye. 'I feal quite overwhelmed.'

'Thanks, Mum.' Mira was glowing. She glanced over at Juliet and signed, 'The scan was all clear.'

Juliet signed, 'Brilliant,' but felt a pang of guilt that she'd forgotten to ask.

Their mother continued, 'I know there are all kinds of mixed feelings, but we will celebrate this new life, we are all here to help you, Mira.'

'We'll have so many things to buy,' said Rosalind, looking thrilled. 'You know, there are some fantastic sites now, you don't need to go around in some enormous smock with a Peter Pan collar!'

Mira laughed. 'I know. In fact, I ordered a new dress, some maternity leggings and a top this morning.'

'Oh, this is going to be great,' said Rosalind, clapping her hands.

Juliet found it fascinating that Rosalind could look suddenly as if she didn't have a care in the world.

Mira glanced over at her sisters. 'I expect you are wondering if my baby will be Deaf. It does seem unlikely, I think. My deafness is like so many with no known cause. I did have genetic counselling, they checked Mum and Dad, but there was nothing they could track down. We shall have to wait and see, I guess, but I don't mind either way. I will be bringing this baby up bilingual, signing and talking.'

'Of course,' said their mother. 'What's most important is that your child knows they are loved and wanted, it's all that matters really.'

'Yes, to be wanted is more important than anything,' said Rosalind, but she wasn't smiling any more.

'You were wanted, you know that don't you?' said Cassie. 'From the moment I knew I was pregnant, I wanted you.'

Rosalind gave a fleeting smile but didn't reply.

The mood had become awkward and one by one they got up and left the room.

Juliet was pleased though to see happiness on Mira's face. It would be good to plan for new life in the middle of so much stress.

* * *

The next day passed quietly until late Thursday evening when Rosalind sent a text in the evening to their mother.

Mum, I'm not coming home for a while. I have taken sick leave from work. I have to leave; I can't bear you all being so nice to me. You don't know what I've done. I'm going to turn this phone off. Please don't contact me. I am sorry I shall miss the funeral on Monday. Rosalind

Her mother was frantic. 'What shall we do? Should we call the police?'

'No, Mum, we can't do that. She's an adult, she can go away if she wants to,' said Cassie.

'But where is she staying? Who is she with?'

'Maybe we threw too much at her too quickly, but what does she mean about having done something awful?'

'She seemed so happy last night when Mira announced the news about the baby. What can have changed since then?' said their mother.

'I don't know. We just have to wait for her to come back to us, I think,' replied Cassie.

Juliet left Cassie and her mother and went upstairs, the words in Rosalind's message ringing in her ears. *'You don't know what I've done.'* What was she talking about? Was it something to do with her work or was it Rhys? Juliet desperately wanted to talk to Rosalind. She remembered her date with Gabriel at the hotel in Southampton that they had planned for Saturday. Would it be possible that Rosalind would turn up as planned, and if she did, could Juliet talk to her then? Juliet sent a text to Gabriel.

Are you still all right to go out on Saturday?

He replied immediately.

Yes, great.

She wondered briefly if she should say anything about Rosalind but decided against it.

Good, looking forward to it.

Tomorrow of course would be Friday, the day she was hoping to see Anwen's aunt again. With everything that had happened she'd almost forgotten about her, but she had to remember that Anwen was still a suspect for Rhys's murder.

* * *

The next day, Juliet left the house late morning. She drove into town, wandered around the shops, and then found somewhere to have lunch.

Eventually she drove up to the hospital, parked at roughly the same time as the week before, and went up to the same ward.

Looking in through the window of the side ward, she saw Jean sat alone. There was a different prison warder handcuffed to the man in the bed this time, but the patient looked no better than he had the previous week.

Juliet left the ward and waited until Jean came out. Walking quickly, she sidled up besides Jean.

'Oh, hello again, this is a nice coincidence,' Juliet said, hoping she sounded convincing.

'Well, how nice to see you,' said Jean. She spoke brightly, but her eyes were red-rimmed.

'Are you back visiting?' Juliet asked.

'Yes, I think that might be my last time though.'

'Oh, um, I'm sorry to hear that.'

'Yes, he's not good. I must ring Anwen when I get back to the hotel. So, you're back here, I thought your friend only had a minor op?'

Juliet noted that Jean might be chatty, but she was no fool. 'That's right, I had to pop into a friend of my mum's this time. Good job we live relatively close. I'm on my way out, are you?'

'I am. I get the bus from out the front of the hospital.'

'I tell you what, do you fancy a cup of tea and I could run you back. It's no trouble.'

'Well, that is very nice of you, yes, thank you. I could do with one.'

The café was close, and Juliet told Jean to sit while she got them tea and scones. Once she was back, Juliet asked, 'So, how was your journey today?'

'Not too bad. I left Swansea at six.'

'Wow, that is early.'

'I know, but it's lovely and quiet at that time and I'm an early riser anyway. Anwen was telling me you are the artistic one of the family. Fancy being one of four sisters. I was one of six.'

'Six! Goodness, that's a lot.'

'Most of us are still in the Swansea area. Sadly, my sister Gwen died young, it's why I come over to see Euan. Someone has to come and visit him, no one else wants anything to do with him, but he's family. He was Gwen's only child, she doted on him, never saw the bad in him.'

'Euan must be very unwell if they are keeping him in so long?'

'To be honest, I'm not sure he will ever come out. We have had a few scares with him. Anwen has been very good. I would not blame her for not having anything more to do with him. I know they say, "for better or for worse", but not everyone will do that, will they.'

Juliet shifted in her chair. Did she dare ask?

'Erm, so... is Anwen married to Euan?'

Jean looked up, a surprised expression on her face, as if she had only just realised Juliet didn't know the full background. 'Anwen hasn't told you all about Euan?' she said. 'Well, in that case, I wouldn't want to break her confidence.'

Juliet could feel Jean backing off and wondered desperately how to keep Jean talking.

'I didn't know about Euan, but I had gathered Anwen had not always had it easy. Rhys had said she had a difficult past. I guess you know about Anwen planning to set up a restaurant with my sister Cassie?'

'Anwen did mention it; it's wonderful of your sister to help her have a fresh start like this.'

'I think it's a mutual thing. Cassie is grateful to Anwen for her expertise and, of course, she has the money from her inheritance. They will be partners.'

Jean frowned. 'I didn't think she'd any of that money left, I was sure her and Euan had got through it. Still, she's a good brain on her. Always was much brighter than Euan.'

'Rhys seemed to have some objections to Anwen going into business with Cassie.'

Jean took a sip of her tea and then a bite of her scone. 'Rhys never understood Anwen. They were so different. The trouble is their parents spoiled Rhys; they were so proud of him going into the church. Anwen rebelled, got into bother. Her and Euan both grew up in our village, you see, so they'd known each other a long time.'

'It sounds like the island.'

'Yes, it's similar, they're both close communities. Anwen may have got into trouble in her youth, shoplifting, stealing cars, things like that, but I don't think she was ever involved in crime like Euan. He wasn't a bad lot really, but he got in with a very nasty crowd, he ended up in prison here on the island the year before Rhys and Mira's wedding. Anwen had been traveling to visit him but she decided to move over here when she came to the wedding, she was tired of all the traveling to see him. People don't realise how difficult it can be getting over here.'

'No, you only need the weather to go bad and it can be impossible to get over here.'

'Exactly. In light of his diagnosis earlier this year it's just as well she is close by. I don't think he has long now.'

'I am very sorry to hear that.'

'Yes, such a waste. Anwen has stayed loyal to him; she really loves him. She came that night we had the big scare. They told us Euan had been moved over to the main hospital from the prison infirmary a few weeks ago.'

'When was that?'

'Oh, let me see, it was a Saturday, the hospital rang me because they couldn't get hold of Anwen. Eventually I managed to contact her, she was cooking some meal, but she got a taxi to the hospital as soon as she could.'

'Do you think it might have been the twentieth?'

'Yes, of course, that was the night Rhys died, wasn't it? That poor family.'

'So, she was here with Euan all that night?'

'Yes, although she phoned me just after half twelve, told me she was going to get some fresh air. The nurse did tell me that they'd been worried at one point because Euan had taken a sudden turn for the worse while Anwen was out. They'd tried to phone her mobile but got no answer and anyway they thought she'd be back up any moment, but she missed it all. They'd had the emergency team up to him, but by the time Anwen was back, it was all over. Maybe it was as well Anwen didn't see that, sometimes these things are meant to be, aren't they?'

'Maybe you're right,' said Juliet and sipped her tea. However, her mind was running on. Anwen had not been with Euan at the crucial time. But even if she'd wanted to get back to the village, how on earth could she have done it without a car?

'It's good of you to tell me all this,' said Juliet kindly. 'It helps me understand Anwen a bit better.'

'She's had it hard, but I hope now she can start again.'

They finished their tea and together walked down to the car park.

'Are you sure about this?' said Jean. 'The bus stop is only over there.'

'No, come on, it will take me five minutes.'

And so they got in the car and drove back to Jean's hotel.

'It's been lovely to meet you, Juliet, and thank you very much for the tea and the scone. I don't suppose I'll see you again if I'm right about poor Euan, so you take care now.'

Juliet said her farewells but was reluctant to go back to the house. Instead, she drove to the Downs, and went for a walk. As she did, she tried to think through what she'd learned about Anwen. She had supposedly been at the hospital on that Saturday evening, but had been missing around the time Rhys was killed. But the problem of getting back to the village could not be ignored. She had no car, there would be no buses at that time, and it would take hours to walk. The only way she could get back was by taxi.

Juliet remembered the card her friend Mike had given her. He'd said they manned the taxi rank at the hospital. She decided to ask Mike if he had a record of Anwen travelling that night.

She picked up her phone to call him, and as she asked him, she knew it sounded odd, but he said he would check and get back to her. All she could do was wait now for a reply.

First, however, she needed to see if she could find Rosalind. Even if Rosalind did turn up to work at the hotel, how was she going to react to Juliet being there too? And Gabriel. What would he think of it all?

Juliet went and looked out of her bedroom window. When she'd been messaging Rosalind from China, she'd had a picture of someone young, pretty but naïve, someone who was, at heart, homely and easy to read. But she'd realised from that first walk on the beach the day her father had died, Rosalind had changed, or maybe just grown up, and had experiences that Juliet had no idea about. And so, who knew what this 'new 'Rosalind was capable of? Was she leading some kind of secret life, or had she actually killed someone? Or, had Juliet got it all wrong, had Rosalind really landed some incredibly well-paid waitressing job and was this guilt about something incredibly minor? Juliet sighed; all she could do was wait now. Tomorrow she would hopefully find out answers, but Juliet was not sure they would be anything she wanted to hear.

28

Juliet dressed carefully for her night out with Gabriel. She wore trousers rather than jeans with her best top, and she actually put on some make-up and jewellery.

Gabriel came to pick her up in a taxi and she was touched to see he looked very smart too, in trousers, shirt and a jacket.

'How are you all doing then?' he asked as they travelled to the Red Jet terminal.

'Okay, I suppose.'

'So, have you backed off the suspicions of your family now?'

She shrugged and then smiled. 'Well, I do know that Dad had nothing to do with Harry's death.'

'Of course he didn't, but I'm glad you know that too now.' He paused. 'Maddie and I saw the announcement for Rhys's funeral in the paper, we will be coming of course.'

'Mira will appreciate that.'

'I hear she is expecting.'

'Now how on earth did you know that? She only told the family a couple of days ago.'

He tapped the side of his nose. 'That's village life for you.'

They arrived at the terminal, and as Gabriel paid for the taxi, Juliet spotted Mike and ran over to him.

'Mike, did you find anything on Saturday, 20 August?'

He grinned. 'I did check, and even though I am not meant to release this kind of data, I can tell you a woman named Anwen called for a taxi from your village at about half ten to take her to the hospital and then she used us to take her home again about six the next morning. She didn't use us in between time.'

'Oh thanks, I suppose she could have rung another company.'

'It's possible but not likely. As I said, we have the contract. Of course, we are not exclusive, people can phone other taxis, and they do in the daytime, but at those sorts of hours, people tend to use us.'

'Of course, right, thanks. That really helps,' replied Juliet, but part of her was wondering if this now completely cleared Anwen of any involvement in her brother's death. It had been clear Anwen had disappeared for some time in the night but how could she have got back to the village if she'd not used a taxi?

'Enjoy your evening. That's Gabriel from the vineyard, isn't it? What a life you'd have up there, queen of the castle and all that!'

Juliet groaned. 'It's nothing like that. We're just going for a meal.'

Mike winked at her. 'I'll believe you.'

She shook her head and said goodbye before going back to Gabriel who was waiting for her now.

'Everything okay?'

'Yes. Just catching up with someone I went to school with.'

As they took their seat on the Red Jet, Gabriel put his arm round her. 'Look, Juliet, try and give yourself an evening off. Let's try and have a good time, okay?'

She pushed the thought of Rosalind to one side and nodded, squeezing his hand.

They chatted about their work, and the island. Gabriel talked about the upcoming harvest and went into a lot of detail about testing the grapes that she didn't understand. He did confess to going up each day and tasting, even though it wasn't his responsibility this year.

'I need to stay hands-on. I walk with Maddie or someone from the winery each day; it's good to keep in touch with everything. It's such a hard balance, cutting back enough to allow the sun at the grapes, but not too much in case they get burnt.' Gabriel carried on chatting as they got off the Red Jet and started to walk through the town.

Finally, they arrived at the hotel.

'Wow, this has got even smarter than I remember; still, I suppose it was a few years ago that I came here last,' said Juliet, glad she'd made an effort but still feeling a little underdressed.

'It has. I came here last year for a meeting – you know, they stock our sparkling white here.'

They went in and Juliet admired the Wedgwood blue walls, the beautiful lamps and a wide oak staircase with thick velvet carpet.

Juliet glanced around for Rosalind, but there was no sign of her. Maybe she was in the restaurant.

A young man in dinner jacket came over and escorted them to the dining room, to their table, and took her jacket.

Juliet grinned. 'It's not quite McDonald's, is it!'

Gabriel looked very relaxed. He may have attended the local schools through his childhood, but he was more used to opulence than her.

He ordered champagne, and together they went through the menu.

When another waiter came to take their order, Juliet glanced around and saw there seemed to be waiters everywhere. She guessed part of what you were paying for were all these people. But there was no sign of Rosalind.

After they'd given their order, she said to the waiter, 'Um, I don't suppose you know a waitress called Rosalind? I thought she would be working here this evening.'

The man looked mystified. 'Sorry, I don't know anyone of that name.'

'Tall, very pretty, blonde hair, comes over from the island?'

'I don't think we have anyone from the island working here; it wouldn't be easy, with the ferries and things at night.'

'I think she stays over sometimes?' Juliet stopped, the story was starting to sound implausible, and she could see Gabriel was getting embarrassed. 'I'm sorry, I must have got it wrong,' she said. So, what now? Rosalind wasn't here; how on earth was she going to find out where she was or what she was doing?

When the waiter had gone, Gabriel asked her what was going on.

'I thought Rosalind worked here, that was all, I was going to surprise her.'

'Well, I'm rather glad she's not here. This is our evening. I have you all to myself and I want it to be perfect.'

Juliet smiled, but she was anxious about Rosalind.

Their first course came – a beautiful dish of crab with thin slices of homemade whole meal bread.

'This is delicious,' said Juliet and she started to relax.

Soon the evening began to feel like a real date. Gabriel told her amusing stories about guests that summer, she told him about China. By the time the dessert came, she was floating on a soft pillow of good company, good food and good wine.

'Thank you for bringing me here, Gabriel,' she said, genuinely meaning it.

'You're welcome. It's lovely to be here with you, you have no idea how much I have missed you.'

She was smiling back at him when she looked over his shoulder and her heart leapt. She sat frozen, holding her glass mid-air.

'What's the matter? Gabriel asked and looked around. 'Oh, isn't that Rosalind?'

Juliet stared at her sister, well, the back of her. Rosalind had obviously not seen her when she'd walked in. The dress and shoes Juliet recognised from the wardrobe; the dress was very tight, short, and obviously very expensive. Rosalind was with a man Juliet had never seen before. She glanced at him as he pulled out a seat for her. She guessed he was in his early forties. He was quite good-looking, wearing preppy cords and jumper, oozing a kind of public-school confidence. She felt like going over and punching him and telling him to leave her sister alone.

'So, she's not working here after all,' said Gabriel, looking puzzled.

'I hope not,' Juliet replied quietly.

At that moment, Rosalind reached down to put her bag next to her chair, glanced around and saw Juliet. The room seemed to fall silent as they stared at each other.

Rosalind recovered quickly, said something to her dinner companion and walked over to Juliet.

'My goodness, what a coincidence,' she said far too loud and bright, glancing over at her dining companion.

'I thought you said you worked here; I was going to surprise you,' said Juliet, trying to look relaxed.

Rosalind leant close to her and hissed in her ear, 'I never told you the name of this place, how the hell did you know I'd be here?'

'It's just a coincidence, we came for a meal.'

'Bullshit, Juliet, you came to spy on me.'

'Who's the secret boyfriend then? Are you going to introduce us?'

Rosalind screwed up her face. 'For God's sake, Juliet, what's wrong with you? Why can't you just mind your own business?'

Juliet had suspected Rosalind might be a bit embarrassed to see her, but she'd not expected her to be so rude. It hurt. 'What's the problem? You don't want me to say hello?'

'No. I don't.'

Juliet was shocked, felt herself blushing. Rosalind, however, was occupied with the man she was meant to be dining with. He was looking over at her now, frowning. Rosalind quickly flashed him a reassuring smile and then turned back to Juliet and scowled. 'Just get the hell out of here. I can't believe you did this.'

Rosalind painted back on the smile and marched quickly away.

'What's going on?' asked Gabriel.

Juliet, bit her lip, picked up her handbag, trying hard not to cry. 'Something's wrong, I know it is. Do you think I should go over there?'

'Of course not.' Gabriel's expression was cold now. 'Did you arrange to come here with me just to spy on your sister?'

'No of course not.'

'I'm pretty sure you did Juliet.' He lent over the table, scowled at her. 'Rosalind asked you how you knew she'd be here – it obviously wasn't coincidence. So how did you know?'

Juliet could feel herself blushing, looked down at the table and fiddled with her glass. 'I found her diary.'

Gabriel threw himself back in his chair, shook his head. 'You've been snooping on your sister?'

'Gabriel, you have to understand, I did it for her own good.'

He threw his hand up. 'Oh God, how often have I heard that! What you were doing was interfering, trying to control your sister's life. I think you resent the fact your family has managed very well without you and now you want an excuse to stick your nose into their lives, take over.'

'That's not true.' Juliet stood up, horrified at the anger she saw on his face.

'It's disgusting Juliet. I thought you were different, but you're not.'

'Different to what, to whom?' she asked.

Gabriel was breathing fast, glaring at her. Suddenly he picked up his serviette and threw it on the table. 'We're leaving.'

He signalled to the waiter and paid the bill.

When they got outside, Juliet said, 'Look, I'm sorry that all went wrong, let me pay half.'

'Don't bother,' he said, clearly still furious.

'I'm sorry I didn't tell you this before, but Rosalind didn't come home on Thursday. She sent a pretty desperate text, and I was really worried about her. All I knew was that she was due here tonight.'

'And so, you set me up. You used me.'

'Gabriel, can't you see this is nothing to do with you. Aren't you at all worried about Rosalind? You saw her clothes; that man must be giving her money for something.'

'You think she's a prostitute?'

'Oh, I don't know...'

'God Juliet, you really despise your family, don't you?'

'No, I love them, and I am sorry you can't see that.' Juliet looked back at the hotel. 'I'm not leaving her here; I am going back for her.'

'You can do it on your own then.'

'Fine.'

Gabriel marched off, flagged down a taxi and disappeared.

Juliet was shaking, but it wasn't going to put her off.

She was about to go back into the hotel when she saw the man and Rosalind appear. Juliet stepped back into the shadows.

'It's all right,' he was saying, 'you need to rest, and I should get back. One of the girls isn't well, I'll text you when I can.'

Juliet watched him walk past and then saw Rosalind walk up

the street. She followed her at a distance, to a smart block of flats. Rosalind used a front door key to get in and Juliet watched the windows. Soon she saw lights in the first-floor window and Rosalind close the curtains.

Juliet went to look at the entry buttons. There were four for the first floor. Eventually Rosalind answered.

'Yes?'

'Rosalind, it's me, Juliet.'

'What the hell? Just piss off.'

'No, I'm not leaving. I can talk to you or I can talk to your friend.'

'For God's sake.' And with a click, the intercom was turned off.

Juliet waited. She saw automatic lights come on in the hallway and heard the door click open. She pushed it and walked up the concrete stairs, which, although smart and freshly decorated, felt anonymous and bleak.

The front doors were all the same, and she found Rosalind standing waiting for her.

'You'd better come in,' she said, scowling at Juliet.

The flat was smart, modern, impersonal. Juliet glanced around, breathed deeply, and was relieved there was no one else there.

There were no photographs, nothing to say who lived here. On the coffee table was a bottle of whisky and a glass.

Rosalind sat down, took a long sip of a drink Juliet didn't even know she liked. Juliet sat opposite.

'You have no right to do this to me,' said Rosalind.

'I understand why you're angry, but I was worried, I mean, your clothes, the money, where is it all coming from?'

Rosalind's eyes flashed with fury. 'Hang on, do you think I'm a hooker or something – my God, you do.'

'I didn't want to think anything of the sort, but what am I meant to make of all this? Who was that man?'

Rosalind was breathing fast and she got up and opened the windows. 'It's none of your business. I'm not your baby sister, you can't come here, demanding answers.'

'It's not fair to interpret my concern as just wanting to control your life or interfere. I care about you; I hate seeing you like this.'

Rosalind walked back to where she'd been sitting. 'I suppose it would be nice to talk to someone,' she said, 'but if I do, you can't tell a soul, okay?'

'Of course.'

'The truth is...' Rosalind took a long gulp, poured herself another drink. 'The truth is I am a mistress. I am the other woman.' She waited for Juliet to say something.

'You are seeing a married man?'

'Yes...'

Juliet was immediately relieved, but a host of worries quickly replaced the feeling. 'How long have you been seeing him? Where did you meet?'

'We've been together, if that is the word, for a year now. I met him, William, at Cowes week. I didn't know he was married at first. He kept that from me for a few weeks, and by the time he told me, I was lost.' Rosalind's voice softened. 'I know I should have walked away, run even, but I was in love, desperately, infatuated, nothing else mattered but me and him.'

'And he loves you?'

'He said he did, he said, don't groan, he said he was unhappy with his wife, he had stayed for the children.'

Juliet grimaced. 'Children?'

'To be honest, I try not to think about them, they are in their teens...'

'And William is well off, hence all the presents?'

'He is minted! He runs an online gambling business. He's spent a lot of money on me, expensive dinners, gifts, he even gave me a credit card with my own account. He likes me to look good. This place is his of course, he said he bought it for me and him, our special place.' Rosalind looked up. 'I know... There is nothing about this that any of you are going to approve of, is there.'

Juliet saw a grey hardness in her sister's eyes.

'There is no way you'll understand any of this,' Rosalind continued. '"What about his wife, his children?" I know, but I try so hard not to think about them, I put them in boxes. I couldn't talk to anyone about this, no one knows, no one at work, no one. It has been so lonely, but even that I deserve, don't I? No one is going to feel sorry for me, even if I've spent all week waiting for our evening, bought the clothes, turned down all my friends and he stands me up at the last minute for family business, because that's what he should do, isn't it? William should be putting them before me, I'm just his bit on the side.'

Juliet heard the hurt, the desperation, in her sister's voice. 'Oh, Rosalind, this isn't all on you, you are much younger than him, he is the one who chose to cheat on his wife. You were wrong to go along with it, of course you were, but you have suffered, and he has used you.'

'And not just me it seems.' Rosalind's words were brittle, sharp, cold.

'Eh?'

Rosalind stood up, she went back to the window, holding her glass, and looked out into the darkness. 'I got a text earlier, not from him though.'

'From who?'

'From another "other woman".' She paused. 'Yes, I'm not the only one. This one had found out about me and she contacted me. She's his new bit on the side, and not as naïve as me. He'd brought her here to the flat and she'd found something of mine... she thought I should know.'

'Oh Rosalind.'

Rosalind sat back down, drained her glass, thumped it down on the table and, by some miracle, it did not break. 'I was so angry, so hurt, I was going to have it out with him at the restaurant, but then you came and I couldn't face the drama.'

'You have to finish with him.'

'I've known that for ages. Rhys was right, it's why I was so pissed off with him.'

'Rhys knew?'

'He saw us together when he was over here one Saturday night not that long ago really. Someone Rhys was with recognised William; knew he was married. Rhys talked to me a few days later, but he had a real go at me before the meal. He had a horrible way of talking down to you and then he said he was going to tell Mum. Well really, how old am I? And how dare he?'

Juliet could see her sister burning with anger and remembered her outburst to Mira.

'I remember you saying you would kill him if he said anything,' Juliet said quietly.

'I was furious with him.' Rosalind paused and her eyes widened in horror. 'God, Juliet, you didn't think I actually killed Rhys, did you? That's absurd. In any case, after reading Dad's letter, Rhys telling you lot about my affair became the least of my worries.'

Juliet nodded and thought she believed her.

'I have started to pack the few things I have here,' said Rosalind. 'I was going to go to the Premier Inn or something, I hadn't thought that far ahead.'

'So, you've not told William yet?'

'No, I'll do it by text, it's all he deserves, isn't it?'

'You handle it how you want, but I really think you should come home.'

Rosalind started to cry. 'But how can I? I am so angry and hurt but what is the point of me talking to them? I'll just make them feel even worse and it's too late to undo it all.'

'But if you are to have any kind of real relationship with them you have to talk, tell them how you feel. The last thing either of them would want is for you to run away from them and I don't think you want to live without them, do you?'

'No of course not.'

'Well come home then.'

Rosalind wiped her face. 'Okay, yes, maybe I will. I'm going to tell them about this mess as well, might as well get everything out in the open.'

'I think you're right.'

'But what if they hate me?' asked Rosalind weakly.

Juliet shook her head. 'No one is going to hate you, but things are going to be different, things have to change. It's something we all have to deal with.' Juliet looked around the room. 'You need to get away from all this.'

Rosalind nodded. 'I know.'

'Okay, well there's a Red Jet soon, so let's go as soon as we can.'

After Rosalind had closed the windows, Juliet noticed a familiar smell.

'What is that scent? I noticed it in your room at home.'

Rosalind raised an eyebrow. 'You must have led a very sheltered life if you don't recognise that.'

Juliet really didn't recognise it but felt too embarrassed to admit it.

'It's weed, Juliet.' Rosalind grinned.

'You shouldn't be smoking that.'

'Everyone I know does, but you're probably right. Still, it's a way to cope with all this. If I'm honest, part of the reason I went to the workshop on that Saturday night wasn't just to look at the musical box, but it was to smoke as well.'

Now Juliet remembered the smell in there. 'Ah, I thought I noticed something. So that explains why you were out there so long.'

'Yes, I sat there smoking, and read the letter. I saw someone go out, was a bit worried actually because I didn't want to get caught. I sat down in the chair after that, and then just sat lost in my own little world, thinking, smoking, and listening to music. I do remember thinking when I was giving my statement to the police that it was a shame I'd not made a call or spoken to someone, it would have shown I'd not left the workshop. But there we are, I know what I did.'

Juliet was watching her sister. She'd given a very good explanation of why she'd been out so long, but Juliet couldn't quite wipe away the anger she'd seen in Rosalind's face when she talked about Rhys.

'Right, I'm ready to go,' said Rosalind.

They went to the front door, but before she left, Rosalind looked back. 'I'm not sorry to leave this.' Then she threw a quick grin at Juliet. 'I'll miss the shoes, and the bags though.'

They walked out of the flat.

Rosalind suddenly looked around. 'Where's your date by the way?'

'You only just noticed? He stormed off; he was furious at being used.'

'Did he pay at least?'

Juliet laughed out loud now. 'Yes, he paid. Poor Gabriel.'

In the taxi to the terminal, Rosalind said, 'I'll tell Mum and Cassie. No more secrets.'

They caught the Red Jet and Juliet sat next to the window. It was very quiet on board; the only sounds were the engine and the splash of sea hitting the windows.

They arrived back to the bustle of Cowes. Juliet glanced over at the taxi rank; Mike wasn't there now. She remembered what he'd told her about Anwen, and so she now knew it was very unlikely Anwen had taken a taxi back to the village. It wasn't even a matter of simply getting there and back either. Anwen would have needed time to steal her car, kill Rhys, set fire to the car, and then get back to the hospital. Juliet wondered if she was going to have to accept the fact Anwen had nothing to do with Rhys's death.

By the time Juliet finally got to bed, Mira was fast asleep. Juliet was only just drifting off when she heard Mira's phone vibrating loudly, flashing, signalling a text, which must have roused her sister. Juliet saw Mira read it, followed by a brief grin flickering on Mira's face.

She expected Mira to go back to sleep but instead, through the subtle light of the nightlight, she saw Mira quietly picking up clothes, and Lola sat upright. They silently left the room, and she knew then she'd been right about the other evening – Mira had gone out. But where on earth would she be going?

Juliet got up quickly and pulled on some trousers and a jumper. By the time she was on the landing, she saw Mira in a coat head out through the kitchen, and she heard the patio doors open and close.

Juliet ran downstairs. The patio doors were unlocked. Lola was sat in her basket chewing a treat, and the dog looked up at her hopefully, but she shook her head and went outside alone.

Mira was opening the gate, so Juliet waited until she had shut it again before going out of it herself. Mira walked down towards the beach; Juliet saw her cross the road and started to follow her. It was so quiet that she felt her footsteps echoing on the path. Juliet crossed the road, stood at the edge of the car park. It was deserted, apart from Mira and a solitary figure who was standing, waiting under the light by the paying machine. Juliet froze. God, no, how could they do this to her?

29

Juliet backed away; her heart thumping, she peered from behind a hedge, frightened they might have seen her. However, they stood very close together both totally absorbed in each other.

Mira was crying and Gabriel had his arms around her.

Juliet put a hand over her mouth to stop herself screaming out. How could they? Tears of anger and rage and disappointment fell. She remembered Mira's face when she read the text, it must have been Gabriel asking her to meet him.

The bastard. How dare he! How long had this been going on? Her mind dashed to the baby, was it possible that Gabriel was the father?

Her father had been right, she shouldn't trust anyone. She would have trusted Mira with her life, but now? Unable to watch any more, she turned and started walking back to the house.

It must have been at least an hour before she heard Mira and Lola return to bed, but she lay trying to strip away the anger and hurt, to understand what was going on. Mira and Gabriel? How long had that been going on? Had Rhys known or suspected? Did any of this give Mira a motive for killing Rhys; had she convinced herself that was the only way out of a miserable marriage?

Mira could have been the person she'd heard leave the house the night Rhys died. Juliet had to face the fact now; Mira could have been the person who had stolen her car and killed Rhys.

She knew, however, now was not the time to be confronting Mira. Rhys's funeral would be in two days, she must leave her sister be until after that.

* * *

The next day, after lunch, Rosalind told the family everything. Cassie was fairly philosophical, her anger aimed at the man who had used Rosalind and betrayed his family. Their mother though was clearly very upset. She seemed less concerned about the man, her hurt more with the fact Rosalind had lied to her, had been leading a life she knew nothing about. However, their mother struggled for words, maybe aware that only days before she'd had to confess to misleading Rosalind for many years. Eventually Cassie and Rosalind went off for a long walk, leaving Juliet's mother sitting hugging her mug of tea looking rather lost and abandoned. Mira moved to sit with their mother, gave her the comfort Juliet felt at a loss to find. And so, Juliet left them together and was glad to have some time alone.

The following day they gathered together in the kitchen, once again preparing to walk up to the funeral together. Cassie had arranged for Anwen accompany them. She arrived with a few minutes to spare. Juliet noticed she was wearing the same black leather jacket with the badges on that she'd worn the day of her father's funeral. However, the walk today felt very different. No holidaymakers made their way to the beach. Instead of people sitting out in their gardens or doing some gentle weeding, there were just a few people sweeping up the orange and brown leaves that had fallen on their tidy paths and lawns.

Even though the church was much fuller, it was cold inside, and people wore coats and gloves. A lot of the villagers from Brookstone and nearby had come, and it reminded Juliet of Rhys's place in the community. As she'd already seen, the ripples of a death, particularly one of such violence, may have gone unnoticed by most in a large city but were felt by all here.

The church fell quiet as the family and Anwen entered and took their seats at the front. Mira took Lola, their mother sat one side, Juliet put her chair at an angle. Mira had asked her to be ready to interpret if she needed it and despite all her mixed feelings towards her sister, Juliet had, of course, agreed.

The archdeacon smiled at them, and introduced the service in a calm, quiet way that was comforting in its formality. Juliet remembered Rhys, nervous, distracted, preaching about the dilemma of what he should keep private, what he should share. Lies and secrets that can fester in a family, a time of reckoning, the truth...

And now they knew at least part of that truth that her father had shared with Rhys. The truth that Cassie and Harry were Rosalind's parents. But it was not the end. There was a chain of events that seemed inextricably linked, going back from Rhys's death to her father's and then back to Harry's.

Unlike in Juliet's family where burial was the tradition, Rhys was to be cremated. Only close family went to the crematorium. The funeral service had seemed very public but here it was a time to pause, cry, and to mourn the loss of Rhys in private.

Juliet stood with her arms around Mira, who sobbed quietly. Mira's grief seemed real – would she weep like this if she loved someone else, if she'd killed her husband? Anwen stood with her arms crossed, her head bent. For a moment, however brief, Rhys was not a victim, he was a husband, the brother, who they had lost.

* * *

They quietly returned to the house. Her mother had arranged for someone from the church to go ahead to put the kettle on and welcome people. Juliet decided to take a breather outside. The day was dry, although the air and the grass were still damp from the rain the previous day.

Juliet could see Gabriel standing alone in the garden while Maddie was busy talking to her mother. It was awkward, how was she meant to talk to Gabriel? There had been the horrendous meal out and now what she knew about him and Mira. She noticed they seemed to be keeping well away from each other today.

It was Gabriel who took the initiative, and he came over to her.

'Can we talk?' he asked.

Not wanting anyone to overhear their conversation, Juliet ushered him into the workshop.

Gabriel continued. 'I wanted to apologise about Saturday, I was annoyed, but I shouldn't have left you in Southampton. I should have understood how concerned you were about Rosalind.'

She found it hard to speak to him, all she could think of was him and Mira.

'You're right, I was worried about her, but it was good I stayed on my own. We got some things sorted out. All is good between us now.'

'I'm glad.' He frowned. 'By the way, could you have a word with your mum? She's been talking to Maddie and putting pressure on her to form some kind of relationship with Rosalind, I don't think it can be forced, you know.'

Juliet blinked. 'It doesn't sound the kind of thing my mum

would do, but I'll speak to her. Is that all, or was there anything else?'

He looked surprised. 'Have I said something wrong?'

'It's not your words that have upset me.'

'Then what is it?'

The words fell out before she could stop them. 'I saw you with Mira, late Saturday night.'

He blinked quickly. 'You were there? What the hell were you doing out there at that time of night?'

'I heard Mira get out of bed and followed her.'

'Good God, Juliet, what has got into you?'

'You haven't answered my question.'

'And I'm not going to. Talk to Mira if you want to know the truth.'

He stormed off and she saw him talk to Maddie, who frowned and then looked over at her accusingly.

Juliet felt close to tears. Was she really going mad? This wasn't her – snooping around, following people, but what else was she to do if no one would talk to her? And, in any case, her instincts had proved her right.

She couldn't face leaving the workshop and so she backed away from the door, stood with her eyes closed and tried to figure out what she was going to do next. Suddenly it was as if she was back down the beach that night, one minute alone, the next aware of someone behind her. It was the same breath, the same smell.

She started to shake, frightened to move.

'You've been following me, haven't you, and talking to Jean about me,' a voice hissed behind her.

Juliet swung around and saw Anwen.

'It was you... it was you who pushed me, wasn't it?' Her voice shook as she spoke.

Anwen laughed. 'You guessed.'

'The frankincense. I'd forgotten, Mum said Cassie gave it you for your hands.'

'It's good, but its stinks, doesn't it?' She looked more closely at Juliet. 'I don't get you. What motivates you? You are prepared to alienate your family, everyone closest to you. What's it all about?'

'I suppose it started with Dad in the hospital, and then Rhys died and all I seemed to have were unanswered questions. I can't live like that. I need to know the truth.'

Anwen shrugged. 'You're a fool to be obsessed with the truth. No one cares about that any more. We all tell the truth if it suits, lie if it doesn't. That's all there is to it.' She sounded harsh, bitter, her eyes dull with the hurt of a life foreign to Juliet.

'I couldn't live believing that,' she replied and then said more gently, 'Your husband looked very unwell.'

'He died last night.' Anwen sighed. 'I know people like Rhys thought he was a waste of space, but he was in the wrong place at the wrong time. I loved him, he's the only person who ever understood me.'

'I'm so sorry, Anwen.'

'Thank you. I thought I'd tell you; I'm leaving the island.'

'Leaving? But what about the restaurant?'

'I've talked to Cassie; I'm pulling out. I've been thinking about it, and the island isn't the right place for me. It's too small. I loved it all when I first came and of course I needed to see Euan. But I've had enough of it now. I need a city; everyone here is watching you all the time. They seem so nice and pleasant, but you never know what they really think, do you.'

Juliet blinked. 'When are you leaving?'

'As soon as I can. I have a few jobs to do first.' Anwen stepped closer to her, her voice quieter but hard, 'Now, for the rest of my time here, I expect you to keep your nose out of my business. Jean told me about your conversation, all those questions about what I was doing the night Rhys died, well, you know now I was with Euan, that's it, no more.' Anwen was prodding her, her finger digging in the flesh of her chest.

Juliet felt a rage inside her. How dare this woman creep up on her, hurt her and now threaten her like this? She grabbed at Anwen's hand, pushed her away. 'I won't be bullied by you. I know you went to Euan, but I also know you weren't with him all night. I don't know how you kept that from the police, but I know it's true. So, where were you? The fact you are threatening me makes me realise that you are desperate – what are you hiding, Anwen?'

Anwen glared at her. 'You have no idea what you are messing with here. You are so innocent, there is a world out there you know nothing about. It's dark, violent and you have no idea how ugly desperate people can get. Watch your back. You think you are some saint on a crusade? Remember what happened to Rhys – saints rarely have a happy ending.'

Anwen turned and left the workshop. Juliet heard a man speak to her, looked out and saw Gabriel holding Anwen's arm, apologising for bumping into her.

Juliet shut the door of the workshop, went to the chair and breathed deeply, her whole body shaking. Good God, what had just happened? This was a family funeral and yet she'd had a row with Gabriel and had been threatened by Anwen. She closed her eyes, took deep breaths; she'd never understood that fear was so tangible, she could smell it in the air, feel it jabbing at her flesh.

Slowly she opened her eyes, looked far into the distance. The sea was greyer today, the colour of the sky, but in a way, this felt more like her sea than the blue sparkling sea of the summer. That was the sea of holidaymakers. The grey, cold sea remained when they left, and it was then she could walk alone along the beach, it was then she could hear the sea talk to her. Today it comforted her, its dullness, sameness, a wonderful contrast to the chaos around her.

She lowered her gaze to the end of the garden and saw Mira with Lola on a garden seat. She knew then she couldn't put this off any longer, she needed to talk to Mira.

30

Juliet walked down to Mira. She looked tired but content. Lola had jumped up next to her and Mira was stroking her silky ears.

'How did you find the day?' Juliet asked, sitting down.

'It went well, didn't it? The archdeacon led the service well. I think it was good for the villagers to have a chance to say goodbye to Rhys. It's easy to forget how many people are affected by his death. It was such a shock for some of his more vulnerable parishioners, they saw him as the strong one, the person they could always turn to.'

'Yes, I suppose it did.' Juliet took a breath. 'Gabriel and Maddie came then.'

'Yes, Maddie attended church regularly. She was brought up Catholic, but she said she was happy enough to come to our church. She liked Rhys and really appreciated the fact he always supported her around the anniversary of Harry's death.'

'And Gabriel? What did he think of Rhys?'

Mira shrugged. 'He wasn't a churchgoer, so he didn't know him well.'

'But he knew what you told him about Rhys?'

Mira pulled her head back. 'Well, yes I suppose. What are you getting at, Juliet?'

Juliet had no option but to blurt it out. 'I saw you and Gabriel the other night.'

'Me and Gabriel. Where?'

'Down in the car park.'

'How on earth did you see us, it was about two in the morning?'

'I know, I saw you get out of bed, so I followed you.'

'Well, why didn't you just ask me?'

'Would you have told me the truth?'

'Of course, you are one of the few people I would have told.'

Juliet waited, steadied herself to hear about Mira's feelings for Gabriel.

'How long has it been going on then?'

Mira frowned. 'Hang on, do you think we are together?'

'He had his arms around you. You were meeting secretly.'

'Oh gosh, I suppose it must have looked like that to you. I'm sorry, it's nothing like that.' Mira's face suddenly changed, she screwed up her eyes. 'That's an awful thing to think Juliet, what has happened to you? First you accuse me of murdering my husband, now of having an affair with Gabriel. Who do you think I am?'

'But, Mira, you talked so much about guilt. I thought maybe something had happened with Gabriel when you were up there for the retreat.'

With her chin on her chest, Mira looked sideways at Juliet. 'I made a terrible mistake...

There was a man who came on the retreat. He was single, and we just clicked straight away. He is Deaf as well, he signed, it was so easy...'

'And things at home with Rhys were hard?'

Mira's eyes met hers. 'They were. I know it's no excuse, but it wasn't until I met this man, found myself laughing, having fun, that

I realised how much I'd missed it, you know, just relaxing, not taking everything so seriously. We drank wine, walked on the beach, had barbeques in the evenings. It was like being on a wonderful holiday away from my life.'

'How far did the relationship go?'

'We didn't sleep together, if that's what you're asking. He came to see me the night before Rhys died in the hit-and-run. We met on the beach, he wanted me to go and live with him. I'd had time to think and knew it wasn't something I wanted. I was also pretty sure I was pregnant. I told him not to contact me again.'

Juliet thought of the bruises. 'Did he hit you?'

'No, no one hit me, he went a bit crazy, told me he loved me and if I didn't go with him, he would walk into the sea and never come back. I thought he was bluffing, but then he went in, he kept walking and so in the end I ended up running in after him, shouting at him. He turned around, I think he was coming back and then I fell, there was this flipping huge rock below the surface and I bashed my arm. He helped me out in the end, apologised. I think he felt a bit stupid, but I was pretty cold and cross. He left soon after, and I made my way home.'

'Good grief, he left you like that? He could have at least seen you home.'

'I knew Rhys was in, it was better I went on my own. Fortunately, I didn't meet anyone on the way.'

'So, what did Rhys say?'

'It was a nightmare. He took one look at me and asked me where I'd been. I told him I'd seen a friend and fallen in the sea. Bit stupid really and, of course, he got really angry, that's when he threw the wedding photo. He said he knew I'd been seeing someone else; he knew, he said, because I'd been looking so happy.'

Juliet's eyes widened. 'He said that?'

'Yes, and I told him I had made friends with someone on the

retreat, I'd not slept with them, but it had made a nice change to have fun. I'm afraid I wasn't very apologetic. He asked me what the name of this man was, and where he lived, and I said it was none of his business. I also told him if he didn't start treating me better, I would leave him. I thought I might be pregnant and the last thing I wanted was to bring up my baby in a miserable marriage.'

'And what did Rhys say?'

'He went on about marriage vows and things, but he calmed down, said we needed to talk again. But we never had the chance the next day and then it was the meal. I really would have liked to have sorted things out with him; he wasn't a bad man, I loved him. I should have told him ages ago how unhappy I was.'

'But he should have realised, he should have taken better care of you. So, tell me, how does Gabriel fit into all this?'

'He has been a really good friend. I got to know him a bit on this retreat. He saw what was happening and was very understanding; I could talk to him. He knew about this man coming down to see me again, and even offered to be there. I told him about being pregnant, and how frightened I was. He was so understanding.'

'If he was just a friend, why all the secret meetings?'

'You know how life works in a village. If we met during the day, someone would see and then the rumours would start. "I saw Mira on her own on the beach chatting to Gabriel. Do you think there's anything between them? I mean Rhys has only just died; it doesn't seem right, does it?"'

Juliet gave a flicker of a smile. 'Okay, yes, I can see how it would be difficult.'

'I needed to talk to someone Juliet, I was going mad.'

'Why didn't you talk to me? You could have told me about this man from the retreat, I wouldn't have judged you, you know that.'

'I didn't want to burden you with all that. And, anyway, with everything our family has been through, it was easier to talk to an outsider, it helped me clear my head.'

'So, have you decided what to do next? Will you contact this man from the retreat?'

'Oh no, that was just a summer fling, that's finished.'

'Well, you're not on your own, you know. Promise me you will let me help you now.'

Mira smiled, signed, 'Thank you,' and then she smiled again. 'Everything has been so awful, I've not had any of the excitement of being pregnant, but I am determined to now that I know things are all right with the scan.'

Juliet gave her a big hug. 'I agree, it's wonderful news and you are going to be a fantastic mother.'

'And what about you and Gabriel?' asked Mira. 'Don't fall out over this, will you?'

'We've a few things to sort out, let's just see how this goes.'

Seeing everyone from the wake had left, Juliet went back inside to her room.

She was incredibly relieved to have cleared things up with Mira and know that nothing had been going on between her and Gabriel. Maybe recent events had been making her paranoid, but she was just glad to be proved wrong. It did make her understand how unhappy Mira must have been, and she felt guilty she'd completely missed that. But she didn't think now that Mira had been so desperate as to have wanted to kill Rhys.

At that moment, her mother came in.

'Could you do me a favour? The people who left their car at Dad's garage have contacted me; they are not going to be back for a while yet, they are extending their stay. I thought I'd drop their keys through the letter box so they can get it when they need. I won't have to think about it then. Could you go up to the garage and pick up their keys please, maybe drive the car out the front for them to collect when they want. I know they don't want it sat outside their house, don't want to attract burglars, it'll be safe enough up there though.'

'Of course, I could do with a walk. By the way, Gabriel seemed a bit worried about Maddie, about her feeling pressurised into seeing Rosalind.'

Her mother let out an exasperated sigh. 'For goodness' sake. I don't understand that woman. I only talked to her at the funeral. I think Mira being pregnant made me feel a bit guilty about all the years Maddie has had to be such a distant relation. Anyway, I asked her how she wanted to play things now, and whether she would like some kind of family get-together or something.'

'And what did she say?'

'I was very surprised. She told me Gabriel had told her about Cassie telling Rosalind, but she didn't want anything to change. She asked me to tell Rosalind that they could carry on as they had done before.'

'Goodness, I know Gabriel said he thought she'd want to stand back a bit, I didn't realise she'd not want anything to change.'

'I think she was just overwhelmed with it all. Of course, there is the vineyard's annual harvest barbecue on Sunday and I wanted to know what Maddie expected of Rosalind at that.'

'Gosh, it's on Sunday. I'd not realised. What will we do, are we expected to go?'

'Maddie made it very clear we were all invited, but she said nothing had to be any different. She expects Rosalind to come, and, in her words, there is no reason they shouldn't be perfectly friendly to each other.'

'How weird.'

'Maybe it's just all too much to take in. Anyway, I will have to have a chat with Rosalind about it all, I don't know what her expectation is.' Her mother sighed. 'Life is very complicated lately isn't it.'

'It is. Have you talked to Rosalind any more about this man over in Southampton?'

'There has not been much chance, and she had a long chat with Cassie...' She paused.

'I suppose it's difficult knowing how to approach some things.'

Her mother didn't answer but Juliet could feel her holding things in.

'Your relationship with Rosalind is bound to change now,' prompted Juliet.

Her mother let out a long breath. 'Exactly. All along I'd been thinking how hard it was going to be for Cassie and Rosalind when everything came out but, and I know I have no right to say this, but, well, I feel like I've lost Rosalind in some ways. Her and Cassie are suddenly so close, and I am left outside of it all. When Rosalind told us about this man, I realised a few weeks ago I'd have been able to speak, well, as her mum. Now, I daren't be angry, or say how upset I am, and I am you know. To think of my daughter, well my Rosalind, taking up with a married man, letting him buy her things... How could she? And his poor wife and children, it's awful. I don't know what your father would have said.'

Juliet saw the grief and turmoil on her mother's face. 'You are bound to have mixed feelings about all sorts of things, but you will have to step back for a bit. As for Rosalind and this man, well, it was a horrible mess. She did love him, and he lied to her, made all kinds of promises.'

'Oh, I know, I'm not completely heartless, I just feel I can't speak about anything.'

'Give it time Mum, things will settle down.' Juliet gave her mother a hug and said, 'Try not to worry. Now, how about I pop to the garage, at least we can sort the car out.'

Juliet found her bag and then walked up to the garage, past the turn-off for the vineyard. She had no intention of going in to see Gabriel but just as she was to walk on by, Maddie came driving out.

'Juliet, I'm glad I caught you,' Maddie shouted through the window.

Juliet went over to the car rather hesitantly, wondering if she was about to get reprimanded by Maddie for upsetting her son or lectured about Rosalind.

However, Maddie was all smiles. 'With everything that happened today I forgot that I wanted to invite your family to come over to the vineyard this Saturday. I am sixty and want to have a small get-together of friends. I would love you all to come, about three in the afternoon.'

'Thank you, that sounds lovely.'

Maddie maintained a fixed smile. 'I know me and your mum had a few words today, but I really think of you all as my dearest friends and hope you all, including Rosalind, will come.'

'Thank you, I will pass on the message,' said Juliet.

'Right, I shall look forward to seeing you all on Saturday and of course I will expect you all at the barbeque on Sunday, we shall see a lot of each other this weekend shan't we.'

'It certainly appears so,' said Juliet, wondering how on earth she was going to cope with seeing so much of Gabriel.

As if reading her mind, Maddie said, 'And that silly tiff between you and Gabriel, you must put that all behind you. Life is too short. So, *au revoir* for now and I look forward to seeing you all soon.' With that, Maddie drove away.

Juliet carried on up to the garage and went inside. The little blue car was still waiting patiently. She went straight to her father's 'office'. However, she saw immediately there were no keys hanging up at all. She looked around, but she couldn't see them anywhere. That was odd, she could have sworn they'd been there before. She phoned her mother, who seemed less anxious than her and accepted that they had 'just got lost'. She told Juliet not to worry, and that she would put a note through the owners' letter box explaining and, hopefully, they had a spare.

Juliet looked around the garage sadly. The workshop was darker today, autumn was creeping in. She went over to her father's desk and remembered she had to empty the bins and sort things out soon. Glancing down, she saw the envelope she'd seen before and picked it out of the bin. On the envelope in neat cursive writing was 'ignition key for VW' and in the corner the numbers 1-9-9-5. There was also a small green cloth poking out.

Her heart was racing; the ignition key used in Harry's accident must have been kept with this cloth in this envelope. That was odd, she'd assumed her father had found it buried away and yet the envelope looked very clean, uncreased. It looked much more like something that had been carefully tucked away.

She looked again at the envelope; there was no way that was her father's scrawl, but she could have sworn she knew that hand-writing with its fancy loops... and then she remembered. Gabriel's handwriting had looked exactly the same. Gabriel had written on this envelope. That could mean Gabriel had handled this key and yet when she'd talked to him about it, he'd acted like he knew nothing.

Juliet looked around the garage and then over on the shelf. She saw a box of drinking chocolate, went and picked it up, examined it. This was a new box, the packing date was this year, and she knew who brought her father posh chocolate like this every birthday, it was Gabriel. She was sure then that Gabriel had brought this to her father on his birthday this year, the day of his accident. He had seen her father and yet he'd denied it. Had he also brought the old key that day?

The big question of course was why he'd had the old ignition key to the car that killed Harry. Her mind raced on. Was it possible Gabriel had anything to do with his brother's death? But why would he?

She tried to remember the times Gabriel had talked about Harry. What had their relationship really been like? When he'd talked about Harry being a bit of a bully he'd hesitated, was there more? Was it possible Gabriel really hated his brother and had killed him? Had he confessed to her father when he'd brought the old key? Had he said her father couldn't tell Rosalind about Harry because it would start people talking again about Harry's death?

Juliet sighed. She was so confused. All she knew was she had to talk to Gabriel. Maybe she'd have a chance to find out more about the night Harry died, find out if Gabriel could have actually gone out. Hadn't Ed said something about Gabriel being wet?

But the last time she'd seen Gabriel she'd accused him of having an affair with Mira. She had got that completely wrong. Was she going off again in the wrong direction?

Well, she would see Gabriel at the party at the vineyard. It was going to be a difficult conversation. On the one hand she wondered if she needed to give him a grovelling apology for the accusation about him and Mira, but on the other she was going to have to be brave enough to ask him about his visit to her father and the business with the old key. He had to explain why he had kept so much from her.

She put the envelope and cloth in her bag and then shut up the garage. Juliet frowned; she wasn't looking forward to the next day.

31

At quarter to three on the Saturday afternoon of Maddie's party, all
the sisters and their mother decided to walk together to the vineyard. The day had started with a heavy fog that still hadn't
completely lifted and the air, particularly when they walked along
the military road close to the sea, felt damp with sea mist.

Juliet and her mother walked a few paces behind the others.

'I managed to speak to Rosalind about Maddie,' her mother
said.

'Oh? How did she take it?'

'She was okay, she was quite glad to be honest, certainly for the
time being. However, I have been thinking about Maddie. I shall
gently encourage her to think about Rosalind a bit more. I am sure
she's got so used to not being able to be involved that she might
need some time to get used to things being in the open.' Her
mother patted her pocket. 'I have brought her some lovely photos of
Rosalind in the dress she gave her; it will be a good memory for
her.'

They were approaching the house, and Juliet started to feel

nervous. How would Gabriel be with her and how was he going to take being asked more questions?

Maddie was dressed smartly as ever in a rust-coloured suit and pearls. She greeted them with a smile saying, 'How lovely to see you all. Please, ladies, if you would like to put handbags over there, feel free. They can be such a nuisance, can't they? Right, do come in.'

They followed Maddie into the main living room where the tea was being held. This was certainly more than the 'small get together' Juliet had envisaged. There were large bunches of autumn flowers and leaves in enormous vases and a buffet of sandwiches, pastries, some delicious lavender scones, which reminded Juliet of her romantic meal with Gabriel. The centrepiece was a beautiful gateau for the birthday cake.

There were a few other people from the village there already, and once the first person had gone to collect food, everyone else tucked in. Juliet could see Gabriel chatting to Cassie quite intensely. He didn't come over to greet her.

Juliet saw Barbara and her son Ed talking to her mother and decided it might be a good chance to try and casually find out a little more about the night Harry died. She went over and said hello. There was never any problem getting Barbara to chat but steering her in the right direction might be harder.

Juliet eventually managed to slip in, 'Nice to see you again Ed.' She looked around at their mothers. 'We were chatting in the pub the other day about things that happened years ago and in particular about that night the old oak tree in our garden was struck by lightning. What a day that was.'

Her mother looked slightly thrown by what appeared to be a random subject change but said, 'Um, yes.'

Juliet turned to Ed. 'You were saying that even though it was years ago you remember that and all kinds of smaller things because of the tragic thing that happened to Harry.' She smiled.

'You were saying you remember being round here playing Game Boys, was it?'

But Barbara answered first. 'They could play with those things for hours! Did your girls have them Helena?'

Juliet was worried the conversation could get hijacked but fortunately a person close by grabbed her mother's arm and started talking to her.

Juliet quickly turned to Ed again. 'The weather was so bad that night. Did you say Gabriel went out?'

'He'd been out before I arrived, yes. He was soaking!'

'And you'd come from the church?'

'Yes, he always went in those days,' interrupted Barbara. 'He'd been confirmed and everything. The vicar then was glad of a youngster to help out. You even helped lead those Bible study groups, didn't you?'

'I did! I was telling Juliet I remember going from there to Gabriel's about eight. It wasn't only Gabriel who got soaked that night.'

'Did he have to keep going in and out to check on the vineyards?' asked Juliet.

Ed paused. 'No, he didn't go out again. I remember Maddie saying to stay in, she didn't want him among the vines in the storm.'

'So, you and Gabriel were together all the time Harry was out running?' She waited, knowing there was nothing subtle now about her questioning.

Ed scratched his head. She was expecting impatience, but he screwed up his eyes in concentration. 'Oh yes. Funny, I remember now. When Harry left, Gabriel said, "Hang on I'll go and nick Harry's new Nirvana tapes," and we listened to them on his cassette player. I'm embarrassed to say we played "air guitar"; we had it on so loud, it was a bit embarrassing when Maddie came in with food for us, but she just laughed and let us carry on. Eventually Mum came for me and then of course the police arrived.' He paused and then asked, 'Why are you so interested in that evening?'

Juliet shrugged. 'Just wondered, so Maddie was in and out?'

'She was around, cooking in the kitchen. It was always the same there.'

She turned to Barbara. 'Were you there long before the police came?' Juliet asked, trying sound casual. She was waiting for Barbara to ask her why she needed to know all this, but, like Ed, Barbara seemed happy to carry on.

'Now, let me think, I wouldn't have normally worried about picking Ed up, but the weather was so bad, and I was coming off a late shift from the nursing home I worked in then, so I think it was about half past eleven. I know the police came soon after.'

'It's so sad isn't it, and to think the very next day Harry was meant to be going to France to start a new life. Mind you, like you say, it was odd him going out training that night in the rain if he was intending to leave the next day.'

'I really don't know—'

At that moment Gabriel came over. 'This conversation looks a little intense!'

'Juliet is asking me about why Harry was training for a marathon if he was going to France.'

Gabriel smiled tightly. 'What a strange thing to be talking about.'

Juliet shrugged. 'It was nothing.' She looked around. 'This is all very exciting; I was expecting a cup of tea and a biscuit.'

Gabriel laughed. 'That would not be good enough for Maddie. Now, please come and have something to eat, there is so much food.'

Juliet looked over to the buffet table where Maddie was talking warmly to Mira. She couldn't sign but she spoke clearly and faced Mira.

'Do eat up, we have so much food; these prawns are so fresh.'

'I'm sorry, I can't eat any seafood. It's a shame because I love it,' said Mira.

'I can't eat crab, but I can eat prawns, isn't that odd? It's like I can eat most herbs and spices but not paprika or mustard, won't have them in the house. But still there are lots of things here you can eat, and you must, Mira. I know what it's like to lose your husband, but you have to pick yourself up. You are young, you have your whole life in front of you. I look out at the vineyard and am so proud of what I've done here.'

Mira smiled. 'You should be. It looks set to be a bumper harvest.'

Juliet saw them walk over to the window, and Maddie was telling Mira about the growing of the vines in detail. Juliet then saw Gabriel go over to them.

'Maddie, this is your birthday, enough of work.' He laughed, putting his arm around her. 'Come on, time for your cake I think.'

Before the candles were lit, Maddie said, 'Thank you so much for coming everyone, and thank you, my wonderful son Gabriel, for organising this party. I am forever grateful for everything you do. Of course, tomorrow night is the biggest event in our calendar. It is our harvest barbeque. Gabriel and I would love to invite you and everyone from the village. It is a wonderful opportunity to thank everyone who works so hard and share our good fortune with you all. I am looking forward to seeing you all there.'

The candles were lit on the enormous chocolate gateau and everyone started to sing happy birthday.

Juliet watched Gabriel and Maddie smiling at each other, both so proud of one another and everything they had achieved. They were celebrating years of hard work. Her mind went back to Harry and Gabriel's protests about him leaving. Didn't Cassie say the land had been left to him? Yes, Gabriel had said he was going to sell his share. Of course, if he'd stayed, it might have been a very different story.

Her eye caught Gabriel looking over at her. His face was serious, it was as if he was trying to read her mind.

She was aware of the envelope, the questions about his visit and suddenly she felt overwhelmed by it all. Could she really face another confrontation?

Juliet went and picked out her bag from the small pile and then backed away to leave, walking quickly out of the house. The sea mist hung heavy over the vines. It looked very different to when she'd stood here the morning after the meal. She remembered having visions of the South of France, the scent of lavender and geranium heavy in the air, no idea that Rhys was lying dead at the church. It seemed an innocent time from long ago.

'Something up?'

Gabriel's voice startled her as he came up behind her.

'No, nothing,' she said quickly.

'I think there is. What's going on?' said Gabriel.

She swallowed and stepped back. 'Look, first I should apologise. I spoke to Mira.'

She saw his shoulders relax.

'I got it all wrong, and I think you have been a good friend to her, so thank you.'

Wrongfooted, he smiled shyly. 'It was nothing. I like Mira and I know she's going through a hard time, but you shouldn't have leaped to that conclusion. It's not flattering, you know, the habit you have of thinking the worst of people.'

'I don't think I exactly do that,' she mumbled.

She saw Gabriel's shoulders hunch up, his face harden. 'Why were you asking about Harry going to France?' His voice was quiet but cold.

'I don't know. I remembered Barbara saying about Harry training that night, it seemed odd if he was leaving.'

'But he was definitely going. I've told you that already.'

'But you've not told me everything, have you? I went to Dad's garage and saw the chocolate I think you took him on his birthday.'

He went to speak but stood with his mouth open long enough for her to know she was right.

'Why didn't you tell me you went to see him?'

'I don't know, I didn't want to upset you.'

'Why would it do that? You know how worried I am about his state of mind that day, you could have told me how he was.' She pulled the envelope and cloth from her bag. 'I also found these. I think that the old car key that was used in Harry's accident, the one my dad found, was in this envelope and I am pretty sure this is your handwriting.'

He scowled. 'What are you implying?'

'I don't know. I just want you to be honest with me.'

He stepped closer to her. 'What is really going on in your head? What are you conjuring up now? First I was having an affair with your sister, now what?'

'Things don't add up,' she stammered.

'I've had enough of all this. I will explain everything, follow me.'

He took her hand rather roughly and walked quickly into the house, up the stairs, the noise from the guests a white noise in the background. They went into his bedroom and he slammed the door. His room was much plainer, neater, and more functional than Maddie's, but there were similar photos on his walls of the vineyards in France, as well as books on management and accountancy. On the windowsill, a bowl of shells and stones from the beach. He opened a drawer in a large chest and took out a box that he put on the bed.

'Right, proof that Harry was going away. Exhibit A.' He took out a hand written letter from Zac, the secretary of the running club.

Juliet read.

21 August 1995

> *Dear Harry,*
>
> *Thank you for your call last evening. I hadn't realised you were going to France so soon. You will be a huge loss to us at the club and the running community here on the Island. I do hope you carry on running in France. I wish you all the best. Do let us know when you are popping home and we will organise a proper goodbye at the club.*
>
> *I know this letter will arrive after you've gone, but I am sure Maddie will post it onto you.*
>
> *Wishing you all the best,*
>
> *Zac*

She re-read it. The line which said, 'after you've gone' disturbed her, but then she got distracted by the stamp on the envelope. It was one of the less interesting ones, the 'boring grey' one her father had tried to persuade her was special. Her mind went to the years of sitting with her dad, looking through his stamps and collections and that nagging sense of loss that never left her, took a grip of her heart.

She was blinking back tears when Gabriel interrupted her thoughts, 'You see? It proves he was going.'

Brought back to the present, she coughed and then glanced again at the date on the letter. 'Of course, yes. But it says here Harry rang Zac the evening before, on the twentieth. That was a bit late wasn't it, if he was going off the next morning?'

'You didn't know Harry. I think he'd been putting off telling them his final plans.'

Juliet put the letter away, and after he'd returned it to the draw Gabriel took out another envelope, a passport and a ticket to Paris dated 21 August.

'But Barbara thinks it was odd him going out training if he was planning to leave the next day.'

'Look, Harry was unpredictable. Maybe he just needed to run off a bad temper, I don't know.' Then he added in a gentler voice, 'I'm sorry for Cassie, but he was all ready to go.'

Juliet opened the passport, saw the picture of Harry, and then handed it back. 'Okay, so he was going, but why all the cover-up about seeing Dad at the garage?'

Gabriel bit his lip. 'I didn't want to tell you, it's difficult.'

'Why?' she demanded.

'Because, you see, a week after Harry died, I went to the garage. The police had shut the place off, and we were allowed back in from the Saturday. Your dad said he'd go back on the Monday, and I thought I'd go and see if I could do some clearing up before he arrived. When I got there, I found the ignition key on the floor in this bit of cloth by the luggage labels. Clearly it was meant to look like it had been there all the time.'

'But why would whoever hit Harry return it?'

'Panic maybe? My guess is the person who did the hit-and-run took the ignition key out of the car and ran off. All I can think is the person froze for a few days, not knowing what to do, then panicked, particularly when the police put out they were looking for the key. Perhaps the driver thought the most innocent place for it to be found was the garage, make it look like it had never been used. I think they also used a cloth, maybe to hide fingerprints, who knows? The person who did this can't have been thinking straight.'

'So, you worked all this out; why didn't you give it to the police?'

Gabriel coughed nervously. 'Because I realised a few things. The break in had happened at the front of the garage. That door was boarded up by the police. So, this key must have been returned without breaking in, by someone with a door key to the old back door...'

Juliet nodded thoughtfully. 'So, it had to be someone with access to the garage?'

'Exactly. I'd seen the state Cassie had been in when I told her about Harry going to France, I was scared she'd done something stupid... The cloth, recognise it?'

Juliet looked at it again and she felt sick. Yes, she knew what it was.

'It's a cloth used for cleaning a violin, isn't it,' said Gabriel quietly.

She sighed. 'So, you suspected Cassie, but you didn't tell anyone?'

'I didn't want to. Look, if Cassie had anything to do with Harry's death, I didn't think she should go to prison, he'd treated her so badly. Also, well, I couldn't be sure it was her, could I? Your parents hated Harry I know that, and your dad had been so good to me.'

Juliet was stunned. 'So, you kept the old key to save them?'

'I did. I was going to throw it away but that didn't seem right, so I put it in an envelope to keep it safe. Just in case.'

'So why did you show it to Dad the day of his birthday, you must have known how upset he would be?'

'I'd seen him a few days before and he'd told me they were planning to tell Rosalind about Cassie and Harry on her birthday. When he said that I thought that, although he'd probably not had anything to do with Harry's death, he ought to know about other possibilities, and know what he was raking up. I didn't expect him to get so distressed.'

Juliet sat very still. 'How have you lived with my family, thinking one of them could have killed your brother?'

'It was difficult, but I believe I made the right decision not telling anyone what I'd found. He was my brother and for all we were so different, I loved him very much. However, I knew Harry had treated Cassie badly. I was sure if she had harmed him, it had been done in the heat of the moment and was something she would have deeply regretted. Going to prison would have destroyed not only her life but all your family. What life would it have been for Rosalind knowing her mother was in prison for killing her father? And your mum, you sisters, your whole lives would have been blighted by this. And then of course I had to think of your father. It would have destroyed him. I couldn't do that to him. It's so easy to forget how grateful I was to him back then. For a time, he was the only person I felt I could relate to. I felt a failure because I was nothing like Dad or Harry. Your father made me realise I had different strengths. He was always so positive and encouraging, I owed him a lot and there was no way I could destroy him. In any case, I feel for Cassie, who I know to be a good person at heart, spending her life trying to live with what she'd done, that has been punishment enough.'

Juliet picked at the duvet cover. 'I don't know what to do. How can I carry on, knowing my sister has done such a thing?'

'I told you, she has been punished enough. We have to protect her.' She looked up, saw deep passion, remembered he'd told her he had strong feelings for Cassie when he was younger. Maybe he still did.

'It's finished. Leave it Juliet.'

She didn't reply but she knew that even if she could try and forget what Cassie had done to Harry, that hadn't been the end, had it? Had Cassie also killed Rhys? Her father had said, *'if they have killed once they can kill again.'* Is that what had happened? If so, surely Cassie was a very dangerous person.

She stood up. 'I need to go.' She paused. 'I don't know if I even need to say this but, well, me and you, it's not going to work, is it?'

He stood up as well, smiled. 'This doesn't have to be the end. All of these things are nothing to do with me and you.'

Juliet shook her head. 'No. Even without them me and you wouldn't work. This vineyard is your life but not mine. I'm the wrong piece of the puzzle.'

'Do you want to go travelling again, is that it? Is it living on the island that makes you feel hemmed in?'

'No, that's not it. The island's not a prison.'

'But you think life with me would be just that, like being locked up in a miserable cell.'

'Of course not, but it wouldn't be a happy place for either of us.'

He nodded sadly. 'I understand, but you will come tomorrow to the barbecue, won't you? Maddie would be so disappointed if you don't.'

'Of course,' replied Juliet.

She turned and left the room; she had to get away now. Putting on a smile, she went down and looked for Maddie. She was talking in a very animated way to Mira. Juliet rushed over, wished Maddie a happy birthday, told her she would see her the next day and then, without any further explanation, she left the house.

She walked back through the vineyard, down the long winding lane onto the main road. Juliet crossed the road and instead of walking along the roadside she went into Compton Bay car park. From here she could see the tide was well out and so she clambered down the steep steps onto the beach. The beach stretched a long way to her right, but she turned left, heading towards Brook.

The mist was still there, and it dampened down any sound. Even the seagulls' cries were softened. There were a few dog walkers, but no one else. The light grey-blue sea merged with the sky, the air, the breeze, the wet sand crunching beneath her feet. The long hot summer had ended. She walked fast, hard, trying to outrun the demons chasing her, but the cold hard facts about her sister kept catching up, kept reaching out to her.

She turned the corner into Brook bay, and stayed down there until finally, exhausted from the furious pace she'd been walking at, she climbed up the path and made her way home.

Juliet pushed open the gate and was about to run into the house when she saw a light on in the workshop. She ran over, looked through the window. She hadn't thought the day could get any darker, but it looked like it had saved the worst till last.

32

Juliet opened the door of the workshop, but her mother was so engrossed she didn't hear her come in.

Rain was hitting the window now like tiny pebbles.

'What are you doing, Mum?' Juliet asked, raising her voice against the beating rain.

Her mother jumped up, startled, the gold glistening in her hand. 'Oh, you shouldn't creep up on people like that.'

'Mum, what's that in your hand?'

Her mother slowly uncurled her fingers.

'It's Rhys's crucifix, isn't it?' said Juliet quietly.

'I just found it down the side of the chair. I thought it could do with a clean. I've not been out here for ages; it must have been here all the time. Like the police said, Mira must have imagined Rhys had been wearing it that night.'

'I don't think so. Mum, why were you hiding it here?'

'I wasn't hiding it,' said her mother, but suddenly she sighed, collapsed onto the seat and put her head into her hands. 'I'm so tired.'

Juliet sat down on a stool and tried to speak calmly. 'On his birthday, what reason did Dad give you for not telling Rosalind about Cassie and Harry?'

'I can't remember.'

'I think you can. I've spoken to Gabriel today. He found the ignition key to the car that killed Harry in the garage after Harry's accident.'

Her mother crossed her arms very tightly. 'Did he?'

'Yes, and he told me that he went to see Dad on his birthday this year at the garage. He took the key. Apparently, he knew Dad was going to tell Rosalind about Cassie and Harry and he thought Dad should know that one of our family was implicated in Harry's death. I think Dad knew then he couldn't ever tell Rosalind the truth, and that is what he came home and told you. He was devastated and later went up to the Downs drinking. Am I right?'

Her mother spoke, her voice flat. 'I don't know what you are talking about.'

'Of course you do. I think you suspect someone in this family of killing Harry, and you think Dad told Rhys who it was. That's why you went to see Rhys the night he died.'

'I didn't know any such thing. I admit I went to speak to speak to Rhys, but it was nothing to do with who killed Harry. I went to try and dissuade him from telling Rosalind about her biological parents. I had no intention that night of telling Rosalind about her true parents, it didn't seem the right time at all to me. But I didn't want him telling her either; it would have been completely wrong for her to hear the truth from anyone other than me or Cassie.'

Juliet pulled on a small tuft of hair. 'I don't think I believe you. I am sure you have your suspicions about Harry's death. Come on Mum, who do you think killed Harry?'

The question shot out, blunt, brutal and her mother swallowed hard.

'A stranger, someone from the mainland,' she blurted out, in the way a child might answer too quickly.

'You have never suspected Cassie?'

Her mother stared in horror. 'Of course not. She told you herself she loved Harry, she thought he was going to marry her. In any case, the night Harry died, no one went out.'

'But you were shut away with Rosalind, you have no way of knowing if anyone else went out.'

'But I saw Cassie, she popped in about eleven, and your father was in and out checking on me and Rosalind.'

Juliet didn't answer but slowly shook her head in disbelief.

Her mother didn't try to defend herself, however. Instead, she asked, 'Does Gabriel still have the old key?'

'No, I have it, Mum.'

Her mother grabbed the arms on the chair. 'You have it? Where is it? We have to get rid of it!'

Juliet was startled by her mother's panic. 'I don't think so, Mum.'

'Give it to me this instant,' her mother demanded, her eyes wide with panic.

'Why are you so bothered about this key Mum? If no one here had anything to do with Harry's death, why do you look so upset?'

Her mother shook her head. 'I don't know, I don't want people getting silly ideas.'

Juliet stood up, crossed her arms. 'I'll give it to you if you tell me the truth about the crucifix.'

Her mother looked up at Juliet, her face hard. 'No, I won't be blackmailed like this.'

'But where did you get the crucifix, Mum? Tell me. It couldn't have been down the side of the chair. I searched the chair the other morning after being with Gabriel because I dropped my phone. It wasn't there then. Where did you find it?'

'I don't need to stand here answering silly questions,' said her mother, who then pushed past her and left the workshop.

Juliet picked up the crucifix her mother had left. She suspected her mother had the crucifix either because she'd found it in the house and assumed Cassie had hidden it, or because she herself had killed Rhys.

However, Juliet realised even those weren't the only explanations. Because someone else had been in and out of the house, and that was Anwen. it had to be possible that Harry and Rhys's deaths were not linked, that while Cassie might have killed Harry, Anwen could still have killed Rhys. She had come to the funeral; she could have planted the crucifix then.

Juliet sat down, suddenly exhausted by it all. What was she going to do?

She opened her hand, looked at the crucifix. Well, at least she knew what to do with this.

Juliet went into the house and up to the bedroom, where Mira was sat reading. In contrast to everything that was happening, Mira looked at peace. She gave Juliet a lazy smile.

'Oh, hi. I'm glad you're back.'

Juliet held out the crucifix. Mira reached out very slowly; her fingers trembled as she lightly touched the crucifix as if she was afraid it would burn her.

'It's Rhys's,' Juliet said gently.

Mira suddenly grabbed it, held it tight, buried her face in it and sat shaking and crying. Lola, who had been sitting slightly apart from Mira, moved closer and put her head on Mira's lap. Juliet explained how she had found her mother with the crucifix in the workshop.

'Where did she find it then?' asked Mira.

'She told me she found it down the chair in the workshop, but I don't think it was there.' Juliet gave Mira a knowing look.

Mira shook her head. 'You mustn't suspect Mum, it's impossible.'

'I don't know, I think she may be protecting someone else.' Juliet looked at Mira, hadn't the heart to tell her what she'd been thinking about Cassie.

'No, there will be an innocent explanation.' Mira smiled weakly. 'At least I have it back. Rhys said, this was the most important thing he owned, he said it spoke of forgiveness. Having it back makes me feel like we have forgiven each other. Thank you.'

Juliet wanted to give Mira some space and so left the room. She could hear rain outside now, heavy, beating on the windows. It was then Juliet saw Cassie. She was in her dressing gown, drying her hair. Juliet felt that burning sensation in her hand and gasped. For the first time she realised the significance of that pain, why hadn't she seen it before?

'What's the matter? You look like you've seen a ghost,' said Cassie.

'I think I have, well, a glimpse of the past anyway. Cassie, think back to the night Harry died.'

Cassie groaned. 'Not this again, Juliet. Let it go.'

'No, seriously think about it. You went out.'

'No.'

'You did, don't deny it. I know you did; I saw you up here, your hair and clothes all wet.'

Cassie's eyebrows shot up. 'How on earth do you remember that?'

'That night has been coming back to me in pieces. I remember I saw you and wondered why you were dressed at that time and why your clothes were all wet. Now I realise of course it meant you had been out in the rain.'

Cassie gestured to her bedroom. 'Let's go in there and talk.'

Juliet followed her in and sat on the edge of the bed.

Cassie sighed. 'You're right, I did go out the night Harry died. Harry had told me he was not going to France, but then, later, Gabriel said he was. I was pretty sure he was staying, but I needed reassurance. Harry had mentioned he would be out running about half ten, and so I went out at that time hoping to meet him. Mum had said she would look after Rosalind; we had decided she would be bottle-fed. I was about to go out when you came out of your bedroom crying. I waited until you were with Dad and went downstairs. Then when you were in the kitchen, I crept out of the front door. I'd wrapped up but not expected the rain to be so bad. I went down to the end of the road that leads to the vineyard, but Harry wasn't there. If we'd had mobiles, we might have been able to talk. I waited for a bit, but it was so wet, and I thought I would see him the next day.' Her voice cracked. 'But of course, I didn't.'

'What time did you come home?'

'I don't know, about eleven. I came up and when I saw you, you showed me your hand. You'd burned it on your milk, not much, it was just a bit red. I told you to run it under the tap.'

'That's right. Dad brought me to bed before eleven with my milk. I drifted off to sleep, when I woke, I had a sip of milk but spilt it on my hand. It hurt, so I came out of my room to find Dad, and that's when I saw you.' Juliet grinned. 'The important thing I'd missed was that my milk was still hot. You know how when you go to sleep you lose track of time? I'd always imagined I'd been asleep for hours but of course it can't have been for longer than say five or ten minutes if the milk was still so hot it burned my hand.'

Cassie shook her head. 'I don't see why any of this matters.'

Juliet explained. 'Harry was killed soon after eleven, and now I know you were here, in the house, not out there in the rain.'

'Of course. Hang on, you hadn't imagined I killed Harry, had you? I loved him, Juliet.'

'But if you'd thought he was going away...'

'But I didn't, I never really thought that.'

'Gabriel showed me proof, he showed me tickets, a letter he'd sent to say goodbye to his running coach.'

Cassie's lips started to tremble. 'Gabriel told me about the tickets, but I didn't want to believe him. Look, I'm not that eighteen-year-old, I see now Harry was no angel, in fact he could well have been a terrible husband. When he died though, I felt like part of me had gone with him. What with that, and all the emotional stress of Rosalind, well, to be honest I'm amazed I stayed as sane as I did.'

'Do you know what Mum thought Harry was doing?'

'Not really. I told her he was staying; I have no idea if she believed me. Why?'

'Did you see Mum at all that evening when you got back, did you go in to see Rosalind?'

'Well, no, I went to my own room. Mum knew how tired I was, she said she would do the night on her own.' Cassie paused. 'Why are you asking?' Juliet looked away and Cassie grabbed her arm. 'You don't suspect Mum, do you? That's absurd.'

Juliet frowned. 'Wait a minute.' She went and found the envelope and the cloth and explained to Cassie about the ignition key.

'So, Gabriel found the key and thought I had killed Harry? He's really believed that all this time?'

'Yes, I think he believes it was one of our family and he thought that in your heart you knew Harry was leaving and you couldn't bear it, and so, well, you killed him to stop him leaving you. The cloth to Gabriel was the proof.'

Cassie picked up the cloth. 'It's the kind of cloth you might use to clean a violin or any number of things, but it's not one of mine. I'd never have a green one, you should have realised that.'

Juliet stared. 'Of course. How did I miss that? So, who put the old key back in the garage?'

Cassie shrugged. 'I have no idea. Look, Gabriel was young,

you know how it is at that age, everyone thinks they are Sherlock Holmes. The key could have been there for all kinds of reasons, maybe it was never used, maybe a perfectly innocent person found it and thought the easiest thing was to put it back at the garage, people hate getting involved with the police.'

'I don't know.'

'You have become obsessed with Harry's death, Juliet, but the police will have looked into everything. Mum and Dad aren't killers, and you know now I had nothing to do with it.'

Juliet sighed. 'Why did Dad get so upset about the key then? Why change his mind about telling Rosalind?'

'I think Dad was always conflicted about telling Rosalind, the key just stressed him out further.'

Juliet shrugged. 'Even if that was all true, Rhys's death needs explaining. I know the police think it is someone from off the island, but every time I want to go with that, something new comes up. Tonight, for example, it was the crucifix.'

Juliet watched Cassie closely as she explained about seeing their mother hiding the crucifix.

'You don't think she was telling the truth about it being out there?'

'No, I think Mum was either hiding it because she'd kept it herself or because she'd found it in the house and thought it implicated someone here in Rhys's death.'

Cassie screwed up her eyes. 'It wasn't me, if that's what you're thinking, and of course Mum would never kill anyone.'

'Well, someone brought it to the house, and that someone I guess was Rhys's killer. Even without Harry, there are plenty of motives for killing him. You and Mum wanted to protect Rosalind from the truth about her parents. Rosalind was furious with him and she was out there a very long time.'

Cassie shook her head violently. 'No way, absolutely no way.' She scratched her forehead. 'Okay, I'll admit to something.'

Juliet held her breath.

'I was the person who went out at half twelve the night Rhys died.'

Juliet stared at Cassie – was she at last finding out the truth about who had left the house? She watched Cassie carefully, trying to judge if she was telling the truth. Because, if she was, then her mother had not gone out a second time, and wouldn't that mean she was innocent?

Cassie continued. 'I wanted to talk Rhys, ask him not to tell anyone about me and Harry. Rosalind had to be the first person to be told the truth and me or Mum were the people to do that. Neither of us felt it was the right time. I wasn't up there long, but I did come back just before one. I went over to the workshop, looked through the window and saw Rosalind. She looked up and smiled and waved to me.'

'Rosalind told me she didn't see anyone.'

'She'd either forgotten or she didn't want to say I'd been out.'

Juliet considered this. Of course, Rosalind did say she'd been smoking weed but not for long at that point of the night and surely, she'd have remembered seeing Cassie. No, either Cassie or Rosalind was lying, and her gut instinct was that Cassie was making this up to give Rosalind an alibi.

'Supposing what you say is true,' Juliet said, 'what about the crucifix? Even if Mum had just found it in the house, why was it here?'

Cassie scowled, scratched the back of her hand. Suddenly she looked up, her face bright. 'What about Anwen? Just say she'd killed Rhys. She could have taken the crucifix and then planted it here in the house.'

'Hang on, you suspect Anwen of killing Rhys?'

'Why not? She was your number one suspect from the start, wasn't she?'

'Well yes, but I know she definitely went to the hospital.'

'Oh, are you sure?'

'Yes definitely.' Juliet frowned. 'I'm surprised you're accusing her; you were prepared to lie for her not so long ago.'

'I know. If I'm honest, I think I've always been a bit scared of her. When she got the message after Rosalind's meal here, she told me she had to go out, that she would be gone all night, but that it was private. I was obviously a bit confused, but she said that we both kept secrets for each other, it was the way we worked. She had a point, she knew about Tim and about why I was leaving orchestra, but I didn't really like the way she was using that. Anyway, she sent me a voicemail later, and again there was an edge to it.'

Juliet sat up. 'She sent you a voicemail? What time? Do you still have it?'

Cassie picked up her phone, flicked through. 'Here it is. Half twelve.' Cassie played the message.

'Hi, remember to stick to the story, I was in all night, it's important. I'm depending on you like you depend on me.' The message ended abruptly.

Cassie looked searchingly at Juliet. 'How can you be so sure she went to the hospital?'

'Her aunt told me and then I spoke to the taxi driver, she was picked up from here at half ten and then brought back about six. There is missing time though of maybe about an hour when I don't know what she was doing, but I can't think of any way she'd have got from the hospital to here and back again.'

Cassie screwed up her face. 'Oh, that scuppers it then.'

Juliet, however, was curious. 'Play the message again, make it as loud as you can.'

They listened and then their eyes met; they'd both heard it.

'Who was that? Cassie asked.

'I don't know,' said Juliet, 'but there was definitely a man shouting Anwen's name in the background, which is odd; she was meant to be on her own.'

Cassie played the message again; there were other voices, but the one calling Anwen was by far the loudest.

Juliet felt the excitement grow. 'So, someone could have met her, brought her back here and then taken her back to the hospital. She had all kinds of friends; I reckon she could pay one of them to do this and keep quiet.'

'Yes, she could have,' agreed Cassie.

'We ought to tell the police about this,' said Juliet.

Cassie shivered. 'I don't know—'

'Look, I know how threatening she can be, but we have to do this. If Anwen killed Rhys, then she can't go free, can she?'

Juliet could see Cassie still looked reluctant. 'Send me the message and I will send it onto Adam, it's up to them then what they do with it.'

Cassie did and Juliet forwarded the message to Adam Smith.

'There. That was the right thing to do.'

Cassie smiled. 'Right, that's the end. Harry was killed by a stranger, and Rhys, if anyone we know really killed him, well, it had to be Anwen.'

Juliet sat back. Was that really it? All the suspicion, the anger, had it come to an end?

It clearly suited Cassie to persuade her that neither Harry nor Rhys's deaths were anything to do with the family. And yet, she knew that Cassie had been lying to her. That business about seeing her mother, Juliet didn't believe it was any truer than her story of seeing Rosalind. Cassie's concern seemed to be to provide alibis for her family and herself. If those stories were not true, it left her mother in the frame for Harry's death, and Cassie, Rosalind or

Anwen for Rhys's. On the other hand, it might have nothing to do with any of them.

Juliet closed her eyes. She was so tired, not just of trying to work things out, but of being the outsider in her family. Why not trust the police, accept Harry and Rhys were killed by people on the mainland? If she did that, everything could go back to how it had been. She remembered Rosalind had said the same thing, to turn back the clock as if nothing had happened. She looked down at the old key. Both her parents had said to get rid of it, maybe they were right, throw it away, bury it, make it disappear.

'I need to go and do something,' she said to Cassie, and before Cassie could ask where she was going, she left.

As she walked out of the room, she almost collided with their mother, and for a moment Juliet panicked; how long had her mother been there?

However, she needed to get out and so, without speaking to her mother, she went downstairs. She picked up an old raincoat from the porch, then put the old key and the cloth in her bag and left the house.

As she walked down the road, she felt the rain seep through her trainers and the seams of the old coat. However, she kept walking, oblivious of the cold, the blackness of the sky. She crossed the road and walked through the car park, down the steep, crumbling path to the beach.

The beach was, of course, deserted and the waves were crashing onto the shore as if the island was angry and hurt. There was no comfort here tonight.

Juliet removed her soaking shoes and socks and rolled up her wet trousers. She took the VW car key from her bag and then found her own car keys with the heart keyring still zipped in the pocket. She took them out, they could go as well. Juliet left her handbag on the stones and stumbled over the small pebbles and shingles that dug into her feet. She crossed the foamy shoreline, dragged her feet into deeper water, not sure now what was making her wetter, the sea or the rain.

She swung back her arm, prepared to throw all the keys and the cloth as far as she could; burial at sea seemed a good way for this to end.

But then she paused, because deep down she knew it wouldn't end here. She felt the cold, stone heart on the key ring in the palm of her hand. For her, mislaying this set of keys with their key ring had been where so many of her doubts had started and she still had no answers as to who took them and who returned them. She would live her life haunted by them, looking at her family, never sure, never quite trusting them, and she didn't want to live like that.

Juliet turned around, looked up the beach at her bag on the pebbles. Her mind went back to that hot summer evening with Gabriel, down here drinking. A soft breeze off the sea, a relief after such a hot day. She'd paddled that evening, she remembered Gabriel getting his camera, taking pictures of them. After the strain of the evening, it had been a slice of heaven.

Suddenly, an enormous, hard, cold wave came crashing against her legs. She staggered forward. Another came drenching her hair, she could feel the cold water seeping through her coat. It was if the sea was shouting something at her.

Juliet gripped the keys tight, staggered out of the water, her trousers sodden and heavy. She trudged up the beach, thrust wet, sandy feet into her dry socks and shoes and then picked up her bag. She looked out at the sea, back down at her things and then, in a flash, she knew what the sea had been trying to tell her. Of course, why hadn't she thought of it before? She started to go through everything that had happened, but this time from a new perspective and found things that had seemed insignificant suddenly took on a different meaning. Pictures flashed through her mind: bags and keys, that day Cassie told them about the restaurant and she'd met Gabriel, the letter, it all started to make sense.

She walked quickly off the beach and up the path. Once at the top she walked into the field, looked over at Rhys's car that she'd parked in the same place she used to park her own car. She remembered the last time she'd seen it, her little car had been so neat and tidy after two years in Mira's care, although it was shame about that awful air freshener, the terrible smell of fake lavender. For a moment, her mind stalled, the lavender, the smell of fake lavender – why did that matter? Her mind stumbled around. She stood very still, putting all her energy into trying to work things out. She glanced back down the beach. Yes, it was possible.

Juliet rushed home. She was soaking wet, but she didn't want to have to explain why to anyone. She went to the porch, hung up her soaking coat and took off her shoes and socks. Then she ran upstairs, went into the bathroom, took off her clothes and threw them in the washing basket, then she wrapped a warm bath towel around herself and started to dry her hair with a hand towel and left. She had started walking to her bedroom when she saw her mother.

'Oh, you've had a shower,' said her mother.

'Yes,' she said, smiled and walked on, and she knew the shower excuse had worked.

Juliet stopped. That should be telling her something, but what?

Juliet went back to her bedroom and glanced over at the corner, saw the box that contained her father's collections, remembered looking through them the day of Rosalind's meal. Her mind started to click through pictures of that day and suddenly she knew there was something else.

Juliet dragged out the box of her father's collections, flicked through books and albums... and there it was. She realised she'd been gathering all the pieces of the puzzle; she'd simply been putting them in the wrong places. There were a few things though she needed to check, to figure out. Once they were done, she would know exactly who had killed Harry and who had killed Rhys.

Tomorrow she would give herself time to think, and then she would talk to people. Juliet felt fear grip her because she knew she would be alerting the killer that she was closing in on them. And with that thought she remembered the warning of her father's that she had pushed to the back of her mind – 'Anyone who has the motive can kill.'

Her father had been afraid, and Rhys had admitted to fear, to a sense of evil. She'd promised her father she would be brave. Now it was time act.

33

Juliet woke on the Sunday morning with a kind of sickening feeling of anticipation. However, she'd promised herself time to think, and she decided to go to the workshop and draw. For her, the process of sketching often calmed her, cleared her mind.

And so, she went out into the workshop, spent her time, drawing, thinking. The morning and then the afternoon drifted away from her, but slowly her mind unscrambled.

Before she went back in the house, she took out a piece of paper which she headed 'The Killing of Harry and Rhys' and proceeded to write in detail everything she had learned. She knew how dangerous the next few hours were going to be, this was her insurance, the truth would not die. When she finished, she carefully folded the piece of paper and tucked it in her draw in the workshop.

Then Juliet went back into the house. It would soon be time to go to the barbecue. She went to find Mira who was sat with Lola, reading.

'HI,' signed Juliet and she lent to stroke Lola. 'Looking forward to this evening?'

Mira shook her head. 'Not particularly. I know it's rather late compared to some, but I've started feeling ever so sick.'

'You could stay home.'

'No, I had a text from Gabriel earlier; I promised I'd go for a short time anyway. I'm not taking Lola though; I think all the smells of food will drive her mad.'

Juliet smiled but then she heard the house phone ring and went to answer it.

To her surprise, it was DC Adam Smith.

'I've been meaning to get back to you about the voicemail you sent me. Could you tell me more about how you came to have it?'

Juliet explained and then he said, 'Right, well, it was very interesting, and we would like to talk to Anwen about it. I was wondering if you or anyone in the family has seen her, we are having problems tracking her down.'

'I don't think any of us have seen her since Rhys's funeral.'

'I see. Didn't your sister Cassie mention her and Anwen were going to start some kind of business together?'

'That's not happening now. When I spoke to Anwen at the funeral, she told me she was planning to move back to the mainland.'

'Ah, well, I hope she hasn't gone yet; we really need to speak to her.'

Juliet hesitated. 'Do you suspect her of Rhys's murder?'

There was a pause and then he answered, 'I'm very sorry, I can't say any more. But I would be very grateful if you could tell me if anyone sees or hears from her.'

Juliet ended the phone call. She remembered Anwen's threats, the talk of violence, of desperate people doing ugly things. If Anwen found out that she'd sent that voicemail to the police, what would she do? Juliet could feel herself getting hotter, a fear deep in her stomach, making her feel sick.

Juliet went into the kitchen where she found her mother, Cassie and Rosalind, ready to leave. She told them about the phone call and Anwen.

'So, the police are taking the voicemail seriously,' said Cassie.

Their mother frowned. 'I do hope Anwen doesn't get blamed in any way for Rhys's death. It wouldn't be right.'

Juliet was surprised at her mother's tone. 'You are being very forgiving, Mum.'

Her mother sighed. 'It's a dark world, it's not easy to see the way sometimes. We can all take a wrong turn.'

Juliet looked at her mother more closely, she could see dark rims under her eyes, she was fiddling with the delicate wristwatch she always wore, but her fingers were shaking.

'Are you all right, Mum?' Juliet asked.

'I've had a lot to think about.'

'You don't need to come to the barbecue you know, you look very tired.'

Her mother nodded, but there was no smile. 'I have to come.' She lowered her voice so only Juliet heard her add, 'We need to be careful this evening, I think.'

Juliet shuddered.

In a far more normal and matter-of-fact way, her mother then said, 'I shall drive us to the barbeque, they forecast stormy weather later. I hope it holds off for the barbecue. Anyway, I don't want to be staggering home in the dark, falling in ditches.'

Juliet took a deep breath. 'Before we go, I just wanted to ask one or two questions about the night Rhys died.'

Cassie groaned. 'I thought we'd settled all this.'

'Almost, it's just handy having you all together.' She looked at her mother. 'Mum, did you find Rhys's crucifix in your handbag?'

She saw her mother's eyes dart between Rosalind and Cassie.

'It's not a difficult question, Mum.'

Slowly her mother nodded her head.

'Right, good. Rosalind did you see Cassie through the window of the workshop that night?'

Rosalind frowned and shook her head.

'You didn't wave to her?'

'No, but—'

'Exactly,' interrupted Cassie, 'Rosalind was, um, preoccupied.'

Juliet shrugged, gave a quick smile. 'It's just easier if people tell the truth that's all. Finally, Cassie, the night Harry died, did you go in to see Mum?'

Cassie blushed, shook her head.

'No, I didn't think so. See, it doesn't hurt, does it? Right, time we went.' She walked away satisfied. At last, her family had started to tell her the truth.

* * *

When they arrived at the vineyard, there were already a number of cars parked on the verges. Fortunately, they found a space fairly close to the house. As they got out of the car, they could hear the strains of French music, see the lights, smell the barbeque.

'I love this,' said Rosalind, 'it's like being transported to France. Shame it's so bloody cold.'

When they arrived at the house, Juliet saw that Maddie had opened the patio doors at the end of the living room, allowing people to easily go between the inside area of tables, chairs and drinks, and the barbeque outside. She had arranged some patio heaters and it looked magical with candles, fairy lights and lanterns spread around. There were also beautifully woven balls and crosses made of soaked vine twigs with autumn grasses entwined in their branches.

In the living room, clusters of chairs had been laid out and the older members of the party had settled in there. The guests' bags were taken by a waiter and put into the room opposite. However, when a waiter approached Juliet's mother, she was surprised to hear her mother speak quite sharply. 'I will hold onto my own bag, thank you.'

Her mother went to join some of her friends and Juliet went outside and savoured the heavenly smell of the barbeque.

Gabriel came over to see her and smiled as he held out a heaped plate of food. 'I'm so glad you all came.'

'Of course, we wouldn't miss it.'

Juliet had also held onto her bag, so she placed it by her feet, took the plate.

'Shall I put your bag somewhere safe?' he asked.

'I think it's safer with me thanks,' she said.

Their eyes met, he frowned at her, stared, but she held his gaze until finally he looked away.

She glanced down at her plate of food; a small, rare steak, marinated chicken, dressed salad, and buttered potatoes.

'Wow, this looks lovely, thank you.' She sniffed the air. 'Now that would make a good scent for an air freshener. Better than the one Mira put in my car.'

Again, their eyes met, the look in his now more searching, but this time she felt unable to hold his gaze and looked away. Her hands started to shake, and she understood that putting together the pieces of a puzzle here was a very dangerous game.

Her mouth was so dry, it was hard to swallow. Cassie came over to them, grinned at Gabriel. 'So is Maddie due to give her annual address soon?'

Gabriel laughed. 'Actually I am doing the honours this evening. Maddie thought it was time.'

Cassie leant forward and kissed him quickly on the cheek. 'There you are, that's for luck.'

Juliet saw Cassie surreptitiously push something into his pocket. Gabriel didn't seem to notice, but blushed and joked, 'Well thanks, that will make all the difference.'

Cassie laughed. 'I'm sure you'll do it perfectly; in fact, people are already pretty pissed – you can't go wrong!'

He grinned and made his way to the top of the steps that led into the living room, where he could address both sets of guests, and the music was turned off. Gabriel clinked the side of his glass and everyone turned his way. Before he started to speak there was the awkward interruption of someone's phone signalling a text. Juliet glanced around, saw it was Cassie, who then left them all to read her messages. Gabriel's speech was short, thanking everyone for coming and sharing in his deep sense of pride in the vineyard and workers there.

Juliet listened, clapped politely but was preoccupied. She had things she wanted to do, but people were in and out of the house. She noticed Gabriel frequently refreshing his glass. There was nothing she could do but wait for things to quieten down. She was careful not to drink too much but went round chatting.

At about eleven, Juliet noticed the caterers were quietly starting to shut things down. The older members of the village began to take their leave and the younger people who might have been tempted to make a night of free food and drink saw that both were running out.

Juliet's mother came over to her. 'I'm thinking of making a move,' she said. 'Are you ready?'

Juliet looked up at the house, she had not done what she needed yet. 'Not quite, you go on without me.'

'Don't worry, I'll wait.'

'No, Mum, really, I'd rather come home in my own time.'

'I want to get back,' Rosalind said. 'I'm expecting to FaceTime with some friends.'

Her mother looked torn, but Mira said, 'I'd like to get back as well Mum, I've left Lola for a long time.'

Cassie came over. 'I have to go somewhere so I don't need a lift back.'

She sounded serious.

'Is everything okay?' Rosalind asked.

'Oh yes, I just need to do something, you all go on without me.'

Their mother frowned. 'I suppose I can't make you two girls come with me.' She sighed. 'It was so much easier when you were children. Anyway, both of you take care, remember there's a storm on its way.'

Cassie left them all and started to walk down the path.

Juliet, sensing her mother was still hesitating, said, 'Go on Mum, I'll be fine.'

Her mother nodded and started to walk away with Rosalind and Mira.

Mira, however, looked back, her face anxious. She didn't speak but signed to Juliet, 'Are you okay?'

Juliet signed back, 'Don't worry, I'll see you later.'

Mira nodded and slowly walked away.

It was then Juliet noticed Gabriel and Maddie seeing people off further along the path. Now was her chance.

She walked quickly into the house and the first thing she did was go into the kitchen and search among the herbs and spices. Then she went up the stairs. First, she went into the bathroom, looked around. Second, she went to Gabriel's room. She opened the drawer where she knew he kept Harry's things, but before she could look inside, she heard a cough behind her.

'Why are you looking in there?' His words were slightly slurred.

He walked over to her, stood very close. She could smell alcohol on his breath. She could hear people downstairs clearing up, but they seemed a long way away. She took a deep breath. *Be brave, I must be brave*, she thought.

'I was wondering if I could see that letter that you said the secretary of the running club sent to Harry.'

His face darkened but he reached into the draw, handed her the envelope. She took out the letter, perused it carefully, re-read that line with 'after you've gone' in it. She glanced at the envelope she'd allowed to distract her before, and then handed it back. She'd seen what she needed.

'Thank you.'

'If that's everything, I think the party has come to an end. I saw your mother leaving, can I offer you a lift?'

She backed towards the door. 'No, it's okay, I'll walk.'

'Be careful then, we don't want any more accidents.'

Juliet stumbled down the stairs. She had to get away.

34

Juliet left the house and hurried along the path. It seemed very dark now, horribly quiet. There was that stillness that hangs heavy with anticipation before a storm, as if nature is holding its breath, longing for the tension to break.

There were no cars parked now; everyone had gone home. Her heart was racing as she left the vineyard and faced the long narrow lane that led down to the main road. There were no streetlights, just darkness. She was completely alone. If anyone followed her down here, attacked her, no one would see.

The road seemed longer than ever. A barn owl screeched above her, a fox let out a cry, creatures rustled in the hedges. She walked faster. It was with a breath of relief she finally reached the main road.

Juliet crossed the road to walk on the grass verge. It felt safer along here even though it was dark and there were still no street lights. She wasn't hemmed in by hedges and the road may be deserted but it was a major, well maintained road. The grassy area that led to the cliffs on her right was wide, she was well away from the sea she could hear crashing on the rocks below.

As she walked, she started to relax, her breathing became more measured. However, suddenly, without any warning, she heard a loud car behind her, obviously driving at speed. Glancing over her shoulder, she saw a small car travelling in her direction, being driven in an erratic manner, swerving all over the place. It raced towards her and to her horror she saw it mount the grassy verge at the side of the road. Fighting her instinct to freeze, Juliet ran onto the grass, but the car kept driving in her direction. Just as she thought there was no escape, she heard the screeching of brakes, and the engine cut out. Juliet turned to see the car, a small Fiat Panda, and stopped. The headlights were still on and enabled her to see a man slumped over the steering wheel. Her instinct was to keep running, but she fought it, she had to see if the driver needed help. Juliet pulled open the driver's door, saw the gash on the man's forehead and then she recognised him.

'Gabriel, my God, Gabriel,' Juliet screamed.

The smell of alcohol filled the small car. Gabriel rested back in the car seat, turned his head towards Juliet, giving her a lopsided, slightly wild grin.

It was only then she fully understood what had happened. Gabriel had been driving the car at her, he had been trying to kill her.

'What the hell?' Juliet shouted, her voice loud, hysterical.

The grin disappeared; his face crumpled in despair. 'I'm sorry.'

Juliet, breathing heavily, left the car door open and collapsed onto the grass besides it, trying to breath. Gabriel touched his forehead and the sight of the blood seemed to sober him.

'You've been asking so many questions, you wouldn't let anything go. I had to do something. I'm so sorry,' he stammered.

She looked over at him, his face becoming clearer as she adjusted to the light. 'I know what happened Gabriel, I know everything about Harry and Rhys. I know Harry was not going to France. That's where it all started, didn't it?'

'But Harry was going to France, I proved it.'

'No, he wasn't.'

'But—'

'For all your covering up, you made mistakes. You were unlucky with one that I noticed, I don't suppose many people would have seen it, but then not many people have fathers who have been avid stamp collectors.'

She saw him shake his head in confusion, and so she explained. 'It was the stamp on the envelope of the letter supposedly from the running club. That stamp on the envelope was not printed until September 1995 and yet the letter was meant to have been sent in August. The secretary would have known within a day or two what had happened to Harry, he certainly wouldn't have been posting a letter in September. The other thing about that letter that disturbed me was that 'after you've gone' but I couldn't work out why. Once I thought about it, re-read the letter, I realised that it was the hand-writing that was familiar. Although you'd tried to disguise your own, the odd cursive 'y' and 'f' had crept into that phrase.'

Juliet paused, shivered as she became aware rain was falling steadily now. She could feel the cold wet drops on her head, driz-zling down her neck, and inside her coat. She pulled her coat more tightly around herself and continued. 'And of course, there was Barbara. She never quite stopped questioning why Harry would be out training in that awful weather if he was leaving. He'd not gone out because of a bad temper; he was back training because the truth was, Harry was planning to stay and make a life with Cassie, wasn't he?'

Gabriel screwed up his eyes. 'Even if Harry was staying, why does it matter? It doesn't prove anything.'

'Oh, but it provides motive. Cassie told me the dream Harry had

had, the woodland and the house, he was going to transform his half of the land up there and that would have decimated the vineyard, but there was nothing you could have done to stop him.'

Gabriel gripped the steering wheel, stared through the rain splattered windscreen. Juliet waited until he finally turned to her, his face stern, lips tight. 'It would have destroyed everything; it would have broken Maddie's heart.'

'And so, Harry had to be stopped.'

Gabriel glanced at her. She held his gaze. Eventually he said, 'I didn't want Harry to die.'

'No, I don't think you did.'

'But he had to,' he said, his voice cold. 'I had to save the vineyard, I had to do it for Maddie.' He sat back, his eyes narrowed, and his voice became harder, more defiant. 'You can't prove anything. Ed will testify I was in the night Harry died; you know that.'

'I know you went out before eight, it's why you were so wet. My guess is you didn't go to see to the vines, you went to stage the break in at the garage, steal the car, have it ready. Timing was everything. And then what happened? Maybe, while Ed was messing about listening to music, you managed to get out without him noticing?'

Gabriel nodded.

Juliet sighed and said, 'So you thought you'd got away with it. You only had a motive if Harry was staying and so you faked the letter. He'd already bought his tickets, you could hold them as proof as well. You held onto the ignition key – was that a mistake or your insurance? It was a useful thing to plant on someone if things got difficult or, of course, one day to use to frighten my father.'

Juliet saw something close to real distress spread across Gabriel's face. His eyes were wet with tears. 'I never meant your dad to have that accident. He'd told me he was going to tell Rosalind about Cassie and Harry being her parents; I couldn't have allowed it all to be raked up. Everyone still talks about Harry. If they knew he was Rosalind's father, if Cassie told them he was planning to stay, well, how long would it take for people to start asking questions?'

Juliet shook her head. 'But it was unforgivable, you know that. My dad was like a second father to you and yet you showed him the old VW ignition key.' She paused, her voice shaking, the pain in her throat making it impossible to speak.

They sat in silence, the waves clawing at the shingle below. In the distance she heard another deep growl of thunder, a crack of lightening; the storm was closing in.

'I'm so sorry,' said Gabriel quietly.

She shook her head. 'You keep saying sorry, but it doesn't mean anything. I despise what you did. Even after Harry and my dad it didn't stop, did it? Because my father told Rhys.'

Gabriel closed his eyes as if trying to shut her out, but she continued.

'Rhys went to see Maddie the day he died. He told her everything Dad had said, and you decided he had to be silenced.'

Gabriel opened his eyes, turned and said, 'So how do you think I did it? You said yourself someone in your house had taken your set of car keys, that indicates that if anyone here had anything to do with Rhys's death it was someone in your family.'

Juliet, aware how wet the ground around her was becoming, stood up. Looking towards the road she saw a car race past, the occupants unaware of the drama they were passing, just thinking of getting home, being safe and warm.

Juliet looked down at Gabriel now as she spoke. 'For too long I let myself assume my car keys had to have been taken out of my bag at the house. But of course, that wasn't true was it? I didn't work it out until yesterday, but now I know. You took them from my bag when we were on the beach, when you'd said you were going to find your phone. But you wanted to return them, continue to throw suspicion on my family. I had to think of a time when you'd had access to my bag, but I wouldn't notice what you were doing. Of course when you gave me the monocular I was completely distracted from what you were doing and I found my set of car keys that evening at home, never making the connection with you.'

She touched the door frame and suddenly she recognised the car. 'I've just realised you hadn't intended to use my car originally.' She paused, gave herself time to think and then said, 'You'd been planning to kill Rhys before you met me that evening and so you must have had a car ready. I think this was that car. I should have realised. I saw the keys hanging up when I went to Dad's garage the evening of his funeral but then when I returned, they'd gone. I didn't give it any thought but now I realise you'd stolen them, hadn't you? I guess you'd held onto your old garage keys, so it was easy enough for you to go up there and steal the keys. That meant that as long as the owners of the car were away, you had quick and easy access to the car whenever you needed it.'

Gabriel shrugged. 'You're right, I had planned to use this car. Still, it was handy to be able to use it this evening, better than coming in my own.'

Juliet lent towards Gabriel. 'If you'd had this car ready, why did you use mine?'

'I didn't get the idea until you came to me and showed me the keys. Suddenly it was all rather ingenious, a useful misdirection as well, got the police checking out your family. I was sure you would never suspect me of taking the car keys, it seemed fool proof.'

She hated the pride in his voice. 'But you made mistakes. You talked about the awful smell of the fake lavender in my car. How would you have known about that unless you were in it?'

Gabriel looked away. 'A mistake. A stupid mistake.'

'Yes, you made a few of them. However, there is one thing I don't know how to explain,' she said. 'How did you manage to video call me at the time you were killing Rhys?'

Gabriel touched his forehead again, flinched. 'You can change backgrounds and things.'

Juliet stood back, crossed her arms and shook her head. 'No, that's not right, is it?'

'It is, that's what I did.'

She shook her head again. 'No. The thing is Gabriel, you may be cowardly, a liar, greedy, morally bankrupt, but one thing you aren't, is a killer.'

There was another growl of thunder, louder, closer and the sound of it merged with the roar of a car engine.

Juliet turned and saw a car tearing across the grass, windscreen wipers clearing the screen so that she could make out the face of the driver. This time the car coming towards her was being driven by a steady hand. If this person wanted to kill her, they wouldn't miss. Juliet looked around frantic to escape but before she could move, the car was in front of her. She froze, waiting to be hit, but instead the car screeched to a halt, inches in front of her. The woman driving leapt out of the car, slammed the door, ran over to Gabriel.

'Oh Gabriel, what have you done?' said the woman, speaking as if to a child who'd just fallen over while playing.

'I'm sorry. I wanted to do this for you.'

The woman shook her head. 'You should have left her to me, you know I take care of things like that.'

Juliet steadied her voice. 'Yes, you are the one who kills, aren't you Maddie? You are ruthless, you were prepared to kill your own son, Harry.'

'Harry was my stepson,' spat out Maddie. She glanced at Gabriel.

'Juliet knows even more that I suspected, even more than I warned you about,' he said. 'She knows Harry was definitely not going to France, she knows the letter was a fake, about the stolen car, everything.'

Maddie turned back to Juliet. 'Harry wasn't my blood. Gabriel is my only son.' Juliet heard the change in Maddie's voice. The French accent was hard, no softening of consonants, no hesitation. 'When Harry came back from that party on the day Rosalind came home from the maternity hospital swearing he would stay, I knew something had to be done. He'd have ruined us, he wanted to destroy everything. Everything I'd done was for Gabriel and no one was going to destroy what was rightfully his.' Maddie paused. 'But, wait, exactly how much do you know about how Harry actually died?'

'I know timing was tight. You'd arranged for Gabriel to steal the car and stage the break in so that all you had to do was get out of the house while the boys were listening to loud music and jump into the car. You drove down the military road, killed Harry, ran home. It wasn't that far and you were a lot younger and fitter then. Back home you threw on a dressing gown, came down drying your hair, using a shower as the cover. The police would never had suspected you, after all, you had no motive. They didn't search your house, find the key you'd brought back. That was a mistake, wasn't it? Why didn't you just throw away the car key?'

'I admit I'd meant to leave it in the car. But Gabriel told me that Cassie had said something about going out to meet Harry. I thought that she might be an insurance policy. It was Gabriel's idea to buy some violin cloths to wrap the key in.'

'But it was the wrong colour, and that mattered. You were going to let Cassie take the blame?'

'We might have had to do that, yes. As it was, no one questioned us; it went very well.'

'Apart from the fake letter and Barbara's questions. But you got away with it. And then Gabriel showed my father the old VW key.

That was stupid, all to stop my father telling Rosalind about Harry being her father.'

'It was not stupid,' said Maddie indignantly.

'Gabriel told me your fears about people asking questions.'

'Of course it would have been a huge risk. However, I'd not expected your father to react in that way, he was just meant to see sense and keep quiet.'

Juliet took a breath, tried to steady her voice. 'Gabriel told my father that someone he knew had killed, I don't know how you expected him to react.' She paused; she couldn't go over that again. 'In any case, when my father knew he was dying, he spoke to Rhys, told him that someone in my family had killed Harry. Rhys was torn apart by this, and finally decided he had to tell you what he thought was the truth. He told this when he came to see you on the anniversary of Harry's death?'

'Yes, he was good like that, he came every year.'

Juliet stared at Maddie. Unlike Gabriel, who sat a crumpled heap in the car, she stood very upright. She was talking to Juliet in a disturbingly casual way, as if they were stood in a garden admiring the borders on a summer's day, not in darkness close to a cliff edge, cold rain falling on their heads, talking about murder.

'Rhys had clearly wrestled with telling anyone about what he knew, but he felt I had a right to know. He had no idea that he'd got things all wrong. He told me he would be speaking to you all the next day and he would be expecting one of you to go to the police. He said he'd give you all a chance to confess to each other. Honestly, these vicars, they can be so naïve.' Maddie shook her head. 'You can imagine how I felt when he talked about the police being involved. I really didn't want it all being dragged up again. Anyway, it was useful, I knew he wasn't saying anything that evening, it gave me the chance to get rid of him.'

'But you'd collected those things at the pub the day of Dad's funeral: the theatre ticket, the travel card, even the lighter you used to set fire to the car. You were planning to lead the police to suspect someone from the mainland. It shows you'd been planning this murder before Rhys came to see you.'

'Oh yes, at the funeral I knew.' Maddie crossed her arms. 'But like with Harry, you have no proof.' Maddie looked closely at her. 'Tell me how I managed to kill Rhys when Gabriel told you, I was very sick in bed? Barbara saw me, I was genuinely ill.'

'Ah I know exactly why you were sick. It was the mustard. I saw it in the kitchen the day after, remember, I came up to see you. Before you went out you took the precaution of video calling Barbara, maybe put on a bit of makeup to make yourself appear ill, then you drove to the church, parked at the bottom of the drive, walked up and killed Rhys. Interestingly, you removed the crucifix, a request for forgiveness? Like the crosses you placed at the scenes where Harry and Rhys died?'

'We all look for a sign God has understood what we've done. I am sure God understood I acted out of love for my son. To be honest, I thought the crucifix, like the key, was something I could use to plant on someone. I thought of Cassie, I saw her leaving the church, you know, close to one o'clock that night. She was already a good line up for Harry's death, if I needed it I could plant the crucifix on her.'

'Yes, you put it in my mother's handbag when she came to the tea party, didn't you?'

Maddie nodded. 'Yes, I thought that was clever. I was sure your mother would never suspect I'd put it in her bag. If she found it, she may suspect Cassie, if someone else found it they may suspect your mother. Most importantly, it all pointed at your family, not mine.' She paused, gave Juliet an appraising glance. 'Still, you did well to work out I'd put it there. You are quite good at this; I can see why

Gabriel was attracted to you. Of course, you would never have been good enough for him.'

Juliet shook her head and continued talking, 'While you were killing Rhys, Gabriel phoned me pretending you were upstairs being sick. When you returned you ate mustard and were then genuinely unwell by the time Barbara came round. But I saw the mustard in the kitchen that morning. However, at the tea party you said you never had mustard in the house, it made you too unwell. Indeed, when I checked your kitchen at the barbecue tonight, the mustard had gone.'

Maddie put her head to one side. 'You are clearly a bright young woman, but I hope you appreciate that what I have done has been very well executed. Nothing was left to chance.'

Juliet stepped closer to Maddie. 'I don't admire anything about you. I despise you. You are a wicked, evil woman who manipulates and kills to get what she wants. You have killed three people and yet you show no remorse.'

'Three?'

'You killed Harry, Rhys and my father.' Juliet clenched her fists to stop herself from grabbing Maddie.

'I didn't kill your father, he was weak.'

Juliet raised her hand to Maddie but was grabbed from behind.

'Don't you dare hurt Maddie,' said Gabriel. She could feel the warmth of his breath as he pulled her back into his body, his face close to hers. The gentle way he normally held her was replaced by a vice like grasp, his strength was frightening. She struggled to breathe, was unable to move.

Suddenly, a crash of thunder seemed to envelope them and a crack of lightening wasn't far behind. Juliet gasped, desperate to get away, but she was held as if tied to a stake, unable to get free, unable to run to safety.

'So, what do we do next?' Gabriel shouted at Maddie. His voice had changed now Maddie was here, a horrible mix of confidence and subservience. He was back on firm ground taking orders from Maddie.

'We'll use the Fiat,' Maddie shouted back as another clap of thunder echoed through the sky. 'I brought that broach you took from Anwen at the funeral, we'll leave that in the car, and we can plant the keys on her mother or Cassie, I've a few things in mind.'

Juliet stood helpless, listening not only to the plan of how they would kill her but even the defence they were planning for themselves. The fact Gabriel had stolen a broach, kept the car keys made her wonder when exactly they'd started preparing for the possibility of killing her.

Juliet was desperate now; her fate had been decided by them. She tried to pull her arms free, to kick, bite, anything, but Gabriel's grasp just got tighter.

'The keys are in the ignition,' he said.

'Good, I'll drive.'

'No, stop,' shouted Juliet. 'You can't. It's not just me, others are working out what you did. Mum knows you planted the crucifix, I have written everything down, Mira or Cassie will find it, take it to the police. They will find start digging. You can't keep killing, you won't get away with this.'

Maddie grinned. 'Oh I think I will.'

She walked over to the car. A crack of lightening lit up the sky but its prongs seemed to reach down to the earth and light up the ground. Maddie was in the car, she slammed the door shut, switched on the ignition and wound down the window.

'You can get in now,' she shouted to Gabriel and instantly he threw Juliet hard on the ground, ran, jumped in the car.

Juliet caught her breath, staggered to her feet. 'You're completely mad,' she screamed.

'I think you'd better get moving,' shouted Maddie, a wild excitement in her voice.

Maddie wound up the window and turned on the lights. The engine roared as she touched the accelerator, but the car stayed stationary.

This is all some cruel game to her, thought Juliet, frantically looking around for a way to escape.

Juliet knew it was useless to run back to the road; there were no cars about, she would be an easy target. She looked to her right, across the grass was the cliff edge, but the terrain was uneven, there were obstacles, as long as she could keep away from the edge, it had to be her only option.

She started to run. The rain was falling heavily now, the thunder and lightning almost in harmony, crashing and lighting up the sky. She ran but at any moment she could stumble fall.

She heard the crunching of gears behind her, screeching of brakes as the car was turned and then the roar as it started to race towards her. She stumbled, felt overwhelmed by the hopelessness of her situation, but kept running, knowing any minute now she would die. But at that moment the sky shot a warning and an arrow of lightening lit up an enormous black rock in front of her. She glanced frantically behind her. She was temporarily blinded by the headlights of the Fiat, but then she saw Maddie's face. She was hunched over the steering wheel, her face close to the windscreen, her eyes wild, her mouth open screaming at her.

Juliet ran headlong at the rock and at the last minute swerved to the side, staggering behind it. As she fell to the ground, her back to the rock, the thumping of her heart banged in her ears. Then she heard it, a sickening sound of metal crunching into the unforgiving boulder.

She sat, petrified, waiting for Maddie or Gabriel to get out of the car, to come and find her.

There was silence. As if in retreat the thunder's grumble was softer, the lightning took refuge back in the sky, no longer sending splinters of light to the earth.

Juliet's head was screaming at her to run and so she tried to stand up. However, as soon as she put weight on her foot, pain shot through her body, making her very aware something was wrong. She tried to ignore it, to start walking, but it was agony.

She realised that there was no noise coming from the other side of the rock. Slowly, using the rock to support her, she managed to get herself around and then she saw the crumpled wreck of the car. To her horror, she saw the faces of Gabriel and Maddie against the windscreen, covered in blood. No seat belts or airbags had been used to save them. Maddie's eyes were closed and she was completely still. Gabriel's face was a thing of nightmares. Eyes open, unblinking, unseeing. Juliet dragged herself to the driver and passenger doors, but they were impossible to open.

She collapsed into a heap on the grass and sobbed. And then she felt familiar, warm, gentle arms wrap themselves around her. She looked up and saw Mira and fell into her embrace.

'I'm sorry we took so long,' Juliet heard her mother say. She pulled herself away from Mira's hold and wiped her face. Mira didn't move, stayed close to her.

Her mother tried the car doors, but she couldn't open them either. Maddie and Gabriel were still frighteningly still.

'I'll phone an ambulance,' said her mother, the slight shake in her voice betraying her sense of shock.

It was only then Juliet saw her mother's car parked at the side of the road.

Her mother knelt down beside her. 'I thought we were too late,' she said and burst into tears, held Juliet tightly to her.

'Oh God, Mum, she was going to kill me. If it hadn't been for the rock...' Juliet stared at the rock, now in darkness.

'It's all right now, you're safe.'

'I think they're dead,' Juliet said, staring at the car in horror.

'The ambulance will be here very soon. We can't do anything.' Her mother stroked Juliet's wet hair. 'I'm so sorry. I've been so slow, got so many things wrong, all these years I've been so frightened.'

'You suspected Cassie of killing Harry?'

'I'm ashamed to say I did. I never asked her if she had, none of us ever talked about that night. I don't think your dad ever thought such a thing, though I never even talked to him about it. Even when he showed me the key, we didn't talk, all we did was agree not to tell Rosalind. I was frantic when Rhys said he was going to tell all, so worried for Cassie. When he died, I didn't know what to think, I couldn't be sure it wasn't Cassie. And then I found that crucifix in my handbag, it seemed to confirm it. It wasn't until I overheard you talking to Cassie that night I realised just how wrong I'd been...' Her mother's voice broke. She held Juliet closer. 'All the time you were trying to find out the truth, I was fighting you, I am so sorry. If you'd given up, we'd have never known what really happened.'

Juliet looked around. 'Hang on, how did you know I was here?'

'Cassie phoned me. She wanted to check when you were home and when I told her you were still out, she told me to go and find you. She was worried about you.'

'But where is she?'

'Just before Gabriel made his speech, Cassie received a text from Anwen, she needed money, so she went to meet her.'

'Oh no, Mum, that's dangerous.'

'It's alright, Cassie had phoned the police. She was scared but she knew the police wanted to speak to Anwen. Anyway, the police went with Cassie, they suspected Anwen of being involved in drug dealing. Anwen was arrested and charged. Cassie is at the police station, she is safe. She phoned me from there about you.'

'Why did she think I was in danger?'

'She said something about a cloth, I don't know what she meant but she said she was getting worried about Gabriel. Apparently she'd put a red cloth in his pocket; it was meant to be a warning. If Anwen hadn't sent that text she'd have stayed with you I think.'

Juliet nodded. She understood now why Cassie had gone off after the barbeque, why she'd looked so serious.

Juliet raised her hand to wipe the tears away, but her mother grabbed her hand. 'Your right arm is bleeding.'

It was then that Juliet saw the flashing lights, heard the sirens. The ambulance, police car and fire engine had arrived. Juliet's mother jumped up and ran over to them, waving. She'd left the headlights of her car on and they quickly came, driving over the grass.

One of the paramedics dealt with Juliet while the others, with the police and firemen, undertook the far more serious work of trying to save Gabriel and Maddie.

Juliet was helped over to the ambulance and, once inside, the paramedic examined her injuries.

'Your ankle will need X-raying, but let's clean that arm.'

As she wiped the excess blood off, Juliet saw a small, deep cut. It made a jagged line across her island tattoo.

'We'll need to stitch or glue that; it'll leave a scar, I think.'

'It's like a lightning bolt, don't you think?' she said to the para-medic. Then, quietly to herself, she added, 'I was struck by lightning, but I survived, and now I am standing tall.'

Juliet walked through the graveyard, past Gabriel's grave; he'd died that night on the clifftop. He had been buried here at Maddie's request, next to his father and Harry. Juliet looked down at the grave but didn't linger. Instead, she went over to her own father's grave. She knelt down and carefully arranged daffodils in a vase, warm yellow, a ray of sunshine.

'Hi Dad, I've popped home again. Work is building up; I have my own customer base now. I love drawing portraits.' Juliet looked around. 'Edinburgh looks great in the spring, but I miss the island, think about it a lot. I took my musical box with me. When I get homesick, I touch it, smell it and it reminds me of you and the workshop. To go to sleep, sometimes I play the music, it can make me smile, it can make me cry, but that's okay. I never forget you, and I know you never forget me. Everyone is home today, I'm on my way there now. They are putting their lives back together very well, and with very little help from me, which is how it should be.' She sat for a few moments and then heard the sweet, high trill above her. 'The swallows are back then, Dad. We all return to the island, don't we? I have to go now, but I'll be back soon, love you.' Juliet quietly got up and left.

She walked down the road, past the houses. Early bluebells clustered under budding trees, that would soon form their own ocean, grabbing the light before it was stolen by the canopy above. She was admiring the tall lilies by the stream, when she heard someone call out. She turned to see their elderly neighbour Kath looking over the hedge of her front garden.

'Good morning, Juliet, I heard you were home today. Lovely for your mum to have you all back. Now, how is Mira? The baby must have been born by now.'

'The baby was born three days ago; Mira is home now.'

'Goodness, these young mums come home quickly, don't they? Well, she has a lovely home down there and your mum will enjoy having them living with her. So, was it a boy or a girl, we're all dying to know?'

'A girl, but I don't know the name yet.'

'That's just perfect.'

Juliet saw Kath's eyes flash around. As her mother would say, *That's the village told.* She smiled. 'I'd better get on then, Kath, lovely to chat.'

She quickly arrived at the garden gate and stopped. To Juliet this was when the garden looked its best. Blossom on the apple trees just starting to open, new leaves on the oak, cowslips and tulips scattered in the boarders. Her family were all outside, Mum on the bench holding the baby, Mira next to her. Cassie and Tim had brought out chairs, but she noticed Cassie's arm outstretched, her hand resting on Tim's. Rosalind lay on the only sun lounger, eyes closed. While the rest of the family wore jumpers and trousers, she was in shorts and T-shirt. They seemed relaxed, at ease with each other and Juliet thought again how fortunate they'd been that the secrets and lies had brought them closer and not torn them apart.

Juliet saw Mira look over and waved to her. Mira ran towards her, Lola close to her side. Juliet flung open the gate, closed it behind her.

'You're home,' Mira signed and hugged her.

Juliet grinned over at their mother. 'I see Mum has the baby. How are you?'

'Exhausted, but happy.'

'Have you finally chosen a name?' Juliet asked.

Mira nodded. 'Seren, it's Welsh for star.'

'Oh, that's beautiful.'

'Yes, star was Dad's name for me, and I chose the Welsh for Rhys. You'll have to come and see the nursery, me and Mum have done up the guest room.'

'I'd love to.'

Mira came closer to her, lowered her voice. 'Anwen's case will be coming to trial soon, they seem pretty sure it will be a prison sentence.'

'I'm not surprised. It wasn't just possession, she was supplying class B drugs, wasn't she?'

'It's so hard to believe her and Rhys's lives took such different paths.'

'I guess it is. Any news about Maddie?'

'No, still in custody. She wasn't in hospital that long in the end. She had concussion and she had a few broken ribs. She reacted very strangely to Gabriel's death, confessed to the killing of Harry and Rhys, said there was nothing to live for any more. In a warped way I think she told herself she'd done it all for him. Still, she's in for a long sentence. I can't say I'm sorry. She took Rhys from me and deprived our child of a father.'

'It was a dark time, wasn't it?' Juliet glanced over at the workshop.

Juliet heard a cry, that unique cry of a new-born, and Mira's face lit up.

Juliet blinked. 'You heard her?'

'Actually, I saw her. I find myself looking over at her all the time and I see immediately when her face screws up or her fists clench. I've also got a monitor with a flashing light, and other devices for the night. I never miss her cry. Right, feeding time,' Mira rushed over to Seren.

Juliet walked over to her mum and watched as she carefully handed Seren to Mira and then stood up to face Juliet.

'You look well,' her mother said.

'And so, do you.' Juliet saw a light in her mother's eyes. 'You look excited as well.'

'I am. I'm going on a break with Barbara.'

'Really, where?' asked Juliet.

'We're off to Verona. Her husband hates holidays and Barbara is very keen.'

'That's brilliant, Mum.'

'Right, I'll go and get some cake for everyone – I made a fruit cake.'

'Dad's favourite,' said Juliet and they smiled. As her mother walked away, Juliet's glance met Cassie's and she went over to her.

'How's the teaching going then?' she asked Cassie.

'It's okay, much better than I expected.'

'And your hands?'

'I've been seeing a specialist; it's been a lot of help. Me and Mum had a long chat about it all, it's okay now.'

Tim grinned. 'And she's in high demand. She can pick and choose with her pupils, no little ones scraping away at Three Blind Mice on their violins.'

Cassie laughed and then gave a little cough. 'Tim and I are thinking of coming up your way sometime.'

'Oh, that's brilliant,' said Juliet, trying to hide her surprise. 'Let me know when, we have some great concerts and things coming up, I'll get us tickets.' They smiled at each other. They were taking the first tiny steps in a new relationship.

Before Juliet could say any more, Rosalind shouted over, 'When are you going to come and speak to me then?'

Juliet grinned and went over to Rosalind.

'You must be freezing,' Juliet said.

'I can't go to Dubai completely pale, can I.' Rosalind grabbed her hand and examined her fingernails, tutted. 'You've not done anything to them, have you.'

'When do you go?' asked Juliet, ignoring her question.

'In a few weeks, not permanent though. The spa I work for in London have a branch out there, so I can come and go. I like to see Mum and Cassie when I can...' She hesitated, and Juliet saw a flash of pain in her eyes and remembered healing takes time.

Rosalind held out her hand, a red gemstone ring caught the light.

'Cassie gave it to me. Harry gave it to her that day of my coming home party.'

'I didn't know that – it's lovely,' said Juliet.

Rosalind glanced down the garden. 'Remember making dens down there? We had some great times, didn't we?'

Juliet heard the plea for reassurance in Rosalind's voice and grabbed her hand. 'We did, I promise you. We can't take the whole thing in, and sometimes we focus on the darker parts, but it doesn't mean all the light, softer parts weren't there.'

Rosalind grinned. 'You've become very profound. So, tell me, have you met any decent men yet? What about this Alistair?'

Juliet laughed. 'We're just friends for now.'

Juliet sat on the grass, took a piece of fruit cake offered by her mother, and they continued to chat until it became too cold even for Rosalind to remain outside.

Much later, once night had drawn in, Juliet quietly left the house and walked down to the beach alone. The moon shone brightly, a ghost on the surface of the sea. She remembered Maddie talking about the ghosts of the past speaking and she knew now she was no longer frightened to listen to them.

She sat on the pebbles, and picked up a stone, ran her fingers over its surface, she could feel the ridges, the spiral, an ammonite. She might be the first person who had seen it for millions of years, but the island had held onto it, kept it safe. She listened to the soft waves breaking on the shore, the island speaking, whispering to her. 'I will never forget.'

ACKNOWLEDGMENTS

Writing a novel during lockdown has been both a challenge and a wonderful escape. Thank you so much to everyone for all their love and support. In particular, I would like to say an enormous thank you to my publisher Boldwood Books, to the amazing team including Nia, Ellie and Claire, whose enthusiasm and patience appear endless! Thank you so much Sarah Ritherdon for an exceptional edit, for all your encouragement and taking my tangle of words and enabling me to craft this story. Thank you to the other editors, Jade Craddock and Candida Bradford, the cover designer, and everyone involved in bringing this novel to life.

On a personal note, I have, as always, to thank my wonderful husband and children, Thomas and Emily, for their unconditional love, support and countless cups of coffee.

Thank you so much to Wendy Coates for allowing me to use the name of her beautiful cocker spaniel Lola.

I would like to thank Isle of Wight photographer Steve Gascoigne of Available Light

Gallery and Gifts for the beautiful photograph he very generously donated to our competition.

I would also like to mention the wonderful work of Hearing Dogs for Deaf People. This is a wonderful organisation that trains very special dogs who transform the lives of the Deaf people they live with.

Finally, thank you so much to you, the readers. Some are my close friends in the 'real' world, some I know through social media. I know every writer thinks their readers are the best, but I know mine are! Thank you for the lovely comments, reviews, the smiley faces on Facebook and Twitter, each means more to me than you could know.

MORE FROM MARY GRAND

We hope you enjoyed reading *The Island*. If you did, please leave a review.

If you'd like to gift a copy, this book is also available as an ebook, digital audio download and audiobook CD.

Sign up to Mary Grand's mailing list for news, competitions and updates on future books.

https://bit.ly/MaryGrandNewsletter

The House Party, another gripping thriller from Mary Grand, is available to order now.

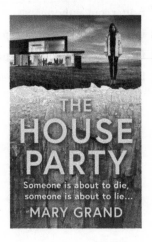

ABOUT THE AUTHOR

Mary Grand is the author of five novels and writes gripping, page-turning suspense, with a dark and often murderous underside. She grew up in Wales, was for many years a teacher of deaf children and now lives on the Isle of Wight.

Visit Mary's website: https://marygrand.net/

Follow Mary on social media:

twitter.com/authormaryg
instagram.com/maryandpepper
facebook.com/authormarygrand
bookbub.com/profile/mary-grand

ABOUT BOLDWOOD BOOKS

Boldwood Books is a fiction publishing company seeking out the best stories from around the world.

Find out more at www.boldwoodbooks.com

Sign up to the Book and Tonic newsletter for news, offers and competitions from Boldwood Books!

http://www.bit.ly/bookandtonic

We'd love to hear from you, follow us on social media:

facebook.com/BookandTonic

twitter.com/BoldwoodBooks

instagram.com/BookandTonic